FORESTS OF THE NIGHT

Also by James W. Hall

Off the Chart (2003)

Blackwater Sound (2001)

Rough Draft (2000)

Body Language (1998)

Red Sky at Night (1997)

Buzz Cut (1996)

Gone Wild (1995)

Mean High Tide (1994)

Hard Aground (1993)

Bones of Coral (1992)

Tropical Freeze (1990)

Under Cover of Daylight (1987)

Hot Damn! (2001)

JAMES W. HALL

FORESTS
OF THE NIGHT

St. Martin's Minotaur ✖ New York

FORESTS OF THE NIGHT. Copyright © 2005 by James W. Hall. All rights reserved. Printed in the United States of America. No part of this book may be used or reproduced in any manner whatsoever without written permission except in the case of brief quotations embodied in critical articles or reviews. For information, address St. Martin's Press, 175 Fifth Avenue, New York, N.Y. 10010.

www.minotaurbooks.com

Library of Congress Cataloging-in-Publication Data

Hall, James W. (James Wilson), 1947–
    Forests of the night : a novel / James W. Hall.—1st ed.
      p. cm.
    ISBN 0-312-27180-8
    EAN 978-0312-27180-0
    1. Policewomen—Fiction.   2. Mountain life—Fiction.   3. Runaway teenagers—Fiction.   4. Mothers and daughters—Fiction.   5. Fugitives from justice—Fiction.
6. Great Smoky Mountains (N.C. and Tenn.)—Fiction.   I. Title.

PS3558.A369F67 2005
813'.54—dc22

2004056650

First Edition: January 2005

10 9 8 7 6 5 4 3 2 1

ACKNOWLEDGMENTS

As usual I'm indebted to many individuals who helped in the creation of this book. I relied extensively on the extraordinary work of Paul Ekman for the facial coding information. Dick Heidgerd, a solid friend from forty years back, provided abundant assistance on legal matters.

C. Walton Johnson was my inspiration in so many matters having to do with the natural world of North Carolina, Cherokee Indians, and summer camps. His memory sustains me in so many ways that it is impossible to note them all. I also must give credit to Reynolds Price, whose masterful novel *The Tongues of Angels* was a guide back to those early days of Camp Sequoyah and its powerful role in my life and the lives of so many young men of that era.

And as always, Evelyn, my wife, sacrificed much during the months of the creation of this book. Her steady and clear advice, her literary perception, and her rigorous honesty kept me marching on the right path.

This book is dedicated to her father, William Francis Crovo, a man who had a stong passion for Native Americans and the natural world. I am grateful for the wisdom and generosity of spirit he imparted to his daughter, for it is through that legacy he bestowed on her that I am lucky enough to know him.

Tyger! Tyger!
Tyger! Tyger! burning bright
In the forests of the night
What immortal hand or eye
Could frame thy fearful symmetry?
　　—William Blake

There is no moral authority like that of sacrifice.
　　—Nadine Gordimer

1838

THE GREAT SMOKY MOUNTAINS

IN HIS SIXTY YEARS, TSALI had never shed the blood of a white man or another Cherokee in anger or defense. But that was about to change.

Sitting on a sunny boulder outside his family's cabin, Tsali was sharpening his ax blade with a wedge of shale. Nearby, his two eldest sons were employed in similar fashion, preparing their own axes for another day in the forest, hewing firewood for the approaching winter.

Already, autumn's crimsons and golds were blazing through the poplars and birches high on the nearby peaks. And from the earth and stones beneath his feet, Tsali could sense the gray advance of winter. Each day the sun grew more feeble. Soon the drifts of snow would mount, a vast stillness would descend, and yet another test of the family's strength and resourcefulness would present itself.

After a while, Tsali's ax blade was so sharp it could shave the sparse hair from his arm or cleave a man's skull in a single blow.

Such would be its use before that day was done, though Tsali had no inkling of his fate or the ruthless men galloping toward them at that moment.

Isolated on his remote riverside farm, the same land his ancestors had cultivated before him, Tsali knew nothing of the harsh changes sweeping the Cherokee Nation. All through the region, to make room for gold prospectors and white settlers, the U.S. government was systematically stripping Cherokees of their land, rounding them up and marching them halfway across the continent to the prairies of Oklahoma, then known as Indian Territory. Those who resisted were killed on the spot.

On the savage trek, which became known as the Trail of Tears, thousands of Cherokees died of starvation or of disease or at the hands of the U.S. Army. A third of the entire Cherokee Nation would perish before reaching that distant land of parched soil and bleak, treeless plains.

But living in his remote woodland valley, Tsali was ignorant of the events already under way and made no attempt, unlike many in his tribe, to conceal his family from capture.

As they washed and mended clothes in the shade of a giant poplar by the bank of the Nantahala River, Tsali's wife and daughters laughed quietly. Their pleasing voices sounded to Tsali like the music rising from the river's endless movement. The day was blissfully cool, the sky a perfect blue canvas stretched tight across the heavens.

Despite her advanced age, Tsali's wife was still a pleasure to his eyes. In their private times, the woman was as eager for the comfort and satisfaction of her husband's body as when they'd first wed. And he was as eager for hers. A comfort beyond all measure.

His contentment was increased by his daughters' full blooming. They were becoming fine women, strong and clever, with the dark, haunting eyes of their mother. Soon Tsali would journey to Quallatown or one of the other far-off settlements, introduce the girls to the clan elders, and set about finding suitable partners.

As Tsali rested his gaze on the women, the rumble of hooves sounded from the west. Garbed in blue woolen uniforms with gold buttons and hats of various shapes and sizes, four horsemen broke through the nearby woods, and whooped and fired their weapons at the sky as they galloped into Tsali's clearing. Their leader took the measure of the gathering of savages, then veered toward the boulder where the old man sat and drew his blocky pistol.

The soldier was tall with black hair. His eyes were close-set and glittered with a bitter fury. His cheeks were densely bearded. Even from several feet away, Tsali could detect the reek of corn liquor.

Barking a command, the soldier waved his pistol for Tsali to rise. The old man pulled himself to his feet and his boys ran to his side. The other three soldiers were a motley collection who more resembled vagabonds than disciplined fighting men.

Having mastered a few English phrases, Tsali's eldest son took charge of the interchange. This sergeant was hereby ordering Tsali and his family to pack whatever belongings they could carry and make ready for a month's journey.

For what reason? Tsali demanded.

By order of President Andrew Jackson and the Congress of the United States, the sergeant replied. You and your people will accompany us to the Bushnell stockade, where you will remain until such time as you begin your march westward.

Tsali began to protest, but the sergeant jumped down from his horse and rammed his pistol into Tsali's stomach, while the other soldiers grinned and aimed their rifles at the family of Cherokees.

You will do as instructed or die where you stand.

After gathering bundles of possessions, Tsali and his family followed the orders of Sergeant Matthew Tribue, the bearded man with the narrow face and eyes of volcanic rock.

Later, as they trudged away from their home, his sons stared at Tsali, awaiting his command. Were they going to surrender to these loutish men, be marched away to the slaughterhouse without a fight?

Tsali made no move to resist but plodded forward with his eyes on the rocky path before him. After only a mile or so, Tsali's wife, a heavy woman, lagged behind, and Tribue, who had been steadily sipping from his flask, jabbed the old woman in the back with his bayonet to hurry her along.

She fell to the ground, bleeding, while the soldiers hooted at their sergeant's antics.

Tsali managed to hide his anger as he tended his wife's injury, then hoisted her to her feet and helped her forward down the trail.

As they marched, Tsali whispered to his sons, telling them to ready themselves for attack. They would take the soldiers' guns and drive them away.

A mile or so later, when the soldiers were joking among themselves, Tsali motioned to the boys and they drew knives from their bundles and threw themselves on the four military men.

In his haste and drunkenness, one soldier discharged his rifle by accident and blew off the side of his own face. He fell from his saddle, mortally wounded. As the sergeant took hasty aim on the eldest boy, Tsali dragged the big man from his horse and, in one swift stroke, drove his ax into the man's forehead, breaking open his skull as cleanly as a ripe gourd.

The other two soldiers tore away from their attackers and fled.

In the sergeant's fall to the ground, a tin locket on a strip of rawhide came loose from around his neck. Tsali's son retrieved it and handed it to his father. Inside the tin heart was the miniature portrait of a young woman. She was round-faced, and her hair was worn in tight curls around her painted face. To Tsali, the woman's toothy smile resembled the cheap, beckoning look of the barroom strumpets he had seen in the white man's settlements.

Tsali closed the locket and placed it on the dead soldier's breast.

Bloodied and weak from the struggle, Tsali stood on that trail, a half-day's walk from his home, and absorbed the certain fact that he and his family were now forever exiled from their ancestral land.

With few choices open to him, Tsali determined they must strike out at once for the nearby peaks, which were honeycombed with caves. There they would hide themselves until some future time, when this difficulty had passed.

In the following days, they hunted the abundant game and harvested the late-season crab apples and berries. Twice they heard shouts from distant soldiers searching below them on the mountainside, but on neither occasion did a white man come closer than a half-day's walk to their hideaway.

Later still, the weather turned gray and cold. Fog and rain thickened the air. The men's hunting skills provided a steady supply of fresh game, while the girls wove baskets and ornaments to decorate their rock-walled home. They were determined to outlast the white man, live in what peace they could manage.

One frigid morning, as the family was awaking, a stranger appeared in the mouth of the cave.

Tsali's sons scrambled for their weapons.

But the Cherokee man showed his empty palms. He meant no harm. He had been searching for Tsali for over a week, carrying a message from the elders of the tribe.

An offer had been put forth by President Jackson. The leader of the white men could not abide Tsali's revolt. He feared Tsali's actions might inspire a wider rebellion. So desperate was the president to end Tsali's insurgence that he was offering the following bargain.

All Cherokee people not already forced from their homes and marched to the desolation of Indian Territory would be granted permission to remain on their tribal land, if only the renegade Tsali would surrender himself and his family to a firing squad.

When the man left, Tsali was silent. Hours passed. Tsali would neither eat nor reply to his wife or children, but sat cross-legged at the mouth of the cave, puffing on his pipe and staring toward the distant blue haze of the mountain ranges.

Two days after the offer was made, Tsali rose and gathered his cherished family before him. Tsali was a simple, practical man, not the least bit superstitious. In his long, difficult deliberation, no great spirit from beyond this world of rock and water and sky spoke to him, guiding him to his choice.

Tsali simply decided that for the greater good of his people, he must surrender. He would lay down his life and the lives of those he cherished so others of his people might have a chance to survive. His family received his decision with quiet calm. No tears, no arguments.

Days later, without ceremony, his strong young sons and handsome daughters were shot down before a firing squad, then Tsali was tied to the same bloody, mutilated tree and killed by a volley of bullets. In a small act of mercy, Tsali's wife and youngest boy were spared.

The federal government upheld its bargain and Tsali's death did indeed save scores from death on the Trail of Tears, and secure a home for the thousands of his people who populate those rugged blue mountains today.

No one would claim this plain, pragmatic Cherokee was a saint. His sacrifice did not atone for the sins of mankind, and no cathedrals were erected to honor his name and pass on his teachings. Although his selfless act changed the course of his people's future, because he was a Native American his story survives only on the margins of the nation's history. A pebble among boulders.

Yet when dropped into the center of a still pond, that trifling stone sent ripples of consequence spreading outward in ever-widening circles until one of those tiny waves, tainted now by a hateful poison, washed ashore a century and a half later in the most unlikely place.

PRESENT DAY— MIAMI, FLORIDA

ONE

Charlotte Monroe had sixty seconds to act.

Starting now.

She watched the red-haired boy raise the handgun and adjust his aim. He had bangs and was heavily freckled. Dennis the Menace hits puberty. Fuzz darkened his upper lip, and a single red pimple festered in the middle of his forehead like a tiny bullet wound.

Charlotte had a long-standing bias against redheaded boys. Blame it on Jake Calvin from her childhood, a gawky kid with maroon freckles so dense he looked like he'd been splashed with acid. He taunted her. Mocked her ratty shoes, her hand-me-downs. Reminded her that her older sister, Marlene, wore the same flowered dress two years before, and how Marlene used to lift that very skirt and flash her panties, sometimes even pull her panties aside. He dared Charlotte to do the same. Show him what she had.

Thirty-five seconds, thirty-four.

The boy she was watching brought back Jake Calvin's face, causing a ghostly interference. This redheaded kid had the same sneer, the same heckling tone as he aimed his cheap automatic at the black cat humped in the corner of the bare room.

"Here, kitty," he called. "Here, kitty kitty."

The cat hunched tighter, as if it heard the same tone Charlotte did—a whine of deceit and hatefulness. The boy's lips were mashed flat, straining to hold back his glee.

Twenty seconds left, nineteen.

One of Charlotte's cats, Max, had the same white spats and tuxedo shirt. She told herself Jake Calvin wasn't the boy before her now and it wasn't Max cowering. No reason to be so worked up. Her job was to see clearly, make a decision and act. She'd been batting a thousand—now this simple situation without even a human life at stake was bedeviling her.

She had no doubt the boy was capable of murdering an animal. An emergent torturer. Serial killer in training. Buried beneath his flattened gaze was a cold, fuming rage.

But for the first time she doubted herself. It felt like a trick, too obvious. She was exhausted, ready for this whole awful scene to be finished. Five seconds left. Four, three.

So, just to be done with it, she pressed the No button and a soft ping sounded behind the mirrored glass.

No was her official decision. No, the little shit wouldn't fire. But this time she wasn't certain. She truly didn't know if the kid would or not. A helpless cat exploding against a wall? It was possible. She'd seen worse in the last two weeks. Much worse.

Pressing the button didn't stop the videotape. The scene played to the end, as they all had. So she could discover how accurate her forecast was. And, of course, seeing all the previous scenarios affected her subsequent votes. Like life on the street, learning from each episode, constantly modifying.

Every video she'd seen for the last two weeks was authentic, real people, real violence. News footage, or grainy, homemade tapes confiscated after arrests, trophies from self-absorbed sickos, or taped confessions. Earlier in the week she'd spent eight hours watching people speaking into the camera. No sound—just their faces, mouths moving. Charlotte's assignment was to pick out the ones who were lying. Then there were the dozens of soundless videos shot from the dashboard cameras of patrol cars doing roadside stops. Is this driver dangerous or not? First thing this morning, with breakfast still warm in her belly, she'd watched a Georgia state trooper get out of his car, walk to the white Toyota he'd pulled over, confront a heavyset man in loose clothes—the man, out of the car, acting passive, head slumped forward, but doing something with his jaw, a nearly invisible grinding of teeth—then, seconds after Charlotte had pressed the Yes button, the attack she'd predicted occurred.

The trooper was off guard. Misreading the danger. Charlotte mashed the button several more times. She felt the scream rise to her throat: *Draw your weapon, step back, you idiot, watch out, goddamn it!*

With dreadful speed, the motorist produced a machete from behind his baggy trousers and hacked the trooper in the upper arm, and when the cop fell to the pavement, the motorist hacked him again. She'd known it would happen. She'd read the approaching spew of rage, an extra blink, a dark twinkle, the subtle grind of jaw. She knew, damn it, she saw it coming. An early-warning system probably instilled by the string of ducktailed men that flowed through her mother's double-wide when she was a kid. More than one of them had eyed her with a slanting smile, and stumbled her way. Jim Beam in one hand, lust in the other. But by then she'd positioned herself near the door and had always managed to escape. Even at that age she could sense some seismic jiggle, see the change of light in their eyes, a spasm in their lips, some clue that came and went so fast she doubted a camera could catch it.

On the screen the redheaded boy fired and the cat screeched and jumped a yard in the air. Plaster exploded. Incredibly, the boy missed. He fired again, then a third time, swinging wildly, shooting in a blind panic, blowing gashes in the drywall.

The cat must have escaped, because when the shooter staggered into camera view again, his arrogance had crumpled into misery. He stared at the lens, shoulders weighted with doom, bitter tears muddying his eyes, and he jammed the pistol against his temple.

"You worthless punk," he snarled at the camera. "Jerry Cox can't even kill a freaking cat. A freaking alley cat. Jerry's a scum-sucking dumb-ass bastard shit-for-brains. Can't even kill a freaking freaking cat."

Charlotte knew he wasn't going to shoot himself. The kid was spent. His eyes were dark vacuums, mouth slack, disgusted by his own grim appetites, his abject failure to accomplish a simple chore. For two or three seconds the boy struggled to pull the trigger, then he lowered the pistol and trudged to the camera and switched it off.

Maybe the kid had wanted to be a voyeur of his own cruelty, or perhaps the tape was meant to win him admission into some ruthless cult of juveniles. Either way, the event turned out to be merely a testament to the boy's utter ineptitude.

The screen went black and Charlotte sagged in the padded chair.

In the observation room, she heard voices, then the door between the rooms opened.

"I should get fifty percent for the last one," she said without turning from the empty screen. "He shot at the cat, but didn't shoot himself."

Dr. Fedderman was silent. She could feel him looking at her. When he spoke, his voice was huskier than it had been earlier in the day.

"When you voted no, you were reacting to the scene with the cat. You had no way to know the young man was going to consider suicide. This will count as an incorrect result."

"Hey, relax, Doc. I'm just kidding around with you."

"Oh," Fedderman said. "I see."

"Why're you so upset? Am I making you mad for some reason?"

She swiveled her chair to catch his face. The room was still dim. Only the weak glow of the blank screen. Fedderman was a short, sleek man with a shaved head and a goatee. For two weeks he'd worn black turtlenecks and sharply creased blue jeans. Nobody in Miami wore black turtlenecks. Like he'd been time-warped in from a fifties Bleecker Street coffeehouse. Him and his bongo drums.

"And why would I be angry at you, Officer Monroe?"

"Maybe because I'm doing too well. Beating the averages."

"It's research. I have no vested interest in any particular outcome."

"What about the software you're peddling?"

"You're participating in a clinical trial. All data is useful."

"But if I keep beating your program, then your system isn't as amazing as you say. Some ordinary patrol officer can do better, why should a department shell out the cash? Isn't that why you're pissed?"

He stared at the empty screen and spoke with what was probably meant to sound like scientific detachment.

"Ms. Monroe, so far you've produced fine results. They may turn out to be a statistical anomaly or they may not. If you continue to score this well over a longer period, then we'll seek to explain how you accomplish these feats, and that information will help us refine our program. That's the purpose of these experiments. Data collection. It is certainly not my intent to try to prove the superiority of my software over ordinary people."

"Your throat's tight. There's a squeak in your voice. You're pissed."

He shifted his gaze and gave her a bleak appraisal. This was a man who knew the name and function of every muscle strand in the face and had learned through arduous practice how to tighten or relax them in every possible combination to signal the entire range of human emotions. Thousands upon thousands of expressions with only the subtlest differences among them.

Facial coding, it was called, anatomical analysis of facial actions. This man knew his infraorbital triangle from his nasolabial furrow, and he was trying to fine-tune his computer program in facial recognition so it could sort out lies from truth, dangerous men from harmless ones. Charlotte had read up on him. Fedderman was renowned in his circle of scholars and researchers. Now he was trying to cash in, it seemed to her, make the jump from academia to where the serious money was, real-life applications.

But at that moment there was no artifice in the good doctor's face. He was so furious he was forced to swallow twice before he could speak again.

"After lunch we'll be doing faces alone," Fedderman said. "Head shots. No body language, no other clues to put the expressions in context. Significantly more challenging than the scenarios you've been watching. More subtle and far more complex. This has just been the warm-up."

"No offense, Doc, but I'm out of gas. Two weeks of this is plenty. There's real-life felons that need attending to."

Fedderman squeezed his lips into a smile that even a blind man could tell was insincere.

"Lieutenant Rodriguez has volunteered your services for as long as I might need them. So we'll see you at one o'clock on the dot. Faces in isolation. Have a lovely lunch, Monroe."

. . .

15

"May I?"

The short man with a rigid crew cut held a cafeteria tray and nodded at the empty seat beside Charlotte.

She said, "Sure," and the man sat.

A Caesar salad on his tray and a mug of coffee. He wore a blue shirt and dark trousers and a smile that was a little too twitchy.

"Charlie Mears," he said. "Federal Bureau of Investigation."

He slid his business card across the table and she took it. Only his name and a cell number.

"Officer Charlotte Monroe," she said, and held out a hand. He took it and for an awkward second he seemed to consider bringing it to his lips. Then he squeezed it and let it go.

She had that effect on some men, bringing out their latent gallantry. Though she'd never understood why. The woman she saw in the mirror was no stunner. Brown hair worn in a no-fuss straight cut that brushed her shoulders. Her eyes were hazel and on first glance appeared gentle, even vulnerable, but with a closer look, people usually caught the metallic flash of the woman she was. Focused, stubborn, with a low tolerance for bullshit. At five-foot-six, she was ten pounds too heavy to be called willowy. Most of those ten she'd earned in the gym, low weight, lots of reps. She'd inherited her mother's jutting cheekbones and bronze complexion. Her mouth was a size larger than the fashion magazines endorsed. She'd been told it was her father's mouth, though she'd never met the man.

Across the table, Mears looked at his watch, then speared a few leaves of lettuce and munched thoughtfully.

"To come to the point, Monroe. We've been following your progress with Dr. Fedderman. You've done quite well."

"Thanks."

When he'd swallowed, he said, "Actually, 'quite well' is a gross understatement. You've had remarkable results. So remarkable that I came down from D.C. especially to meet you."

She had a sip of tea and looked around at the bare walls of the cafeteria.

"It's just instincts," she said. "Intuition and a little luck, no big deal."

She took a bite of her turkey sandwich, then laid it aside. Tried one of the potato chips. Stale.

"Oh, no. It is a big deal, Monroe. A very big deal."

"Not to me it isn't."

"Reason I'm here is, I'm heading up a new, somewhat unorthodox task force at the bureau. By traditional criminal science standards what we're doing might be considered experimental. It's forensics, but not the tweezers, microscope, black light variety."

"Forensic pathology."

"In that general area. But more specialized. Profiling serial killers, that's still important, but we're pioneering some new territory."

"If this is a recruiting pep talk, you wasted your trip. I'm a police officer, plain and simple street cop. I have no other professional aspirations."

He gave her an empty smile.

"My team's responsible for everything from forensic archaeology to the paranormal."

"Oh, come on. ESP? You guys believe in that horseshit?"

"We believe in what works, whatever it may be based on. Skills like yours, for instance, may appear to be clairvoyant at first glance, but they aren't. They're simply skills. Highly developed, perhaps. But still skills. You're a gifted code cracker. Only your codes are human and emotional. It may be instinctive for you, but it's nevertheless a very, very rare talent."

He ate more of his salad. Took a long swallow from his mug. He patted his mouth with the napkin and looked around at the room full of cops and secretaries. A couple of her friends were looking over at her curiously.

"Let me ask you a couple of questions, Monroe?"

"The answer is no. I'm happy doing what I'm doing."

"I understand that. But would you say that your ability to anticipate behavior and read body signals and facial expressions has benefited your police work? Perhaps even kept you safe at times?"

"Maybe. That and good training."

"Think about it, Monroe. If we could learn more about these skills you possess and improve our methodology in teaching them to others, the applications would be immense. Take a Customs official at the airport, stamping passports, making eye contact, asking a couple of innocuous questions. He has maybe ten seconds to make a judgment about each person passing before him, an individual entering the country. He's the last line of defense.

17

What if that official was able to correctly distinguish honest answers from dishonest ones seventy, eighty percent of the time? Think of the impact, what catastrophes that might avert."

Charlotte was silent. Weighing his argument, but not buying it fully. Catching liars at airports was a long way from preventing catastrophes.

"Could you do something for me right now, Charlotte? A small favor."

"I'm listening."

"When you look at me, at my face, my eyes, my mouth at this particular moment, what do you see?"

"Hey, I'm off duty. It's lunch, okay?"

"Officer Monroe, from the results I've seen, I don't think you're ever off duty. Yours is the kind of gift that doesn't shut down. I believe you're always watching, evaluating, making highly informed judgments. Maybe it's happening just below the surface of your awareness, but it's there."

"Everybody does it."

"But few do it so well."

"Two weeks of tests. What does that prove?"

"What I'm guessing is that you're relieved to know you have this skill. Most of the time it probably feels like you're eavesdropping on people's thoughts. Invading their privacy. That's how I've heard it described by one of the other members of our team. A man who's incredibly good at reading faces and body language. Our most gifted associate. That is, until you cropped up. The best results we've ever come across, by the way, are from a Tibetan Buddhist monk. Thousands of hours of meditation have apparently given him the empathy and focus to detect and decode those fleeting facial expressions that can give away true emotions. Forty milliseconds, that's how fast they come and go. But he can see them. And apparently so can you."

Charlotte put down the rest of the chip and looked into Mears's eyes.

"Fedderman said prison inmates were the best."

"That's true, inmates score very high. Surrounded, as they are, by world-class deceivers and liars, it's life or death to figure out who to trust."

"Buddhists and convicts, that's quite a brotherhood."

"Like it or not, Monroe, you're at the top of the class."

"So if I read your mind you'll leave me alone?"

Mears held her gaze but said nothing. His face neutral.

"Okay. I see a guy who's so good at hiding his feelings, he's not sure what they are anymore."

Mears nodded, lips relaxing, then tightening.

"Fair enough. Though that would be true for a lot of men. Especially in my profession."

"And I see a guy on edge. Anxious. Not as poised as he comes across. Like right at this moment, it's like you're waiting for a bomb to go off. Those tension lines below your eyes, a twitch in your right eyelid. The way you dab your tongue at the corner of your mouth. Four times in the last two minutes. You're anxious, and I'm guessing that's an unfamiliar feeling for you."

"You should be banned from the poker table, Monroe."

The cell phone on his belt chirped.

Mears held her eyes for a moment and let it ring.

"I believe this may be the bomb you were referring to, Ms. Monroe."

Mears snapped the phone open, listened, and said, "Yes, sir, she's right here."

He handed the phone to Charlotte and a second later she was listening to a gruff, familiar voice. She'd never met the man, but she'd heard him speak on television often over the last nine years. Harold Benson, director of the FBI.

He was courteous but aloof. Giving her a brisk speech that had the practiced rhythm of one he'd made a few hundred times before.

As Charlotte was surely aware, the world had recently become a far more dangerous and unpredictable place than it was a few years before. And the FBI was responding aggressively and creatively to these new challenges. One way was by assembling teams of uniquely talented individuals with a variety of highly developed skills. Along those lines, the director had examined the results from the two weeks of testing Charlotte had undergone and he was highly impressed. She had an extraordinary gift, and he hoped she would consider the offer that Deputy Director Mears was making.

His pitch was short and ended abruptly.

"We know you have commitments in Miami. We could work around that. We need you, Monroe. Used properly, your skills could save lives and make a fundamental difference to your country. We'll be in touch."

And without waiting for a response, he was gone.

She handed the phone back to Mears. He smiled at her. No more tongue dabbing.

"Triple your salary, big step up in your benefits package. Maybe a trip to D.C. now and then, but you'd be based here in Miami with Fedderman and a few others we'd send down. We'll even give you a three-month grace period to try it out, see if it works. If for some reason it doesn't suit you, your job's still open at Gables PD. No need to decide right now. Tomorrow is fine."

TWO

JACOB BRIGHT SKY PANTHER PARKED the red Ford pickup he'd stolen in Daytona Beach three blocks north of the Palm Beach address, tucked his Smith & Wesson .357 under the front seat, and set off down the beachfront boulevard, unarmed for the first time in months. He'd been told by his contact that the woman was harmless but would not do business with him if she found he was armed. Though it had been his experience that no man or woman was truly harmless, he took the risk and left his weapon behind.

The sun floated in a cloudless sky, turning the Atlantic a flat, perfect blue. On the sharp line of the horizon Jacob watched a half dozen slender clouds glide southward like a war party of ghostly canoes. As if the ancient chiefs were monitoring him from afar, wagering on his chances for success.

At the front gate of 267 Ocean Drive he buzzed the speaker button, and moments later a husky voice asked who the hell it was. Jacob gave his alias and the voice thought about it, then growled, "You're twelve hours early."

Across the street, on the beach where the ocean crashed and foamed, white-haired people with big bellies marched back and forth as if guarding their stretch of sand from any riffraff who might try to sneak ashore.

"I'm here now," he said.

Jacob waited. He watched the clouds thicken and re-form into clumsy battleships, and he listened to the explosions of surf. He watched the sea-gulls circle and splash.

At the end of the broad avenue a white patrol car with a blue stripe appeared and came prowling his way. Motionless, Jacob watched it pass, offering his face to the policeman. Cowering wasn't his way. If it was his fate to be captured at this place and time, then so be it.

But the cop was gazing out to sea, missing an excellent opportunity to advance his career.

When the gate finally buzzed, Jacob pushed it open and stepped through, shut it, and walked down the long brick pathway toward the main house.

Scattered about the walkway were courtyards and columns topped by gargoyles. In tiled fountains, lazy goldfish circled the lily pads and naked cherubs pissed into the sultry air.

Jacob advanced along the shaded walk, trailing his fingers across the cool braille of the stucco. It felt thick enough to withstand cannon fire.

While he waited beside the double doors, Jacob turned and stared back through the front gate, watching the waves shatter against the white sand. He breathed the ocean air. Salty, with a hint of fresh oysters and sandalwood.

Jacob blinked and drew a disciplined breath.

He had spent his life in the mountains and hadn't been prepared for the sea. It was bigger than he'd imagined. It went out so far, it disappeared into itself. A blue empty distance.

Jacob wasn't sure how long he waited on the front porch. He'd never worn a watch. What mattered was day and night, summer, winter, not the second or minute. What good were the clicking gears of a timepiece, pulverizing each day into fine, meaningless powder?

He had a natural talent for keeping himself occupied. His senses perpetually alert, like now, feeling the prickle of sunlight on his skin, inhaling the mix of ocean scents and the new-cut grass. This instinctive watchfulness served him well this last year. Hunted as he was, his first impulse when arriving somewhere new was to chart the best path of escape.

Behind him the hinges squealed, and he turned to find a woman, darkly tanned with tattoos circling her upper arms. Except for a tiny swatch of glittery green fabric over her crotch, she was naked.

She eyed the length of his body, her gaze returning slowly to his face.

"Who sent you?"

The password ritual.

"Levi," Jacob said.

The name clicked the tumblers in her eyes, and her jaw muscles eased.

"You're early. I don't like early."

It was the voice from the speaker box, harsh and croaky as if she'd been gargling beach sand.

She turned and padded barefoot across the red tile floor. He followed her through the house, the rooms cool with high ceilings and exposed beams, chandeliers dangling in their diamond halos. She led him outside onto a sunny patio next to the largest swimming pool he'd ever seen, and she turned to face him. Her eyes were bloodshot and muddled as though she'd just awakened and was still sorting out her nightmares.

"How do you know Levi?"

"We found each other on the Internet."

"The Internet? Levi said you were a dumb-ass Indian, living in a tepee or a mine shaft or some shit."

Her lips were halfway to a grin, testing how easily he got pissed off.

"Even dumb-ass Indians use the Internet," he said.

Her smile tightened.

"My name's Shirlee. That's with two e's."

"So that makes you special," he said. "Not like all the other Shirleys."

"You got that right."

"Do you have something for me?"

"You're just a kid. I was expecting an adult."

She craned her neck to the left and right, as if working out a kink.

Her breasts were small, with tiny raisin nipples standing up, and at the edges of the strip of green shiny material across her crotch, black hair coiled out. Now that he had a better look, Jacob saw that the tattoos on her arms and circling her ankles were oversize scorpions with their barbed tails poised to strike.

"I'm almost thirty. Do you require ID?"

"Oh, I'll make an exception this time, honey. But if it's frog toxin you want, forget it. Big order last week wiped me out. More diaperheads on their jihad—Saudis, Iranians, whoever the hell they were."

In the swimming pool, a large gray fish swam in circles as though searching for a way out.

"Then you have no venom."

"Did I say that? I have venom. Just not from frogs."

Jacob said, "Frogs, eagles, donkeys. It doesn't matter."

"As long as it's lethal, right?"

She smiled at him and stroked her left breast, keeping that nipple awake.

"Nudity bother you?"

"I'll let you know if it begins to."

Jacob watched the brittle light bounce off the surface of the pool. The fish rose from the water, cast a look their way, then plunged beneath the surface. It was four or five feet long, gray and silky. In the mountains, Jacob knew the name and habits of every insect and sentient creature, but the ocean and its residents were a mystery.

"When Levi said 'Indian,' I asked if he meant Gandhi or the tomahawk kind. Know what he said?"

"That I'm no Gandhi."

She smiled and picked up a Baggie that lay on the table next to a brass pipe. She opened the ziplock, took a pinch of weed, squeezed the fibers into the bowl of the pipe, lit it with a plastic lighter, sucked down more than seemed possible for such a skinny woman, and blew the smoke toward the empty sky.

She held out the smoldering pipe.

Jacob stood motionless. She released the last of the blue smoke.

In her scratchy voice she said, "All business, huh? No time to socialize."

"I have the five thousand," he said. "In hundreds as Levi suggested."

"Five thousand buys a lot of socializing."

She had short, spiky black hair and dark eyes. Skinny arms and legs with her ribs showing. Like one of those women who starved herself, thought that was pretty, or maybe just forgot to eat, all the drugs she was using.

Either way, she wasn't Jacob's idea of sexy. Even with the long nipples and the crotch hair showing, she was no more attractive to him than a bundle of dry kindling with a cottonmouth lurking inside.

"You know, kid, you've definitely got that exotic thing going on."

Jacob waited. She had to say what she had to say. She had to get it out before they did their business. So Jacob waited. Savoring the fertile air, taking it in, letting it out. Sandalwood and saltiness.

"So you're what, part Cherokee? Like a half-breed or whatever the trendy word is these days?"

Jacob watched the fish rise and fall from the sleek water.

"Your skin, it's not all that red, maybe a little rusty, that's all."

She reached out and dabbed her fingertip against his temple, then looked at her finger like his makeup might've come off.

"I mean, I see it in the forehead, how broad it is. And your eyes, that hooded look. But the hair, no way. I don't think there's any blond Indians, are there? Unless that's peroxide, which it doesn't look like."

She brushed her fingers through the hair at Jacob's temples. It was sandy and coarse, and in the last year he'd let it grow till it touched his shoulders. Back when he was young and vain and wanted more than anything for a woman to fall in love with him, he'd kept his hair short and tried to style it in the modern way, but it was so thick it ruined combs and defied brushes. Now he simply used his fingers when it was snarled.

"And those slick baby cheeks, yeah, I can picture how it happened. Some dark-eyed Pocahontas gets down and dirty with a square-jawed Irish stud. Quite a mix. I know a guy, a photographer down in South Beach, one look at you, he'd faint. He's always searching for that one-of-a-kind primitive mojo. Of course, you probably wouldn't want your picture in a fashion magazine, would you? Post-office walls, that's more your style."

Jacob waited. Polite. He forced himself to smile.

"Tell me something, okay?"

Jacob was silent.

"You're an Indian, you live in the goddamn forest, commune with the birds and beasts. How come you don't go milk a rattlesnake or something? You gotta buy your poison from people like me?"

"That's not a skill I have, milking rattlesnakes."

"But you know what I mean. Your ancestors, they didn't have to buy venom. They got their own. Brewed it up, whatever the hell they did."

"I have my own ways," Jacob said. "My own reasons."

"What happened to self-sufficient? That's what Indians do, right? They live off the land, commune with the spirits, rub two sticks together."

"Those days are a long time gone."

"Well, you're a disappointment," she said. "You're my first Indian and look at me, I'm standing here full of disillusionment."

"Venom from the forest would provide clues to those who pursue me."

She considered it for a moment.

"Yeah, okay," she said. "That makes sense. Throw them off."

Jacob watched the fish circling the pool, rolling and diving.

"You know about cone snails?" Shirlee said. *Conus purpurascens.*"

"I'm prepared to learn."

"I found this kid, he's doing a postdoc down in Miami, studying neuropharmacology. They're producing some shit-kicking hallucinogens these days, painkillers you wouldn't believe. One taste, you're gone for a week, flying wherever the hell in the universe you want to go, then you wake up, you're fine, no hangover, nothing. Amazing shit. This kid, he's hard up for cash, got some kind of habit, poor guy. So we worked out a deal, our mutual benefit. And yours, too."

"I don't want to hallucinate," Jacob said.

"Yeah, yeah, I know. You want to wax somebody, ship 'em to the embalmer. Sure. That's what I'm talking about, cone-snail venom. Same stuff, different strength, that's all. A tiny bit gets you high, a little more kills the pain, and a teensy bit more gets you dead. It's all about portion control."

She drew on her pipe and blew out a stream near his face.

"First phase hits like cobra toxin, second phase like puffer-fish venom. Different peptide fractions cause different nerve reactions. Paralysis, numbness, total shutdown of neurological receptors. One peptide targets skeletal muscle sodium, another does neuronal calcium channels. Bottom line, this is seriously bad shit. A little dab'll do. Three seconds your guy is frozen, can't breathe, three seconds later, you got yourself a corpse."

Jacob nodded again.

"That's what you want, then? A cone-snail cocktail?"

"How much does five thousand dollars buy?"

"With or without the blow job?"

"Just the venom."

She drew on the pipe again, but the weed had gone out, so she tapped out the remains into the flowering red plants that filled the beds behind them.

"What're you, sexually challenged?"

"I'm on a tight schedule," he said.

The scorpions on her shoulders were blue and green and they seemed to be moving, a slow dance across her tan flesh. Maybe it came from breathing the cloud of dope, or maybe it was some leftover trace of his old self warming to this twisted woman, making his eyes play tricks. A year ago Jacob Panther would've seized the chance. Happy to test his stamina against this she-devil, fly to whatever planet she was from, plant his flag in that ground. But not now. That Jacob was gone. Only some last stray molecules left.

"Just the cone venom."

"All right, all right. Christ, you don't like girls, whatever, fine."

She got up and marched into the house and when she returned, the vial she handed him was full to the brim. Jacob peered at the liquid, tipped the tube to the side. The fluid was oily and thick, with the tint of weak tea.

Shirlee lit her pipe again and said, "Stab a needle through the membrane, leave it a second or two, pull it back out. Whatever traces are left on the point should do the job, unless you're trying to kill an elephant, then maybe you'll need two jabs."

Jacob jiggled the tube. A faint coppery vapor hung in the air.

"There's enough in that vial, you could put a dent in the Hundred and First Airborne."

Jacob slipped the ampoule in his shirt pocket and reached into his jeans and pulled out the envelope. A bank in South Carolina had provided the funds. Five thousand, Jacob told the terrified teller. No more, no less.

"What're you, anyway?" Shirlee said. "Hit man, terrorist, or just some guy gonna whack your wife's boyfriend? My bet is terrorist."

"You lose."

"Aw, come on. You think I'm going to the cops?"

"None of those," Jacob said. "I'm just trying to stay alive."

"What's that mean? This is for self-defense? Give me a break."

"What's that thing in the pool?" Jacob nodded toward the water.

"What?"

"That fish."

"It's not a fish, it's a mammal," Shirlee said. "It's a goddamn dolphin. You never saw a dolphin before? Jesus, you *must* live in a mine shaft."

"So that's a dolphin."

"Yeah, yeah. Big brain. Smart as you and me, maybe smarter, that's what they say."

"If it's so smart," Jacob said, "what's it doing in your pool?"

At Miami International Airport, Jacob Panther found a bank of TV monitors and checked the arrival time of the US Airways flight from Charlotte. On time, arriving in forty-five minutes. He located a Burger King and bought a large Coke and got a plastic lid. At the first trash can, he dumped out the Coke and ice, then snapped the lid back into place. In the men's room he locked himself in a stall. He pricked the rubber membrane with the dart, and swished the fluid over the point. After a moment more, he withdrew the needle tip and slid the dart, point first, into the white tube. He drew a pipe cleaner from his pocket and poked the projectile down the barrel of the blowgun until a speck of the shiny tip was exposed and the fletching was secure. When he had it positioned correctly, Jacob inserted the white tube through the plastic lid of his empty Coke cup.

He flushed the pipe cleaner, then walked out of the bathroom to the head of Concourse H and eased in alongside the chauffeurs with their signs.

Jacob held the cup, and every few minutes he touched his lips to the white straw that poked through the lid and moved his cheeks as if he were swallowing. The arriving passengers streamed out of the concourse exit, some of them stopping to hug loved ones. Most in a hurry, on cell phones, jostling toward the waiting cabs.

Jacob watched the crowd and sucked on his straw that was not a straw.

Hundreds of people passed by before the man appeared.

Jacob saw his face through the swarm, on a route that would bring him only a few feet away from Jacob's position. Jacob gripped the mouthpiece of his blowgun and drew it a few inches from the cup. But just as his target entered killing range, he made a sudden cut behind a group of women and Jacob lost the shot.

The crowd swarmed, and the man passed by only two yards away, but shielded by women in bright dresses. He walked with his usual cocky strut, passing quickly with his long, even stride.

Jacob swung around, bumped a tall woman holding up a welcome sign. He apologized and slipped through the crowd.

At the head of the escalator, his target halted for an elderly lady who was balking, as if this were her first experience with moving stairs. A moment of providence.

Jacob headed down the fixed stairway that ran between the up and down escalators. He slowed his pace, watched in his side vision as the elderly woman glided past, then the tall man with the familiar face. Jacob timed his descent to stay even with the man. Two feet away.

Choosing the largest patch of exposed flesh, he used the move he'd rehearsed a hundred times. Drawing the straw smoothly from the cup, taking only a second to aim, then he puffed hard into the mouthpiece.

The dart lodged two inches below the man's left ear. In half a second, the blowgun was back in the plastic cover of the cup.

Grabbing at the sting in his neck, the man looked directly at his killer. Recognizing Jacob, his eyes flared with dark lightning. A second later the light drained away, and his mouth opened into a savage yawn, and he tumbled forward just as the old lady was stepping from the escalator.

Behind Jacob a woman shrieked. Two men in dark suits hustling down the escalator halted at the bottom and stared at the body sprawled on the linoleum before them. One of them glanced at his watch, spoke in Spanish to his friend, and they tiptoed around the dead man and hurried on.

Jacob pretended to take sips while he mingled with the crowd that gathered around the man. Edging backward little by little to the perimeter of the throng until a security guard arrived, kneeled over the man, felt for a pulse, and began to bark into his radio.

Jacob walked out the exit and headed for the airport's Flamingo Garage, where he'd parked the red pickup. One more stop. Another man to deal with.

This one he'd been wanting to meet for a long, long time.

THREE

CHARLOTTE MONROE DIDN'T RECOGNIZE THE red pickup truck parked in her front drive. It didn't belong there, that was for sure. In fact, it was illegal. One of the nitpicky rules of the city of Coral Gables was that no pickups were permitted to be parked in residential driveways overnight anywhere within the city limits. Workmen were okay in daylight hours, as long as they returned to their own shabby neighborhoods before nightfall. Charlotte had never written a ticket for a pickup truck parked overnight, and she didn't know anybody on the Coral Gables PD who had. But still, the law was there and at least once a week a good citizen called 911 to turn in a violator. City Beautiful. This was her beat. Protecting people who spent way too much time spying on their neighbors. Her beat and also her home.

Her patrol car was in the motor pool for its sixty-thousand-mile service and there were four officers waiting ahead of her for spare cruisers, so when she saw Jesus Romero pulling out of the parking lot, she flagged him down. Her old partner, back in the early days.

Now as Jesus stared at the ornate wrought iron gates blocking the drive, he grunted as if marveling at an attractive woman crossing his path.

"Yeah, yeah, I know," Charlotte said. "Go on, give me some shit."

Charlotte drew the remote from her purse and aimed it through the windshield and, as the heavy gates rolled back, Jesus chuckled.

"Say it," she said. "Why the hell do I keep slogging along in the sewers when I could stay home all day and boss around a dozen maids?"

When the gate was open, Jesus pulled into the brick drive and eased up to the front door. But Charlotte sat there for a moment looking at the red pickup truck in the headlights.

"If I could afford a place on the Gables waterway, I sure as hell wouldn't buckle on my piece one more day. I'd be trolling for sailfish from dawn to dusk, perfecting my margarita recipe."

"I live here, Jesus. It's a house, not a way of life."

He waved his hand at the Mediterranean villa.

"I see you every day, but I always forget you come from this."

"I don't *come* from this. I *live* in this."

"It's just weird, that's all. Being a cop, for you it's like some volunteer thing. The Peace Corps, missionary work. You don't need it."

"Screw that," she said. "I need it all right."

He looked at her for a moment, then nodded. Jesus was one of the very few who knew her story and understood where her need was rooted.

High school, her senior-year spring break, she'd ridden to Florida with Teddy Miles in his rusty Olds Cutlass. Him to get drunk and ogle bikini babes, Charlotte to escape Murfreesboro and for the tan. All the way to Lauderdale, Teddy bummed gas and food money from her, so she knew he was flat broke and pissed off about it, but she didn't know exactly what he intended to do about it until their first hour in South Florida.

Teddy pulled into a Qwik Mart for more beer, Charlotte looking for crackers, sandwich meat, anything cheap and filling. When she wasn't paying attention, Teddy drew a handgun on the clerk, a black woman in a dashiki and tons of jewelry. Down the cracker aisle, Charlotte screamed at him to put it away, but he ignored her. Grabbed the cash, yelled for Charlotte, then noticed the surveillance camera on the way out, firing at it but missing. By then the cashier was howling like a wounded dog. Teddy turned and shot her twice, just to keep her quiet, he said later. First slug kicked her against the cigarette case, the second one killed her.

Thirty minutes later the two of them were in jail. Next day Charlotte was assigned a young public defender named Parker Monroe. In the deposition, she gave him her complete hard-luck story back to the beginning of time, went on to describe her total shock that Teddy Miles would commit robbery and murder. She didn't even know the jerk had a gun. Parker listened, nodding. Then he told her quietly about the get-tough policy of the current DA, a woman running for reelection. Usual sentence for accessory in felony murder was twenty-five to life. The new sentencing guidelines made no distinction between the shooter and his accomplices. Everyone was charged the same. And given the current politics, the DA might press for the death penalty. But he'd give it a shot, see what he could do. Saying it all in his gentle, measured voice. Reassuring, but no guarantees.

Three days passed before he showed up again. By then Charlotte had cried herself dry. He sat down across from her at the stark metal table and smiled. Parker had done his magic in judge's chambers. The surveillance tape backed her up. He gave himself no credit, but Charlotte was forever convinced her freedom was due to Parker Monroe's gift, his utter faith in his client's innocence, and his plainspoken style. Teddy got thirty to life. Charlotte's record was expunged. An innocent party to another's vicious impulse.

After a year of steady dating she moved in with Parker, and three years after that, when she graduated from the local university, they eloped to Vegas. Giddy in love. This handsome Harvard boy rescued her from prison and an equally tawdry future back in Tennessee. She had to love him. No choice. Two parts gratitude, an equal measure of love and attraction all churning in her gut. Now, almost two decades later, she was still doing penance for her sins, serving and protecting, and still feeling indebted to this man who'd won her freedom. It nagged at her sometimes, Charlotte unsure what portion of her love for Parker was based on thankfulness. And why the hell a man like him had married down, plucking her from the lower classes, anointing her. What had she done to deserve any of it? Most of the time she managed to let it go. Knowing how goddamn lucky she'd been to draw Parker Monroe that day, not one of the harried public defenders she'd met since.

In a quieter voice, all the macho drained away, Jesus said, "Fact is, I'd get bored with fishing. A week or two, I'd be begging for my shield back."

Max walked into the flare of headlights and rubbed his back against the rear tire of the pickup. The red truck had Volusia County plates—Daytona Beach area. None of their friends drove pickups.

Romero's radio crackled and they grew quiet and listened. Suspicious character sighted in front of a jewelry store at Merrick Place—the hoity-toity shopping center in the heart of Coral Gables.

"Suspicious character," Charlotte said. "At Merrick Place that would be anyone not wearing Manolo Blahniks."

"Manolo what?"

"Shoes. Expensive shoes."

Jesus nodded, tried to smile.

It was their longest conversation since her rookie days, when Jesus was her mentor. In the years since, Charlotte had passed up promotions, choosing to stay on patrol while Jesus worked his way up to major-crimes detective. Bully for him. He had five kids, needed the extra pay, and had no problem with the dismal crime scenes, investigations going cold, getting filed away. Charlotte preferred the tang of the street. Eight edgy hours, no two days alike. People in need, panicked, confused, jacked up on fury. Drunks, heart attacks, family violence, robberies in progress. Volatile situations, brief windows when it was still possible to make a difference.

"You hear what your husband did today?"

She grimaced and nodded. She'd caught a glimpse of Parker on the waiting room TV on her way out. Lead story on the five o'clock news.

"I don't get it." Jesus thumped his knuckles against the steering wheel. "Kid shoots his coach in the face and doesn't even get thirty days. No probation, nothing. Little turdball struts out of the courthouse smiling."

"Parker's good at what he does."

"Too good, you ask me."

"There's always two sides."

"You starting to lose your way, Charlotte? I'm talking about a nine-millimeter slug in the face. In through the nose, blows off the back of his head. Kid's sixteen, he knows from right and wrong. Coach reprimands him for some bullshit thing, kid goes home, gets his Glock. Runs back. Don't be dissing me, old man. Bang, bang."

"I believe it was his uncle's Glock. Left unlocked in a dresser drawer."

"Oh, come on. Right and wrong, Charlotte. Justice, injustice."

"Can't blame Parker. It was a bad Miranda. Some Metro rookie, stopped halfway through his rights, answers a personal call on his cell, never finished reading the card. His partner testified. Talking to some girl he'd just met instead of doing his business."

"Technicality."

"Chain of evidence was spotty, conflicting eyewitnesses. Other kids in the locker room were all over the goddamn place. Shooter was just trying to scare the coach, never meant to fire the pistol. Coach went for the gun, there was a struggle, gun fired accidentally. Guys who were there, watching the whole thing, even they couldn't agree what happened."

"Some of them were lying. Protecting their buddy."

"Maybe, maybe not. Either way, it blows the case."

"Your old man's got you brainwashed. He's whispering to you in your sleep, converting you to his brand of Satan worship. Goddamn trial lawyers."

"We do our jobs right, Parker's got nothing to work with. We screw up like the yahoo stopping halfway through the Miranda, the bad guys walk."

"Did the kid shoot the coach?"

"You know there's more to it than that."

"Not for me there isn't."

She huffed and shook her head. Acting more put out than she was. But this is how she managed it. Took Parker's side. Repeated his set phrases. Tried damned hard to see it his way. And usually nobody called her on it, or got in her face like Jesus was doing.

She'd been doing it for years, whenever one of his cases made news. Another bad guy let loose. She trotted out the speeches. Parker's arguments were valid, of course, and she believed them to a point. Even scum were entitled to counsel. Crafty lawyering made for smarter police work. Yeah, yeah. Still it wore on her to mouth the words. Frayed the strands of her self-respect. Marriage vows in direct conflict with her other sacred vow—to serve and protect. Ride the bad guys to their bloody knees and haul their asses in.

"There he was on TV while I was eating my black beans and rice, standing out on the courthouse steps, taking questions from that blond babe on

Channel Six. All humble, no smiling, no high fives or any of that garbage. Came off pretty well, considering he'd just given the justice system a good reaming."

"Look, he's a decent guy. More than half his cases are pro bono."

"Like this guilty fuck today."

"That's not fair and you know it."

"Half are pro bono, the other half are rich-ass swindlers and drug lords. Nothing personal, but your husband's playing on the wrong team."

"Goofy as it sounds, Parker believes everybody who walks through his door is innocent."

"You're shitting me."

"Every single one of them."

"I knew he was some kind of bleeding-heart lunatic, but man. Everybody's innocent? What kind of outer-space bullshit is that?"

"One night soon, come over to dinner, bring Maria. I'll make that lasagna you like so much. You can talk to Parker, hear his side, call his bluff. Then afterward feel free to badmouth him all you want."

"Christ, I have dreams about your damn lasagna. Been years since I had it last, but some nights I wake up, I'm salivating."

"So we'll do it then. Get together."

"Hell, if I got in the same room with that guy, he'd work his voodoo on me, next thing you know I'd be down at the jail throwing open the cells."

Charlotte smiled and looked over at the house. She could see shadows through the gold curtains. Two tall men walking through the dining room, heading for the patio. A shorter shadow tagging along. Gracey.

Jesus tapped out a *café cubano* rhythm on the steering wheel.

"I heard Gracey was having trouble. How's she doing?"

"Depends on the meds. She skips a few, it can get rowdy."

"She still into oil painting?"

"It's acting now. She goes to the fine-arts magnet downtown. Got a teacher who thinks she's a genius. Mr. Underwood."

"So what's wrong with that?"

"You ever seen *Double Indemnity*? Fred MacMurray and a beautiful blonde murder the blonde's husband?"

"Sure, Barbara Stanwyck. Tight sweaters and an ankle bracelet. I've seen it maybe twenty times."

"Well, Gracey's been consulting with Barbara on acting matters."

"What? She watches her movies, studies technique?"

"More than that. The two of them have heart-to-hearts. Sometimes it's Joan Crawford."

"She could've picked better actresses."

"It's from the class she's taking. Film Noir. So my daughter's learning how to wear a mask. That deadpan, shell-shocked look they all used back then, the Humphrey Bogart thing, hide your feelings, cover it all up."

Jesus shifted, looking uncomfortable.

"So she talks to Barbara Stanwyck? How does that work?"

"She hears a voice in her head. Barbara Stanwyck's got a hotline to my daughter, sending her inspiration."

"She's got an artistic temperament. Hell, one of my girls acted pretty weird for a couple of years, making all these creepy-sounding voices. Role-playing or whatever. Just a phase, part of that teenage hormone thing."

Charlotte shook her head.

"Now you sound like Parker."

"Well, what is it then? It have a name?"

Charlotte hated the word. She could count the number of times she'd spoken it aloud.

"Schizophrenia," she said. "That's what I'm told."

"Oh, Christ. I didn't realize."

"One percent of the population worldwide."

"Yeah, that's the one percent that keeps us busy."

Jesus winced when he realized what he'd said.

"It's okay," Charlotte said. "She's not that bad yet. It could happen, but there's drugs, therapy. She may turn out to have the high-functioning variety."

Jesus stared at the red truck in his headlights, his voice going quiet.

"You know that guy Ray Hamersley, the basketball coach the kid shot? Well, about a hundred years ago I played for him at Miami High."

She turned to look at Jesus's profile.

"Junior year, he caught me smoking a Camel behind the gym, kicked my ass off the team right there. Did I go home and get a fucking gun? Let me think. No, no, I don't recall that. I think I went home and smoked the rest of the case and puked in the backyard and never smoked again."

He looked at her and then turned back to the pickup in his headlights.

"It's what he does, Jesus. He's not a bad man. He does it because he believes in it, same as we do."

Jesus turned in his seat, pointed at her face, and wagged his finger like she'd been naughty.

"Don't you be going over to the dark side now."

She grabbed hold of Romero's finger and bent it backward, not enough to hurt, but close.

He groaned and pried loose from her grip.

"Okay, okay. You women, shit, first time you burned a bra, we should've been all over you. What were we thinking?"

"Too late now, Jesus."

"Don't I know it. Don't I fucking know it."

Charlotte opened the door and got out. Jesus popped a two-finger salute and rolled out the drive. She left the electric gate open, then squatted down to pat Max. The rest of the troop emerged from the shrubs purring and whining like they hadn't been fed. She gave each of them a stroke, then unlocked the door and the whole gang scampered inside around her ankles.

FOUR

CHARLOTTE THREADED THROUGH THE MAZE of hallways to the bright kitchen, set her purse on the granite counter, and peered out the French doors. Gracey and Parker were out on the patio tending a small bonfire in the brick barbecue pit. Floodlights off, the fire cast a rippling halo across the flagstones and the wide waterway that ran behind the house.

Parker and Gracey both held long twigs and seemed to be roasting marshmallows. Beside them stood a burly man with shoulder-length hair. He had on khakis and work boots, and when he turned to the side briefly, she saw on the back of his denim shirt some kind of colorful embroidered insignia. The firelight fluttered on his face, and though he was a hundred feet away in bad light, an old brain cell woke from its timeless nap and fired off a sharp tingle of disquiet.

Charlotte watched the man sip his beer. She burned the image on her retina, closed her eyes, and tried to summon a name, a situation, any distant echo of this man. Nothing came. Blankness. Then an ugly snippet replayed from one of today's videos, the trooper lying on his back, one hand rising like a feeble plume of smoke toward the downward slice of the blade.

She opened her eyes and stared some more. The guy was probably just an electrician or plumber bidding on a job. Their house was eighty years old, ancient by Miami standards, and required constant attention. She was simply oversaturated with violent images, having a flash of paranoia.

After another few seconds, when no recollection hardened into focus, Charlotte turned to the counter, got out the cans of tuna, opened them one by one, and fed the tribe. When they'd taken their positions at their bowls, she poured herself a glass of cabernet and walked outside.

Parker was in his after-hours uniform. Faded jeans, boat shoes, and a T-shirt from his vast collection. This one, bright yellow with red lettering, was from Duffy's Tavern over in West Miami, a beer joint they used to frequent when they were first married and burning so many calories in the bedroom they could eat all the fries and greasy burgers they wanted.

He opened his arms, and Charlotte rocked in and out of his embrace, planting her shoulder briefly against his chest and managing a quick bungled kiss on the edge of his mouth. The prickly conversation she'd had with Jesus was making her feel ungainly and self-conscious. An impostor in her own life.

"Won the Drury case." Parker made a self-deprecating smile.

"I heard."

"Botched from start to finish. Metro should reprimand that patrolman, their crime-scene people. But they won't. A total mess—Miranda, everything."

"Which you exploited successfully."

Parker leaned away from her and squinted at the hint of disapproval.

"You okay?"

Gracey extended a twig capped with a fresh marshmallow and waved it near Charlotte's face. For the moment the sullen tautness in her cheeks had relaxed and she looked like the sweet, sincere girl she'd been a year earlier. Charlotte couldn't tell if this mood was genuine or not. Maybe Gracey was making progress, chanting some new mantra she'd learned from her therapist. Or more likely it was simply a short-lived burst of artificial serenity brought on by the miracle of pharmaceuticals. For the last year their lives had been ruled by the endless skirmishes between the drugs and Gracey's biology. Almost as quickly as they found a new pill that eased her back to normalcy, her condition mutated and the wild eruptions began again.

When Charlotte opened her arms, Gracey stepped in and embraced her with such simple warmth that, against her better judgment, all her caution and reserve dissolved and Charlotte felt a rush of unadulterated hope. Maybe this was it, the watershed moment when the storm finally passed and the sun broke through and all would be well again. She would have her Gracey back, the demon exorcised, not even a memory of its terrible possession lingering on.

Gracey drew away and gave Charlotte a cheerful smile.

"We're having white-trash hors d'oeuvres," she announced.

Charlotte took the twig and had a nibble of the white foam.

"Oh, Mom, you're supposed to roast them first. I'll do one for you. Didn't you ever go to summer camp?"

"No, I didn't. I was deprived."

Gracey took the twig back and walked over to the fire and held the white flesh near the heart of the flames.

The large man shifted in the half-light.

"Oh, I'm sorry." Parker stepped beside her, lay a hand on her arm. "Charlotte, I'd like you to meet Jacob Panther."

The big man nodded hello. His sandy hair brushed his shoulders, and his features were strong and distinctly mismatched. While there was a boyish smoothness to his skin, the sum of his features radiated the weariness of someone far older. His quiet blue eyes were heavy-lidded and moved with lazy ease. But the man drank her in with unsettling frankness. She felt the touch of his gaze like an insolent hand trickling across her cheeks.

His sharp jawline and finely etched nose clashed with the blunt chin, the wide, bullish forehead. Belligerence and gentleness in equal measure. Crude yet refined. A face at war with itself.

Now that she was only a few feet away from him, the tingle of uneasiness had grown to a bristling apprehension. She knew this guy from somewhere, and the bell it was ringing was sharp and discordant.

Charlotte managed a guarded hello and shook the man's thick hand.

She had a sip of wine and could feel Parker watching her.

The memory was there, hovering just out of view like one of those silly sayings trapped inside that fortune-telling eight ball from Charlotte's youth. Ask a question, turn the ball over, and wait for the answer to float up through the thick liquid with the same painful sluggishness as this man's face and identity were emerging from the sea of memory. Maybe his was a face from the pages of the countless mug shots she'd pored over, or one of the black-and-white printouts handed around at roll call. Or perhaps it came from some other realm entirely.

Parker said, "I went to summer camp with Jacob's uncle. We were cabin-mates. Jacob's passing through town and decided to look me up."

"Tsali?" Charlotte was holding the stranger's solemn stare.

"Camp Tsali, yeah," Parker said. "You know."

Yes, she did. Knew it damn well.

"That's why we're doing marshmallows," Gracey called over. "In memory of summer camp. It was my idea."

Charlotte broke free of the man's eyes and smiled at her daughter. Then she turned to Parker. He was gazing off at the swirl of sparks rising into the humid evening, though she could see enough of his face to know he was transporting himself to that mountain retreat his father had run for twenty years. For a man so city-tough, such an uncompromising realist, Parker Monroe could turn into a dreamy doofus in a micromoment.

Mention summer camp and a blush came to his cheeks, a shy smile surfaced, eyes looking off toward those summery fields where his best self still drew the longbow and planted arrows dead center from fifty yards away. She'd heard it all. Seen the Kodaks. Even gone with him once up to the fog-shrouded Carolina mountains and hiked over cow pastures and streams and a bald precipice to reach the gravel road that led to the padlocked gates of Camp Tsali. The place had closed for good the night Parker's father died.

That day Charlotte and Parker had climbed the gates of Camp Tsali, hiked up the steep entrance drive through a green tunnel of pines, then wandered for hours around that ghost town of log cabins and weed-infested playing fields and Indian ceremonial rings. She'd listened to the stories, and was genuinely touched by Parker's zeal. It would be easy to mock the whole thing as a bunch of spoiled country-club boys dressing up in beaded loincloths and face paint, while in their spare time working on their backhands and chip shots. But Camp Tsali was anything but cushy. It was a hell of a lot more primitive than she could have handled at that age.

She would've bailed after a single night on those unforgiving cots, and peeing without privacy in open latrines. The Coral Gables holding cells had more creature comforts.

"Indian lore," Parker said to Gracey. "That was the big thing. Tribal dances, songs, Cherokee history. Lots of woodcraft. How to survive in the wilderness. Which berries you could eat and which would kill you. Making fires, lean-tos, all that stuff."

Gracey rolled her eyes and gave Charlotte a look. Here we go again. Stouthearted man time.

Charlotte returned the look, then had a sip of her wine and angled to the left of the fire for a better view of Jacob Panther. The name as haunting as the face.

"Jacob's a Cherokee Indian," Gracey said. "Aren't you, Jacob?"

He nodded and smiled at the girl and she answered his smile with a gesture so provocative not even Stanwyck would have dared to use it.

Basking in Panther's gaze, Gracey stroked a fresh marshmallow against her cheek and in her sauciest voice she said, "Wouldn't it be nice for your lover to have marshmallow skin? So soft and powdery."

Charlotte flinched and spoke her name in warning, but Gracey ignored her.

"Your skin's already beautiful," Panther said. "Better than any marshmallow."

With a sly smile, her daughter turned away, giving Panther a full view of her ample profile. She wore a tight gray top that left a five-inch band of flesh exposed at the rim of her black jeans. A dress code ordained by the reigning pop diva. She had Parker's pale gold hair, which was parted on the side and hung straight to her shoulders. More Veronica Lake than Stanwyck. She'd inherited Charlotte's nothing-to-brag-about hazel eyes but little else. Lately, Gracey had been making droll remarks about getting lucky in the boob department—taking after her daddy's side of the family.

It was true enough. In the past year Gracey had begun to assume the figure of Parker's mother, Diana, a sinewy, athletic woman with wide shoulders, a narrow waist, and inexplicably heavy bosoms. But the hormonal gush that was reshaping Gracey's body had yet to touch her face. Her complexion was as flawless as warm crème brûlée. And her childish, pudgy cheeks and trusting eyes seemed absurdly at odds with what was appearing below.

Charlotte thought of her as treacherously beautiful, but still thankfully lacking in the vanity of most teenage girls who were so endowed. The boys at her school had gotten the message and were calling nightly. Polite enough when Charlotte answered, but in a hushed fever to get past the gatekeeper and whisper their secret charms in her daughter's ear.

"I noticed the plates on your truck," Charlotte said to their guest. "I take it you're from Daytona Beach?"

He looked at her, but the question tripped nothing in his eyes.

"You'll have to excuse Charlotte," said Parker. "She's a cop. Spends her days interrogating people, she comes home, can't turn it off."

"It's all right," Jacob said. "No, I'm not from Daytona. I move around. I'm a traveling man."

Gracey drew another marshmallow from the fire. She plucked at the shriveled black mess and pinched a bit into her mouth. Charlotte caught her eye and waved her back over to join in, but Gracey shook her head and resumed her scrutiny of the blackened goo in her hand.

Pressing his beer bottle to his sweaty cheek, Panther smiled at Charlotte. Though there was nothing overtly wolfish in the grin, his eyes lingered too long, becoming familiar, challenging.

"You have anything in mind for dinner?" Parker asked her.

"If you mean am I cooking, the answer's no. I'm done in."

"I was thinking of Norman's. A little celebration. Wouldn't need a reservation on a Thursday this early."

Jacob Panther turned from them and gazed out at the swath of moonlight on the polished water of the wide canal. The embroidery on the back of his shirt was red and black, a series of concentric circles, some interlocked, some broken, like a maze seen from high above.

Charlotte stared at his broad shoulders, urging the recollection up through the murky depths.

Nudging her arm, Parker gave her a quick "What's wrong?" wave of his hand. But Charlotte just smiled and looked away.

"When we go to Norman's I get the yellowtail snapper with garlic mashed potatoes," Gracey said to Panther. "It's the best. Norman always comes over to our table. He's cute. I'd *so* marry him. He could cook for me every night."

The big man nodded, still wearing the bold smile he'd given Charlotte.

As she studied the man's profile, his identity finally began to clarify, a shape congealing from the fog. Of course, of course. Jacob Panther. Sweet Jesus Mother of God.

"You know you look like somebody," Gracey said. "Doesn't he, Dad? Doesn't he look like somebody we know? I can't think who."

Panther turned slowly from the darkness.

"I get that a lot. I must have a common face."

"Anything but," Charlotte said quietly. Parker heard and turned in her direction. She set her wineglass down on the arm of a lawn chair, saying, "Norman's sounds fine. I just need to freshen up. Back in a sec."

Parker shot her a puzzled look, but she didn't field it, didn't even hold his eyes for an extra tick, not wanting anything to trigger Jacob Panther's sensors.

Charlotte ambled to the kitchen, then, when she was certain she was out of sight, she jogged down the hallway past the master suite to the back guest room where she stored her work files and her laptop.

She sat down at her desk, switched on the IBM, opened the DSL connection, and a second later she typed in the Web address for the Federal Bureau of Investigation. With two clicks she was looking at a thumbnail photo of the man on their patio. He hadn't even bothered with an alias.

Though the FBI didn't number them anymore, counting down from the top of the page their blond guest held the eighth position on the Most Wanted list.

FIVE

"So I hear you're one tough son of a bitch," Jacob said.

"What?" Parker stiffened.

"You're a rough-and-tumble guy."

"I don't know what you're talking about."

"That's what Uncle Thomas said. Lots of fistfights, hell-bent to prove yourself. Chip on your shoulder."

Parker poured the dregs of his beer onto the dying embers.

"That's what he said. Don't turn your back on Parker Monroe. Only makes sense a guy like you would turn out to be a lawyer."

Parker was floored.

In a profession so shamelessly belligerent, he'd always prided himself on the opposite virtue, an unassuming manner, a quiet though tenacious passion for fairness. In the courtroom he adopted an old-fashioned pace, dawdling, meandering. Unfailingly serene and polite in cross-examinations. When he had no choice but to object to a prosecutor's line of questioning, he was courteous to a fault. No irony, no sarcasm, 100 percent sincere. A twenty-first-century Atticus Finch. And that, he believed, was the source of his success. He was a man out of time. His hyped-up adversaries with their eye-gouging tactics didn't know how to respond. Next to Parker either they came across as grossly aggressive or—by trying to compete with his approach—they assumed a laid-back pose that struck juries as totally bogus.

"Win at any cost." Jacob was still smiling. "Hiking, felling trees, rope climbing, starting campfires, whatever it was. Had to do it bigger, better, faster. Super gung ho."

"Funny," Parker said. "I don't remember it that way."

"Like you needed to prove yourself to all those other rich snots, you being the owner's kid. You had to make up for it some way. That's what Uncle Thomas said. I'm just repeating."

Jacob sipped his beer and stared out at the moonlight glazing the canal.

"I remember a couple of fights. No more than anyone else."

"No need to be defensive. I don't believe he meant it as a criticism," Jacob said. "I think he admired you for it, 'cause that's how he felt himself. Out of place. Not one of those prep-school types with their silverware manners. Then, of course, he was the token redskin, all those boys spying on him day and night, trying to see if he pissed and shit like regular human beings."

"I suppose that must've been hard."

"Being a fighter," Jacob said, "sometimes it's the only way to survive."

Parker waited for him to continue, to make his point, but Jacob went silent, and his face turned again to the water.

"What's all this about, Jacob?"

The big man glanced his way briefly, then looked back into the glittering darkness.

"Looks to me like you're still that way, Parker. Gung ho, competitive."

Jacob Panther gazed across the canal at the McCollums' brightly lit backyard, their Great Dane enlarging the excavation it had been working on all week. When he turned back to Parker he had a quiet smile.

"You in some kind of trouble, Jacob? Because that's what I do. I get people out of trouble."

"I know what you do."

Parker could see that Gracey was transfixed by the conversation. Allowed to stay and witness an unguarded adult encounter. It was one of the areas of disagreement in child rearing between Charlotte and him. Parker argued they should treat Gracey as an equal, include her as much as possible in family decision-making. Charlotte lobbied hard the other way. Wanting to prolong the girl's childhood as long as possible. Adults ran the show, children followed the rules. Lately it had turned into a good cop, bad cop situation. Parker the permissive one, Charlotte the enforcer. Gracey sensed it, and was exploiting the friction between them to negotiate herself the best possible outcomes. Daddy's little bargainer.

"You're not passing through town, are you? This isn't a social call."

"No, it's not."

"Well?"

Jacob glanced at Gracey for a moment and his face relaxed.

"You got yourself a handsome family. You're a lucky man."

Then he stepped close to Parker and spoke with such grim authority that Parker felt something lurch and stumble in his gut.

"You're next."

"What the hell is that supposed to mean?"

Parker set his beer bottle on the edge of the barbecue pit and took a moment to gather himself.

"This have something to do with your uncle Thomas?"

"Thomas, no." Jacob's eyes flashed to Parker's. "The spider dragged Thomas off to the darkening land."

Parker repeated the phrase to himself, fetching through the fog of years.

"Thomas is dead?"

"Well, you remember *something* they taught you at camp."

Tilting his head back, Jacob looked up at the first faint stars.

"Heart attack, six years ago. Too much whiskey."

Parker chose that moment to pose the question he'd been wanting to ask since Panther showed up at his door.

"And your mother, Lucy? How is she?"

"I'm forbidden to speak of her."

"Whoa," Gracey said, coming closer. "What's that mean?"

Without taking his eyes from Jacob, Parker said, "It's a Cherokee thing."

"Forbidden to speak of her. Like what, she's being shunned or something? Kicked out of the tribe. She did something bad?"

48

"Not shunned." He looked at his daughter, reached out and lay a hand on her shoulder and maneuvered her to his side so the two of them were facing Panther. The man's face had lost the last wisps of amusement. A defiant stare emerging as though he was daring Parker to explain this to his daughter.

Even though it had been almost thirty years, the words came easily, those strange, foreign lessons imprinted in his marrow.

"The Cherokee are one of the few cultures where women have as much power as men. Women were held in such high regard among the Cherokee people that long ago, if a woman's name was so much as mentioned when warriors went into battle, the fighter's resolve was thought to be seriously weakened. So the warriors on the edge of the battlefield were forbidden to speak the names of women."

"Cool," Gracey said. "That's a tribe I'd like to belong to."

Jacob looked around at Parker's home, at the canal, the palm trees rustling. Then his eyes drifted back to Parker.

"You ever been back to Tsali?"

"Once."

"Log cabins are still standing," Panther said. "A few rotted away, but it looks a lot like it did. The fire tower you guys built. Tetherball stands. The dam's still holding, but it doesn't look real solid. Dining hall's there, infirmary. Not in great shape, but standing."

Parker watched him hold out his palm and stare down at it as if he were trying to read his own fortune in the frail moonlight.

"You remember the Sequoyah Caverns? Up on Bald Knob?"

Parker said yes, he remembered them.

"Thomas said you two used to sneak up there and smoke dope."

"Dope?" Gracey said. "You smoked dope?"

"I was young. It was a long time ago."

"Caverns are all grown over. Kudzu, laurel bushes." Jacob fanned a night bug from his face. "Walk right past them, never know they were there. Good place to hide."

In a huff, Gracey pulled away from Parker, pitched her marshmallow stick into the moonlit water, and stalked toward the house.

Parker raised his hand to call her back, try to explain the dope thing if that's what was upsetting her, but she'd already disappeared into the shadows.

"Okay," Parker said. "Now talk to me, Jacob."

"I'd say you've got a few things to figure out."

"What things?"

"About your family. Where you've been, where you're headed."

"Come on, cut the double-talk."

"You know who I am? That'd be a good place to start."

Parker looked into the young man's eyes. His mind blank.

"I can't help you if you won't tell me what's going on, Jacob."

"Looks to me like you might've gone a little soft, living like this. Citified. Fighting with words instead of muscle and flesh."

He looked from left to right, searching the darkness.

"I've done what I can," Jacob said. "Slowed them down. But there's no stopping it. They'll show up eventually. They will."

"Who?"

"You say you're good at getting people out of trouble, and I can see you make a damn fine living at it. Now you better see how good you are at getting your own self out of trouble."

"What kind of trouble am I in?"

"Worst kind there is. You've probably got a few days. Two, three maybe."

"Are you saying my family is in some kind of imminent danger? How would you know such a thing? Talk to me, Jacob."

Panther opened and closed his right fist several times as though pumping a tennis ball.

"Look," he said. "You got a john around here? I need to get rid of this beer."

Parker motioned vaguely toward the French doors.

"Through the kitchen, down the hall, first door on your left."

For a long moment in the half-light, Jacob studied Parker's face. Cocked forward, tense, he seemed to be debating some long-standing argument, his eyes making difficult calculations as they roamed Parker's features. Finally he reached out and put a warm hand on Parker's bare arm. Flesh to flesh.

At that moment Parker thought it was only the snap of static electricity passing between them, but afterward, for as long as he would live, the nerves on that patch of skin prickled as though he had been forever branded by Jacob Panther's handprint.

Jacob took his hand away and lowered his eyes to the flagstones, cleared his throat gruffly like a man trying to choke back an unwelcome emotion, and glided away toward the house.

SIX

CHARLOTTE CALLED LIEUTENANT RODRIGUEZ AT home but got his answering machine. Then she dialed the Gables special weapons and tactics number, and a rookie answered. He was manning the phones while the rest of the SWAT guys were out assisting a Metro hostage situation that was turning into an all-nighter.

So she broke with chain of command and called Frank Sheffield.

A couple of sentences into her explanation, Frank put her on hold and kept her there two minutes, three, while she stared at the thumbnail photo of Jacob Panther.

When Sheffield clicked back on, first thing he asked was if she had her handgun nearby.

"In the next room."

"It's to be used for self-protection only. Okay? No heroes."

"You're sending your people?"

"That's right. SWAT."

"Shit, Frank. By the time they get in gear, I could have a dozen Gables cops here. This part of town we've got less than a two-minute response time."

"Forget it, Monroe. This is ours. It's already in motion."

"I'm going to catch shit from Rodriguez."

"Rodriguez will be fine. You called him first, did it by the book."

"How soon?"

"Choppers on the pad, firing up. Perimeter's going up right now. I'm already in my car—five, ten minutes tops."

For the last year Sheffield had been special agent in charge of the Miami field office. Ten years back she'd met him for the first time at a Miracle Mile bank robbery when the feds took over. Nice guy, not the usual stiff-backed hotshot. In fact, he was the only slacker she'd ever met in the FBI. Notorious for his maverick approach, his laid-back style. Everybody she knew in local law enforcement was amazed the guy hadn't been canned long ago, and doubly amazed he'd been promoted to the top slot of one of the largest regional offices in the country.

"Can you tell if he's armed?"

"You already asked that, Frank, and I said no, not that I can see."

"Whatever you do, don't let Parker in on it. No offense, but your husband's liable to have Panther bailed out of jail before we can arrest the son of a bitch."

"This isn't funny, Frank. My family's at risk. My daughter."

At the groan of a floorboard in the hallway, she shot a look over her shoulder and in the same moment clicked her mouse to kill the FBI page. Nobody there. In that old house the oak planks were always creaking from the muggy air swelling the wood, the constant breezes stressing the rafters.

"This is a bad dude, Monroe. Eight homicides."

"I've read the stuff on the site. I've got the picture."

"Blown five banks so far, every other month for the last year. We got half a dozen agents with the Southeast Bomb Task Force out of Atlanta working full-time on the guy. Those boys are going to be pissed we made the takedown."

"Got to wonder," she said, "why the hell someone blows up banks."

"We'll ask him in a few minutes."

Charlotte's breath burned her throat. Chitchatting while FBI's Number Eight was on her patio.

"I got to go, Frank."

"Keep him distracted. Give him some wine, truffles. Whatever you people eat in the Gables."

"Not funny."

"Well, I guess this explains the airport thing."

"What airport thing?"

"What, your power go off over there? A guy got assassinated at MIA this afternoon. Blowgun, poison dart. Eyewitness got a look at the boy who did it. Tall, heavyset, long hair. She thought maybe a Miccosukee or Seminole from the design on the shirt he was wearing."

"Why do you say 'assassinated'?"

"Dead guy was the son of some congressman, in town for some fund-raising thing. Gets whacked going down the escalator to baggage claim. Media's playing up the political angle."

"A blowgun? You can't be serious."

"Dart lodged in the neck. Unless the perp walked up and smacked him with a dart, which doesn't seem likely, it was some kind of air-pressure weapon. Tribue went down—five, six seconds later, he's cold."

"And that fits Panther's MO, a blowgun?"

"Not really. But he's one of the names that popped when we ran the eye-witness stuff. Now here he is, standing in your living room eating liver pâté. So hey, two plus two."

"Bye, Frank. I'll leave the front door open. No need for the battering ram. Parker's touchy about that front door. You damage it, he'll sue."

She slapped the phone down and turned to see Gracey in the doorway.

"So who was that, your boyfriend again?"

Gracey was holding a sheet of paper. The serene look had dissolved. Now her lower lip jutted, eyes frosted over as if the dizzy white noise was filling her head. In only a few moments her daughter had been swept up by the storm of molecules and mitochondria and assorted unruly chemicals. A cheerful, imaginative teenage girl body-snatched and replaced by a warped, fun-house-mirror version.

"I was discussing work," said Charlotte.

"Yeah, right, Mom, whatever you say. But I don't care if you have a boyfriend. Be kind of nice, really. Make you less boring. Give my life a little texture and dimension."

"There's no boyfriend, Gracey. Now stop that."

She held out the paper and rattled it.

"Dad said I should get you to sign this."

"It'll have to wait."

"It's so I can do a ride-along with a Metro cop. An eight-hour shift with a real police officer. Go into the ghetto, the down and dirty world."

Charlotte stood up, came over to Gracey, took her by the upper arm, and tugged her into the room. She leaned out, peered down the empty hallway, then shut the door.

"Steven thinks I need more life experience. Breathe some exhaust fumes. Experience some hard knocks."

"Listen, sweetie, something's come up. We can talk about this later."

"I'm your daughter," Gracey said. "Don't my needs count?"

"Of course they do, you're the most important thing there is, but . . ."

"Yeah, right. You spend all day pulling winos out of Dumpsters, you don't have a lot left for your family when you get home."

"Don't say that, Gracey, you know it isn't true."

"Steven had a shitty childhood. Mega personal pain. He thinks I'm too sheltered to be a real artist. I'll never get the depth into my work without more heartache, struggle."

"Steven thinks this. Some friend from school?"

"Spielberg, stupid."

"Oh, Gracey. Come on."

"*Jaws*, you know, Mom. *E.T., Jurassic Park*. Just the biggest movies of all time. That Steven."

"I know who he is."

"Steven's made me his protégée. He sees what I'm capable of. He's chosen me."

Charlotte measured a breath. Stay logical, the shrink said. Don't buy in to her fantasy. Keep showing her the real world, its shape, its hard contours.

"You've spoken with him on the phone?"

"We talk all the time. He's considering me for a project."

Charlotte stopped, listened. She thought she heard the heavy thud of a helicopter but then wasn't sure.

"I have to go, sweetie. If you want to do a ride-along, I'm not ruling it out. But we need to discuss it."

"Rules," Gracey said. "Everything's against the rules. Rules, rules, rules. You know all the rules, don't you, Mom? You got them all memorized."

"I know some of them."

"Well, Steven didn't get where he is by following rules. No real artist does. They make their own. That's what creativity is, Mom, in case you haven't heard, breaking the rules. What you're trying to do is suffocate me. Push all the air out of my lungs, sit on my chest, and turn me into some kind of mushroom fungus. A goddamn toadstool, that's what you want me to be."

"Okay, I've listened to you, now you listen to me. Go to your room right now, Gracey. I'm not mad at you, I'm not punishing you, and I won't try to keep you from doing what you want with your life, but right now, this second, you have to go to your room, lock the door, and stay there till I come for you. Okay? There's something going on. It's a volatile situation, sweetie, and I want you to be safe. In your room. Now."

Gracey bent her arm backward and dug her thumb at her bra strap, tugging it back into place. The artless gesture of a child wrestling with a twenty-year-old's body.

When the strap was fixed, Gracey swung toward the built-in bookshelves in the corner of the room.

"I told you what the bitch would say. Didn't I tell you?"

"Gracey, stop that."

Staring at the bookshelf, she lowered her voice to a whisper, only a few words audible. "My life. Bruises. Haven't forgotten."

Charlotte reached out for Gracey, then let her hand fall. Fighting the instinct to wrench her daughter's arm, shake her hard, do whatever it took to drag her back from that dark oblivion.

Gracey stared at the spines of the books and listened to the phantom voice, and nodded and mumbled some reply, then by slow degrees her eyes resurfaced and her gaze drifted from the shelves and settled on Charlotte. A grim mask tightening into place on her child's face. Stanwyck, Bogart, the lifeless look.

"This is about him, isn't it? That phone call, how you're acting. It's about Jacob."

Charlotte glanced up at the ceiling, hearing it, the thrash of blades somewhere within a few blocks.

"I know who he is, Mom. I've got eyes. I'm not a kid you have to hide things from. You should've come out and told me. But no, you think I'm this little girl in gingham frocks, some goody-goody you have to protect. Well, it's too late for that. I can see who he is. I'm not stupid."

"I don't know what you're talking about, Gracey."

"You're such a liar. I just talked to him in the hall and asked him straight out, and he said yes. He admitted it."

"In the hallway? Just now?"

"Goddamn it," Gracey said. "Why doesn't anyone listen to me? You think if you ignore me, I'll just go away. That's what you really want, isn't it? Well, okay, maybe I will. Maybe I'll just leave. I'm wasting my time here anyway. The way you've tried to turn me into a privileged little brat. Always so goddamned worried about protecting me. Well, it won't work, Mom. Know why? Because I don't need any of this shit, and you know what else? I don't want to be protected. Not by you. Not by anyone."

Gracey gestured at the room and the house beyond it, then her head rocked back, shoulders trembled, eyes blinking rapidly. A full-scale meltdown. The tears welling, quickly brimming over, her nose running. Gracey fragmenting.

Charlotte put an arm around her shoulder, pulled her into a hug, spoke into her hair, into the smell of clover and rain. The girl shivered and twisted against Charlotte's embrace, a token resistance, then she grew still.

"Look, sweetie, I want you to stay right here in my office till I come back for you. Don't go anywhere. Don't move. You've got to promise me."

Gracey spoke through her tears.

"I need to e-mail Mr. Underwood, tell him I'm going to do ride-alongs. He agrees with Steven. I need more seasoning, more bumps and bruises."

"Nobody needs more bruises, honey."

Gracey tore away from the hug, her eyes wild and scarlet.

"What do you know? Driving around in your bulletproof vest all day, reading the rule book. What do you know about anything?"

"Okay, fine, e-mail your teacher. Use my laptop. Just stay here till I come back. Promise me."

"Sure, Mom. Whatever."

SEVEN

"HE'S IN THE BATHROOM, OKAY? He had to piss. Jesus, Charlotte, what the hell's going on with you?"

She stepped over to the front window and tugged the drapes aside. Panther's red pickup truck was still there.

"Charlotte? Talk to me, damn it. What's going on?"

She swung around, brought her voice to a hoarse whisper.

"FBI SWAT team is on the way. We've got a minute or two at most."

"What!"

With a slash of her hand she silenced him.

She gave him the two-sentence version. FBI Most Wanted list. Eight homicides. When she was done, Parker stared up at the glitter of the crystal chandelier. His lips parted but no words came.

"Gracey's in my office. You go stay with her, Parker, and I'll keep Panther occupied till they get here."

Parker clamped his lips and shook his head.

She gripped Parker's elbow and tugged him toward the door.

"Stay with your daughter. I'll handle this."

He roused himself from his daze, stared at her hand, and shrugged loose.

"No," he said. "No fucking way."

She pointed a finger at him and he stared at it, bewildered.

She angled away from the door, lowering her voice to an airless hiss.

"This is my territory, Parker. When Panther's in custody, feel free to take charge, habeas corpus to your heart's content, but this situation right here, right now, this is what I'm trained for. This is what I'm about. Okay?"

He stepped back from her, hand rising to brush his cheek as if a bullet had skimmed his flesh. She'd never pulled rank on him before or used her cop voice. Never tried it, never had to.

Something shuddered in Parker's eyes. Perhaps he felt the faint slip and buckle of the tectonic plates, no earthquake yet, but a crack in the foundation of their bond.

Charlotte found a softer voice, as close to gentle as she could manage.

"Go stay with Gracey. Please. It'll be over in minutes."

"Okay, okay." He showed his palms. "But no gunfire, right? Taking him alive, that's the idea."

"Always is."

She shot a look at the door. Empty.

"It's got to be more than that this time. You've got to protect him, Charlotte, you've got to be absolutely sure."

"Keep your voice down."

Parker backed off to a harsh whisper.

"Don't let this get out of hand. Go the extra mile, okay? Promise me. You've got to promise."

"What the hell, Parker?"

He dabbed his tongue at his upper lip and stared again at the empty brilliance of the chandelier.

"That boy . . ." Parker swallowed and couldn't go on.

"That boy what?"

Parker shook his head and lowered his gaze to hers. He shook his head another time as if refusing some command.

"What is it, Parker? Talk to me."

"He's my son, Charlotte. My flesh and blood."

.   .   .

It wasn't Frank Sheffield's fault. He repeated Monroe's address twice to the airfield dispatcher and thought he heard the confirmation behind the layer of static. But the MTS handhelds the chopper personnel used were regularly desensed by the Nextel site a half-mile away from where they were stationed. Depended on the weather, number of cell-phone calls coming and going. Miami field office had been complaining to D.C. long before Sheffield took over. Memos and more memos. Get them better equipment or move the chopper field somewhere out of the dead zone, or else blow the goddamn tower.

Finally, last year D.C. sent down two geeks to run a check with their spectrum analyzer. But after a week of crisscrossing the territory in question, the techies couldn't identify any discrete interfering signals.

"How about the Nextel tower?" Sheffield said. "You know, that twelve-story object that's taller than anything within ten square miles. Bouncing a few thousand microwave signals every second. Think that might be it, fellas?"

The techies couldn't confirm it. They left, and no one got back to Sheffield. Papers shuffled. Budgets cut, funds diverted to more pressing needs. Same old shit.

So tonight the chopper dispatched to Parker Monroe's address hovered ten blocks east of its objective, and its enormous spotlight scanned the front and backyard of Dr. and Mrs. Jeffrey Silberman's two-story Mediterranean, while seven black-suited, heavily armed federal agents battered down the heart surgeon's front door.

Considering how fucked their radios were, it was a miracle the rapid-response guys got as close to the target as they did.

With a steadying hand against the dining-room table, Charlotte said, "Panther's in his late twenties." Struggling with the simple math, her head so fogged. "So you were, what, fourteen?"

"Fifteen," he said. "It's a long story, Charlotte."

He crossed the room and offered his arms. She hesitated, feeling her own geologic tremors deep beneath their common ground. She retreated a step, and Parker lowered his arms.

"You've known this how long? For years? That you had a son?"

"Not until tonight."

"He told you that? He told you he was your son?"

"No one told me. I saw it in his eyes, his bone structure. Who his mother is, his age. Look, I'm just now sorting it out myself."

"So you're not sure. You're guessing."

"We don't need a blood test. He's my son, Charlotte."

Outside in the driveway, tires screamed.

She got to the window in a second, yanked the curtains back, and caught a flash of the rear lights of Parker's Mercedes swerving onto Riviera Drive.

"Goddamn it."

Before she turned away, she saw, above the oaks and royal palms, a helicopter's searchlight washing across a neighborhood at least a mile away.

"Aw, shit. Shit, shit, shit."

She sprinted to the kitchen. Dug her cell phone from her purse and speed-dialed Gables emergency. Getting Mary Troutman, thank God, a veteran of twenty years.

"They've got the wrong address, so the perimeter's off. And it's not the red truck I told them he was driving. He's in Parker's Mercedes. Silver sedan, heading north on Riviera toward U.S. 1." She spelled out Parker's vanity plate, DFENDR.

Mary kept her on the line while she patched into the FBI. As Charlotte drummed a finger against the stove top, Parker passed through the kitchen, heading down the hallway.

With the line still empty, Charlotte grabbed the Cabernet bottle from the counter and took a slug. She put the bottle down, wiped her mouth, and craned to see from the kitchen window if the chopper was still there, but a hibiscus bush blocked her view. One of many chores Parker had been neglecting, working all that overtime to get a guilty kid off a murder rap.

"Everything's busy," Mary said. "They're probably calling each other, a lot of backslapping."

"Keep trying. Call me when you get through."

When she snapped the phone shut, Parker was at her side, out of breath.

"Gracey's not in her room, not in your office. Nowhere."

Charlotte's throat shut. Something hot and hard lodged there.

"We've got to go," Parker said. "Now, Charlotte."

"He took her? The bastard took her hostage?"

"We don't know that. Now come on."

Charlotte clawed through her purse, grabbed her holstered Beretta Cougar. Then sprinted after Parker.

By the time she reached the truck, he was revving. Charlotte threw herself in the passenger's seat as he peeled toward the street.

"Left," she said. "Left, north. Go."

Parker slammed through the gears, fishtailing onto Riviera.

"Your headlights," Charlotte shouted at him.

He found the lever, got them on, bumped to high beams. Roared down their street, toward a four-way stop.

"Which way?"

"Straight, I don't know. Yeah, straight. Best thing for him is to head for traffic. Up to Dixie. Assuming he knows his way around."

Parker fired through the intersection.

"I don't get it," Parker said. "Why would Jacob take her? It just complicates things, slows him down."

"Maybe he got scared, thought he needed a hostage."

"Doesn't make sense."

"Or maybe she went willingly. God knows. She was having a major mood swing."

Three or four blocks ahead, the Mercedes had pulled two wheels onto the shoulder. Parker was doing seventy through a twenty zone, maybe half a minute behind.

"They've taken off on foot," she said.

But as Parker closed to a hundred yards, the Mercedes swerved back on the street and roared north toward the busy thoroughfare.

"He was waiting. Like he didn't want to lose us."

"Not good," she said. "Some kind of game."

Her cell phone chirped and she pressed it to her ear.

Sheffield was yelling over engine noise. Men shouting.

"I'm standing in your living room, Monroe. What the hell's going on?"

She hesitated a moment, then began to fill him in, Parker waving no, grabbing for the phone.

Charlotte leaned out of range and gave Sheffield their location, told him they were giving chase, and snapped the phone shut.

"Goddamn it, Charlotte."

"It's my duty. I have no choice."

"Your duty? Putting your daughter in jeopardy, those gun-happy cowboys."

"Getting my daughter *out* of jeopardy."

"Jesus Christ, Charlotte." He hammered the wheel. "Jesus H. Christ."

Two blocks ahead, the Mercedes weaved back and forth, then took a sharp right into someone's front yard, disappearing into the shadows. Probably trying to duck down one of the narrow alleys that laced the area.

As Parker sped up, a pair of reflective eyes flashed in their path. A dog, a possum. He swung the wheel, hit the brakes, and the high-riding truck bounced over a curb, blowing through a hedge. Parker wrestled it back to the pavement and accelerated.

Behind them she heard the chopper coming low and loud. A moment later their windshield turned to blinding white light. Parker flipped down the visor, used one hand to shield his eyes, kept going.

"Those morons."

A booming voice ordered them to halt, step out of their vehicle.

"What the hell're they doing?"

"Goddamn it. Sheffield doesn't know about the car switch. They think we're Panther."

"Great. Just great."

Charlotte flipped open her phone, then snapped it shut. It was useless now, things unfolding too fast.

"Will they fire?"

"Not the chopper, but *they* might." She waved at the half-dozen cars peeling out of side streets, blue lights whirling, assembling a hasty barrier.

"The Benz. That yard two houses down. Something's wrong."

Parker took his foot off the gas, staring out at the men and cars, coasting at fifty-plus.

"Don't do it, Parker. Stop right here, let them take over."

But Parker shook his head. He grimaced so hard, the outline of his skull rose as if through the cloudy waters of his flesh. He was crossing some ancient line. Animal self prevailing over man-of-the-law.

He flattened the gas and picked his spot. Helmeted men in black were still piling out of their cars and vans, shotguns and assault rifles. But they were seconds too late setting up. Parker hurtled through the blockade, clipped a white Ford, nearly lost control. Their rear glass exploded and the slug blew out Charlotte's window, filling her lap with broken glass.

Twenty yards from the Mercedes, Parker stood on the brake and the pickup got sideways and began to tip, but he cut the wheel and brought it down. As they spun, Charlotte caught a glimpse of Parker's silver car. Front end crumpled against a tree.

Their truck finished its 360 and came to rest with its big bumper against the driver's-side door of the Mercedes.

Sirens howled behind them, and the chopper trapped them again in its dazzling lights. Through the shattered window, Charlotte saw long blond hair, longer and blonder than Panther's. She wiped her eyes, threw open her door. Her daughter was slumped behind the steering wheel of the Mercedes, air bag deflated in her lap.

Gracey's head lolled against her half-open window.

Charlotte unholstered the Beretta, held it two-handed above her right shoulder, and approached.

Rumbling from above, the voice in the chopper commanded her to throw down her weapon. Her last chance or they would commence firing.

Charlotte ignored him and stooped to aim inside the car. Her heart taking a wild flight around her rib cage. Just Gracey. No Panther.

She heard Sheffield yelling at her. To her right she glimpsed Parker on his knees, hands raised. Visored men slammed him facedown into the grass, a knee in his back.

Charlotte lowered her Beretta. As she reached out to grip the door handle, Gracey jerked upright.

She straightened slowly, then turned her head to look out the half-open window and she smiled.

Then Charlotte's daughter began to giggle.

"Gracey!"

Powerful hands gripped Charlotte's shoulders and struggled to force her down. Sheffield ordering them to stop. It was okay. This woman was a cop.

"I fooled you," Gracey said. "I told him it would work. You're so smart, but you weren't smart this time, were you, Mom? Were you? You played by the rules and see where it got you. Jacob escaped, didn't he? He just walked down the sidewalk and left."

"Gracey, good God, what were you thinking?"

She pulled open the door and hauled her daughter out.

Her eyes flaming, Gracey looked around at the circle of men, guns drawn. Her father with his face mashed into someone's lawn. In the blaze of the overhead light she extended her right forearm and admired it.

"Look," she said. "It's turning blue."

"What's she talking about?" Frank Sheffield was staring at the girl.

"This is awesome. Steven's going to love it. He's going to freak."

EIGHT

AFTER GRACEY'S SCRAPES WERE TENDED by the paramedics, she and Charlotte and Parker sat for an hour in Frank Sheffield's car while the hunt for Jacob Panther ran its futile course. Then Frank drove them to the FBI field office in North Miami Beach, and until well after midnight they were confined in a small conference room, grilled by Sheffield and two other agents and a female federal attorney, a prematurely gray woman in her forties who was annoyed she'd been summoned so late in the evening.

One of the agents wanted very much to press charges: aiding and abetting, reckless endangerment of federal officers for Parker's storming of their barricade. For well over an hour Parker quietly picked apart the agents' arguments with questions delicately phrased to suggest that the recklessness and endangering had been brought on by the FBI's failure to arrive at the correct address in a timely manner, and by their gross negligence in firing their weapons on innocent civilians. Parker had feared for his own life and his wife's life because of the mistaken identity, and he felt he had no recourse but to run the barricade. A suit for damages wasn't out of the question. The federal attorney said nothing, but kept shaking her head in reluctant admiration of Parker's rebuttals.

Early on, Charlotte managed to get Gracey excused from the interrogation. The girl sat in the waiting area watching Leno, while Parker and Charlotte were cross-examined. First and foremost, the agents wanted to know what information either of them had about Panther's current whereabouts, his plans, his destination, anything he might have said that could help them focus their dragnet while he was still in the vicinity. But the Monroes could offer nothing helpful. Sorry. Panther hadn't revealed any clues whatsoever about his destination or the location of his hideout.

Then the federal attorney joined in. She wanted very much to learn why a notorious fugitive, the subject of a yearlong national manhunt, would show up at the door of a well-known defense attorney. Was Parker Monroe by any chance offering his services to the young man, or had his services already been engaged by Panther?

Certainly not.

Well, be that as it may, was it possible that Mr. Monroe was in a position to negotiate a surrender of this man?

No, he was absolutely not in that position.

Then what the hell was the purpose of Panther's appearance at the Monroe home?

A simple social call, Parker had repeated, over and over. Panther's uncle Thomas and Parker had once been close friends, and Panther was simply stopping by to say hello. Charlotte kept silent on that one. Technically it was true. Throughout the whole ordeal, Parker continued to be scrupulously honest in answering every question, yet somehow he managed to avoid revealing that Jacob Panther was his son.

In a way she was grateful. Because Charlotte knew the revelation would keep them in that conference room for hours more, covering and re-covering the same ground. And their coming days and weeks were likely to be monopolized by more interrogations. She would no doubt be suspended from work until the FBI was satisfied that she and Parker had told all they knew. And, worst of all, Gracey would be subjected to a whole new set of stresses that were very likely to worsen her condition. So Charlotte had deferred to Parker's knowledge of the law and his skillful dodges, at least for the moment.

Withholding such information might or might not be illegal, though she knew it was at the very least unethical. Even though it wasn't immediately clear to her how the FBI's investigation might be aided by knowing that Panther was related to Parker, she still had to work hard to restrain her cop instincts. Her training told her that every scrap of information mattered in an investigation. It was impossible to foresee how one fact or another might pay off.

But by that hour of the night she was exhausted and bewildered and wanted desperately to bring an end to their ordeal, and get Gracey back to the safety of her home. So she kept her mouth shut, telling herself it would be better to sort this out with Parker in private before she came clean with Frank Sheffield. There was time enough for that tomorrow.

After they returned home, Charlotte stayed by Gracey's bedside until her mutterings died away and she fell into a heavy sleep.

Then she went to their darkened bedroom and slipped into the sheets beside Parker.

"Okay," she said. "Let's hear it."

"Not now, Charlotte. We can do it tomorrow. You know I'm not going to bullshit you. I need to absorb this first, get it straight in my head."

"Screw that, Parker. Talk to me."

"Look, I know you're angry and you have every right to be, but please, let's do this tomorrow, okay? Whole truth, nothing but. I promise."

She rubbed at her eyes, tried to soothe the thudding pain.

He rolled over and kissed her good night. A quick, dry touching of lips. Not the most memorable kiss, or the warmest. But it was their unspoken pact. Never in their seventeen years of marriage had they gone to sleep without that kiss. Whatever arguments may have estranged them during the day were to be resolved by bedtime. And the kiss had always served to put their petty squabbles officially behind them.

Although, on this night, no kiss on earth could have accomplished that.

"No, Parker," she said. "It's going to be now. Not tomorrow, when you've had time to polish it up. I want the whole thing. Unvarnished. Now."

A slant of moonlight cut across their sheets. Parker took a long breath and blew it out, then began the tale.

Charlotte had heard most of the story so many times before that it had taken up residence in the recesses of her mind, living alongside her own memories with such heft and vividness that sometimes she found herself unintentionally mingling her own youth with Parker's.

The violence, the fire, the trial, all of it he told the same way she'd heard it a dozen times before. But tonight he added something new. The story of the Cherokee girl. The youthful love affair. And hearing that part, that missing thread that interwove the rest of the events of that terrible summer, changed everything.

NINE

PARKER'S FATHER WAS NAMED CHARLES Andrew Monroe, but to the two hundred boys who filled the log cabins of the summer camp he owned and operated for more than twenty years, he was known simply as Chief. Camp Tsali occupied two hundred acres of mountaintop land two days' hike west and south of Asheville, North Carolina. Meadows and old-growth forest laced with clear streams and ancient Indian trails, all perched on a craggy knoll that gazed out at the very heart of the Great Smoky Mountains. From the front porch of the tribal lodge or the open-air dining pavilion, a boy could stand and gaze out at the silhouettes of eight mountain ranges stacked back to back. Forty miles of misty wilderness in every direction.

Chief was six feet tall, with a mane of black Irish hair, wide shoulders, an outdoorsman's ruddy complexion, and the resonant voice, the hard blue eyes, and the quiet but commanding presence of a four-star general who had never lost a battle and by God never would.

Each June another crop of innocents journeyed up the steep gravel road and dragged their duffels from expensive cars and trooped like pilgrims before Charles Andrew Monroe. Their fathers and mothers stood shyly in the background, entrusting their sons to Chief with the understanding that he had two months to transform their boys into men, or at least accomplish that part of the task they themselves were incapable of. And he rarely disappointed them. Before the summer was done, he would anoint each of his boys with a powerful dose of his manly charisma, a wafer of himself on every tongue.

As his only child, Parker could have expected some larger share of his father's attention, but instead he got only that one wafer, and only when it came his turn. But it was no hardship. For those summer months, he moved out of his own bedroom in his parents' two-story log house and blended in with the other campers, and he was more than content to bathe in the distant shine of his father's magnificence. The luckiest boy alive.

Until that moonless August night when Parker was fifteen.

Like all the other cabins, Parker's was constructed from oak logs, unchinked and unscreened, open to the cool night air. Eight simple canvas cots, arranged bunk bed–style. A single lantern hung from the ceiling, and big luna moths danced in its sputtering light until taps was blown each night.

That summer a college boy named Corky Bondurant was the counselor for Parker's cabin. Corky was a fleshy man whose flatulence was ceaseless and toxic. Consigned to the bunk below him was Nathan Philpot, a slender boy from Durham who had spent most of that summer whining to be removed from the gassy chamber beneath Corky. Across the cabin and well out of range of Corky's farts, Parker occupied a breezy top bunk by the door, and below him was Thomas Dark Cloud Panther, a full-blooded Cherokee.

Thomas Panther was one of the handful of hard-luck cases that Chief admitted to camp each summer. Thomas and his family lived in a one-room, tar-paper shack on reservation land down in the valley. Badly schooled, sullen, and unskilled in white man's sport, Thomas Panther clashed daily with one or another of the affluent kids from Atlanta, New Orleans, and Charleston who populated the camp, cocky boys with prep-school breeding and shocks of blond hair, who played expert golf and tennis on their private-school teams and studied diligently so one day they could partner up with their fathers in law practices or surgeries at the best hospitals in the South.

Thomas, like most of his tribe, seemed to know far less about the myths and history of his own people than Chief did. Parker's father was an ardent student of all things Cherokee. He embraced the myths and lore and magic of those native people so fiercely it was as if he were determined to substitute their noble ancestry for his own Scotch-Irish lineage.

At Camp Tsali a large portion of every summer day was spent in diligent imitation of primitive Cherokee life. The boys bathed in the icy lake, prepared and cooked much of their own food. They felled giant poplars and locusts and maples, then worked the wood, turning the larger portions into logs to be used in building projects and the smaller pieces into bows and arrows, blowguns and hatchet handles. For two months those suburban boys prowled the forests like young warriors, their ears tuned to the slightest vibrations of animal life, slipping through the pathless woods as surreptitiously as moonlight.

They killed and skinned squirrels and other small game, and from the pelts they fashioned loincloths, vests, moccasins, and fur caps. From yellow pine they carved dugout canoes and tested them on the lakes and whitewater rivers. They whittled dance masks from buckeye and basswood and once a week performed in the big ceremonial ring the Green Corn Dance or the Eagle Dance, chanting in Cherokee and whirling around blazing bonfires.

It was on a lightless evening at the end of August, only moments after Corky Bondurant began to snuffle and snore, that Parker Monroe ducked beneath his blankets and shone his flashlight on the slip of paper he had discovered moments earlier beneath his pillow.

Meet me, it said, in her careful script.

Parker switched off his light. He lay listening to his cabinmates until he was certain they were all asleep, then he slipped from his bunk and dressed in jeans and sweatshirt and tennis shoes, and eased out the open door. In a light-footed sprint he zigzagged across the dark, familiar campground, ducked behind the infirmary, took a narrow footpath within yards of his parents' log home, then opened up to a full-speed dash down the gravel road toward the main highway.

Five miles he trotted down that hill, then another half-mile along the serpentine asphalt road that passed through the small town of Cherokee.

With his heart thrashing as it had from his first moment with her, he climbed up the running board and slipped into the aromatic darkness beside Lucy, his Cherokee lover.

Parker had first glimpsed her two months before, in the outdoor pageant that ran all summer at the nearby amphitheater: *Unto These Hills.* The drama portrayed the history of the Cherokee Nation from the Indians' first encounter with white men till their forced removal from their native mountains and the violence and heroism that followed. It was required viewing for all Tsalimen, for it told the story of the camp's namesake, a simple Cherokee named Tsali who had sacrificed his life so hundreds of his people would be allowed to stay in their native hills. Tsali's sacrifice was the moral gold standard of Charles Andrew Monroe's summer camp—that every man must be ready when the crucial moment came to lay down his life for a greater good.

Though Lucy's role in the play was minor, when she first moved across the outdoor stage Parker was mesmerized. The footlights sparkled on her long black hair. She stepped lightly and spoke no lines, but she held herself with such artless dignity that she lodged deep in Parker's mind, and back in camp that night he could barely sleep.

The next evening he went AWOL for the first time. Stealing back to the amphitheater, he talked his way backstage and fumbled through an introduction so clumsy Lucy and her friends barked with laughter. But he persisted, and the two of them wound up strolling in awkward silence down a nearby footpath that meandered beside the Oconaluftee River. On that clear night the rippling water was coated with gold, and trout rose in multitudes as if to feast on the dense moonlight. Fireflies hovered in the grass, and the air was lush with honeysuckle.

Overpowered by the moment, he tried to kiss Lucy, but she shoved him roughly away. He blurted that she was the most beautiful girl he'd ever seen, and she laughed at him again. Foolishly he reached out to touch her cheek, but she caught his wrist in a grip as powerful as any boy's and wouldn't let go until he apologized for his forwardness.

"You're an idiot," she said. "You think because I'm Cherokee you can do or say whatever you want."

"It's just that you . . ." He stared at her face gleaming in that gold light.

"I'm so exotic. So mysterious. My long black hair, my cinnamon skin. You're swept away and can't restrain yourself."

"I'm sorry," he said. "I'm not usually this way."

"Yeah, Thomas says you're real polite."

"Thomas?"

"My brother Thomas. I believe he sleeps below you."

"You're Thomas Panther's sister?"

"That's right," she said, and smiled. "But more important to you, I'm the oldest daughter of Standingdog."

Parker stared at her speechlessly.

Standingdog Matthews headed a faction of Cherokees who had been campaigning fiercely to annex several parcels of land adjacent to the reservation—land they considered sacred. One of those parcels was the meadowy knoll on which Camp Tsali stood.

In the last year Standingdog and his people had organized the local merchants to boycott the landowners. Campers at Tsali were no longer welcome in certain shops, and several grocery stores had refused to supply Tsali's kitchen with fresh produce. That summer there was a sudden rash of vandalism around the campground. Fires broke out, and machinery failed and had to be replaced. The new camp bus blew an engine. An avalanche of boulders destroyed the archery range. It had reached the point where any mishap around camp was blamed on Standingdog Matthews and his gang.

"If he's your father, why does he have a different name?"

"My mother threw Standingdog out years ago and took back Panther."

"Goddamn."

"Yeah," she said. "It complicates things, doesn't it, Romeo?"

Lucy Panther smiled at him and stepped back from Parker and turned to watch the river's golden passage.

"It doesn't have to." He reached for her again, but she skipped away.

"What I suggest, Parker, is that you go back to your camp and get more practice being a Cherokee, and if you ever get any better at it, maybe we can talk again."

That week he wandered in an airless trance. Nothing he knew about girls had prepared him for her. Parker had a glib and easy manner, and he'd always found girls his age to be plentiful and compliant.

But Lucy was something else. She'd spoken to him with the scorn of an adult chiding a misbehaving child, and stared disdainfully at his white skin as if it were a fatal affliction.

Finally he cranked up his nerve and snuck down the mountain a second time and waited in the parking lot until the pageant was over. She was wearing blue jeans and a white T-shirt, and her hair hung to her waist. She met his eyes but didn't alter her path to her pickup truck. She got inside, started the engine.

Parker stood nearby and waited. The truck idled for several minutes until the parking lot was clear. When finally the passenger's door squeaked open a few inches, he let go of a breath he'd been holding for the last week and moved quickly and slid into the seat beside her.

For the next hour he said little, but listened attentively as she told him of her younger brother who collected butterflies, a little sister who suffered from epilepsy.

As she talked, Parker stayed on his side of the truck, reining in his pulse as best he could. He spoke only when she posed a specific question. Late in the evening, after she parked on a bluff that looked west toward the dark mountains, Lucy went silent for a long moment, then suddenly leaned her face to his and rewarded his restraint with a kiss.

Another week of nights passed before their kissing deepened and Parker touched for the first time the dusky silk of her hidden flesh. Then in the unforgettable summer nights that followed they made love dozens of times in the tall, flickering grass beside the Oconaluftee. Her hair smelled like the river's lush perfume and her body surged like its dark currents and together they were swept along at the river's raging pace.

Lying together afterward in the high, fragrant grass, they watched the constellations shift and listened to the Oconaluftee move across the boulders with a deep, steady rumble, and Parker felt that new feeling steal through his body like that mysterious river noise, a deep resonance that swelled inside his chest and brightened the stars and gave the breeze an unbearable sweetness.

For two months their romance flourished, then on that moonless night in August, an evening when they were not scheduled to meet, her note brought him racing down the hill, breathless and sweating and full of the amazing certainty that Lucy Panther had come to need him as much as he did her.

He climbed into the truck, gave her a quick kiss, and as she drove him silently to their spot beside the Oconaluftee, he felt again the airless heat of his passion, the mad roar fill his ears.

"How did you get the note to me?"

"Thomas," she said simply.

When she parked the truck and swiveled on the seat, he saw from her expression that there would be no kissing tonight. No words of love. He drew a careful breath.

"What is it?"

She brushed the hair from her face, set her mouth, and looked away.

"Standingdog knows about us," she said. "He knows everything."

"How?"

"It's a small town, Parker. A small tribe. People talk."

She stared out the windshield at the black, gleaming water, moving so quickly but moving not at all.

"I'm sorry, Parker. But this is finished."

"He's not even your father anymore. He doesn't live with you. Why should it matter what he thinks?"

"He's my father. He'll always be my father."

"Hell, I'll talk to him. I'll tell him how I respect you. How much I respect your customs, everything about you and your people. I'll just tell him."

"He already knows who you are. He knows what you respect."

She turned her head and showed him the other side of her face. Her eyes and lips were puffy, and a lump disfigured her forehead.

"He beat you."

She didn't reply.

"Shit, I'll kill the son of a bitch."

She raised her hand.

"No."

"This isn't about you and me. It's about my father. The land."

"It's all the same. You can't help who you are. None of us can."

"I'm his son, but he and I aren't the same person. Don't do this."

"It's done." She wouldn't look at him.

It was nearly two in the morning when she pulled up to the entrance road to camp. Parker had not tried to argue her from her decision. She had taught him the power of silence, and now it was all he had to use.

When she'd brought the truck to a halt, she turned and looked at him. In the green glow from the dash, her face was slack, a withered mask.

"Lucy, I love you. You love me. Don't throw that away."

"Go on," she said quietly. "Get out of my truck. It's finished."

She reached across him and opened his door.

"Go," she said. "Go."

Parker stepped down and had to jump aside as her tires threw a storm of gravel. He watched her taillights swerve around the first bend and disappear.

The rest of the tale was exactly as Charlotte had heard it a dozen times before. When Parker reached the campground, he found his parents' home in flames. No one in the camp had awakened yet, for the house was more than half a mile from the cabins. He hesitated for a moment, staring at the flames, then drew a deep breath and rushed into the burning house.

Fire ringed the living-room floor, springing up from a glistening trail of what smelled like kerosene. Flames climbed the walls, feeding on the drapes and his grandmother's quilt, which hung from the wall below the stairs. The heavy oak logs had not yet caught, but the fire had already risen up the stairway and was fluttering at the upstairs floorboards.

With the smoke growing more dense at every step, Parker could barely see by the time he reached the bottom of the stairs that led to the sleeping quarters. Before he started up, he looked back through the dense smoke of the great room. There was still a narrow path of escape, but the flames were closing fast.

He screamed to wake his parents. But his voice was swallowed by the roar. As he mounted the stairs, a heavy beam from the ceiling gave way and fell in his path and the shower of sparks set his shirtsleeve ablaze. A second later, another rafter gave way and clipped him on the side of the skull.

When he came to, Diana was kneeling at his side in the grass of the main yard. Her hair was singed, and a gash on her cheek had been hastily bandaged.

Chief was consumed in the fire that night, along with Nathan Philpot, the boy from Parker's cabin, and a handyman who'd been hired only a week before. A man named Jeremiah. It was assumed that Jeremiah had been awakened by the noise of the fire and tried to rescue the Monroes, only to perish himself.

During the trial, the prosecution argued that the unlucky Nathan Philpot had changed bunks to escape the noxious fumes coming from his counselor, slipping into the cot that Parker Monroe had vacated. Before setting the fire, the culprit had gone to Parker's cabin, mistaken Nathan for Parker, and dragged him back to die with the rest of the family.

The prosecutor claimed it was clearly Standingdog Matthew's goal to wipe out the entire Monroe clan because of their refusal to part with their land.

Parker did not take the stand and refused to tell anyone, even Diana, where he'd been that night.

Standingdog offered no defense. In a buckskin jacket, he sat erect but showed no sign that he understood the words spoken against him or in his behalf. And he sat impassively when the prosecutor pointed at Standingdog Matthews and named him as the killer and listed the evidence against him. A boy in Parker's cabin who had seen him wake Philpot and drag him away. The kerosene-spattered shirt found hidden in his shack, his long-standing feud with the Monroe family, his lack of an alibi on the night of the fire, and the testimony of several other Cherokees who confirmed that Standingdog had made repeated threats on the Monroe family.

The defense attorney cross-examined no one, and Standingdog continued to listen placidly as a parade of witnesses praised Chief as the most inspiring man they'd ever known.

None of the Panthers attended the trial. One evening Parker could endure it no longer and stole Diana's car and drove to the Panthers' home in Horse Cove. The place had been stripped to the bare walls. The Panthers long gone. None of the neighbors would speak a word to Parker.

When Parker was finished with the story, Charlotte rolled onto her side and put her back to him. He reached out and lay a hand on her shoulder, but she didn't respond. She lay listening to the night sounds, the hum of distant traffic, an incessant dog barking a few doors away. Her heart felt as if it had swollen to such a size inside her chest that it was cramping against her ribs.

All she had ever believed about Parker Monroe now had to be reconsidered. Over the years, she had never caught him in an overt lie. But after hearing his story, she saw he'd been treating her as he'd dealt with the FBI interrogators. Omitting the crucial facts, giving her the bare outlines of truth, but not its whole weight.

As far as Charlotte was concerned, leaving out the girl and the love affair amounted to something worse than a lie. For Lucy Panther was the very heart of the story, the meaning of it. Charlotte lay unmoving, her blood cold in her limbs, as if she'd just discovered the man she loved was a charlatan. A man who had pretended to be simple and honest and true, but was actually far more complex, more darkly haunted than she could have known.

And worse than that, far worse when she considered its consequences for the future of their marriage, Parker Monroe was a man who very possibly had used up a crucial portion of his lifetime supply of passion before Charlotte ever walked onto the stage.

TEN

TEN O'CLOCK ON TUESDAY MORNING a blinding thunderstorm brought the traffic on Dixie Highway down to five miles an hour, though some maniacs were still cutting and weaving at five times that, as though it were full sunshine. Diana Monroe hugged the far right lane and crept along, leaning forward to peer through the smeared window of her Jaguar.

A few hours earlier, bedraggled and reserved, Parker had called a cab and left the house at seven.

With her cruiser still in the motor pool, Charlotte had little choice but to call her mother-in-law for a ride downtown. Gracey sat in the backseat muttering to herself while the two women rode silently in the front. Charlotte had called into work and been granted a temporary reprieve from her next session of facial videos. She wasn't due back at the station until after lunch.

Normally, Gracey took the Metrorail downtown to the New World Center, Miami's school for the artistically gifted. But after the drama last night, Charlotte had decided she needed to speak with Mr. Steven Underwood, make sure he realized the enormous strain Gracey was under. If there were other teachers besides Underwood who held sway in her daughter's life, Charlotte hadn't heard their names mentioned.

Charlotte also wanted another look at the young teacher, to decide which of her impressions of him was accurate. On the three other occasions they'd met, the young man seemed to fluctuate between sincere concern for Gracey's welfare and smug amusement at Charlotte's worry. It was possible both Underwoods existed. At twenty-five, the young man might identify a little too closely with his students. Smart enough to make nice to parents one-on-one, then later undermining the hell out of them, scoffing at their old-fashioned values to score points with his students. Charlotte was determined to find out. It was time to start plugging holes in the dike, no matter how minor they might appear to be.

As soon as Diana slid into a parking space outside the New World Center for the Arts, Gracey popped out of the back door and without a word hurried up the stairs into her school.

"I can't park here," Diana said.

"There's a parking garage around the block, near the courthouse."

Diana looked over at her and shook her head, something vaguely disapproving in her eyes, although Charlotte knew if she called Diana on it, there would be denials. "I don't disapprove of you, darling. I'm on your side one hundred percent." Though it never felt that way. Never in all these years had Charlotte considered herself a full-fledged member of the Monroe clan.

As odd as it seemed, part of her alienation had to do with Diana's appearance. Her mother-in-law carried herself with such a straight-backed dignity, something so close to haughtiness, that she managed to radiate a superiority and distance that Charlotte could never quite bridge. Her face was all patrician sharp angles. An aristocratic geometry made more severe by her arching eyebrows and neatly composed mouth and piercing brown eyes. She had rich black hair with only a few stray strands of white. Miraculously, her deep golfer's tan had not damaged her complexion. She had the velvety skin of a woman in her twenties. Her daytime wardrobe consisted almost exclusively of bright pastel pants and polo shirts with the insignia of the Granada Country Club. She was handsome in a way that no one in Charlotte's shabby Tennessee family was. It was a beauty that was handed down reverently through the generations along with the family silver and crystal and a few rare gemstones.

Her maiden name was Parisi. And every so often, when a certain wistful look overcame Diana, Charlotte imagined that her mother-in-law was revisiting the grand family villa back in Tuscany, with its endless vineyards and happy peasants who tended the groves of olives and persimmons. The rich Mediterranean sun beamed down on all the dukes and countesses invited over for exquisite dinners in the rustic courtyard with its view of Parisi land stretching all the way to the sunset.

"Charlotte, could I ask you something?"

"Of course."

"About the television appearances, Parker, I mean. All that coverage."

"What about it?"

"Is it necessary? To have such a high profile? So much publicity."

"I don't know what you're saying."

"It's just . . . I don't know. Unseemly. I know he's ambitious. But all that exposure . . . is it really necessary?"

"What in the world are you talking about?"

Behind them a taxi honked, and Diana glanced into the rearview mirror with a distracted air.

"Oh, never mind," she said. "I just worry about the silliest things. Don't pay any attention to me. Forget I mentioned it."

Diana recomposed her face, but Charlotte could detect a lingering strain around the eyes, a wrinkle of anxiety that seemed rooted in some faraway thought. As if some haunted memory was dogging her.

Charlotte guided Diana to the parking garage and the two of them, huddled beneath Charlotte's umbrella, walked back to the school.

"You're sure you don't mind if I come along? I'd really like to meet this man, too. Give you my impression."

Charlotte considered asking Diana to stay in the background, to let Charlotte handle this, but she knew even if Diana agreed, it wouldn't matter because when she felt so moved, Diana Monroe could be as ballsy and assertive as any man she'd ever met.

They climbed the stairs and entered the building. Charlotte led the way to the main office and spoke briefly with a secretary and learned that Mr. Underwood was in the auditorium at the moment but would be free to talk with her in fifteen minutes or so, after his ten o'clock class.

Charlotte located the lecture hall and was choosing an out-of-the-way spot in the hallway to wait when Diana pushed open the doors and swept into the dark room.

"Shit."

Charlotte followed and found her mother-in-law in a seat in the back row, leaving the aisle seat free.

The movie was just wrapping up. Joan Crawford in *Mildred Pierce*. Recently Gracey had rented the film and for the last week had been watching it in fits and starts, rewinding a section, playing it again, freeze frame. It was a forties melodrama, a mother-daughter movie that Charlotte had watched as a child, fantasizing that she had a mother like Joan Crawford who spoiled her daughter religiously, sacrificed her own marriage, worked endless hours so her Veda might have a fancy new dress, piano lessons, all the trappings of the wealthy upper classes that Mildred Pierce had been denied as a child. But as Charlotte watched a crucial scene play out, she realized that Gracey must have been viewing a totally different movie.

In the confrontation between Veda and her mother on the stairway of their house, Veda damns Mildred, calls her a common frump. Throws back in her face all those years of wretched self-denial. And second by second, as the tirade unfolds, Joan Crawford's rigid mask softens. Tears shine her eyes, and Veda, in a burst of utter contempt for her mother's weakness, slaps her face.

Then comes the moment the movie has been building toward. The instant that Charlotte must have discounted long ago because it didn't fit with the fantasy she'd constructed around the film.

At that insolent slap, Joan Crawford's facade is torn away and her anger erupts with such raw pain that Charlotte pressed herself back in her seat and almost turned away. Crawford screams at her child, "Get out before I kill you." But Veda ignores her and walks blithely up the stairs, and Joan Crawford, in full fury now, barks out the girl's name with such terrible force the little brat, the vicious heathen, stops dead.

And when Veda turns to face this terrifying woman that she has clearly underestimated, Joan Crawford slowly reassumes the neutral, zombie mask, a bit of acting that Charlotte had never noticed before, but that now chilled her to the core. That such monstrous rage could flash into view, then so quickly be concealed behind a bland half-smile seemed hideous and inhuman.

When the lights came on and the rustling of the forty or so students had stilled, Underwood bounded up the stairs to the stage and looked out at his class. He wore jeans and a black T-shirt, and his long ponytail was clasped by some brightly colored bands.

Underwood was silent for a moment, then he spread open his arms as if basking in a tumult of applause. Turning, he swept one hand at the empty screen.

"Did you see that?" he shouted. "You see what she did? Joan Crawford, that last moment. Who saw it? Who can describe it?"

In the second row, Gracey sat up so straight it was as if every cell of her being were focused on the young teacher. Underwood didn't give the class time to answer, but hurtled on.

"We're acting all the time," he said. "None of it is real. We make it up, all of it. Some of us are just better at it than others. There's no such thing as an authentic gesture, a real smile, a true emotion. Everything we do and feel is awash in ambiguity and the thousand conflicting emotions. We're liars, all of us. Lying twenty-four hours a day, even our dreams are lies. Joan Crawford knows that. That's her genius. She shows that at the end of the film. She's the terrible mother and the saintly mother. She's beautiful and damned. Both slave and master. She can make her face do anything. She can scream and contradict that scream in the same instant.

"Can you do that? No, of course you can't. Only one or two of you can even come close. That's why you're here. That's why I'm here. To guide you to that place. To teach you how to be anybody and everybody in the world. Not just the sad, limited person you were born as. Or the person your parents are trying to mold you into. Why would anyone surrender to a single identity when you could be an infinite variety of people? All people. But to accomplish that, you need to expand. Open like frail flowers to the ruthless sun, to expose yourself to the brutal poetry of the world, the lethality of reality."

He smiled triumphantly at his turn of phrase. And then his voice grew oily with sarcasm.

"Unless you throw yourself into that harsh, soul-piercing struggle, you'll never amount to anything. You'll be normal. Normal. Think of it. Oh, what joy you'll have being normal."

Titters ran through the room.

"Normal, normal, normal. Is Joan Crawford normal? Is Ann Blyth normal? Or Barbara Stanwyck or Fred MacMurray or Bogart?"

He was strutting now. A tyrant rallying his troops to battle.

Charlotte stood up, stepped into the aisle. For a giddy moment, she considered pointing her umbrella like a lance and rushing to the stage to run the idiot through.

Underwood squinted into the lights, and as he recognized her, his mouth arched into a smile.

"I see we have an audience today," Underwood said.

Forty heads turned. Gracey glanced over her shoulder and when she saw her mother and Diana, her mouth turned sour and she crossed her arms over her chest and slumped down in horror at their grotesque intrusion.

"Well, okay then, let's give them something to see."

Underwood summoned a student onto the stage, a tall thin girl with braces and stringy black hair. He told her that she would be Veda. Did she know her lines? She nodded shyly that she did. And then he pointed at Gracey and curled his finger. With fuming reluctance she rose from her chair and joined her classmate on the stage.

Underwood posed them, spacing them as movie mother and daughter had been, then showed them where they would pretend the stairway to be, then he stepped away and clapped his hands as if waking them from a trance.

"Action!"

They played the scene, quietly at first, too fast and out of sync, but when the tall girl called Gracey a common frump, then cocked back her hand and unloaded a slap so hard that Gracey staggered back a step, the big room was hushed.

Charlotte found herself drawn forward down the aisle, edging closer to see her daughter's face, to intervene if necessary.

But when Gracey shouted Veda's name and the tall girl turned to stare at her "mother," the fury in Gracey's face was utterly real, and when it drained away to something approaching the same unnerving nonchalance as Crawford's had, Charlotte was paralyzed, and it took the whispers of Gracey's classmates to wake her from her daze and find herself only steps from the lip of the stage.

"Bravo!" Underwood cried out as the scene ended. "Bravo, my little elves."

Charlotte turned and marched up the aisle and out of the auditorium. A minute later Diana joined her in the corridor.

"Let's go," Charlotte said.

"What about the conference?"

"I've seen enough. I have the picture."

"She's wonderful, isn't she? A real talent for acting. That was something very fine indeed."

"That was a horror," Charlotte said.

Diana followed her out to the street. The rain had passed, and the sun was in full force, humidity so dense she was instantly sheened with sweat.

"Well, you do have to agree he's a charismatic young man."

"A fool," Charlotte said. "A dangerous, self-absorbed adolescent."

"Oh, good," Diana said. "Now everything can be Underwood's fault."

Charlotte halted. Around them the manic hustle of downtown Miami rushed on. A man hawking plastic Baggies of limes weaved in and out of the logjammed traffic. By the front door of the pawnshop behind them, a mutt lifted its leg and pissed on the wall a few inches from a sleeping man. The harsh tang of high-octane coffee. And from a dozen tiny stores lining the street came competing rhythms and lyrics. Bob Marley and hip-hop, Sinatra and Dylan.

"All you need to do is love her, Charlotte. Love the girl. That's all."

"Is that right? And that'll fix everything?"

"Yes, it will. It will fix everything that can be fixed."

Charlotte's chest was splitting like some deep-sea diver who'd gone down too far, then come up too fast.

She nodded. The quickest way past this moment was not to engage. Take the advice in a silent gulp like a shot of hundred-proof wisdom.

"Thank you, Diana. I'll work on it. I'll try to love her better."

And though she meant to keep the words free of irony, some of it must have seeped through, for Diana gave her a prim smile and nod, the way you might reply to a servant who has failed for the umpteenth time to perform the simplest of tasks.

ELEVEN

"YOU'RE NOT CONCENTRATING, OFFICER MONROE."

It was four-thirty and she'd been staring at faces for four hours. Mainly men. Small variations. Getting another lesson in the basic units of facial coding. She was supposed to master Dr. Fedderman's jargon so she could communicate to him exactly what she saw and why she was anticipating the outcomes of the videos so accurately. He had a very precise set of terminology and her impressionistic shorthand was no help to him.

"There's a flicker in his smile," she said. "It's there for a half-second and then it goes away like a smoke signal."

"That's another microexpression," Fedderman said. "Now watch it in slow motion and tell me what you see anatomically. Use the right words, so later on you and I can communicate accurately."

Like that all afternoon. Learning the first few phrases of a foreign language, one that seemed hopelessly simplistic. Inner brow raiser. Outer brow raiser. Upper lid raiser. Lip tightener. Nose wrinkler. Dimpler. Lid droop. Fedderman gave her some of the physiological terms for the muscular actions but passed over them quickly. First things first. Layman's terms, then the muscular transactions behind those terms. Forty-four different muscles in the face. Using just five of those forty-four muscles, a person could produce ten thousand discrete facial configurations. Some were meaningless, but most communicated some subtle emotional message.

"Later on? Don't get ahead of yourself, Doc. I haven't decided yet if there's going to be a later on."

Fedderman did a lip stretcher. Not quite a smile, not quite a frown.

"I understood the offer had been made and accepted."

"Made, not accepted."

"Well, we're all hoping you choose the right path."

"Let me ask you something, Doc."

"Yes?"

"I've got this natural ability, right? This instinctive skill."

He waited in silence.

"What if all this jargon and study makes me so self-conscious, distorts things in my mind so much, it actually interferes with what I can do naturally? You ever thought about that?"

"Doesn't work that way," Fedderman said.

"You're sure?"

"The more you know, the more you see."

"It's that simple, is it?"

"It's that simple."

Charlotte gave it fifteen more minutes, then pled a migraine. Fedderman told her they were almost to the end of the first cycle. Twenty more minutes.

Charlotte rose and headed for the door. Behind her, Fedderman remained coldly silent.

She marched directly to Rodriguez's office. But according to his secretary, Marie Salzedo, the lieutenant was hashing out budgetary shortfalls with the mayor and couldn't be disturbed.

"Did the FBI guy find you?"

"What FBI guy?"

"The cute one with the tan. Body of a twenty-year-old."

"Sheffield?"

"Yeah, Frank. Boy, oh, boy."

"Sheffield was looking for me?"

"I told him you'd be out soon. I think he's down in the lobby."

She gave Charlotte a swoony smile.

"He stays in shape, that one. Sensitive eyes, too."

"He's married, Marie."

"Oh, I know. That writer, Hannah Keller. Yeah, I've read her books. They're kind of slow for my taste. Anyway, a man like Frank, he looks like he might need more than one woman. A whole harem, probably."

"A little heads-up, Marie. You might want to cut back on the romance novels. Rodriguez hears you salivating over FBI agents, you'll be in the warehouse alphabetizing cold-case files the rest of your twenty."

"Oh, don't be that way, Charlotte. A girl can fantasize, can't she?"

When the elevator doors opened in the lobby, Frank was leaning against the water fountain near the front door talking to a couple of detectives. She'd intended to hit up Romero for another ride home. But she guessed it was going to be Frank.

When he saw her, he broke away from the guys and held open the door.

"Need a lift?"

"Matter of fact."

He led her outside to a black Porsche parked next to a fire hydrant.

"Borrowed it from my wife," he said. "Little effeminate for my tastes, but my pickup had a flat."

She got in and he drove down the tree-lined section of the central Gables, then swung in at Alhambra and cut over to the Venetian Pool and parked in the shade of an oak, angling his car so they had a view through the fence of kids jumping from the coral boulders into the giant lagoon.

With its caves and overhangs and dozens of nooks, the Venetian was a dream pool for kids and paddlers who wanted to dawdle in the shadows rather than swim laps. Gracey had once loved that pool, playing princess and dragon among those watery lairs, but now she could barely be coaxed outside into the sunshine. Swimming, like most things she'd once enjoyed, was for silly juveniles.

"What's on your mind, Frank?"

She watched a small boy in blue trunks climb the tallest boulder at the pool and wait his turn behind the bigger boys, a bunch of rowdies who were cannonballing some late-afternoon sunbathers.

"Got an intriguing phone call this afternoon."

"Collection agency pestering you again?"

"Caller made some pretty startling claims. I would've tossed it in the kook pile except for who it was, which gave the claims a little more credibility."

"Come on, Sheffield, you got something, just blurt it out."

"Now if a lawyer, especially one known for his genius in getting scumsuckers out of jail, if he were to withhold evidence in a criminal investigation, it might give us pause. Do we want to go after a guy who's into fancy legal footwork and probably has some tricky explanation for why the fuck he withheld evidence? Guy like that could turn it all around and find some way to sue us for upholding the law. No, I think we'd probably think twice about that guy."

He polished his hand across the gleaming walnut shift knob.

"But a sworn officer of the law," he said, "now that's another story."

Charlotte watched a heavy older woman in a skirted bathing suit from the last century pick her way up the boulder and join the teens on their perch.

"Gracey called you, didn't she?"

"Yep, your daughter. Turned in her own mom. Did it reluctantly, she said, though she didn't sound all that reluctant to me."

"I was tired last night, Frank. Confused. That's no excuse, I know."

"No, it's not."

"So what are you going to do?"

"First, I need to know if it's true. Is Panther related to Parker Monroe?"

She nodded.

"Parker thinks so, yes."

"Well, then it's a terrible plight I find myself in. I like you, Monroe. I even like your slimeball husband. But the law's the law. Withholding evidence, that's a hard one to just turn the other cheek on. Fugitive from justice, Top Ten Most Wanted, he's your own stepson, and that didn't strike you as potentially relevant?"

"So go ahead. Whatever I got coming, I'll deal with."

"I guess I had the mistaken impression you loved your work."

"Maybe *love's* a little strong. But yeah, I like what I do."

"Well, there's the rub. Because a little problem like withholding evidence on a Top Ten guy, if that got out, now that would just about blow your career all to shit. There's no coming back from that into police work. You'd be done."

"Am I smelling a deal here?"

"When did you first learn your husband was the father of Jacob Panther? Like where was the big hand and the little hand?"

"Five minutes before you threw me in the back of your car last night."

"That's the truth?"

"Why don't you ask Parker?"

"Against the advice of my inner voice, I'm going to respect your privacy. For one thing, I'd hate like hell to see how the papers would play it. The snarky headlines. Dragging the two of you through all that."

"You're a saint, Frank." She watched the old woman pinch her nose and throw her body off the ten-foot rock. A bigger splash than any of the teenage cannonballs. "Now what's the game?"

"Excuse me." He reached across her and popped open the glove box and took out a small black felt pouch and shook free a rectangular gadget. Aerial on one end, buttons on the other.

"I'm not wearing a wire, Frank. Forget it."

"Not a wire. This is cutting-edge James Bond stuff, straight from geekville. Your tax dollars working overtime."

He held it up for her to inspect.

"I already got a cell phone."

"Not this kind, you don't. This is next generation walkie-talkie. Pull up the aerial, press this button for two, three seconds, it speed-dials your friendly federal agent. Just talk into the receiver like you're ordering a pizza, and about twenty of my colleagues from here to Los Angeles and everywhere in between will be listening with bated breath. Sends your GPS location and everything."

"What the hell is it?"

"Microwave beeper, I think. Hell, I can never remember that gobbledygook. Point is, you're a button-push away. Thing's got unlimited range. Works off cell towers, satellites, roams to fetch whatever's out there. Press, bing, we know where you are, we mobilize. It could work anywhere on the planet, the Sahara, or smack in the middle of five hundred thousand acres of forest wilderness in western North Carolina. Which might come in handy, seeing how that's where Panther is from and exactly where we suspect he's been hiding this last year. Not many cell towers out in the middle of that national forest, but this gadget will still get through."

"I'm not spying on my husband."

"Not spy, hell no. He'd catch on to that. You try to wheedle something out of him, he'd snap shut like a giant clamshell, we'd never get another word."

"What word are you looking for?"

"From what you told us last night, during that highly unhelpful interrogation, it appears that earlier in the evening, when you and I were speaking on the phone, your hubby and Mr. Most Wanted were having a dialogue on the patio, right? And you weren't privy to that conversation, but your daughter apparently was."

"She's not reliable, Frank. Whatever she told you, ten grains of salt. The whole shaker."

"At this point, I don't think anybody in your fucking family is reliable. Reliable isn't the issue. I'm grasping for whatever I can get, so the white-hot poker that was inserted in my rectum last night doesn't get hammered any deeper. If you'll pardon the metaphor."

"Your passion for your work is touching."

Frank drew the aerial out and dabbed it back down.

"I think your husband knows where Panther is. And if I'm not mistaken, he's spent most of his professional life extricating dirtballs from their legal distress. So how I reason it is like this. He's going to meet his dirtball son somewhere and they're going to do the lawyer-client thing face-to-face and when they do there's a good chance you'll be in the vicinity. You can work that how you want. Push hard, push soft. Up to you. I trust your instincts."

"I'm honored."

"So you get a second chance, Monroe. I don't have to write your script, you know this guy—what works, what doesn't. You obviously landed him successfully in the first place, kept him happy all these years. Despite you coming from slightly different backgrounds."

"And what's that supposed to mean?"

Frank looked off at the swimming pool, choosing his words.

"Apparently you didn't realize, Monroe, when court documents are expunged, they're never wiped completely clean. That's another thing in this equation. Way back at the dawn of time, you kind of fudged your employment application. Never arrested for a crime? Well, not convicted, maybe. But arrested—well, we both know that ain't true."

She took the device from his hand.

"This is how you guys work? Blackmail, threats, intimidation."

"To name a few."

"Fuck you, Frank."

"Can I take that as a yes?"

She watched the heavy woman climbing the rock again. All that work for three seconds of free fall and the watery explosion at the end. In that instant of flight her weight must evaporate, the woman turning to air. Some bright blossoming of joy as she plunged.

"Is this thing for real, Frank, this gadget? You're not conning me, are you?"

He gave her a full-on look, a disappointed smile. She held his eyes for several seconds, probing, but she saw not even a shadow of deceit. Waiting for the dodge of eyes, the deep swallow, or his hand rising to touch his face. All signs of perjury. But his frustrated smile held firm.

"You're a shit. A real shit, Frank."

"So you're not going to run for president of my fan club. I regret that. But this is the deal. Brass ring is coming around, you got one shot, then I go dump what I know on Rodriguez's desk and let nature take its course."

She closed her eyes, hearing the happy cries from the pool.

"Okay, okay," she said. "I'll be your snitch."

"Yeah? And why am I waiting for a punchline?"

"One condition."

"Oh, boy. Here we go, the counselor's wife cutting a deal."

"I want the files on Panther. I want to know everything. What we're dealing with. If I agree to do this, I'm not going in blind."

"Oh, man. No way. No way in hell does that happen."

"I'm serious, Frank. No files, no James Bond."

"That's a serious, class-A violation of procedure. You got no clearance.

I'd be courting major disaster. Even a guy like me, a highly valued member of the law-enforcement society, if anybody sniffed that out, man, it'd be Frank Sheffield day at the gallows."

"Every page. No edits. No blackouts. Everything you have."

"What, so you can leak it to your old man? Get a jump start on Panther's defense? Yeah, like I'm going to do that."

"I'm talking self-protection. If I get into this and it leads to another encounter with the guy, I want to know which way he jumps when he's shot at, whether he's right- or left-handed. Everything you got."

She held up the black device.

"You wouldn't send one of your own guys undercover without a briefing, right? He's got to know the names, the evidence, what to look for, what to discount. You know I'm right."

"Problem is, you're not one of our guys."

"Well, then take me home—this date is over."

"Not even a kiss at the door."

"The files, Frank. I'll take your gizmo home with me tonight, okay, but tomorrow my in-basket better be stuffed with Panther's files or I'll toss this sucker into the nearest canal."

He started the car and put the shifter in drive and eased out of the lot.

"No can do," he said. "That's a line I can't cross."

"Have a couple of drinks," said Charlotte. "Lube up your morals."

"Oh, yeah," he said. "Speaking of morals."

He circled the fountains on Granada and headed south.

"Just to get the ball rolling on this share-and-share-alike thing. Seems our Atlanta field office took down a man by the name of Charles Levi last night."

"And this is relevant to what?"

"Mr. Levi apparently ran a Web site, kind of a switchboard that hooked up customers with suppliers."

Charlotte was quiet. Frank had his own pace. Nothing she could say would change it.

"The dart Panther used to bring down this Martin Tribue, it was coated with something, I forget the name, comes from seashells, deadly, fast-acting. They're using it in pharmaceutical labs, tinkering with it for some reason, cancer or something. Seems this Levi character was offering this god-awful shit for sale. Our Atlanta guys been monitoring his e-mail the last few months, snooping on his transactions. A lot of the shit he's selling is perfectly legal. Poison for hunters, if you can believe that. There's a whole blowgun culture out there. Militia types, the Nazi crowd. I mean, for chrissakes, this guy is doing a couple of thousand dollars a week in cobra venom alone."

"Panther was on his mailing list."

"Exactamundo."

"And you've traced the e-mail?"

"Public library terminal in Bryson City, North Carolina."

"Which is where you've been looking for Panther."

"Maybe it doesn't sound like a big deal to you, Monroe. But it's always nice to have a little confirmation you're turning over rocks in the right forest."

"I want the files, Frank."

"That's a no. Can't be done. Not even me, with my slipshod ways and my notorious don't-give-a-shit view of life, it's the big impossible."

"Okay, then, call a number for me."

She dug through her purse, found the card, then reached out to Frank's visor and tore off a sheet from his memo pad. She scribbled the number on the sheet and handed it to him.

"What's this, dial-a-fantasy?"

"A guy named Mears. He's up your chain of command. One of those Washington types that calls the shots."

"You don't mean Charles Mears?"

"When you get him, tell him the situation you're in. And tell him this. I'll agree to join his gang of wackos, but I want the Panther files."

"What gang of wackos?"

"Just call him, Frank. Just call the guy."

TWELVE

"YOU DID WHAT?"

"You should've heard this kid, Parker. He was practically inciting a riot, mocking parental authority, telling these impressionable kids they should work on developing multiple personalities. Expose themselves to the brutalities of the world. That's where Gracey gets this stuff. I wanted to strangle the kid."

They were in Parker's study. He was at his oak rolltop, looking up at her from his old swivel chair. It was just after seven, Parker home early for a change, still in his work clothes, tan slacks and a French blue shirt, his red tie undone. Outside in the drive a white rental car was parked.

"Why didn't you go to the principal, an administrator, someone in charge? Or you could've spoken directly to Underwood and confronted him."

"I was too angry," she said. "It wouldn't have worked anyway. They're not going to fire this guy because a parent doesn't like his teaching style. And the guy's not going to change on my say-so. He was bad, Parker. He's a sick, twisted, immature little shit and even if he's not the sole cause of how Gracey's been behaving, he's an accelerant. Gasoline on her personal bonfire."

"You had no right, Charlotte."

"I'm her mother. I have a perfect right."

"What about consulting with her father? Or maybe sitting down with Gracey and me and the three of us talking it through? We don't do things unilaterally. At least we never have."

"I made a command decision."

"This isn't about Gracey, is it?"

"What's that supposed to mean?"

"It's not about Gracey and it's not about her having a bad teacher. This is about last night. You're angry about Lucy Panther, the story I told, and you're angry at Gracey for helping Panther escape, and this is how you're going to punish us both. Pulling your daughter out of a school she loves without even a word to me. Just a couple of weeks left in the academic year. It's just spite, pure and simple."

She was dizzy with rage. About to spit back at him, when she caught herself. Because she knew some portion of what he said was true. She'd been angry at Underwood, sure, and justifiably, but that anger was compounded by the swarm of emotions buzzing in her gut, most of it brought on by Parker's confession last night. Just why a teenage fling should be so devastating, she wasn't sure. All night and all day she'd pushed the thoughts away, though she'd been feeling something happening inside her, some trapdoor springing open, and Charlotte falling through a place she'd always believed was solid and true, plummeting through cold, airless space without any sign of bottom.

She sat down on the gold couch across the room.

"Where is she now?" Parker cleared his throat, shifted in his chair, composing himself.

"At Diana's."

"Why?"

"She was screaming. Hysterical. Diana stopped by in the middle of it."

"So you shunted her off on Mother?"

"Yes, I did. Diana suggested it, but I agreed she could go over there and cool off. We can pick her up after dinner."

Parker bowed his head and touched a hand to his temple. Prayerful, patient. But from her angle she could see the flash of anger at the edge of his mouth. Another expression for Dr. Fedderman's list. A teeth-baring jaw-grinder. But as he raised his head and looked at her again, all that disappeared behind his patient face, his mouth finding a forgiving smile. Saint Parker.

Even though she hated to admit it, that stupid punk Underwood was right about one thing. Everyone was acting. Everyone was a bundle of conflicting feelings, and we were sorting through them constantly, editing, repressing, selecting the best face to show the world. Not necessarily the one that expressed our truest self. We were all simply getting by, coping with conditions. Most people were only passable performers who'd settled into a lifetime role, ignoring the constantly shifting needs and grievances and urges and fantasies that skated below the surface.

Parker was peering at her curiously. For all appearances he was a reasonable man who simply wanted to understand his wife, to come to some peaceful resolution. A harmless, unthreatening look.

"So it's Gables High, then, just a regular, mainstream public school? And you believe she'll be better off there? She'll fit in, find friends, inspiring teachers, all the things that matter to a teenage girl?"

"I went to a regular public high school."

"Yes, you did."

But there was nothing affirmative in his tone.

He let his words hang there for her to absorb.

He was maddening to argue with. Two steps ahead, laying his logic traps, blithe and sly in his delivery, but dealing stunning blows when you least expected. Yes, Charlotte had gone to public high school. And yes, only a month before she was to graduate she'd been jailed as an accomplice in the murder of a woman in a convenience store. All that echoed through his simple yes. And yes, if it had not been for Parker Monroe's legal expertise, where would Charlotte be today? Yes. Yes. Yes.

"We need to put this aside for the moment."

"All right," she said. "I'm for that."

"You need to take a look at something."

He held out a scrap of yellow paper. She rose and took it from him and sat back down. It was a Post-it note, the same size they kept by the phone in the kitchen. She looked but could make no sense of it. She held it upside down, then the other way. Tried holding it up to the light and squinting through the paper but could make no sense of the hieroglyphics.

"It's Cherokee," he said. "It was on the mirror in the guest bath."

"And of course you didn't report it to anyone."

He shook his head. No, he certainly hadn't.

"What does it say?"

"I spent the day trying to figure that out."

"And?"

"I can tell you what it says. But I can't tell you exactly what it means."

"One thing at a time. What does it say?"

He swallowed and looked away toward the darkened windows, then back at her.

" 'We have lifted up the red war club.' "

She repeated it. Then repeated it again.

"Tell me the truth, Parker. What did he say to you out on the patio?"

"You mean while you were calling your buddies at the FBI?"

"Parker, don't do this. We're both dealing with this the best we can. Let's don't make it any worse with cheap shots, okay?"

"Like changing Gracey's school."

"Okay, yes, you're right, I was angry. I'm still angry."

"Because I never told you about some summer romance a lifetime ago."

"Because you fell in love with some girl and you're still in love with her."

"What! I never said anything like that."

"You didn't mean to, but you did. The way you told the story last night. How your voice was. It's true, Parker. Whether you know it or not. It's true."

"Jesus Christ. You hear something in my voice and that incriminates me? I betrayed you before I even met you?"

"Can we move on?" she said. " 'We have lifted up the red war club.' I think that's the priority of the moment."

"All right, but we're going to get back to that, Charlotte. You can't just take a potshot like that and then run off like it didn't happen."

"The red war club, Parker."

He loosened his tie another notch, and reached behind him for a heavy volume. He closed his eyes for a moment as if wiping away the echo of her words. Releasing a long breath, he held the book out to her. *Sacred Rites of the Cherokees.*

"I spent the day in the university library," he said.

Charlotte came over and took the book and paged through it.

He'd tagged a half dozen pages with more Post-its.

"Panther left a message that he wanted you to decode. Why?"

"I don't know why, Charlotte. It has something to do with what he said while you were in the other room, something about being next."

"Next? Next what?"

"Goddamn it, if I knew I'd tell you the whole thing right now. I'm not playing games. I'm telling you what I know. He said we or I was next. The way he phrased it, 'you're next,' it could've been singular or plural. I'm not sure. He was vague, whether it was intentional or not, I don't know."

"Like we're in some kind of danger?"

"I took it that way and I asked him that very question, and he said he'd done what he could to slow things down, that we had a few days probably before anything happened."

"Jesus Christ, Parker. This goddamn killer comes into our house and tells you all this shit and afterward you just button up and go on your merry way to the fucking library?"

He touched a fingertip to his forehead again. Maybe it was a gesture he'd used a thousand times, and she was just noticing it. Maybe Fedderman was right, and his facial coding bullshit was making her see things she'd missed before. Either way, the gesture suddenly grated like hell. This man communing with his private gods, pleading for divine assistance in dealing with his wife.

" 'Slow things down?' What's that supposed to mean?"

"I don't know."

"Anything else you forgot to mention?"

"He might've told me where he's hiding out."

Charlotte groaned.

"Again, it's the way he put it," Parker said. "The way it came into the conversation. He mentioned a specific spot at summer camp, a place a couple of us used to go, you know, a private hideout."

"More sex?"

"Not sex. When I was a kid, I smoked dope there a few times. It was a good spot because it was the highest point around and you could look down all the trails leading to the place so no one could sneak up on you. None of the other boys knew about it, even the ones who'd been there a long time. I don't think Dad even knew it was there."

"And Panther mentioned this place."

"It came out of left field, a non sequitur. We were talking about the other thing, being next, and then he was reminiscing about this place. Like he wanted to insert it into the conversation, something for me to remember later. But he didn't want to be blatant about it."

"And where is this place? What is it?"

Parker shook his head. He glanced suspiciously around the room.

"You think we're bugged?"

"It's entirely possible."

"Well, if we are, they should be here in another minute or two and put both of us under arrest for withholding."

"Lawyer-client," he said. "They're out in the cold on that one."

"Christ, Parker. You're going to play legal games with our lives?"

"Jacob's innocent."

His look of certainty was so deeply rooted, it almost swayed her.

"That's absurd, Parker. The FBI has it all wrong? They made him one of their most sought-after fugitives by mistake?"

"It happens every day. People falsely accused."

Charlotte reached out, stuck the Post-it to the edge of a side table.

"What about this red club thing?"

"Like I said, I spent the day in the library. I scanned a dozen books before I came across the phrase. It's part of a Cherokee chant. But I don't understand its connection to us. I mean, I have a general idea about the interpretation. But there are nuances I'm missing. I know people I can ask. People I can talk to if I can locate them. People versed in these things."

"Or you can turn this over to the people it belongs to."

"It belongs to me, Charlotte. You understand that. Let's say we *are* in some kind of danger, that it was a plural *you,* and all of us are at risk, you, me, Gracey, all of us. Is that what you want? For a bunch of Frank Sheffields to insure your safety?"

"You'll do a better job?"

"I'm not the expert Dad was, but I still remember a lot of the Cherokee lore from back then. I've got the resources, and I sure as hell have the motivation. I'd bet on me before Frank Sheffield. Damn right."

"Okay, yeah, Frank's a cabana boy," she said. "He's one margarita away from dancing on the table at any given moment."

"So you agree?"

Charlotte drew a deep breath and blew it out.

"We have lifted up the red war club," she said.

"It's a war chant," Parker said. "It was repeated for four nights in a row by the warriors before they left for battle."

"That's it?"

"It's a paragraph long, full of traditional Cherokee symbols, colors and images. Red and blue and black. 'There under the earth the black war club and the black fog have come together for their covering.' That kind of thing. A sacred song to prepare the warriors for battle, protect them from their foes."

Charlotte got up and walked to the liquor cabinet.

"Red or white? Or something stronger?"

"Whatever you're having," he said.

"I'm going with strong."

THIRTEEN

SHE POURED THEM BOTH TWO inches of Patrón tequila in old-fashioned glasses and handed him his. He took a sip, then stared into the glass for a moment and threw back the rest of it. After a gasp, he raked his hands through his hair and began.

"Spent an hour on LexisNexis, researching the newspaper accounts of the bombings." Parker swiveled in his chair and lifted a sheaf of printouts. "I remembered them vaguely, but I was hazy on the details. Same wire stories over and over, not much independent reporting. And a lot of contradictions. Vague stuff about security videos, but no detail. Bottom line, no one seems to know about his motivation. No notes left behind, no phone calls taking credit. All five banks were in North Carolina. Of course, the stuff we could use wouldn't make the paper.

"Question number one is, how'd they arrive on Jacob Panther as their prime guy? And question two is, why does someone blow up banks? If it's not to steal the cash, which it isn't, then it must be to make some political point. If it's that, why hide it? Abortion clinics, gay nightclubs—there's a clear motive, no notes required. We'd be dealing with some kind of fanatic. But banks?"

Back on the couch, Charlotte nursed her tequila, savoring the glow that was working down her throat and spreading golden warmth through her chest.

"Maybe there's some private crusade going on between Jacob and the bankers," she said.

"That occurred to me. But there's no evidence of that in the public record. The fact is, we could speculate forever. We need some hard facts."

"We?"

He waved his hand as if clearing smoke.

"Okay, okay. I'm not expecting you to get involved. I understand your position. This is my son. My fight. You've got ethical conflicts with what I'm doing. I respect that."

"What you need at this point, Parker, is a look at Panther's dossier."

"Not much chance of that."

She sat back on the couch and crossed her legs.

"I'm working on getting the boy's file."

Parker straightened, and she watched his face grow bright.

"You are? How?"

She explained about Charlie Mears and his recruitment attempt.

"Harold Benson? You spoke with the goddamn director of the FBI?"

"That's the deal I offered. I get the file, I give them a pound of my highly intuitive flesh."

Parker shook his head and smiled.

"Jesus, I knew you were good at reading people. But that's a little scary. I'm living with a human polygraph."

"That's right. So don't even try your bullshit with me anymore."

His smiled softened, and she saw his eyes dodge to the side and close briefly as if shunting away an uncomfortable thought. Perhaps a pang of worry about how many more of his dark secrets she might uncover.

He got up slowly and came toward her across the room, and she rose from the couch. As he opened his arms, she felt a confession rising from her gut. Go ahead and tell him about the gadget in her backpack, join forces with this good, sweet man she loved, become a double agent, screw the feds.

And maybe she would have done it exactly that way if they'd kissed, and if that kiss had ripened as it had so often before into a communion of identities, a warm blurring of the distance between them.

But at that moment the phone rang, and Parker halted, lowered his arms, shrugged an apology, then headed back to his desk and picked it up and looked at the caller ID and said, "It's Mother."

Charlotte forced down a long breath and sat back on the couch.

Parker told Diana hello, then was silent and went strangely stiff.

"When did this happen?"

Charlotte stood up. With both hands she made a questioning gesture, and Parker waved at the hallway phone.

She was there in seconds. Diana paused midsentence.

"Is that you, Charlotte?"

"What happened?"

Parker said, "Gracey ran away."

"When?"

"I'm not sure exactly. Fifteen, twenty minutes ago maybe." For once Diana's voice had lost its imperious edge. "She took the Jaguar."

"Did you see her leave?"

Diana said that no, no she hadn't. She'd been cooking dinner, lost track of time, and went out on the patio to see how Gracey was doing. That's when she found the note.

"Oh, Christ."

"What'd it say, Mother?"

"I'll read it to you if you want."

"Just tell us," Charlotte said. "We need to get moving."

"It was a couple of sentences, that's all. Very garbled. It didn't make any sense. She was still quite upset, sobbing and cursing. I've never heard her talk like that before. The foul language."

"Diana, please."

"She said something about bruises."

Charlotte came down the hallway with the portable phone and sat on the couch again. The blood was draining from her limbs.

"Bruises?" Parker looked at Charlotte for help.

"I'll explain later," she said through the phone. "And what else, Diana?"

"Something about her brother. She was going to live with her brother. In a cave like a bear."

"Oh, Christ Almighty."

"What's she talking about, Parker? What brother?"

Charlotte dropped the phone and trotted to the kitchen and dug out her cell and called Gables emergency. Mary Troutman two nights in a row.

She gave her the story, describing Diana's car.

"It's Gracey?"

"Right—sixteen years old, shoulder-length blond hair, five-five, a hundred and ten pounds. Blue jeans and a yellow top. Probably headed north on I-95. I'll call you back in a minute with the tag number. Pass it to the Highway Patrol. Tell them it's about the Jacob Panther case. That should get them humping."

A few seconds later she was back on the phone with Diana and Parker. But the line was silent.

"What's going on?" Charlotte said into the mouthpiece.

Across the room, with the phone pressed to his ear, Parker said, "She heard something outside, glass breaking or something. She's spooked. Don't be hard on her, Charlotte. Gracey'll be fine. She's only been gone a few minutes. She's probably already turned around and heading home."

On Diana's end of the line there was a heavy thump, then a squeal.

"Mother?" Parker took a clumsy step toward Charlotte.

The line was still open, but there was no sound.

"Diana?"

Diana's phone tumbled from its perch and clattered against the tile.

"Mother, are you all right?"

A moment later a rustling wind blew across the mouthpiece, then Diana spoke.

"A hatchet." Her voice was light and drifty, almost bemused, as if she were giddy with champagne. "My neck."

"Are you injured? Diana, are you cut?"

"Oh, Lordy. Oh, Lordy, Lordy."

"Lie down," Charlotte said. "Lie down, don't move. Stay perfectly still, take deep breaths. Cover yourself if you can."

Parker dropped his phone on the carpet and sprinted toward the front door. Diana's house was eight blocks away. Not more than five minutes.

Charlotte spoke Diana's name, and the woman responded with a wet, rattling cough.

"Stay calm, Diana," Charlotte said. "You're going to be all right. Just be still, try to relax. Parker's on the way."

She could hear Diana straining for breath, a low, gasping wheeze. Then two words spoken in the hoarse voice of someone strangling on smoke.

"Beloved woman."

"What?"

Diana sputtered and heaved and was silent.

"Diana? Mother, hang on. Parker's on the way. Hang on, Mother."

Charlotte listened as the tread of heavy footsteps echoed across the floor of Diana's house. Growing louder as they approached. She heard the rough scrabble of someone lifting the phone from the floor.

Then a man was breathing faintly in her ear. Charlotte concentrated on the rhythm and texture of his breath, struggling to form a picture of his face, but nothing came. After a moment's pause the man inhaled deeply, then blew out the long sigh of someone with a great deal of work left to do.

While the Metro crime-scene techs worked the scene, Charlotte stood on the flagstone patio staring into the lit swimming pool. Diana's body lay in the kitchen and would remain covered until the ME arrived. The killer had left behind his weapon. A primitive ax whose head was a dark, triangular stone with a blade sharpened to a brittle edge. The ax head was lashed to the wooden handle by a complicated weave of strands that looked like animal hide.

One blow was all it had taken. A deep gash at the base of her neck near her collarbone.

A single pane of glass was broken in the French door leading from the kitchen to the pool area.

Charlotte's instant theory: The intruder saw Diana on the phone and was impatient to do his job, so he broke the glass to draw her outside. When she stepped onto the patio, he chopped her from behind.

Why that side of her body, that angle, that shape of wound? The crime-scene gurus would work up a theory. Use their software to make a cartoon out of it, position the victim and the culprit, analyze the geometry, determine height and strength of her killer. Right or left hand. Read some secret message in the Rorschach of the blood spatter.

After Diana was dealt the fatal blow, she'd managed to stumble the five steps back to the kitchen, grab the phone, and speak her final words.

Her killer followed her inside, watched her fall, then picked up the phone, listened for a second, and put it back. Arrogant son of a bitch. Cool and smug. No hurry, no worry. Didn't try to prevent Diana from talking to whoever was on the line. Which meant he was either a stranger or masked.

Maybe he even wanted Diana to pass on some detail about the killing. A teaser for the cops. Which made him more than arrogant, made him a truly pathological fuck. Bragging, chest-thumping while a woman died at his feet.

There wouldn't be fingerprints. Wouldn't be any fibers or DNA, footprints, no fairy dust of any kind. This guy was clean. If he wasn't a seasoned professional, at least he'd seen enough cop shows to wear his booties and latex gloves. Fucking cop shows.

Sheffield took her statement, what she'd heard over the phone, Diana's words, the sound of the killer's footsteps. Nothing helpful, she knew that, nothing to nail the son of a bitch. She started to describe the sound of the guy's breath, but even in her jangled state she knew that was ridiculous, so she gave Frank her theory about the killer—his egotism, arrogance—and Frank scribbled something on his pad. She could see he wasn't totally buying it, but was treating her like every other grief-stricken relative of a homicide victim—numb, out of it, unreliable.

Charlotte brought up Gracey, and Sheffield assured her they were doing what they could: be on the lookout for the bulletins, state troopers making it a top priority. Which she also knew full well was the reassuring bullshit next of kin always got, but she was too goddamn weary and desolate to call him on it. And anyway, Sheffield assured her that the biggest percentage of runaways turned around and headed back home within twenty-four hours.

When Charlotte ran out of words and began to stare off at the sky, Frank gave her a buck-up pat on the back and went to speak with Parker. Diana's spacious, well-appointed house was full of people, one last party.

Gables cops, Metro, South Miami, an FBI squad. More than a dozen cars outside—red lights, blue lights pulsing in the high limbs of the oaks. The entire gang working with a hushed professionalism. No crime-scene humor tonight, showing some respect for a fellow officer. Or, if they were joking, at least they were concealing it pretty well.

Charlotte stared into the pool and watched the automatic cleaner move aimlessly around the bottom, sucking up leaves and debris. With her mind perfectly blank, she stood watching the mindless robot do its work while the cops combed Diana Monroe's home for fairy dust they wouldn't find.

FOURTEEN

IT WAS NOON THE FOLLOWING day, Wednesday—roughly sixteen hours since Gracey had fled and Diana was murdered, and when Charlotte and Parker were leaving the house for Diana's hastily arranged memorial service—that Charlotte found the manila folder cocked against the front door.

She waited till they were rolling before opening it. After a minute of riffling through the pages, she could see the feds had upheld their end. It was unedited, with no blackouts, a document running to eighty-three pages, including black-and-white stills from some of the bank security cameras, and eyewitness testimony. Even with a cursory look she could see the narratives were composed by no-nonsense agents who'd taken their time and written in complete sentences. Not the sketchy, dashed-off police report lingo she was used to seeing and guilty of writing herself more than once.

"The file," she said, in answer to Parker's questioning look. "Panther's."

They were both dressed in black, riding in the Toyota rental. A single morning to throw together Diana's service, phone all her friends, write the obituary. Aching every second for any word on Gracey. But nothing came.

The affair was at the Granada Country Club. Manhattans and vodka gimlets, finger sandwiches. How Diana would want it, Parker said. No church affiliation. No other surviving kin to invite. Just her golf friends and her bridge cronies. A few toasts and everybody could trot off to the front nine.

For the last sixteen hours every throb of blood through Charlotte's brain had spoken Gracey's name. A fog had settled over her, a twitching impatience to kick it into gear, be doing something, anything, to find her runaway girl. But what was there? Drive aimlessly up I-95, searching for a silver Jaguar? Go rummaging through every goddamn cave in the Carolina wilderness?

That's what Mildred Pierce would have done. Let go of everything, rush off in a blind, flailing, self-destructive panic, crazed to rescue her Veda. But Charlotte wasn't Mildred. The last fifteen years of police work had made her averse to impulse.

In his dull-eyed state, Parker continually repeated Sheffield's bullshit about twenty-four hours, eighty percent of all runaways turned around and came home. Like some statistical mantra could soothe their anguish.

All through the night he had sobbed beside her in their bed. For hours at a time Charlotte held him tightly as the rhythmic waves of grief crashed over him. But she had shed no tears. From the very moment she'd seen Diana's body, her emotions had shut down. A professional detachment had kicked in, that central dogma of good police work—stay cool. But this time, distancing herself from the events didn't quite work. She was feeling dizzy and dislocated, as if floating several feet above her body's current position.

As Parker was pulling into a space in the country-club lot, Charlotte's phone vibrated and she plucked it out of her purse.

In a sober voice Sheffield said, "They found the car. Your mother-in-law's Jaguar. Northern outskirts of Jacksonville. Parking lot of a Holiday Inn along I-95 near the airport. No sign of struggle. Just sitting there."

"When?"

"Sunup this morning. It might've gone unnoticed for a while except a delivery truck bumped the back fender and the driver filed a report. Took a few hours, but eventually the crack law enforcement types up there ran the plates and we got the call."

"Jacksonville." She said it half to Parker, half to herself, trying to unravel it. Then to Parker, "They found the car, nothing else."

"Oh, there *was* something else," Sheffield said. "Activity on her credit card."

Charlotte said, "Tell me, Frank."

"Just got off the phone with MasterCard security. A fill-up at an Exxon station in Vero. Breakfast at a Cracker Barrel near Daytona."

"Ate at Cracker Barrel," Charlotte said to Parker.

"She loves that stupid place," he said.

"That sound like her?" Sheffield asked.

Charlotte said yes, it did.

"Is it normal these days," Frank said, "a sixteen-year-old girl has her own credit card?"

"Normal, Frank? What's that?"

"You sure she didn't witness the murder? That she was gone already?"

"That's what Diana told us. She could've been gone for as much as half an hour before it happened."

He thought about it for a second, then said, "Daughter of a cop. Knows there'd be an APB, so she ditches the car. Or maybe Panther gave her instructions to do that."

"We don't know her note's true, Frank. We don't know Panther is involved in this in any way. The girl's delusional. She could scribble down one thing in a note, do something totally different. Meeting her brother in a cave, that could be a complete fantasy."

Charlotte watched the parade of old folks entering the country club. Most wearing the bright, unnatural pinks and lime greens of the golf course. In solidarity with Diana. What she would've worn for their funerals.

"You check the Holiday Inn, surrounding motels?"

"No need for that," he said. "Same credit card was used for cab fare from a location near that Holiday Inn to the Jacksonville Greyhound station."

"And the bus ticket? There a record?"

"Apparently she used cash."

"The cabdriver?"

"One of our guys talked to him, yeah."

"She was alone?"

"That was our first question, too. Yeah, she was by herself. So she's not being coerced. Officially, we can't treat this as a kidnapping. It's a runaway.

In fact, the cabbie said she seemed in good spirits. Talkative. Very upbeat. A smart girl, full of sass, that's how he put it."

"What'd she talk about?"

She heard Frank paging through his notes.

"Movies, actors. That sort of thing. Small talk."

"What about the bus station? Somebody had to notice her."

"Mexican woman, one of the cleaning crew, notices a girl—seventeen, she thought, maybe eighteen—blond hair, pretty. Girl took a nap on a bench at the station around dawn this morning, then apparently hopped a bus sometime after that. Somewhere between dawn and right now."

"How many buses we talking about? Morning departures."

"Way too many to flag them all down, if that's what you mean. Locals, express. She could've already switched from one bus to another. They do a lot of business through there."

"You bastard. This suits you just fine, doesn't it?"

"Why would you say a thing like that?"

"You're banking on Gracey leading you to your boy. Probably got agents at every bus stop along the way from Jacksonville to North Carolina. See if she gets off, then follow her."

"If we find your girl, we return her immediately. The government doesn't use sixteen-year-olds as decoys. You think I'm that kind of asshole?"

"I hope not, Frank. I sure as hell hope not."

Charlotte was trying to imagine Gracey's state of mind. Full of sass? Was that real or an act she was doing for the cabbie? At least her head was clear enough to navigate three hundred miles north along a busy interstate at night. She was a very smart girl, very competent in lots of ways despite having a serious mental illness. There was no way to know if the note was true and Gracey was headed to see Jacob Panther. No way Charlotte could read the girl's intentions at this distance. It was hard enough to do that when she was in the same room.

"I'll let that slide," Frank said. "So tell me, Monroe, she have a driver's license? Maybe some kind of fake ID says she's eighteen?"

"She's got a learner's permit. No fake ID I know of."

"But she looks eighteen?"

"Depends on who's looking. But yeah, she could pass. Why?"

"I was thinking she might appear young enough, it could register with somebody along the way. They'd think something wasn't right, make a call, stop her, and ask some questions."

"She could pass," Charlotte said. "The right makeup. Even without it."

"She have access to a lot of cash? Savings? Or anything missing from your mother-in-law's?"

"Not that I know of. She might've saved a little from her allowance. But not more than a hundred or so. She's not a thrifty girl."

"Well, that's it then."

"What about the ax? No prints were there?"

"They're looking at some fibers, hairs. But nothing yet."

Parker was staring out the windshield, submerged in his dull trance.

Still staring forward, Parker said, "Ask Sheffield why the guy uses a blowgun one time, hatchet the next."

She passed along the question, and Sheffield said, "Different locations. He has no choice in the airport—got to use something that gives him a chance to melt away. At your mother-in-law's he didn't care if things got messy."

She relayed that to Parker, but he shook his head firmly.

"Different MO equals different killer."

Already building his case.

"And for godsakes, Diana was his grandmother. Why would he attack her? Where's the motive?"

"Why would he blow up banks, Parker? Kill some guy at the airport?"

Parker shook his head firmly, having none of it.

Charlotte asked Frank if there was any more. There wasn't. He did a quick condolence on Diana.

"I got your package," she said. "Thanks."

"Which package was that?"

"Panther's files."

"All I did," Sheffield said, "I passed on the message to Mears, and stepped back out of range. For the record, this little deal's between you and the high-and-mighties, okay? If there's blowback, it's going to singe their butt hairs, not mine."

"I appreciate it anyway, Frank."

"Thing is, Officer Monroe, and let's underscore this in big red Magic Marker, okay? I'm keeping you in the loop because you're the anxious parent of a runaway kid. But if a parent was all you were, you know damn well I wouldn't be sharing as much detail. I think you understand what I'm saying."

Charlotte choked back a flare of anger, then drew a measured breath.

"Thanks for keeping me informed, Frank. Anything else you get, day or night, I want to hear about it."

"That goes double for you, Monroe. Double. And please tell me you got that gizmo on you?"

"I got it, Frank. Everywhere I go."

"Press it, green light comes on, bingo, we're there. Don't even have to say a word."

"Bye, Frank. Always a pleasure."

FIFTEEN

FRANK SHEFFIELD SHUT HIS PHONE and joined Special Agent Joe Roth at the walkway in front of the Cherokee police department. Local tribal cops in their navy blues were coming and going, shooting Roth and him surly looks.

Across the street was the Cherokee history museum, and on the other side of the road there was a shabby restaurant and a ticket office for the local outdoor pageant. Frank could see the silver flicker of moving water through the trees. The Oconaluftee River, he'd been told. Strange turf, all in all. Mountains, giant trees, cold dry air for June. Hardly any traffic except around the casino. And all those Indians drifting around—handsome people, but not a lot of cheerfulness in the air.

Roth was winding down his own phone call, the last few "okays" before signing off. Joe was a stocky man—five six, five seven—and built like a Little League hammer thrower. Thick neck, stubby arms. Sheffield and Roth might've been a comic tag team. Chop them high, chop them low.

Both agents were in jeans and different shades of blue button-downs. The Carolina uniform, he'd been told. Try to blend in. Though Sheffield could see that wasn't working worth a damn.

Roth finished his call and nodded to two more officers passing by. Got the same frosty response as they pushed open the front door and went inside.

"Friendly town."

Roth shook his head helplessly.

"Local law enforcement hasn't taken a cotton to us city folks."

"Taken a cotton?"

"I'm trying to adopt the native tongue."

"Oh, I bet that goes over big."

Roth clicked his phone, looking for messages, then slid it into his pocket.

"We've worn out our welcome. Last year looking for Panther, all the questions, poking around, city attitude. Bound to happen."

"From the looks of it, if one of these guys knew where Panther was, you'd be the last person they'd tell."

"I'm afraid you're right."

"So we going in or what?"

"Quick warning, Frank. You knew the sheriff's an identical twin to Martin Tribue, your victim."

"I heard that, yeah."

"Just thought I should warn you. Walking in, seeing this guy after you been looking at photos of his mirror image on a slab, it might spook you."

"You're a warm and caring person, Joe."

"One other thing," Roth said. "Sheriff's kind of an oddball. Got a serious case of the weirds, but he's competent enough. Runs a tight ship."

"I take it he's not a Cherokee?"

"No." Roth smiled. "Only white guy on the force."

"Elected?"

"No, hired by the tribe. An employee. They got themselves a sovereign nation here. Write all their own laws, got their own employment practices. Affirmative action times ten. It's total Indian preference, written right into the statutes. Casino, fire department, anything operated by the tribe, got to let the Cherokee get first in line."

"I got no problem with that. Time they had a break."

"Sure, whatever." Roth checked his watch. "The guy's waiting."

"So let me guess how he got the job, being a white guy. It have anything to do with his old man being Otis Tribue?"

Roth nodded at a couple of cops coming up the stairs to the office. Same sullen hellos came back.

"Didn't hurt," Roth said. "Last thirty years his father runs the show around here. Eleventh district, Republican congressman."

"So much for Indian preference," said Sheffield.

"Never hurts if Daddy breaks bread at the White House now and again."

"Man, I could use one of those daddies," Sheffield said.

The interior of the police department had all the charm of a fifties ranch, with brown shag in the offices and an avocado refrigerator in the lunchroom. Stone Age computers atop all the desks. Tacked up on one wall was a kid's finger painting, but that was about it for artwork.

The sheriff's office was a little better. A window that looked toward the river, a wide desk cluttered with papers. Some family photos. But still frugal, all in all a gloomy-ass place to work, in Sheffield's estimation.

Sheriff Farris Tribue was indeed an identical copy of his brother. Taller than Sheffield by a few inches, with the kind of body Frank associated with bronc riders. All gristle and tendon. Late forties. A long, bony Abe Lincoln face with a bulky jaw and dark, close-set eyes. His ears cupped out like small hands, and the bluish shadow of his beard was showing already at noon.

Two white standard poodles that had been lying on the linoleum behind the sheriff's desk rose, came to attention, and sauntered around the desk.

"Don't mind them," Tribue said. "They're harmless."

While the dogs took turns sniffing Sheffield's crotch, Sheriff Tribue held out a huge mitt, which swallowed Frank's hand as they shook. The sheriff held the grip a few seconds longer than necessary. Tugging Frank an inch or two off balance till his thighs were pressed awkwardly against the edge of the sheriff's desk. Maybe on purpose, maybe not. But Sheffield was still pissed off even before the guy opened his mouth.

"Special Agent Sheffield's up from the Miami field office."

The sheriff nodded his greeting.

"My sincere regrets on the loss of your brother, Martin."

The sheriff thanked Sheffield, his face blank. He waved the agents into the folding metal chairs across from his desk. Sheffield's was a size too small, making him feel suddenly like a third grader called before the principal. Which he supposed was the intention.

The two poodles stood side by side watching Frank, at eye level now.

They were weird-ass dogs, sizing him up like he might be on the dinner menu.

"I assume you want to know if I have any thoughts on why Jacob Panther might want to murder my brother."

"Good place to start."

"I have absolutely no idea. I've given it a great deal of reflection, but I can't fathom it."

"Did they know each other? Before Panther went on the run, I mean."

"It's a small town, Agent Sheffield. Everyone knows everyone."

"But there was no history between them? Animosity?"

"They traveled in different social circles," the sheriff said. "As far as I know, Martin and Panther had no contact whatsoever."

Sheffield shifted in his puny chair and watched the guy. He wore the same dark-navy uniform as the other cops. Nice, crisp Windsor knot hugged tight to his throat. A little more gold sprinkled around than on the noncoms. Sidearm was a chunky SIG Sauer .357 in a polished leather holster. Sheffield wasn't sure why the guy irritated him so much. The undersized chair, that handshake game. But it was something more than that. Smugness radiating off his flesh like a bad smell.

As if following some silent command, the dogs turned away from Sheffield and returned to their spots on either side of the sheriff's desk.

Roth was quiet, letting Sheffield take the lead.

"Your brother, Martin, he ran a construction company? Tribue Engineering?"

"That's right."

"Office buildings, that sort of thing?"

"Commercial, residential, parking lots. Whatever needed building, Martin could handle it. Housing developments, swimming pools, anything."

"Successful business?"

"Like any company, there have been good times and bad."

"Maybe Panther did carpenter work, day laborer, anything like that? He might have a run-in with the boss?"

The sheriff shook his head.

"Barroom fights, girlfriends? Something out of left field that might tie them together?"

"If there was anything like that, I can't think what it is. Believe me, I've racked my brain. But no, I'm aware of absolutely no reason why Jacob Panther, or anyone else for that matter, might want to kill my brother. He was a gentle spirit. A kind and generous soul."

"You and him, you shared a house?"

The sheriff stiffened for a moment, as if Frank was implying something deviant.

"Martin and I lived in the home where we were born. Where my father was born and his father before him. Is that relevant?"

"At this point, I don't know what's relevant. I'm just collecting data. You know how it is."

The sheriff nodded, but there was a new rigidity in his manner. Sheffield had crossed some line. Getting personal. Something.

The dogs seemed to sense it, too. They lifted their heads, giving Frank the dead man's stare.

"So Martin was down in Miami setting up a fund-raiser, that right?"

"He was scouting locations for a future event. Motels, conference rooms, banquet halls. Looking for the right venue where some of my father's loyal supporters could gather."

"Strange thing," Sheffield said. "Going through his papers, we found he was booked on a flight coming back the next day. Hits Miami Monday midday, schedules his return for Tuesday. I'm wondering, can he accomplish all that in less than twenty-four hours? Banquet halls, motels, conference rooms. I mean, Miami's a big place."

"I'm not sure I'm registering your point, sir. Is there some other agenda here I'm not aware of? I find your tone somewhat inappropriate."

"I'm just trying to understand. Fact-checking, that's all."

The sheriff picked up a ballpoint and drummed it on his ink blotter.

"I'm not certain of Martin's schedule. You'd have to query one of my father's aides about that. But Martin was a very competent businessman. I'm sure his travel plans were suitable to his task."

Sheffield said, "He always travel with a handgun? Your brother?"

The sheriff cocked his head and looked at Frank with a cold smile.

"I believe he was concerned about Miami's reputation for crime and disorder. So it wouldn't surprise me if he would choose to carry a legally registered handgun for protection."

"Like for the motel room?" Sheffield said. "Somebody tries to break in? That sort of thing. Or a mugging on the street."

"You're free to conjecture, of course. But we'll never know for sure exactly what scenario Martin feared."

"Had to ask," Sheffield said. "You got a victim of a violent crime; he's got a Glock nine in his checked luggage. That's a red flag. Like there might've been something else going on. More than looking for banquet rooms."

"A reasonable line of inquiry, of course," the sheriff said. "Pardon me for being defensive. But he was my twin—a good, honest man. Naturally I bristle at the suggestion that he was engaged in suspicious activity of any kind."

"Naturally," Roth said.

"So you'd know what your brother was into? If it was something hinky."

"Hinky?"

"Illegal, weird, kinky—anything along those lines."

"He was a good man. A solid citizen. Nothing hinky about him."

"Way I hear it," Sheffield said, "Martin could get a little emotional. Like a serious go-getter. You were the quiet brother, he could get worked up. Short fuse, too much hot sauce."

"Where'd you hear that?"

"Agent Roth and his people have been up here for a year. All that time, you pick up a few things. Is it true?"

Farris looked down at one of the poodles.

"I've heard that characterization before. It's not uncommon in identical twins. A brash one and a quieter one."

"So then maybe it is possible, you two being so different, Martin might've been into something you didn't know about. Something that got him worked up and he didn't tell you, 'cause you're the quiet one, the one in law enforcement, you might not approve. Is that possible?"

He looked up from the poodle and gave Frank a hard stare.

"Absolutely not—we were very open with each other. He had legitimate business in Miami. Carrying along a sidearm was not uncommon for him."

Sheffield was quiet for a moment. Scrounging around in his head for anything else. The older he got, the harder it was to keep more than a handful of questions floating in his mind. It might be time to consider a notebook, jot a few things down, see how it felt.

"You done, Frank?"

"For now, yeah. Take it away."

Roth drew the photos from his shirt pocket and lay them before the sheriff. Two black and whites, three colors. The ax that killed Diana Monroe propped up against a white background. Different angles, a couple of close-ups.

With a fingertip, the sheriff fanned the photos across his ink blotter and put on a pair of reading glasses.

"All right," the sheriff then said, taking off the glasses. "So what is this? Am I supposed to hazard a conjecture?"

"A conjecture would be fine. It's kind of an unusual weapon."

"Well, it looks Cherokee to me, if that's what you're asking. But I'm no expert. There are people across the street, over at the museum—they could tell you. That's what I'd suggest."

"We'll do that next."

"Some kind of glorified tomahawk," said Farris. "That's what it appears to be."

"Got no prints or other forensics tying the weapon to Panther," Roth said, "but there's other linkage."

"You're suggesting Panther killed Martin, then struck down someone else as well, employing this weapon?"

"Could be," Frank said. "We're looking into it."

"Well, naturally, this is your case, gentlemen," said Tribue. "Forgive me if I'm going beyond my bounds, but I believe you're headed in the wrong direction." He tapped the ballpoint against one of the photos. "This weapon doesn't match Panther's profile."

"How you figure?"

"The blowgun, yes. Yesterday, when I received word of my brother's murder and your suspicions that Panther was involved, I immediately spoke to some of Panther's former cohorts. And yes, apparently he was known to have used blowguns on several occasions while hunting for small game. According to those same friends, he also owns a deer rifle. But an ax? No, I'd have trouble putting that together with what we know of Panther. Such proximity between Panther and his target is not within the man's personality pattern. He hits from a distance, and runs. A coward."

"Okay," Roth said. "So noted."

"So we'll take our pictures, go across the street," said Sheffield. "See what the museum people have to say."

The sheriff gathered the photos and held them out.

"I thank you for stopping in. Your concern for keeping me advised is a welcome professional courtesy."

Roth got up and reached for the photos, but at the last second the sheriff drew them back. Roth lowered his arm and sighed.

"I do see one thing here that might be of interest." Tribue fanned the photos like a poker hand and plucked one out and held it up.

Sheffield clamped his jaw. He'd seen Tribue's type before. Had to milk every situation for its maximum one-up potential. The kind of dick-measuring smart guy Frank had lost all patience with in his grumpy midlife.

Roth sat back down and shut his mouth.

"It's a construction technique I've seen employed before around these parts. A traditional Cherokee method. Make a slit in the limb of a cedar, insert the ax head through the slit, and over time the limb grows around it and creates a strong seal. Then for additional support, the head is lashed in that crisscross fashion with sinew, rattlesnake skin, buckskin."

"Lab results said deerskin, but not the others," Roth said.

Sheffield said, "Take a long damn time to make something like that, wouldn't it? Letting a branch grow around an ax blade. Years, maybe."

"Time, patience," the sheriff said. "The Cherokees have a different clock than you and I do. Theirs runs a little slower."

The sheriff came to his feet, held out the photos. Another cute move. Playing traffic cop in his own office. You're dismissed—I'm done with you.

Sheffield kept his seat. The guy wanted to play? Okay, he'd play.

"And those cross-hatchings on the handle, the grooves? Got any thoughts on those?"

"Simply to improve the grip, I would suppose. A method for turning a

slick piece of cedar into a more effective implement. All that would be required is some careful whittling."

The sheriff continued to stand. Arms behind his back, legs spread. Parade rest. The large white poodles were standing as well, poised on either
side of the desk like a couple of stone lions outside a big-city library.

Aw, fuck it—Sheffield was tired of the schoolyard bullshit.

He got up and nodded for Roth.

"You think of anything else, you know how to reach us."

The sheriff walked them to the front door. Cordial, pointing out the museum from the front steps. Wishing them well in their endeavors.

When he'd gone back inside, Sheffield said, "What'd you guys do to
piss these people off so bad?"

"Just hung around too long. Got on their nerves."

"Works both ways," said Sheffield. "Give me a city asshole any day over
these swaggering coon dogs. I wouldn't last a week up here."

"Let's hope you don't have to."

They headed across the street to the museum.

"You got guys covering the bus stops, right?"

"Two guys at every stop from here back down to Asheville," Roth said.
"That little girl shows up, one second later my phone rings."

"Well, shit. Between the girl and her parents, we're going to nail this asshole, Joe. I got that feeling."

"Hope to hell you're right, Sheffield. I could use a break from this shit-
poor food."

"By the way," Frank said. "*Oddball* isn't the word I would've picked."

"Yeah?"

"I'm thinking more along the lines of *fuckhead*."

SIXTEEN

FRANCES WOLFE, THE CURATOR OF the Cherokee Native American museum, was out sick, but her assistant, Randy Forbus, was filling in. Randy led them to his cubicle, where he sat down behind an old army-surplus desk.

Long, dark Cherokee hair hanging loose down his back. Round-faced, pudgy kid, about twenty-five, in a checked shirt and scruffy jeans.

Roth spread the photos out on his desk, and the kid got an eager look and bent forward like he thought he was going to see a naked body.

"Ever come across one of those?"

The kid's sparkle evaporated.

"Yeah."

"You tell us where?"

"This way," he said, and got up and led them back into the museum area, moving through the maze of small rooms filled with glassed-in exhibits, to a dimly lit room near the back.

They had to wait till a family in matching T-shirts moved out of the way. Frank and Roth stepped up and surveyed the three-window display. Window one showed a life-size tableau of a group of six Indians being prodded along by U.S. soldiers. Civil War era, Frank figured, maybe a little earlier.

In the next case, one old Indian had his arm raised to strike at one of the soldiers. And in the final display the same old man was standing up against a tree, hands bound, with five men aiming their rifles at him. An execution.

Forbus looked puzzled. Stepping close to the glass, he said, "It's gone."

"What's gone?"

"That ax. It's supposed to be in Tsali's hand. It's gone missing."

"An ax like this one?" Roth held up the stack of photos.

Forbus looked at the photo, then back at the old guy's hand, which Sheffield could see was half open like he'd been gripping something.

"Same ax," Forbus said. "Or damn close."

"How long could this thing be gone?"

Forbus was getting a queasy look.

"Not long," he said. "Somebody would've noticed."

"What, like a day or two?" Sheffield said.

"Couldn't be any longer than that. All the people coming through here, somebody would've said something."

"How secure are these things?"

Sheffield tapped on the glass.

Forbus went over to the wall beside the case and peeled open a handle that lay flush against the black wall. He drew open a door and stepped through it and, a second later, he looked out at them from behind the exhibit.

"We're not talking Hope diamond here," Frank said.

"He can't just use a gun like any other killer. He's got to steal an ax from a museum."

"This guy's got an agenda," Sheffield said. "Something weird's going on in his head."

Forbus came back out and Frank said, "It's always like that, unlocked? Anybody can get in?"

Forbus nodded.

"It's not like anything here is worth stealing."

"Somebody thought so," Sheffield said.

Forbus said, "I got to call my boss."

He started to go, but Frank put a hand on his shoulder and halted him.

"We're cordoning this area off. No one gets in or out till our fingerprint guys are done."

"I'll call them," Roth said, and stepped aside to flip open his phone.

"Should be done in a few hours," Sheffield said to the kid, and the boy nodded meekly.

"Whatever you say."

"So what's the deal here?" Frank said. "What'd that old Indian guy do?"

"That's Tsali," the kid said. "You don't know the story?"

"I got a minute if it's not too long."

Roth shut his phone and moved beside Sheffield.

The kid's voice took on the bored tone of a tour guide.

"The Cherokee people were being forcibly removed from their home-land, and Tsali resisted. He killed a couple of soldiers, then fled into the mountains and hid. Army couldn't track him down, and they were afraid other Cherokee people would try the same thing, so they made an offer. If Tsali would come out and give himself up to execution, the government would give a few hundred Cherokee amnesty, let them stay up here in the mountains instead of driving them like cattle to Oklahoma."

Roth said, "The guy's a big deal around here. Local hero."

"Yeah," Forbus said. "So will that be all?"

The kid started to go, but Sheffield had a couple more questions.

"So this Tsali character. He was a murderer, and after he got caught and executed, he was promoted into what, like a saint or something? That's what we're talking about?"

The kid looked at Frank for a few seconds and said, "Maybe he was a saint a long time ago. Now he's more like a tourist attraction."

"Tell me this," Frank said. "If I wanted to find out more about this guy, can you suggest a book, somebody to talk to, an expert?"

"Dr. Julie Milford," the kid said. "She's at Asheville Women's College. We have some of her books out front. Anything about Tsali, she's knows it."

SEVENTEEN

SHERIFF FARRIS TRIBUE STOOD IN the doorway of Julius Weatherby's office and waited silently to be noticed.

Maybe fifty years old, bald, a hundred pounds overweight, and red-faced, Julius Weatherby was a buffoon who blathered so incessantly he hardly had time for a breath.

Finally the man looked up, saw the sheriff standing there, popped up, and hustled around his desk, giving the poodles a quick, uncomfortable look.

"Sheriff Tribue, oh my. I was so terribly sorry to hear about Martin." Weatherby pressed his palms flat as if he meant to recite a prayer.

Ordinarily Farris would have kept his distance from such a fool, except that Weatherby Travel Agency provided the Tribue family bargain rates on their travel needs. The glamour of arranging a congressman's occasional junkets to Aruba and the Caymans and the frequent airline travel back and forth between his home district and the nation's capital more than offset any lost profits.

Farris glanced across the open office area. Three women were sitting at their computers busily typing. No one looking his way.

Farris stepped into the office, signaled the poodles to follow, then shut the door.

"Is something wrong? I mean besides Martin, of course."

Farris drew up the customer's chair closer to Julius Weatherby's desk. Sweat had begun to erupt on Weatherby's pink forehead. The poodles lay down on the bare floor beside Farris, both of them assuming the same position, resting their snouts on their extended forelegs.

"Is the congressman all right? I'm sure it was a terrible shock to lose Martin in such a heinous way. I mean, is he all right, your father? His health?"

Farris drew a breath and brushed a strand of lint from his blue trousers.

"Would you like some water? I'm having some."

Weatherby got up from his desk and shuffled to a small refrigerator near the front window and drew out a plastic bottle of water. He held it out to Farris, but Farris made no move. The man said, "Yes, of course. How about the dogs—would they like some water?"

Farris remained silent and Weatherby apologized again and went back to his desk and sat down and screwed open the bottle and drank half of it in one swallow.

"Who handled Martin's accounts?"

"I'm sorry?" Weatherby put the bottle on his desk and leaned forward.

"Which of your girls made Martin's arrangements? His airline tickets, that sort of thing."

"Oh, the girls. Which of my girls handled Martin's account? That's what you want to know? Is this a police matter? Is that what it is? Something about the murder investigation?"

Farris gave Weatherby a thin smile.

"I can't discuss police business, Julius. I'm sure you understand."

"Oh, yes. Yes, of course."

"Which girl?"

"Well, Nancy Feather handled Martin's accounts. His travel. Actually, Martin was kind of sweet on her. Asked her out once or twice, but Nancy always said no. I told her, go, Nancy, go on, he's a nice young man. So successful in his business affairs. You should be honored he singled you out."

Farris stood up. The two poodles rose and stood behind him, waiting, watching his movements.

"Do you have to go so soon? Did Nancy do something wrong? I'll fire her if you want. I mean if she did something wrong in any way. I'm very strict with the girls. Those Indians are so scatterbrained. If there's something she did, just say the word and she's gone."

"I need to know," Farris said, "if Nancy Feather has any association with Lucy Panther."

"Oh, my, so that's what this is about. Of course, of course. The Panther investigation. Yes, a terrible thing, all the banks. Just terrible. But of course, I have to say, with all these federal agents coming and going, it's provided a healthy uptick in business around here this last year."

"Julius."

"Oh, yes. I'm sorry. Nancy Feather and Lucy Panther. Yes, yes, I've heard talk that they were friends. Went to school together way back when."

"And do they have contact currently?"

Julius drew a wadded hankie from his rear pocket and dabbed his throat.

"I wouldn't know about that, Farris. I mean, I realize Lucy Panther is under suspicion for aiding and abetting her son. In cahoots, as they say. But Nancy never speaks about her. Very tight-lipped."

"You understand, Julius, not to speak of police matters. No gossip."

"Of course, of course."

He hurried around the desk, prattling as he came.

"I told Nancy, I said, Nancy, men like Martin Tribue don't come along every day. And you're no homecoming queen, Nancy. I said that. I said that to Nancy."

Farris turned to the door, opened it, and stepped outside.

"Once again, Sheriff, my deepest condolences. And tell your father I send my very warmest wishes for continued prosperity."

Farris parked his cruiser along the shoulder of Stillwell Branch Road, let the dogs out of the backseat, and locked the doors, then cut through an open field and, with the poodles tagging along at a respectful distance, crossed Little Bear Creek at the footbridge he'd built with his own hands nearly thirty years earlier.

For a hundred yards the trail ran level, then dipped into a small basin where the white double-wide trailer sat among the freshly leaved maples.

His son, Shelley, was sitting in the tall weeds just outside the door, scratching with a twig at the ground between his outstretched legs. He wore a yellow T-shirt and baggy diapers, and even from thirty yards away, Farris could see the bug bites pimpling his bare flesh.

The two large white poodles trotted over to the boy and stopped ten feet away, lifting their noses to catch his scent. Farris had trained them not to approach his son. He trusted the dogs, for he and Martin had trained them rigorously. But he also knew what violence they were capable of, so it was only prudent to keep a buffer between the boy and the animals.

Hunched forward on an aluminum lawn chair a few feet away from the boy, Margie Hornbuckle spooned lemon yogurt into her mouth. She looked up as Farris broke through the bushes and stepped into view but said not a word to this intruder in her small encampment.

Farris went over to the boy, thirty years old, with the milky, translucent skin and dreamy green eyes of his mother. His head was shaved, and the silky black hair on his arms and legs waved in the cool breeze like the tentacles of some undersea creature.

Farris squatted down beside the young man. In the red dust between his legs were a dozen oval shapes.

"And what are you drawing today, boy?"

The lad looked at Farris and smiled the crooked way he could manage. He stammered something, but as usual Farris had to await Margie's translation.

"Flowers," she called over. "He's been a-drawing flowers all week long. One flower after the other. 'Cause of it being springtime, I reckon."

Farris peered at the boy's handiwork and spoke his approval.

"It's a beautiful bouquet," he said. "You're becoming quite an artist, Shelley. Quite gifted."

Margie got up from her chair and came over. In her toothless old age, yogurt and soft-boiled eggs made up the bulk of her diet. He'd hired the woman shortly after Shelley's condition became apparent and Farris's young wife decided she wanted none of it, deserting both husband and child. For nearly thirty years Margie had been the boy's caregiver, Farris making visits whenever he felt a need to peer again into the boy's depthless eyes.

"Got another of them postcards from your missus," Margie said.

"Have I not made it clear? I want to hear nothing about the post-cards."

She ran her spoon around the inside of the yogurt container and licked it clean.

"Care for any yogurt? I got all the flavors."

"Nothing, thank you."

"You happen to bring along anything with you today?"

The boy continued to draw in the dirt, the petals of roses and lilacs and daisies. Circles within circles within circles, a field of endless blossoms. Once more Shelley lifted his eyes to squint at Farris, this tall man who had appeared from thin air.

"Good work, lad. Good work."

The boy grinned, and when he had his fill of Farris, he took a new grip on his stick and applied himself with fresh enthusiasm to his sketching.

Farris stood up and reached into his back pocket and withdrew his wal-let and peeled out three hundred-dollar bills. Margie took the cash and stuffed it into the pouch of her apron.

"Don't imagine you notice, living up in the big house, but prices is go-ing up and up. Them groceries is about to break us little people. 'Lectricity, too, damn, you wouldn't believe the cost of current. And diapers, yes sir, I go through near five a day. They ain't cheap either. Those ones you got me using."

"Buy some antiseptic for his bites. Then remember to apply it."

"Yeah, yeah, I'll do that. The boy's got such sensitive skin, you know. Flares up over just a chigger. Then he scratches at 'em till they're bloody. I try to stay after them, but he gets such a kick out of rolling around in the grass, you know."

"Antiseptic," Farris said.

He drew out two more hundred-dollar bills and held them out while he watched his son draw garlands in the red Carolina dust.

EIGHTEEN

IN THE BULKHEAD SEATS OF first class, on the three-fifteen Delta flight to Atlanta that connected to Asheville, Charlotte studied the FBI field report on Jacob Bright Sky Panther while Parker buried himself in one of the Cherokee reference books crammed in his carry-on.

He was wearing scuffed hiking boots he'd hauled out of the recesses of his closet, along with heavy khaki pants and a flannel shirt, an outfit that was grossly out of place for the muggy Miami afternoon. He'd badgered her into swapping her summer lightweights for a pair of dark jeans and a medium-weight sweatshirt over a cotton blouse. And good, heavy tennis shoes for the rough terrain. Spring weather in the mountains was unpredictable. They were going on a hike tonight. Up to Camp Tsali to get Gracey back.

About a half an hour into the flight, she set aside the legal pad she'd been using to take notes on the FBI report, and nudged Parker's elbow.

"How'd he do it so quickly?"

He looked up from the text, took off his glasses, and rubbed his eyes.

"Do what?"

"Gracey left you and Panther on the patio and came into the house, then a little later Panther goes to the john. Gracey and I were in my office for a couple of minutes, which means she and Jacob only had a couple more alone."

"So?"

"Jacob sells her on the diversion with your car, and he manages to make enough of an impression on her that the first chance she gets she runs off to join him. Three, four minutes he accomplishes all that."

"So what're you saying? He had it worked out ahead of time? His sole reason for being there is to get Gracey alone and seduce her into running off?"

"I don't know what I'm saying. It just seems fast, that's all."

"Jacob's got a forceful personality."

"Bullshit. Gracey is ill. She's not responsible for her actions."

"I don't accept that diagnosis."

"Jesus, I can't believe you, Parker. Everyone's innocent, and no one's sick. How can a smart man like you have such a simplistic view?"

He swallowed back his first response and drew a long breath.

"Our daughter ran away from home, okay, it's upsetting, sure, but it's not that uncommon. She's almost legal age—another year she could go anywhere she wanted without our permission."

"She's a year and three months shy. And she's ill, Parker."

"You ran away from home. Same age."

Charlotte cleared her throat and drew a calming breath.

"Yeah," she said. "And look what happened."

"It didn't turn out so badly, did it?"

Charlotte felt the old refrain crawling up her throat: *I'm grateful, Parker. I wouldn't be here today without your help. You saved my life.*

"Difference is," she said. "I didn't run away to join up with a killer."

"Even if it wasn't your intent, it *is* what happened."

"Oh, so this is karmic payback. She's repeating the sins of her mother."

"Never said that. Never entered my mind."

"Sure it didn't."

"You keep saying I believe everyone is innocent, but that's not true, Charlotte. I would have to be an idiot to think that. Totally out of touch."

"That's how it comes across."

"I take people for who they are. Innocence, guilt—that doesn't come into it. People deserve a second chance. That's my job, to see they get it."

"And Gracey?"

"I'm not blind. I see what you see. I just deal with it differently."

Charlotte was silent. Not quite fuming, but getting there.

"Diana said all I had to do was love Gracey and everything would be fine. Is that what you believe?"

"Yes," Parker said. "Yes, it is."

"That would cure her? A big dose of uncritical love?"

"You're talking about fixing Gracey. That's not what I'm saying."

"Then what?"

"Changing her school isn't going to fix her. Changing her meds won't do it either. The only thing you can fix is yourself, how you're dealing with it."

They stared at the bulkhead. Charlotte's ears were ringing. She reached down and picked up her backpack and found a Kleenex and blew her nose. As she was setting the backpack back on the floor, Sheffield's gadget spilled out and bumped Parker's right boot. She unsnapped her seat belt and bent forward and palmed the thing, checked it quickly to make sure she hadn't activated the green light, then dropped it back into the bag.

When she arose, Parker was still staring straight ahead.

She drummed her ballpoint against her notepad. Watched the flight attendant delivering another Bloody Mary to the guy across the aisle. Already soused and getting louder by the minute.

"We should call Frank. This is too risky, Parker. Waltzing into some cave in the middle of the night."

"You want to get Gracey back, don't you?"

"Don't be a shit, Parker. You know I'd do anything."

Parker polished the lenses of his glasses with the edge of his shirt-sleeve.

"If Jacob Panther wanted to kill us, he could've done that in Miami."

"He got scared off before he could."

"No, Charlotte. He was there to warn us of something."

"This guy leaves a note about a red war club, the next night Diana is murdered by a hatchet. What more proof do you need? And by the way, you're withholding again. Not telling Sheffield about the red war club note."

"It's not relevant."

"Bullshit."

"That was not a war club. A Cherokee war club has a two-sided blade. The weapon that killed Mother had only one. A garden tool for cutting firewood."

"You're incredible, Parker. You won't accept the obvious."

"He came there to warn us, Charlotte, but when he needed to use the john, I sent him to the guest bath across from your office. And I assume you had your office door ajar, right?"

She nodded.

"He walked by, saw the FBI page on your screen, realized he was in jeopardy, and threw together whatever scheme he could to get out of there."

Charlotte drew a fierce circle on her legal pad. Round and round in the same orbit till she'd scratched a hole in the yellow paper.

"So now I'm also responsible for Diana's death?"

"Oh, come on."

"If I hadn't called the feds, Jacob could have told us the whole story and we could have done something to prevent Diana's murder. That's how you work, Parker. You don't say things straight out. You leave things dangling, lead people right up to the edge. Then you back away and see if we poor idiots come to the right conclusion on our own. I've been watching you do it for years, in and out of court."

Parker clamped his lips, damming up the words he wanted to say until his neck seemed to bulge from the effort.

It took a while for the swell to subside. Then, with the same subdued tone she'd heard him use on Gracey after some outrageous remark, he said, "So, you learning anything from the file?"

"Seventy-five pages of padding, only a few facts."

"I'm not surprised."

"Well, I am. A lot of generic bullshit about the lab results on the bomb materials. All this boilerplate about incendiary devices and explosive ones."

"Which were used on the banks?"

"Combination. An explosion, then a fire. Nothing high-tech about this guy. He blows out a window with a shotgun, heaves a one-gallon ceramic jug filled with gasoline, a kerosene-soaked handkerchief for a fuse. Pretty damn crude. A moonshine jug, for godsakes. Redneck C4.

"But most of the file is filler. Law-enforcement trivia. Of the twelve hundred bombing incidents nationwide last year, only seven were banks. Public high schools were bombed seventy-six times. Government offices twelve. Most common time of day for bombings—there is none. Morning, noon, and night in equal percentages. Useless stuff."

"It's political," Parker said.

"What?"

"The Most Wanted list. It's about power, not crime."

"Power? What're you talking about?"

"Oh, come on. Who owns banks? Same people who make campaign contributions. A few well-placed phone calls from politically connected business types, Panther gets promoted to the list."

"Eight homicides don't count for something?"

"If it was five liquor stores in the Liberty City ghetto, eight African-Americans killed by the same suspect, you think he'd make the list? Or eight Native American victims for that matter? Of course not. It's political."

Charlotte looked down at the FBI field report and shook her head.

"So what if it *is* political. We're still talking about eight homicides."

"Politics, banks, money," Parker said. "The guy at the airport. He was a congressman's son. There's a pattern."

"You're stretching."

"Tell me about the videos," Parker said.

She raised her feet and pressed her soles flat to the bulkhead.

"Security cameras. On three occasions they show a large man with shoulder-length blond hair leaving the bomb sites. Cherokee, Waynesville, Bryson City. In all three there's a pickup similar to Panther's and a partial view of his plates."

Parker had to tangle with that for a moment.

"They have Panther's face?"

"Profile in one, back in the other two. All of it's pretty fuzzy."

"They include an outtake photo in the report?"

Charlotte found the pages and showed him the black-and-white stills taken from the video.

"That's not Jacob."

"Parker, give it up."

"This man is taller, thinner. It's not Jacob."

"You saw him for half an hour max, and you can positive ID him?"

"These are worthless," he said. "Could be a wig. Could be anybody."

"It's the sum of the evidence. The preponderance. Right?"

"You get to the sum by examining the parts. If the pieces aren't true, the sum can't be either. Now what about the license? How partial is it?"

"Three or four numbers. The others are obscured by tree limbs, shadows, other objects."

"Which is it? Three or four? Big difference statistically."

"Jesus, Parker. You're a cop's worst nightmare. Going for every chink in the armor."

"You'd rather live in a police state? Whatever you and your FBI pals say, that's what goes?"

"Those are the only two choices?"

"Three or four, Officer Monroe? Which is it?"

"It's four, Counselor."

"Same four numbers repeat every time?"

"Hell, I don't remember. What difference does that make?"

Charlotte paged through the document until she found the pages. Ran her finger down the margin. Then paged forward to the other two citations.

"Yeah, as a matter of fact. Same four—1773. Turns out there's only one white Ford pickup registered in the entire state of North Carolina with those last four numbers. Registered to Jacob Panther."

"Well, that's kind of coincidental, don't you think? Same four digits. Others obscured in each of the videos. Doesn't that have a funny odor?"

Charlotte coughed out a half-chuckle.

"So that's your fancy strategy? This is all a grand conspiracy. Someone is setting up poor Jacob? Wearing a wig, phonying up license plates. Going to elaborate lengths to fabricate a case against him. That's your defense? Some boogeyman hangs eight homicides on this guy? Why?"

"Doesn't matter why. The license wouldn't stand up. Juries don't like coincidences. Good cop like you, you shouldn't either."

"Jesus Romero was right. You're so far gone, there's no bringing you back to this world."

"Who made the initial ID on Panther?"

"Local sheriff up there. Why's that important?"

"Once a name gets attached to a photo, it sticks. Things become self-perpetuating. One long, self-fulfilling prophecy. What you look for, you see."

"So the sheriff's in on it, too?"

"What about the profile?" Parker said. "What motive do they have?"

"He's an angry member of an oppressed minority. An outcast. He's striking back at a symbol of authority."

"That's it?"

"Pretty much."

Parker laughed.

"And you buy that, Charlotte?"

"I've seen people do worse things for more trivial reasons."

"He blows up banks because he's a member of an oppressed minority? Jesus Christ. Then why aren't a thousand banks being blown up every day? We've got enough oppressed, angry outcasts to sustain a hell of a lot of bank bombings. That's crackpot forensic psychology."

Charlotte watched the heavyset man across the aisle chug the last of his Bloody Mary and raise his glass and clink the ice at the attendant. He caught Charlotte watching him and gave her a sloppy smile and a full-frontal wink.

"Buy you a drink?"

"They're free up here," Charlotte said. "Hadn't you heard?"

"Then, hell, I'll buy you two."

She turned back to Parker. He had his reading glasses on and he'd turned his attention back to the volume spread open in his lap.

"Two eyewitnesses," she said, "picked him from photo spreads."

"I remind you, Charlotte, that Panther is only in those photo spreads because some local yokel sheriff made an initial ID."

"Two eyewitness agreed with him, Parker."

He stared down at the page and shook his head.

"I assume the bombings all happened after midnight."

"Ranged between two and four A.M."

"Victims all rent-a-cops?"

"Five security officers, one young couple passing by, and one employee working late."

"Those eyewitnesses, what were they doing out at that time of night? Maybe a bottle of wine with dinner? Just how intoxicated were they? How's their eyesight? When was the last time they visited an optometrist? What were the weather conditions—windy, misty rain? When's their bedtime? Were they tired, in a hurry, anxious to get home?"

"Two different eyewitnesses, two photo spreads."

"Weak," Parker said. "Never met a photo spread I couldn't dismantle." Charlotte groaned.

"What's wrong, I'm too sleazy for you?"

And again Charlotte heard it, embedded in the question, the faint reminder of her long-ago deliverance from jail. When she was behind bars, she sure as hell hadn't cared if Parker was sleazy or not. And she hadn't given a good goddamn about the finer points of jurisprudence that secured her release.

"Get serious, Parker. This is no setup. This is about Panther blowing up banks for his own twisted reasons. Real flesh-and-blood men and women dying, like that guy at the airport. I'd like to hear you explain that one away."

"That one's different," Parker said. "That one he did."

"You're kidding? Panther did that, but not the banks?"

"I believe Jacob killed the man as a last resort. This man, Martin Tribue, what if he was working in tandem with whoever killed Mother? Say Jacob knew what was coming down and he intercepted the killer before he could carry out his mission. He got one but not the other. Or maybe he didn't know about the second killer. I don't know."

"The son of a congressman is an assassin? That's your premise."

"Gut instinct. Hunch, whatever you call it. It's my operating theory. Jacob intercepted the man at the airport, then came immediately to warn us. He was just getting around to it when Sheffield and the Keystone Kops arrived."

Charlotte shook her head.

"All that's based on Jacob saying 'You're next'? Jesus, Parker, for a logical, rational man, you're flying off into the ether."

"I have Cardoza looking into Martin Tribue. We'll see where that goes. But that's my guess. Jacob's trying to save our lives."

Miriam Cardoza had been Parker's investigator for more than twenty years. Pre-Charlotte. A police academy washout. Couldn't take the push-ups, the running. A large lady, out of shape and getting heavier every year, but as smart and dogged as Parker and with endless aunts and uncles scattered through Little Havana and Hialeah. An indispensable virtue in South Florida.

"There's something we need to discuss, Charlotte."

He set the book at his feet, and out of his briefcase he pulled out a manila envelope.

"That thing Mother said on the phone." He cleared his throat, his voice parched. "Her last words."

NINETEEN

"I MIGHT'VE GOT IT WRONG," Charlotte said. "Diana was mumbling."

"You didn't get it wrong."

"I said she should lie down. I was trying to keep her calm, and she called me a beloved woman."

Parker shook his head.

"This wasn't about you. She wasn't giving you her blessing."

He unlooped the string on the envelope, opened it, and held it out. She looked inside, inserted a finger, and tugged the opening wider, then reached in and drew out a flat, woven disk of beaded embroidery the size and heft of a silver dollar. Solid red on one side, a design on the other in beadwork of black and white and red. A pattern that struck her as vaguely familiar.

Staring at the bulkhead, Parker said, "This was in her safe-deposit box."

"Something you made at summer camp?" Charlotte said. "A treasure from her little boy that she saved all these years."

Parker looked at her and smiled, but his eyes were elsewhere, as if he'd sprinted a long way ahead of her on the logic path and was absorbing a different view entirely from what she saw.

Charlotte held the disk at arm's length and squinted.

"What is this? Some kind of Nazi crap?"

"That's a swastika, yeah," he said. "But they were around forever before Hitler perverted them. Roman, Greek, Chinese. A good-luck image, symbol of power. This particular version is Cherokee."

Charlotte recalled where she'd seen the design before, and a cold prickle radiated down her shoulders.

"This was on Panther's shirt."

He nodded.

"All right, Parker, talk to me. What's going on?"

"This isn't a kid's summer camp project. Look at that beadwork—no gaps, perfect lines. You can't see knots or any sign of thread. It's seamless. This is as close to Cherokee high art as you can get."

Parker bent forward and scooped the book from the floor and flopped it open to the page he'd tagged. A glossy color photograph showed a collection of embroidered disks. He pointed at one identical to the one in her hand.

"What are they?"

"These are facsimiles. Archaeologists have never actually found a real one. Only drawings, oral reports."

"And this one, it's real?"

"I'm no expert, but my guess is that it is, yes."

"All right. So what is it?"

Parker closed the book and slipped it back in his briefcase, and groaned as he hauled up a heavier volume. He paged through the book until he came to another section of color plates.

Tilting the book in her direction, he pointed to the same design of thick interlocking lines she'd seen on Jacob's shirt. The swastika shape was elegantly made, with rounded edges like the overlapping blades of two scythes.

In the color plate the design decorated an Indian's shield. The man wore a headdress of red and black feathers, and from the bottom of the shield dangled several more feathers. His loincloth was red, a scarlet cape hung across his shoulder, and in his right hand he gripped a bow and quiver of arrows. His chest was wide and rippled with heavy muscles, and around his neck hung some sort of amulet.

"A warrior," she said.

"Not just any warrior. That's the Great War Chief in full regalia. For the Cherokees he was nearly a deity. President, general, pope, all in one."

Parker's voice had grown raspy. She'd heard that happen during interrogations just before a hard-ass suspect broke down and confessed, as if so unaccustomed to admitting the truth, the words burned his throat with their own fierce bile.

"What's it doing in Diana's lockbox?"

Parker took extra care drawing a breath, as if priming himself for a tricky admission.

"Okay," he said. "The phrase she used on the phone, Beloved Woman, that's an honorary title. It's pronounced 'Ghi-ga-u' in Cherokee. A Beloved Woman was equal in status to this guy." Parker tapped a finger against the Great War Chief. "Over thousands of years of Cherokee history, only a handful of women ever earned that title. Like a goddess, a kind of sainthood."

Saint Diana, the Haughty, was on her tongue, but she restrained herself.

"A Beloved Woman might come along once every other century. She had to be extraordinary in some way. Distinguish herself, make some enormous sacrifice, take a heroic risk. She became the subject of legend, stories that were passed on for generations. *Ghi-ga-u.* The Beloved Woman."

Charlotte mumbled the phrase under her breath.

"Your mother's dying words were about Cherokee folklore?"

"It's not folklore. The Beloved Woman was real, she had true power. She sat in the Council of Chiefs. Had an equal say in all matters about the future of the nation. And she was the ultimate judge of all captured enemies. She decided their fate. Life-and-death authority. She was a central part of their culture for thousands of years, long before our benighted civilization built its first cathedral. The Beloved Woman was deciding who lived and who died."

"Thumbs up, thumbs down."

"Exactly."

Parker closed his eyes, and his head dropped back against the seat. His expression was such a complex mixture of sadness, frustration, and fear, she was certain even Fedderman couldn't parse it.

"The tradition died out centuries ago," Parker said. "The last Beloved Woman was Nanye-hi of the Wolf Clan. You want me to read her story? How she achieved her status?"

"Paraphrase is fine."

He laid his head back against the seat and stared straight ahead.

"In a battle with the Creeks, when her husband was struck down, she ran onto the battlefield and took up his weapon and waded into the enemy, against overwhelming odds. Inspiring the other Cherokees, she single-handedly turned the tide and saved her people. For that, she was elevated to Beloved Woman."

"So she becomes an honorary man."

He gave her a swift, slicing look.

"This isn't about gender politics."

"So what is it about? Say it. Speak the words."

Parker shifted in his seat so he was facing her.

"I think it's pretty obvious, the common denominator here."

"Not to me it isn't."

"Red war club," he said. "Great War Chief. Beloved Woman. I don't know who the combatants are or what it's about, Charlotte, but it looks to me like we're in the middle of some kind of war."

Charlotte was silent, staring at Parker, waiting for him to smile, give her the punchline.

"That's what Jacob's trying to tell us. We're at war."

"You're serious."

"Very serious."

"That's nuts, Parker. Totally and completely wacko."

"I don't think so. I think Diana was a casualty. And I think we're out on the battlefield, too, in the line of fire."

"And what's that make Gracey, a goddamn POW?"

"I think Jacob's trying to protect her. Get her out of harm's way."

"By enticing her to run off to his cave in the forest?"

"He's on our side. I can't prove it, but that's what my gut says."

"Your gut *always* says that."

"This is different. We can trust Jacob."

He brushed invisible crumbs off the lap of his khakis. He turned to her, but his eyes dodged away. Not the gesture of a man about to tell a lie, but a man about to tell a truth that was more than he could bear.

"There's something I never told you about Mother."

"Oh, God, here we go."

Charlotte stuffed the pages of Panther's file back in the folder. She looked across the aisle at the drunk. He was smiling at her. Not only flexing his zygomatic major, but also tightening his orbicularis oculi, pars orbitalis, the muscle encircling the eye. A genuine smile, impossible to fake. A 100 percent, no-bullshit, big, sloppy, alcoholic grin.

Charlotte raised her hand and caught the flight attendant's attention, and pointed to the man's Bloody Mary, then pointed at herself. The attendant nodded and set to work making her drink.

"Okay," Charlotte said, turning back to Parker. "Hit me."

"Diana's father was Giovanni Parisi."

"Yeah, and her mother was Millie Walker."

"Walkingstick," he said. "Millie Walkingstick. A full-blooded Cherokee."

The flight attendant came around the edge of the galley and handed her the drink. Charlotte thanked her and took a healthy taste, then another.

"You sure you should be drinking?"

"Damn sure," she said.

He sighed and brushed more crumbs from his lap.

"Both my grandparents were dead by the time I was five. I may have met Millie Walkingstick once or twice, but I have no clear memories."

"I don't get it. Your dad revered Cherokees. Why would he go along?"

"Maybe Mother was ashamed of her heritage. I don't know why, exactly. But Dad honored her wishes. That's how he was."

"How long have you known this?"

"A few years. She wanted me to know my roots. I got the feeling there was something more she wanted to say, but she lost her nerve."

"Your roots. So she was half Cherokee, which makes you, what, a quarter? And Gracey an eighth? That how it works?"

"I suppose it does."

"And this Beloved Woman thing, let me get this straight. Because this badge is in Diana's lockbox, you're suggesting she's one of those? A female war chief?"

"What I think is . . ." He reached out and took the drink from her hand and swallowed what was left and set it down between them. "I think Mother did something heroic, something extraordinary for her people. I don't know what, I don't know when, but it's part of this thing."

"Part of this war, you mean."

He nodded and his eyes drifted shut. His lips flattened as if he were straining to hold back a howl.

TWENTY

FOR THE LAST HUNDRED MILES Steven Spielberg had been whispering inside Gracey's head, challenging her to quit whining about the smell that rose from her unwashed body, the lanky mess that her hair had become, the broken nail, a small ragged tear that continually snagged on the bus seat beneath her. He wanted her to embrace her discomfort, learn from it. She mumbled back that she was trying. Try harder, he said. You want to open up the depths of your inner life, you need to be on a first-name basis with pain.

Okay, okay, she was working on it. She was. Steven went on talking, same theme, same words, over and over.

Gracey felt herself drifting away.

She had no idea buses were so slow, that they stopped so often, let people off, took more on. She could have walked the same route almost as fast. After ditching the car, she'd gone to the Jacksonville bus station, sleeping on a bench for a while, then leaving at eleven, and now it was late afternoon, the bus stopping at one little nowhere town after another. Ever since the stop in Hardeeville, South Carolina, she'd been wedged in beside a young black man in overalls and a white dress shirt buttoned to his throat. He was muscular and kept his hands cupped in his lap, and he smelled like a smokehouse where hams were cured or perhaps the insides of a barn where tobacco dried. He smelled like the Deep South, like red clay baking in the endless sun.

Gracey'd been smelling the man and listening to Steven's plans for her, his urgings, his wild flipping of the channels in her mind. She adored Steven and respected his artistic work but was beginning to have faint doubts about things working out between them. Their partnership.

He was so different from her. So much older, so much more accomplished. She could hear Mr. Underwood talking, too, like a voice on a phone line bleeding in from the background.

The bus stopped in downtown Columbia, but Gracey stayed in her seat, didn't even get off to pee, stretch her legs, buy crackers, or anything, because Jacob Panther had begun speaking to her.

His words were shaped with perfect edges, like photographs in supersharp focus. Every word he'd spoken to her still hovered like a tangy flavor that wouldn't die.

She sat on the bus and finally it pulled away and chugged back onto the highway and she sat back and watched the miles.

Gracey was tired and her back ached and she smelled the black man next to her. His honest scent. She listened to the voices flipping the channels in her head. Listening to them all, but she kept returning to Jacob's words, which burned deeper, brighter, and seemed louder somehow than even Steven's voice. Though she knew Jacob had made no movies, probably had not even seen a movie. Still, it was Jacob's voice she heard above all else.

He repeated everything he'd said in their one meeting. The exact words in the exact order, like a memory, only newer and more real than it had been the first time. He repeated it all—where she could find him, the names and numbers she should look for, the towns along the way, the mountain ranges, telling her all of it again in his fast, efficient, effortless voice. Jacob Panther. Her half brother.

With Jacob Panther's voice speaking to her, Gracey rode through the late afternoon with hunger crawling cold and irritable in her belly, smelling herself, the scent of Gracey Monroe, her true nature seeping past the layer of deodorant, the dab of cologne, the fabric softener in her blue cotton top, the stink of her own humanity rising into the air all about her.

She rode into the heavy gray dusk, the bus leaving the straight four-lane interstate and going into the mountains, where the road began to snake upward and on every other turn she was rocked against the black man, her shoulder bumping his and every time he said "Excuse me" and again on the next bump "Excuse me" until his voice became music in her head, a bass accompaniment to Steven's and Mr. Underwood's and Jacob Panther's and her own mother's voice, too, chiming in, begging her get off the bus and call her and tell her she was all right, which Gracey knew was the right thing to do, but she wasn't about to do it, she was so mad at her mother, at all the rules, at the way she'd tried to capture Jacob, send him to prison without even knowing who he was, Gracey thinking about her mother, all the time with the music going in the background, the black man like a deep bass, excuse me, excuse me.

Excuse me, as the highway twisted back on itself and the bus seemed way too big for the narrow, snaking road and the night darkened and then she was dozing, still swimming in voices when the bus stopped again, and Gracey opened her eyes and looked at a small outpost in the cool, damp mountains, a lit store with bugs swirling at the lamps and men standing around doing nothing, a general store with a sign out front that was the sign Jacob Panther had mentioned, the name of the little town, and the black man said "Excuse me" as she climbed across his legs and dragged her knapsack and she said "Excuse me" back to him and walked down the aisle with the others, mostly gamblers going to the casino, for she'd heard them talking about slots and blackjack for the last hour, and she followed them down the steps, the bus driver saying "Good luck" to each of them as they stepped down, but Gracey didn't reply because she was listening to Jacob Panther's voice, what he'd said in the hallway in her house in Coral Gables, about a specific location where he could be found, a place that she had to keep very very very secret, could tell no one about except her dad, only her dad, because if anybody else found out about it, the men with guns would come for him and handcuff him and send him away to the gas chamber.

She wanted to see him again. She wanted to hear his voice in the flesh. "Excuse me," she said to one of the men standing doing nothing, "excuse me, could you give me directions?"

"I can give you more than directions," the man said.

The other men chuckled. Gracey looked at the man carefully. He didn't seem dangerous. He was short and dumpy and had sideburns down to his chin. He chewed on something in his cheek.

"More than directions?" she said.

It was dark and cold. Nippy, her father would say, sweater weather. Up in the mountains in June with bugs swirling at the lights, battling to be warm, to burn themselves up in the electric glow. She looked around at the men doing nothing. Men in overalls and baseball hats and sweatshirts that didn't cover their big bellies, a couple of them holding small paper sacks, some sitting on benches outside the general store. No women she could see. But no one looked dangerous. Not really. Not like dangerous men looked in Miami. These men looked lazy and slow and slightly comical.

"You need a lift?" the man said.

"She ain't even told you where she's aheaded."

"Don't matter," the man said. "I'm going that way."

The men chuckled.

"I'd sure as shit head that away if I had me a fucking car," a younger man said. "I'd head that way in a red-hot minute."

"Don't be talking like that, Seth. Don't be spoiling his fun."

"You can just point the way," Gracey said. "I don't mind walking."

"Suit yourself," the man said. "But if it's around here, I'll be knowing where to find it. Don't listen to these nitwits. Trying to put worrisome ideas in your head."

Gracey decided the man was okay and followed him to his truck and climbed inside. A green Chevy that smelled like mud and wet dogs and stale cigarettes with trash on the floor at her feet.

She told him where she was going, the place Jacob had told her, and he thought about it a second and said, sure, he knew where it was. Kind of out of the way spot, but it wasn't more than ten, fifteen minutes.

He drove her up a dark, winding road, his headlights were dim like they were filmed with crud, and he drove slow, looking over at her as they went, Gracey keeping her eyes forward, the man whistling to himself, the man driving slower and slower, peering into the dark at each of the narrow lanes that disappeared into the trees like he was choosing the place to take her and do what he wanted, with Gracey hearing silence in her head, no one talking to her, no one advising or warning or anything, like they'd all gone off together, Steven and Jacob and Mr. Underwood, Joan and Barbara, to gossip among themselves and left her alone with this man who hadn't told her his name, and kept glancing over at her.

"You in some kind of trouble with the law?"

Gracey said no, not that she knew of. "Why do you ask?"

" 'Cause I think that's Johnny Law on our tail right now. It's one of them cars they drive."

Gracey looked back and could see only a single set of headlights.

"You want me to stop, see what they want?"

"No," she said. "I want to go where I said."

"All right, then. I'd best lose these peckerwoods."

As the road swung hard to the right, the man shut off his headlights and swerved his wheel the other way and bumped onto a gravel road. Gracey hadn't seen it coming. She saw no sign out on the road, listening hard now to her own head, to catch any shred of voice that might be counseling her what to do. Jump out of the door, run? What?

Behind them out on the highway, the headlights went flying past.

The man continued to drive down the gravel lane. Then another one that was even narrower. He made two more turns and then stopped in the middle of the muddy road and looked all around.

"Are we lost?" She heard her voice, how shrill it was and that frightened her more.

"No, ma'am. I don't get lost. These are my woods back here."

He drove on for a while, making more turns down bumpy roads, deep potholes sending paper cups and crushed beer cans tumbling off his dashboard onto her lap.

"Where we going?"

"I reckon this is where you said."

He turned down an even narrower lane, branches clawing at the truck's sides, rocks kicking up against the bottom of the truck.

Then she saw the sign, hand-painted and nailed crooked to a tree, the name of the campground Jacob had told her.

And the dumpy man, her driver, helped Gracey find the exact camping spot, shining a flashlight out his window at the silver numbers nailed to wooden posts. It took him ten minutes more, and Gracey knew she couldn't have done it without him. She would've gotten lost, been attacked by bears, she would have died of cold and fright and loneliness, withered up in a pile of leaves and blown away in the first winter gale. The man in the truck wasn't dangerous. She'd been right, her instincts about him. He was a good man. She'd trusted him and he was good.

"I expect that's it, yonder. Right there in the headlights."

It was a camper, like a Winnebago only half the size. There was a stone pit next to it with the last of a smoldering fire. Dim lights shone inside the camper, and someone moved behind the curtains. It had started to sprinkle, smearing the dirty windshield.

"You going to be all right out here in the dark, little girl?" the man asked.

"I'll be fine," Gracey said. "Thanks for the lift."

"Name's Earl. You need any help while you're in these parts, ask anybody. Ain't but one Earl for miles around. You hear me now?"

"I hear you." And she shook his offered hand. He held on a little too long, then let go and smiled at her with something sad in his eyes. Like he'd been scared, too, but couldn't admit it. Scared of himself, what he wanted to do.

Gracey walked to the camper and stepped up to the door.

Earl waited till her knock was answered and the door opened a crack.

It was a woman. Dark hair cut short, pretty face with dark, glossy eyes. Her slender hand holding the door.

"I'm looking for Jacob Panther."

"Are you now? Then that makes you one of many."

"My name's Gracey Monroe," she said.

The woman frowned and look past her into the night.

"Where's your dad?"

"It's just me. I'm alone."

Earl tapped his horn and called out to see if she was in the right place.

"Am I in the right place?" Gracey asked the woman.

The woman waved at Earl and he backed his truck into the night.

"You were supposed to tell your dad to come, not come yourself."

"What?"

"Did you tell your father where to find this place?"

"I didn't know I was supposed to."

"Goddamn it," the woman said. "I told Jacob it wouldn't work."

"You wanted my dad? I thought Jacob asked me to come."

"Hell, no," the woman said. "You're just a girl. What good are you?"

Tears burned Gracey's eyes. She took a backward glance at Earl's taillights disappearing through the trees.

"Aw, hell. It's all right, don't sweat it," the woman said. "We'll work something out."

The woman opened the door a few inches and Gracey could see she wore blue jeans and a black tank top. She was beautiful in a dark-eyed, foreign way like Cuban women sometimes were, but this woman wasn't Cuban. A Cherokee maybe. A little too old to be Jacob's girlfriend, but pretty enough for the job.

"I'm Lucy," the woman said, putting out her hand out for a shake. "Lucy Panther. Come on in out of the damp."

TWENTY-ONE

THEY PARKED THE RENTAL CAR—another Toyota—at the entrance to Camp Tsali. Parker's key wouldn't work the rusted padlocks, so they climbed over the gates and tramped up the steep path. It was half past nine, but dim yellow light filtered through the trees from a security lamp burning out on the two-lane road.

"You're not going to tell me where we're going?"

"Why? So you can call Sheffield, tell him where to meet us?"

"Maybe you should pat me down, check for a wire."

"Are you wired?"

"Jesus. You really don't trust me, do you?"

"I trust you to act in accordance with your beliefs."

They trudged in silence. A layer of pine needles coated the trail. Cool rain drizzled from the black heavens.

After another hundred yards the roadway light faded to gloom, and Parker halted and held up his flashlight, pointed it into his face, and switched it on to check the strength. Looked pretty weak to Charlotte.

The odor of pine and hemlock was heavy, and there were birds fluttering in the high branches and a stream running somewhere nearby.

Parker set off and Charlotte put herself in motion, found a steady pace, heart thumping, a layer of sweat building beneath her three layers, despite the chill. Maybe mid-forties.

Parker settled in beside her and laid a hand on her shoulder.

"I love you," he said. "It's been a while since I said it. But I do. I love you, Charlotte. Pisser that you are sometimes, I still love you."

"I love you, too. Pisser that you are."

"This shit we're dealing with," he said, "Gracey running off, Mother's murder, Jacob Panther showing up, a son I didn't know about. This whole war thing, whatever the hell's going on with that. It's a goddamn avalanche of major catharses. Only natural we'd be at each other."

"Only natural," she said.

They plodded on for a half-mile, then Parker said, "I do love you."

But it sounded like he was speaking more to himself than her, so she didn't reply. She reached into the backpack slung over one shoulder, touching the hard plastic gadget Sheffield had given her. The nubby button on one end.

Decision time.

She dug around in the pack and found the Beretta. She'd filled out the forms at airport check-in, showed her badge, but still was relieved to find the pistol made it through in their checked luggage without being stolen or confiscated.

"You worried?" he said.

"About what?"

"Gracey might not be here. We might have this all wrong."

"Are you determined to jinx this?"

"I'm just saying I might be mistaken about what Jacob meant."

"All right then, let's turn around, go back, call the FBI, like we should've done to begin with."

"They're bunglers, Charlotte. The other night, going to the wrong address, that whole scene, you want to repeat that?"

"The other night was sloppy, yeah, but this is different. We have no idea what we're walking into. Stumbling around in the dark, we could be putting Gracey in more danger. Not to mention ourselves."

"If that's what your conscience says, then go back to the car and wait. I won't be upset. But I have to do this, Charlotte. And I have to do it this way."

"This guy's a killer, Parker. I'll back you up on this, but if it starts going bad, it doesn't matter if he's your son, I'm not hesitating."

She shifted the holster so she could draw the Beretta smoothly, then hitched her backpack over her shoulder and settled into the dark climb.

He got their flight number with one phone call, pretending to be an FBI special agent working the Panther case, fooling Parker Monroe's big-city secretary with ease. Their plane arrived in Asheville on time, and he followed them from the rental-car parking lot out to the interstate.

For the last hour he'd been looking for the right moment. Running their car off the road was too uncertain. They might survive the crash. He might be seen, might even crash himself. Dying didn't worry him, but he had more to accomplish than just killing these two.

So he followed at a distance, thinking they might stop for something to eat, or a bathroom break, and he could take them against a well-lit background. But they didn't stop. Instead they led him through the town of Cherokee and then out the narrow country lanes toward the old summer camp. Where everything had happened. The fire, the deaths, the cowardice.

When the Monroes pulled over at the front gate of the summer camp, he passed by and parked down the road on a narrow cattle path.

He got the Heckler & Koch rifle from its case and hiked back down the highway and climbed the gate, then headed up the path after them.

He couldn't have designed a better killing ground. So remote. But even better was the possibility that the two of them should die at Camp Tsali—a delicious synchronicity.

Moving off the trail, he angled into the woods, treading lightly and moving with ease through the dark. He could hear them talking up ahead, taking no precautions as they moved across the ghostly landscape.

The path up to the camp was steeper than Charlotte remembered, and by the time they got to the main grounds she was winded and her butt muscles burned. She was trying not to think about Gracey—where she was, her condition—trying to keep her face out of her mind. But it kept surfacing. Little snippets of their heated exchange the night Jacob appeared in their house. Replaying Gracey's remark. Rules, rules, rules.

"You sure you can find this place in the dark?" she said.

"I used to get there in the dark all the time. Get back, too."

"Thirty years ago, you mean."

"I grew up here, Charlotte. I spent my first fifteen years in these hills. It's hardwired in my head. The layout of the camp, the trails, the smells. Like I never left."

Stumbling along, she could just make out the vague shapes of buildings, low cabins, a long, open pavilion. More rain was coming, as light as mist but without pause. She felt her hair clumping, cold dribbles down her neck.

"You hear that?"

Parker halted. Charlotte came up beside him, trying to keep her breath quiet. Not easy after that climb.

"Shhh." Parker raised his hand. Then motioned behind them, at the road they'd just traveled.

They stood for several moments listening. But she could hear only the light breeze and the rain pattering from the branches and the rustle of last year's leaves across the ground.

"You're spooked, Parker."

"It was something," he said. "I'm not spooked. A raccoon maybe."

"You know where we are? Can you see?"

"I know exactly where we are. The dining hall's over there. The lodge." He waved into the dark. "The ceremonial ring that way."

"We could break a leg out here."

"Listen to you. Are you with me or not?"

"Goddamn it," she said. "I'm not saying stop. But maybe you could use the flashlight once in a while. You know where you are, but I'm at the bottom of a goddamn well."

He lifted his head and listened again.

"Aw, shit, Parker. Let's just get there, okay? Let's just move."

She followed his back through the murkiness, stumbling now and then, grateful she'd worn the heavier clothes. The temperature was plunging and even the heat she'd generated from the climb didn't balance out against the chill.

The trail got steeper and narrower, then grew as rocky as an old creek bed. Branches whipped her face, and something stung her cheek an inch from her right eye—a nettle, a thorn. She wiped away the ooze of blood and licked the remains off her fingertip.

Now and then Parker stopped and listened to the dark woods. The rain had stopped but still dripped from leaf to leaf.

"If I lived up here," Charlotte said, "all this uphill, downhill, my butt would be tight as a fourteen-year-old's."

"Your butt is perfect," Parker said. Sounding like he meant it.

The trail leveled, then grew steep again, a half-dozen switchbacks, then a long stretch across a ridgeline.

As they climbed, the air grew cooler and damper. Even though the rain had stopped, the night was still moist with its remains and the trail slick. If there was a moon somewhere, it wasn't doing them any good.

Every few seconds Parker flicked the flashlight on and off, focused on their feet. She caught glimpses of rocks and branches, dizzy swirls of gnats, skittering shadows. Though she'd been born a country girl and spent her first seventeen years in hilly terrain, hanging out for lonely adolescent hours in a nearby forest, she felt no sense of homecoming. This place was as foreign to her as if she had been transported to a remote corner of the galaxy.

"It's not far," he whispered.

"It's already far."

A rock ledge loomed up, and the trail narrowed to only a foot across and rimmed the ledge. They had to duck under an outcropping four feet high. Charlotte didn't want to know what was to her right, off in the darkness, but her senses told her it was a sheer drop and the distance to the bottom was exactly equal to the last hour's upward trek. A swirl of vertigo made her stumble briefly, but she caught herself and plodded on. Gracey, Gracey.

They bulled through a sticky-leaved bush and picked their way down a shallow dip in the trail.

"Watch your head."

Parker took her by the shoulders and steered her through a narrow cleft in the rock, a fissure that required them to turn sideways. She smelled the damp and Parker's sweaty scent, something that even after nearly two decades still gave her a prickle below her navel, his pheromones, that distinct aromatic signature. Whatever else was wrong between them, that wasn't an issue.

She bumped into his back and he whispered, "This is it. Sequoyah Caverns."

Behind them, Charlotte heard pebbles trickling down the cliff face, or maybe above them, higher on the peak.

He took her hand and guided her into the clammy reek of the cave. She heard the hushed music of running water and the squeak of a startled creature, tiny claws scurrying over rock. He let go of her hand and moved away.

"Jacob?" he called out quietly. "Gracey?"

He was scuffing to her right. She drew her handgun and panned it across the darkness. Though a lot of good it would do her. She was dead blind.

As she was swung the Beretta to her left, she saw a red flicker on the distant wall. She squinted till her eyes found the focus. A dot. A single red dot.

"Down, Parker. Down!"

She heard him stumble from ten feet away.

"What?"

Then a man's voice. The booming command of someone armed and fully in control. A gang of men tromped through the cavern entrance, and lights exploded around her. She was tackled and thrown flat against the damp clay floor, her captor's full weight on top of her and his hands scrabbling to disarm her and pull her wrists behind her back.

She shut her eyes against the dazzle, enough candlepower to turn midnight instantly to noon. She didn't struggle against the man's iron grip, though he fumbled with his plastic handcuffs as if he was more nervous than she.

"On the ground! Everybody flat on the ground!"

Pinned to the damp earth, she managed to tilt her head enough to see the far wall dancing with red dots, the laser sights of high-powered weapons.

Troops filled the room with their heavy breathing and the reek of cheap cologne and failed deodorant.

The space was smaller than she'd pictured. Twenty by twenty. The men filled it to capacity, stamping like Thoroughbreds burning off nervous energy in a tiny corral.

Gold FBI lettering on their jackets, a half-dozen men all cut from the same Superboy chunk of granite. The one atop her shoved her head back down, then she heard Sheffield's voice.

"Let her up. Cut her loose."

"Him, too?"

"Him, too."

She blinked against the brilliance, ducking her head, shielding her eyes. Someone hauled her to her feet, snipped the plastic band from her wrists. She and Parker were nudged together, ringed by a special-ops team in blackface, and nonreflective clothes, night goggles, featherweight automatics.

Charlotte stooped to retrieve her backpack, and a barrel banged her arm.

"It's okay," Sheffield said. "They're clear."

She picked up her backpack, dug out the black gadget, and looked at it. No green light. Nothing. She hadn't accidentally tripped the switch.

Frank shook his head in annoyance. Another man drew up to his side. His superior or counterpart. They were dressed in civvies. Same blue jackets, none of the killing tools that hung from the other men.

"Special agent in charge of the Carolina Bomb Task Force." Sheffield gestured at the man. "Joe Roth. Joe, say hello to Mr. and Mrs. Parker Monroe of Miami, Florida."

Roth looked at them, then back at Sheffield. Growled under his breath.

"Where is he, Monroe?"

"Who are you looking for?"

"Don't be cute. Where's Panther?"

"What makes you think he'd be here?"

"Whose name were you calling out just now?"

Parker shrugged. No idea what he was talking about.

"Don't fuck around, Monroe. You came all this way for a face-to-face. We both know that."

"Told you," said Roth. "Guy's smarter than that. Didn't I tell you that? This Panther's one slippery bastard."

"You told me."

"What is this thing, Frank?" Charlotte held out the black gizmo.

"Okay, so I tinkered with the truth. But only a little."

She saw one of the men at the edge of the pack holding a small GPS by his side, a pulsing dot in the center of the screen.

"You son of a bitch."

"Transmits a steady signal," he said. "What could I do, let you go running off? You could've hurt yourself. Think of the lawsuit."

"And if I'd had a real emergency and was counting on your help, I'd have been screwed, huh?"

"We knew where you were at all times."

"Well, that's reassuring. You could've located my body. Great."

She sidearmed the gadget at him, and it bounced off his chest.

Sheffield rubbed at the spot while some of his team fought off smiles.

"You were in with him?" Parker said. "You tricked me?"

"Sheffield tricked both of us. And for what?"

She looked around the empty cave. Nothing but bare rock and clay floor and the ooze of water down the broken face of one wall.

She glanced at Parker and saw that he'd shifted his gaze and was staring at the smooth wall behind her. She turned to look.

At eye level there was a primitive drawing in what looked like chalk: a tall, thin dog standing upright on its hind legs, looking perfectly at ease.

"What's that?" Roth said. "Some Indian thing?"

"Kids," said Sheffield. "Rich summer camp kids."

"Where's the naked girls then?" Roth said.

Sheffield went over and touched a finger to the edge of the drawing and tried to smear it. He looked at his finger, but nothing had come off the wall.

"Isn't chalk," he said.

"No more touching," said Roth. "We got a crime scene here."

"What crime?" Charlotte said. "We're out for a hike and you guys come out of the trees to terrorize us. That the crime you mean? Police harassment?" Taking one of Parker's lines.

Frank shook his head and gave her a wincing grin. Nice try.

"Your daughter showed up," Sheffield said. "Couple of hours ago."

Charlotte swung around.

"Where is she?"

"We lost her."

"What!"

"Pickup truck she was riding in turned off on a side road, disappeared."

"You bastard. You had her in your sights but didn't stop her. Just the thing you promised you weren't going to do."

"Hey, I'm sorry."

"You son of a bitch."

"Look, Charlotte, your daughter's in the vicinity, that's the good news. We're homing in on her. Got our people interviewing some yokels who were standing around when she got off the bus. She looked okay to our guys. Looked healthy, maybe a little frazzled from the trip but healthy."

"How would your guys know what healthy looks like?"

Charlotte pushed past Sheffield and stalked to the mouth of the cave.

"So how about it, Counselor?" Frank stepped over to Parker and brushed the crumbs of clay off the front of his shirt. "That drawing have any significance to you? Some scrawny dog standing on its hind legs?"

"None," Parker said. "None whatsoever."

He lay flat on his stomach and watched through the telescopic sight. The agents of the federal government were standing on the trail now, their harsh lights keeping them in bold relief. They were joking and talking loud. He passed his sight across the faces of four of the men. Square-jawed with tight military haircuts. He could probably nail three of them before they knew what was happening. With his flash hider and sound suppressor and his dark clothes, he could no doubt stay concealed through the whole tumult and, in the chaotic aftermath, sneak away down the hill.

It was tempting. If only to have something to show for the evening.

But he maintained discipline, waiting for the group to clear the mouth of the cave and head back down the trail. He waited an hour more, until the forest had begun to whir and rustle with the activities of nocturnal creatures, and the darkness once again reclaimed its rightful domain.

TWENTY-TWO

"CALL OFF THE DOGS," CHARLOTTE said to Charlie Mears.

It was nine-thirty on Thursday morning. In her jeans and bra, she was perched on the edge of the rumpled bed, using the phone in their room at the Holiday Inn in the village of Cherokee. She'd been put on hold for ten minutes, then handed off to three other hard-ass secretaries before she worked her way to FBI Assistant Director Charles L. Mears.

"Which dogs?" Mears said.

Charlotte had slept fitfully. From the shadows under Parker's eyes, she knew he'd shared the mind-churning darkness with her.

Charlotte described Sheffield's raid the night before, the storm troopers. His use of Gracey as a decoy.

When she was finished, he was silent.

"You there?"

"Frank was acting on his own authority. I may have a slightly grander title than Special Agent in Charge Sheffield, but when it comes to fieldwork, I can't intervene in the investigative process. It's his show to run."

"My daughter's a runaway. I'm doing what any reasonable parent would do, go out and try to find her. I don't give two shits about some fugitive you guys are after. If I happen to bump into Jacob Panther, I'll arrest the son of a bitch because I'm a sworn officer of the law. But finding my daughter is number one. And there isn't any number two."

Parker stood in the doorway with a bath towel wrapped around his waist. His cheeks foamed with shaving cream.

"My husband thinks we should call the FBI's Office of Professional Responsibility and put a very large turd in Sheffield's file."

"He was simply performing his duties. I doubt you'd make much headway with OPR."

Charlotte said, "Well, then you should rethink how much you need my assistance in Fedderman's project."

Charlotte listened to Mears silently consider the issue. She had no way to know the politics of the situation. But she understood from her years with Gables PD that people up the food chain could damn well interfere whenever and however they wanted.

Though she was playing the Fedderman card, it was hard for her to imagine that some simple intuitive quirk she possessed was worth enough for the feds to compromise their goddamn procedures, jeopardize a case on their Top Ten.

Thankfully, she was wrong.

Mears said, "The director very rarely takes the kind of personal interest in recruiting individuals that he has taken in you, Officer Monroe. He saw something remarkable in your test results, as we all did. So I suppose that qualifies you to have one wish granted."

"Thanks."

"I'll do what I can to see that Sheffield leaves you alone. No tails, no surveillance, you'll be out of his sights. You and your husband are private citizens with all the rights and privileges and responsibilities. You may do what you need to do within the bounds of the law to secure the return of your daughter, keeping in mind that you are a sworn police officer and you must not in any way knowingly interfere in the efforts and actions of federal agents."

"Is that off a TelePrompTer?"

"My wife says that all the time. I have a robotic delivery. Talked that way as a kid. What can I say? I'll get Sheffield to back the hell off. You do what you have to."

Charlotte thanked him again and hung up.

"Free at last," she said to Parker.

He gave her a don't-be-so-sure smile and said, "Standingdog Matthews has been having a series of strokes. He's in a hospice run by the tribe. It's a few miles west of Cherokee."

"How'd you find that out?"

He held up his cell phone.

"Reception sucks, all these mountains. Miriam ran down that stuff and a few things on Martin Tribue, the airport vic. He operated a construction company, Tribue Engineering. His father's the congressman, brother's the sheriff for the tribe. Named Farris."

"They have this place sewed up."

"Seems that way."

"So I'm still on the payroll?"

"Probation." He ran a finger through the foam on his cheek, sizing up his bristles. "You break my balls about being honest, not telling you about Lucy Panther, about Mother being part Cherokee, but meanwhile you're off consorting with the feds, making private deals."

"Probation, huh?"

"End of the week you come up for review."

"You sure about that cave drawing? It *could* be kids."

"It could be, but it's not. That's a likeness of Standingdog. Jacob left it. He's guiding us."

"I don't like games."

"Well, he was right not to trust us. If he'd shown up last night, he'd be in jail right now, or dead."

"What you mean is, Parker, he was right not to trust *me*."

"You keep giving everything I say the worst possible twist."

"Do I?"

"Yeah, I think you do. I think you're severely knotted up about all this shit, and I've become the fall guy."

Then a phone was ringing. So muffled it might be in the next room.

"Yours," Parker said, and pointed at her backpack on the nightstand.

She got it out, looked at the caller ID: OUT OF AREA

When she answered there was static, then a disconnect.

"Nobody," she said.

Parker swung back to the bathroom mirror and went to work with his razor. She looked at his back—the V still there, waist trim, shoulders wide. A body maintained on the Salvadore Park tennis courts three nights a week and weekends, when he wasn't at trial. The body still stirred her. It was his mind that was giving her trouble.

His goddamn persistent, all-embracing optimism and faith in the goodness of humanity despite all evidence to the contrary. His sneaky bargains with his mother, his hot and heavy teenage love affair. When she ticked off the list, ran it through her head, it seemed paltry. Certainly nothing worth shaking the foundations of their marriage. And maybe he was right about her giving everything he said the worst twist. Like the way she kept hearing him invoke the Qwik Mart holdup and her legal salvation. It might simply be her own guilty projection. An unwillingness to come to terms with the fact that she owed him her life, always would. She had to consider that. Bite on it a while, see if it was real.

Her phone peeped again and she picked it up, still looking at Parker's trim torso, the muscles working under the flesh as he reached out and wiped a path across the foggy mirror.

"Hi, Mom, it's Gracey. Your daughter."

She froze. Barely recognized the voice. A prank?

"Gracey?"

Parker turned from the mirror.

"So I called Dad at work and he wasn't there, then I called home and Fredericka was there feeding the cats and she told me you'd gone on a trip. Lucy was after me to call you guys. Joan, too. Everybody said I should, that it was the right thing, so I did. You know, to check in. Make you feel better."

Too bubbly and alert. Not the picture she'd built in her head, a kid on the run, unraveling.

"Where are you?"

Parker came over and sat beside her on the edge of the bed.

"Where are *you*, Mom?"

"We're in Cherokee, North Carolina. Where are you, Gracey?"

The reception faded, and Gracey's words turned to garble.

"Gracey?"

Her daughter was talking to someone else, and in the background a woman's voice answered her.

"Same place, Cherokee," Gracey said. "That's pretty amazing, you tracked me down. I'm impressed, Mom."

"Are you okay? Do you have your meds?"

Parker stuck his hand out for the phone.

"We have to keep moving, Mom. Lucy says to tell you to meet us this afternoon at five P.M. Jacob and Lucy have something they need to talk to you about. It's like really important. Life or death."

Charlotte waved his hand away.

He lowered it and looked up at the ceiling. Patience, patience.

"Lucy?"

"Yeah, Lucy Panther."

The breath lodged in Charlotte's throat.

"Butts on the Creek barbecue," Gracey said. "Five o'clock. It's on the main drag in Maggie Valley, whatever that road is, where all the tourist shops are and everything, moccasins, tom-toms, all that crap."

"Butts on the Creek barbecue?" Charlotte repeated for Parker.

He looked at her and nodded. Knew the place.

"We'll come now. We'll come wherever you are, right this minute."

"Lucy and I have a few things to take care of first. Five o'clock."

She drew a long breath.

"Let me speak to Lucy."

She heard Gracey relay the request.

"She doesn't have anything to say. Just meet us at the barbecue place."

"Your dad wants to talk to you."

"We gotta go. Tell him I love him."

Charlotte waited, listening to the silence.

"This is fun, isn't it?" Gracey said.

"This is not fun, Gracey." But her words were spoken to an empty line.

"Fun?" Parker said.

"She's having fun. This is a game. Her and Lucy Panther."

Charlotte repeated the little Gracey had said, and Parker flinched and turned away.

"So what do we do till five o'clock?" Parker said.

"We go see Standingdog. What we planned."

"But that's irrelevant. We get Gracey back, to hell with the rest of it. We'll just go home and be a family and turn this over to the authorities."

"Give up on your son?"

"This could be putting us in danger. And for what? We're just flailing."

"In the first place, we don't have Gracey back yet." She walked to the bathroom, picked up his razor, and beckoned for him. He came into the room, and Charlotte steadied his chin with one hand and began to rake the blade through the dying foam.

"And in the second place?"

In the mirror he held her eyes while she drew the blade across his cheeks in long, smooth strokes. Then tipped his head back and worked on his throat.

"In the second place, this son of yours appeared out of nowhere and warned us we're in danger and the next evening your mother was murdered. We can't slough that off, take our daughter home, pretend none of this happened. I don't like it a damn bit, but we have to resolve it, follow through. Would you ever feel safe again if we didn't?"

"Yeah, yeah," he said. "You're right. I just lost my nerve for a second."

Charlotte rinsed his razor, took the towel from the back of the door, and patted his face dry.

"By the way," she said. "Gracey told me to tell you she loved you."

"And you?"

"She was silent on that issue."

She dabbed a fleck of foam away from his eye.

"She loves you, Charlotte, she does. I see it all the time."

"In her way, sure. I suppose she does."

He slid his arms beneath hers and drew her to him. She dropped the hand towel on the floor, and for a moment she thought his fingers were moving to unsnap her bra. Then she felt on her shoulder the warm flow of his tears and, against her chest, the long, unbroken shudder of his release.

TWENTY-THREE

"I DON'T THINK YOUR PHONE call worked." Parker was staring into the rearview mirror as they pulled into the hospice parking lot. "Sheffield's still on our butt."

Charlotte checked the view in her outside mirror but saw nothing behind them for a mile or more.

"A light-colored pickup truck," Parker said. "Two cars back all the way from the motel over here. It just pulled over when we turned in."

"Or maybe somebody else," Charlotte said.

Parker gave her an impatient glance.

"Like Jacob, you mean."

"Well, we are letting this killer lead us, Parker, from point A to point B."

"A few minutes ago you were gung ho to go ahead with this. What? You change your mind?"

"Going ahead, yes, but let's be realistic. Jacob Panther's a murderer. There's no way around that, Parker."

"He means us no harm. He wants to talk. What Gracey told you on the phone is what I've been saying all along. He wants to warn us about something."

"Your gut tells you that."

"Yes."

"Well, my gut's not as confident."

Parker made one of his give-me-patience gestures, head hanging, one finger touching his forehead. Then he looked up, blew out a breath, and fit the car into a space near the building and set the hand brake against the steep grade.

They got out and Charlotte scanned the lot and adjacent highway but saw no pickups.

"Okay, I defer to your cop training. What do we do if it's Frank back there?"

"At this point it probably doesn't matter. If it's Sheffield, we should've never pulled in here in the first place. After we're gone he and his people will be all over the hospice trying to figure out what we were up to."

"But you don't think it is Frank."

"Let's just be cool, okay? Maybe you saw something, maybe you didn't. From here on we'll do a better job of looking over our shoulders."

Although Standingdog Matthews would have been Parker's father's age, around seventy, the man at the hospice looked a hundred and ten. Severely shrunken from the dark-haired, blocky man that Parker described, he was now an emaciated, white-haired spirit with gaunt cheeks and bony hands.

His wheelchair was parked beside a dim window with a view of a half-filled parking lot. Nearby, in the dayroom, a TV blasted the latest news and a dozen or so men sunk into padded chairs watched and smoked, the haze from their cigarettes hanging near the ceiling of the sunroom where Standingdog sat.

The short, round nurse who led them down the hall spoke in a mountain drawl so dense it reminded Charlotte of the Chaucer fragments Gracey had to memorize for school. An ancient, nasal variety of the mother tongue.

Apparently, Standingdog had been in the hospice's care for a month. He was declining fast after his series of strokes. He seemed awake at times, but the one hand that could still move was palsied and he could no longer perform even the simplest bodily functions without assistance. The nurse told them she had to get back to the bedpan shift but if they needed anything else, just come get somebody at the front desk.

"Is he asleep?"

"Can't rightly tell," the nurse said "Jiggles his hand, 'at's about it."

She pivoted and left, her rubber soles squeaking against the dismal black linoleum.

Charlotte glanced at her watch, as she'd done every five minutes since Gracey's call. Ten fifteen. Less than seven hours till they got her back. She fanned the cigarette smoke from the listless air and stepped back to let Parker handle the questioning.

Standingdog's eyes were a diluted blue, watery and distant. He stared out the window and seemed not to know they were there. The cane he held in his skeletal right hand shivered and tapped against the dusty linoleum. It was a blond wood, intricately carved from tip to handle like an elaborate totem pole, interlaced figures, bears and birds and other forest animals. Prison scrimshaw of the highest caliber.

Parker caught Charlotte's eye and shook his head at the futility of this.

"We're here," she said.

He squatted down in front of the old man and spoke his name.

The quivering hand did its dance, the cane tip drumming the floor.

From the dayroom a tall man in a red-and-white-striped gown drifted over. His legs were bony and bowed so severely he looked like he'd never recovered from an early bout with malnutrition. His eyes were gray, and his hair was black and lanky and brushed his shoulders. His cheeks smooth and tinted with the rouged tan of his race. From the tip of his chin a handful of silky hairs sprouted, the look of a Chinese mystic.

"Ain't no use," the man said. "The Dog don't talk."

"You know him?"

"Shared a double cell with him for a while, till I got shipped to max."

Charlotte glanced at the man. He was sizing her up with an inmate's highly refined radar.

Parker leaned close to Standingdog's ear.

"It's Parker Monroe, Charles Monroe's son."

Remember? Charlotte wanted to say. The man you burned alive.

The cell mate leaned forward, entering Charlotte's comfort zone.

"You a badge, huh? Fucking law."

Parker stood up.

"I can always spot you assholes. You can't hide from me."

"Why don't you go on back to your television. Have a smoke. We don't need any help."

"Boss me around on my own fucking turf? Think you're up to that, big man?"

"It's all right, Parker. I can handle this."

She'd caught a flash from behind the man's angry facade, a crack of somber light showing through the attitude. Something closer to grief than anger.

"My cover's blown," she said. "I'm a cop, yeah. But I'm on vacation."

"Fuck vacation. You guys never rest."

She laughed and the man tightened his fist at what he took as mockery.

"Never rest is right," she said. "All you tough guys getting in my face dawn to dusk."

That relaxed his eyes a fraction. Not disarmed, but backing off.

"We just need to talk to Standingdog." Parker edged between them. "A few questions and we'll be gone."

"He don't talk. He's crippled up with a fucking stroke. You can't see what's sitting in front of you? That's a dead man with a pulse."

Standingdog's hand rattled against the arm of his chair.

"Can he recognize you?" Charlotte asked. "His old cell buddy. Communicate in any way?"

The man shook his head. He tugged at the hem of his gown as if suddenly self-conscious.

"Blink his eyes yes and no? Anything like that?"

"Fuck no," the guy said. "He's frozen. Just the hand shaking, that's all. Had some fucking army veteran in here a couple weeks back, asshole thought the Dog was doing Morse code, tap tap tap, you know, with that fucking cane. Hung around him day and night, scribbling on his little pad, trying to figure it out. Tap, tap, tap. Didn't get shit."

Parker stooped forward and examined the intricate carvings on the cane. Studied the floor next to the tip.

The inmate dug a pack of Camels from his pocket and lit up. Blew his first drag over Charlotte's head. As close to polite as this guy knew.

"So you're the Monroe kid? One of the fuckers that framed him."

"Nobody framed him," Parker said.

"Fuck they didn't."

"He burned down my parents' house. Killed three people."

"Not how I heard it."

"Everybody's innocent," Charlotte said. "Especially in the joint."

"Not me," the inmate said. "What I went down for I did. And then some. Worthless shits had done their homework, gotten off their asses, I wouldn't be talking to you right now. They would've sniffed out the really bad shit, and dropped the cyanide on me."

Parker blew out a breath and stared down at Standingdog.

"You got something you want to confess," Charlotte said, "call a priest."

"Dog's a goner," the man said. "Why the fuck he's hanging on, that's the question."

Parker squatted down and spoke to Standingdog in his quiet courtroom voice. A faraway tone, as unthreatening as the croon of a sleepy child.

"You have anything for us, Standingdog? Anything we need to know?"

The crippled man was silent and still. Charlotte leaned forward for a better view of the old man's face. Paralyzed but not empty. The eyes drained of spark and the facial muscles gone slack for so long that his flesh had begun a downward slide. But there was still something left. The remnants of a lifetime of tics and emotional habits embedded in the tissue. The smiles, the frowns, the laughter, the crippling boredom of prison life. What she saw was a face still full of thought. A man fading into darkness but holding to a rigorous integrity.

Parker reached into his shirt pocket and drew out Diana's beaded disk and held it in Standingdog's range of vision.

Nothing.

Then a second or two later the old man's hand began to rattle, and it rose from the arm of the wheelchair, hovering for several moments, spasms that struck Charlotte as eerily controlled, like a hand cupped over a computer mouse, the subtle twitches of a video gamer firing at a stream of ogres.

"Dead man with a pulse." The inmate expelled a blue gasp of smoke toward the window.

"How long's he been like this?" Charlotte was watching the hand rattle.

"Like what?"

"Frozen up like this. Can't talk."

"Strokes been coming last couple months. It's how he wound up here. About the same time I started puking blood." He held up the glowing butt of his cigarette. "These fucking poison sticks."

"He had any visitors? Friends, relatives?" Charlotte glanced at Parker, but he was staring off at the television room.

"Dog ain't got no friends but me."

"What about relatives?"

"The girl came once."

"Which girl?"

"His little girl, all grown up. Nice-looking broad."

Parker shifted beside her, paying attention again.

Charlotte said, "When was that—before or after he stopped talking? When his daughter was here?"

"He talked okay then. Slurring a little, but you could figure him out. Couple more strokes, now he's what you see."

"And the daughter hasn't been back and seen him like this? No one's notified her?"

"You fucking cops and your questions, man."

"Has she been back and seen him like this?"

"No."

"So they don't know," Charlotte said to Parker.

"Dead end," he said.

Charlotte drew a business card from her backpack. Cell-phone number.

"She comes back to see him, call us, okay? Or anything else you want to talk about. How Standingdog got framed, anything."

He looked at the card and made a spitting motion off to the side.

She let it flutter from her hand, and it landed near his bare feet. He turned and walked back to the dayroom and the raucous TV.

She looked at Parker and nodded that she was done. They headed back down the corridor, Charlotte glancing at her watch again. Five minutes later than her last look.

As they were rounding the bend to the front desk, behind them something clattered on the floor. She stopped, came back a few steps, and saw that the old man had dropped his cane. It lay on the floor in a swatch of light from the window.

Charlotte squinted and moved closer, stepping to the right, two yards away from the wheelchair. She tilted her head to one side as if peering around an obstruction.

At first she saw only the layer of dust and crumbs on the dark linoleum and more dust sifting through an angle of window light. But from the fresh position it was clear.

She drew a sharp breath.

"What is it?" Parker was behind her.

"The light," she said. "The floor."

Parker came alongside her and traced her line of sight.

"Not Morse code." She pointed with her chin. "By the tip of his cane. A few inches to the right."

"Jesus."

In the film on the linoleum beside his wheelchair, the rubber tip of Standingdog's cane had drawn a set of wavering lines. She moved a step closer, waited for a cloud to clear the sun, then the writing appeared again. The letters snaked and wobbled as though scribbled during a rough ocean voyage.

She studied it, then said, "Is that Cherokee?"

"Yes," Parker said. "*Echota*. It means 'refuge.'"

"Refuge. I don't get it."

"There's a place at Camp Tsali. A cabin. It was called Echota."

Charlotte retrieved the cane and handed it back to the crippled man, and Standingdog locked it in his claw and held it firm. She bent forward to peer into his eyes, to see if there was another message there, but his gaze was fixed on a spot far from that room, far from any place or time she had ever known.

"Thank you," she said. "Thank you."

A couple minutes later, as they were climbing in the rental car, Parker's phone rang and Charlotte answered while he started up the car and drove.

It was Parker's investigator, Miriam, full of Miami hustle, a quick hello, then, when she discovered Parker was busy driving, without preamble she began to rattle off her notes. Nothing more on the airport killing, Martin Tribue, but still working that, and nothing else on Standingdog Matthews.

"We got that one covered," Charlotte told her.

Miriam said the reason she'd called was to brief Parker on Lucy Panther.

It was news to Charlotte that Parker had assigned her the task.

"Go ahead," she said, and Miriam filled her in.

When she was done, Charlotte asked if there was any more.

"I'm halfway down the counselor's to-do list. I got some calls out, should be hearing anytime."

They said good-bye and Charlotte set the phone in a cup holder.

"She have anything?"

"Your old friend Lucy graduated from Appalachian State University with a teaching degree. Next twenty years she taught fifth-grade English at the tribal school. Tutored kids in the summer. Her credit history is spotty. Lot of late payments on her car. Never married. No police record."

He considered that a moment, then said, "Anything relevant?"

"As for relevant," she said, "a year ago, when her son started blowing up banks, she walked away from her job. Feds think she's aiding and abetting Jacob's bombing campaign. Every month or so they get a warrant, track her down, and toss the place where she's living. But they haven't turned up anything."

He was silent for a while, concentrating on the steep rise, the sharp turns. Tailgated by an SUV that finally barreled by in a short passing lane. She kept working over the rearview mirror, and thought once she saw a white pickup a long way back, but with all the twists in the road she wasn't sure.

"This Echota, what is it?"

"Nothing special. A single-room log cabin on a little knoll my dad named Inspiration Point."

"Well, great, I've been needing some inspiration."

She looked out her window at a stream rushing alongside the road. A man fly-fishing around some smooth, gray boulders. So calm.

"Every summer a man we called Uncle Mike stayed in that cabin. Piled with books, snakeskins, arrowheads, all kinds of stuff. He and my father were very close. Uncle Mike handled all the folklore stuff. Taught us the tribal dances, Cherokee history. I revered that man. Next to Dad, he was my role model. Echota was off by itself. It'd be a good place for Jacob to hole up."

They were quiet while Parker navigated the steep, narrow road. Then Charlotte remembered something from the night before.

"I had a dream," she said. "In the ten minutes I was asleep last night."

"Yeah?"

"I was supposed to read these faces, you know, like the Fedderman thing. Only these weren't whole people, they were just a bunch of heads sitting on a shelf. Like severed heads, you know, disembodied but still alive, looking at me. And it's my job to see what's going on in their minds. And it's important. Like life or death. You know how dreams get. You're not sure why it's life and death, but it is. Ten faces, eight or nine. I don't remember."

"Gothic," he said.

"Yeah, it gets better. Because I couldn't do it. I studied their faces and I wasn't sure. All these weird pumpkin heads on a shelf, and I couldn't tell a damn thing about who was thinking what. So all of a sudden I've got an ax in my hand. The ax from the other night, at Diana's. It just materialized, and I'm going down the row and splitting open all the heads. Melons, pumpkins, whatever. Splitting them open to see what's inside."

"And?"

"Just seeds. Seeds and pulp. Nothing. Empty like half a dozen scooped out jack-o'-lanterns."

Parker was quiet.

"So what's it mean—you got any idea?"

"I'm a lawyer, not a shrink."

"Take a stab, go on. I won't sue for malpractice."

"You're angry, frustrated, under stress. You doubt yourself. Losing faith in your abilities. Like you thought you had Frank Sheffield figured out, and it turns out you were dead wrong. Now you're not sure of yourself."

She looked at her watch. Three hours left.

"That's good, Parker. I wouldn't give up the day job just yet, but that's good."

TWENTY-FOUR

THE SKY WAS A DEEPER tone of blue than Miami could manage. An icy cobalt that seemed to soar at a greater distance from the earth than any sky Charlotte remembered. More ancient, more vast, as if this was the same sky that had witnessed the first dawn.

The breeze was cool and scented with pine and last year's decomposing leaves, with a faint undertone of wood smoke and old leather. Like the smell of a horse barn long abandoned.

As they crossed the Tsali campground, Parker and Charlotte took a quick look around before hiking the rest of the way up to Echota. The abandoned cabins appeared remarkably intact after decades of neglect. Some decay here and there, lots of head-high patches of jewelweed, and clumps of pines growing from the pitcher's mound and more in center field. Only a few of the larger buildings were beginning to sag on their foundations.

The remains of Parker's family home had been bulldozed to level ground. Over the years the charcoal from the fire had leached into the dirt and clay, and the grass grew patchy there. Jutting from the earth, a few large foundation stones formed the outlines of the old dwelling.

Parker's pace slowed and his gaze swiveled from side to side.

"Lot of ghosts?" she said.

"Like you can't imagine."

The trail to Inspiration Point was only about a mile long, but far steeper and more rugged than the climb they'd tackled the night before. Her haunches were throbbing already and going to be worse tomorrow. Despite a temperature in the low fifties, she'd soaked through her green top. Parker wore a blue denim shirt, a different pair of khakis, same boots. Preppy woodsman.

When they mounted the final hump in the trail, the land leveled and spread into a grassy meadow with a tiny cabin perched near the edge of a drop-off.

Inspiration Point had a 180-degree panorama of mountain ranges, miles of jagged ridges stacked back to back, blurring away into the smoky distance. Charlotte started to count them, just to keep her mind busy, anything to distract herself from her wristwatch. She gave up at six ranges. There were more behind those, but her eyes were burning from the effort.

Above her head, in a maple tree, a mockingbird ran through its playlist. The first wispy leaves of the new season jittered in an accompanying breeze.

Parker was silent, absorbing the view, or perhaps traveling back to the thousand other moments he'd gazed out at those same timeless hills.

"Looks deserted."

A small stone chimney ran up one side of the cabin, and a single window faced their direction. Its greasy panes were opaque, faintly reflecting the dull shine of the sun like a mirror that had lost its silver backing.

The cabin was two hundred yards off, no way to approach it except across that open field.

"Hear anyone in the woods on the way up?"

Parker shook his head, taking the question seriously.

"You knew those SWAT guys were out there last night, didn't you? You heard them, but you kept on going."

"I heard them," Parker said.

"I never thought of you as having acutely sensitive hearing."

"Apparently I'm more gifted than you know."

"I'm finding that out."

The rough edge between them was still there, but smoothing. His worry lines had loosened, his eyes letting go of the strain, the knot in his brow coming undone. She assumed it was because of their imminent reunion with Gracey, or maybe his crying jag in the hotel.

As they crossed the meadow, Parker continued to gaze out at the peaks, a solid span of green broken only here and there with giant boulders or cliff faces. A hawk circled the valley between their position and the closest hills.

"The name doesn't do the place justice," she said.

"I made a bunch of promises up here. Right in this field. Things I vowed to accomplish."

"That's the kind of place it is."

"I haven't done half of them yet," he said.

"Those are hard promises to keep. Ones we made so young. When we didn't know if the earth was flat or round."

He looked at her, mouth drawn into a reluctant smile.

He looked at his watch, and damn it, she gave in and looked at hers. Another fifteen minutes burned. Still a long way to five o'clock.

She marched ahead, the final twenty yards to the cabin, Parker following. If there was anybody in there, they'd had plenty of time to get ready.

At the steps, she drew the Beretta from her backpack, set the bag in the grass, lifted the metal latch, and with a foot against the base of the door, she toed it inward. Creaking hinges and a rush of stale air.

She jammed her pistol into the opening, ducking in behind it, looked around, and drew back.

"Nobody's home," she said. "But somebody definitely lives here."

She held the door open, then followed Parker inside, standing behind him while he surveyed the room.

Two stuffed owls sat high on a shelf. A kerosene lantern hung from a center beam, and books and magazines and newspapers littered the floor. In one corner a cot had been wedged flush against the log walls, the sheets rumpled and thrown open. In the center of the plank floor there was a red and green serape stretched out as a rug. Leather sandals and rumpled clothes were scattered here and there. The windows at the front were missing.

Charlotte drew open the door to a wardrobe and found a half-dozen pin-striped suits hanging neatly and a full shelf of shoes, black and cordovan polished to a high military gloss. On the back of the door were several clip-on bow ties in floral prints and paisleys.

Parker looked at the clothes and shrugged.

She shut the door and turned back to the room.

Beneath the largest window was a solid oak table that had been converted to a desk. It was cluttered with papers and narrow green books that had the look of ledgers.

In the midst of the mess sat a laptop computer with a wire running from its modem to a bright blue cell phone, its aerial extended. On the computer screen was an elaborate spreadsheet, columns of numbers.

She said, "Those sure as hell aren't Jacob Panther's clothes."

"Whoever it is, he has no right to be here. Property's been closed for thirty years. It's private land, no trespassing."

"So arrest me," a man said from the doorway.

Charlotte swung her aim to the man, but he held out his empty hands and she lowered it.

He was short and stooped, and his wispy white hair draped forward over his bent shoulders and brushed the middle of his chest. His clothes appeared to be stitched from animal skins, shapeless and loose. Simple moccasins, no jewelry or adornment. He had a hawkish nose and his face was a moonscape of crags and wrinkles. A desiccated Merlin in his mountain lair, his flesh as pale and filmy as an apparition's.

He smiled at Charlotte and held out her backpack.

"This would be yours?"

She took it and slipped her pistol back into place as Parker was saying, "Uncle Mike? Is that you?"

"Thought I'd died?"

"My god."

"A lot of people make that mistake. See me one day, can't believe I'm around the next."

Parker came forward and opened his arms and the man stepped into the embrace and returned it, both of them clapping the other on the back.

When they broke apart, Parker introduced the old man to Charlotte. No last name, just Uncle Mike. And he took her hand and held it in his dry grasp and looked into her eyes with such penetrating frankness that for a moment she thought she felt him roaming through her thoughts.

"I have so many questions." Parker had begun to pace the tiny room, from desk to cot and back again.

Charlotte glanced at her watch. Three hours left.

"After the fire, and the camp closed, you stayed behind?"

He nodded. In a fey gesture, his left hand swayed through the air at waist level as if his palm was riding bumpy currents of wind.

"Nowhere else I wanted to be. Now I look after things around the old place. Chase off the occasional real-estate developer."

Parker drew the beaded disk from his shirt pocket and extended it to Uncle Mike. The man held his ground but drew his head back an inch or two.

"You know what this is?"

"I do."

"It belonged to Mother."

"Apparently she was a Beloved Woman."

"Why? What did she do to deserve this?"

"I suppose she did what all of them did. She was valiant and took grave personal risks that changed the course of Cherokee history."

"You're kidding," Charlotte said. "Diana?"

"I don't do much of that," said Uncle Mike. "Kid."

"Specifically," Parker said. "What did she do specifically?"

"I'm not privileged to the inner workings of the tribe. A select group of elders make these decisions. Their identities are secret. But from what I gather, Diana showed great courage on the night your father died. And this honor was bestowed on her as a result."

"You don't know any more than that?"

"My guess would be no better than your own."

But his eyes dipped as he spoke the words. A slippery man.

"You know something," Charlotte said. "Go on, say it."

Uncle Mike brought his gaze to hers and waved away the thought like a housefly.

"So tell me, Parker. Where did you and Diana go after you left Camp Tsali? Where in the world did you vanish to?"

"Florida," he said. "Miami. But why do you say 'vanish'?"

"Because Diana cut off all contact with her old friends. The two of you left and that's the last anyone around these parts heard from her."

"Maybe she couldn't face the reminders of Dad's death, even old friends."

"Perhaps," said Mike, looking away. "I'm sure she had her reasons."

"What're you driving at? You got something to say, stop being cute and say it." Charlotte watched the stippled shadows move across Uncle Mike's face from a cloud's quick passage. He caught her scrutiny and dropped his eyes, ducking his chin, and Charlotte saw something flicker across his face in the half-second before his look was transformed by a smile.

It was a flash of some feverish emotion. A fleeting squeeze of brow, the fierce, unmistakable glitter in the eyes and the tightening around them, as though a wince of memory had knifed through him but he had shunted it aside.

And there was something else, a simpler observation based only on quantity of eye contact. He was favoring Charlotte two to one over Parker, as if he had sized her up as the greater threat or else the harder sell.

"Please, Uncle Mike. Mother was murdered and my daughter's run away. She's up here somewhere, and we believe she's in danger."

"Diana murdered? When did this happen?"

"Tuesday night," Charlotte said. "What do you know about it?"

He looked at her and shook his head slowly and the inner corner of his eyebrows rose and his lower lip pouted out. The physiology of generic sadness. Honest enough, but the look passed too quickly to be deeply felt, the way one registered the death of someone who'd been gravely ill for years. A death already processed—meaning either he had known about her murder, or else suspected such a thing was imminent.

"Look, Uncle Mike." Parker reached out and took hold of the old man's sleeve. "Anything you might've heard about this Beloved Woman thing could be helpful. We're running low on time."

"And patience," Charlotte said.

Uncle Mike's expression relaxed to its neutral state. The half-smile of someone adroit at staying out of range of the difficulties of others.

Gently, he tugged his sleeve from Parker's grasp and pulled out his chair and took a sideways perch, looking at Parker for one tick, Charlotte for two. His free hand continued to smooth the air like a conductor keeping the woodwinds on tempo.

"May I suggest that if you find yourself with some free time on your hands and a hankering for some enlightening entertainment, you purchase tickets to the pageant?"

"Pageant?" Charlotte looked at Parker.

"You mean *Unto These Hills*," Parker said.

Uncle Mike nodded.

That particular drama was, as Charlotte knew, the reenactment of Cherokee history, with special emphasis on the life of the namesake of the summer camp where they stood. And it was also, of course, the site of Parker's first encounter with Lucy Panther.

"I've seen it a dozen times, Uncle Mike. What am I going to learn I don't already know?"

"A man sees different things at different stages of life. You're familiar with the story they were telling, but I suspect you missed the hidden one."

"What's your game?" she said. "Why won't you talk straight?"

Uncle Mike held Charlotte's gaze.

"Did you happen to notice the view off Inspiration Point, young lady?"

She said yes, of course she'd noticed it.

"You hiked all the way up here, just over five thousand feet. Florida people like you, flatlanders, your legs must be sore."

"We're surviving," she said.

"Think that view would look the same if you'd driven your car?"

As Uncle Mike's hand undulated through the air, she heard a cardinal on a limb just outside and realized the old man's hand moved in time with its song as though one of them, bird or man, was in service to the other.

"If you had used your car," Mike said, "you wouldn't appreciate the view half as much. It was a core belief of Parker's father, as it is of mine. Unless you earn it, it's not truly yours. Simple as that. The rest is spiritual burglary."

"Come on, Parker," she said. "This is a waste."

"If I simply blurted out to you everything I know," said the old man, "you would find it unfathomable. It would be like describing that view to a man blind from birth. A challenge that neither of us could meet."

"Try us."

Uncle Mike shook his head.

Charlotte stepped across the room and planted herself inches from the delicate man.

"Listen to me, Uncle Mike. If I find out you had anything to do with putting my daughter at risk or prolonging her distress, anything at all, I'm hiking back up here and I'm going to start by snapping little bones in your body and work my way up to the big ones till I get to your goddamn skull."

"Your frustration is perfectly understandable."

"You don't understand shit. You're some squirrelly creep who's been hiding from the world so long, you forgot there was one. Blathering Zen hocus-pocus like a wise old man on the mountaintop."

Parker stepped to her side and drew her back.

"We better go," he said.

"Yeah, before I really lose my temper."

"When you see the pageant," said Mike, "remember there are two sides to every story."

She was already out the door, Parker just behind her, when Uncle Mike said, "Wait."

They came back inside, and Charlotte saw his mouth had tightened into an anguished scowl and his eyes were fogged over as if he were revisiting some unspeakable vision from his past.

"Last chance," she said.

He resurfaced by slow degrees, lifting his gaze and settling it on the open window beside her, the green view.

"All right. Although it was my fervent hope that you would unravel the truth in your own way, I'm afraid there may not be time for that any longer."

"Go on."

He glanced around the cabin with a vague longing, as if searching for some reassurance from his collection of keepsakes. He took a swallow of air and spoke with his eyes floating from object to object throughout the room.

"First, you should know that not everyone is as courageous as Diana. Some of us will never win awards for heroism. But I want you both to understand that in my way I've always done what I could to help."

"Like what?" Charlotte said.

188

The old man stared down at the planks of his cabin for a moment, then drew a breath and brought his eyes to Parker, and finally to her.

"Sometimes a sin can dwell so long in a man's heart it burrows like a larva into the deepest tissues of memory. While it may have disappeared from view, it is always there, festering."

"So let it out," Charlotte said.

He licked his lips, and the hand that had been smoothing the air was now limp at his side.

"You're in mortal danger, Parker. Your daughter as well."

"What about me?" Charlotte said. "I get a pass?"

"Not you. Just Parker and your child."

"How do you know this?" Parker said.

"A year ago my daughter, Sissy, alerted me. I'd taken care to position her in a job where she could spy on my behalf, fearing this very thing might happen. In that year since she warned me of the danger, I have been searching for you, Parker, without success."

"Why? Who's after us?" Charlotte said. "It's Jacob Panther, isn't it?"

"It is . . ." Uncle Mike closed his eyes and shook his head as if grappling with the dreadful words. "It is family against family."

"What does that mean?"

As he opened his mouth to speak, something plucked hard at Charlotte's backpack and she staggered to the left. And as though a phantom had seized him by the throat, the frail old man was tossed backward against the wall. A ragged hole burst open in his chest.

From the shelf above, a stuffed owl tumbled down and landed at his feet. Parker took a step toward the wounded man, but Charlotte grabbed his arm and dragged him to the floor. The second shot tore into Mike's shoulder and sent him sprawling to his right, knocking over the makeshift desk.

Charlotte had the Beretta out and was on her hands and knees. She'd heard no rifle shot, so clearly the weapon was silenced.

Only one window of the four allowed a sight line on Uncle Mike—the one where she'd been standing. Rising from her position on the floor and peeping through the window, she made out a small knoll where pines mingled with boulders. Maybe a ten foot elevation above their own position, fifty yards off.

She scooted across the dusty planks and flattened herself against the wall beneath the window. She held in her mind a snapshot of the layout of the hill and the boulders, and spent a few seconds scanning it for the most likely sniper's nest. But nothing stood out.

Parker was on his cell phone, frantically punching numbers, apparently getting nothing.

She set her grip on the Beretta and drew a breath. Before she could take her shot, two more rounds shattered the computer and the far window.

Slumped on his side, Uncle Mike wore a vacant smile.

She glanced around at the flimsy, decaying logs that formed the cabin's walls. Hardly the Alamo. As isolated as they were, if the shooter had enough patience and ammo, he could riddle every square inch of the room. With only the eight shots in her Beretta, their best chance might come down to making a desperate sprint across open ground.

Charlotte rose up to the corner of the window. She inched her barrel upward, then brought one eye into the frame, cranked the pistol into position, and squeezed off two rounds, bracketing the hillside left, then right.

Before she ducked back down, she managed to glimpse the results of her shots. On the left she'd blown a gash into the trunk of a poplar tree, and on the right her shot had carved a chunk from a gray boulder.

Staying in a crouch, she heard no movement outside.

A bird was calling. Miles away a small plane droned. Cool air flooded through the cabin walls and, in the spears of sunlight dust churned.

Parker finally got reception on his phone and spoke to someone in harsh whispers. When he was done, he said, "Frank's on the way."

She touched a finger to her lips.

She was listening to the crackle of leaves and twigs, a shuffling, uncertain gait that was drawing closer. She inched to the doorway and stayed in a crouch, a two-handed grip on the pistol. As the rustle approached, she held the warm barrel next to her cheek.

When the noise halted a yard or two beyond the door, Charlotte took a grip on the door's edge with her left hand, rehearsed a move in her head, gave herself a second more to still the rattle in her pulse, then threw open the door, flopped on her belly, and aimed out at an emaciated chocolate Lab.

She spun back to a position behind the log wall and stayed there while the dog wandered into the cabin and walked directly to a tin dish that sat in a corner and began to lap.

It drank until the bowl was empty, then turned, looked blankly at Charlotte and Parker, shuffled over to sniff at Uncle Mike's cooling flesh, then shook itself hard and walked back out the door and headed into the woods.

They waited another fifteen minutes in aching silence before hearing Frank Sheffield shouting and a herd of federal agents trampling through the woods.

TWENTY-FIVE

THE FORENSIC TECHS WERE WORKING the hill where the shooter had been, but from a quick look Charlotte could see there was little sign of his presence left behind: some crushed leaves, a heel print in the hard dirt. Large shoe, but the sole pattern was murky.

"So let's run through this one more time, shall we?"

Sheffield was sitting on a boulder halfway between the cabin and the shooter's lair. He was staring at the notebook in his hand. It appeared new, unused. He scribbled something on the first page and underlined it twice.

"So you two came up here to visit an old friend."

"That's right. A friend from Parker's past."

"And the victim is that old friend?"

Parker was taking a long look at the distant mountains.

"Frank, you can run us around this same track till Christmas, but you know damn well we're just going to give you what you already have."

Sheffield smiled at his notebook.

"The victim in the cabin is the person you came to see?"

Charlotte sighed and recited it again. "His name is Uncle Mike. He and Parker's father worked together thirty years ago."

"At this summer camp?"

"Exactly."

Frank looked through the cabin door again, at his men probing the walls for slugs.

"And since you just happened to be in the area, you had a wild hair to come visit this guy. Social call, like for old times' sakes and all that. Sing a little 'Kumbaya,' tell ghost stories around the campfire."

"A wild hair," Charlotte said. "Yes."

"Didn't have anything to do with your runaway daughter."

Charlotte was silent. She didn't need to tell him the obvious. Anything and everything they were doing had to do with Gracey.

Frank drew some more lines in his notebook.

"Frail old guy like that, living up here in his deerskin clothes, playing Davy Crockett. Boggles the mind. No heat, no electricity, no water."

"You know everything we know, Frank. Now we're out of here."

"The hell you are. You're not going anywhere till I'm finished. Got it, Monroe? In fact, your smug-ass attitude is starting to grate."

Charlotte was about to bite back, but Parker brought his gaze from the mountain range and shook his head at her. Just play along, get this over with.

"So tell me again, if you'd be so kind, Counselor, about this white pickup you saw following you. You got a make, model, approximate age? Any distinguishing features? You know the drill. Dented fender, busted headlight. Anything that makes it pop from all other white pickups."

"It might have been tan or pale blue," Parker said quietly. "It might not have been following us at all."

Sheffield sighed and glanced over at Agent Roth, who was supervising the forensic techs on the hillside.

"Uncle Mike," Frank said. "That's the sum total of what you know about this guy? His name was Mike and he worked with your dad thirty years ago."

"Jesus Christ, yes, that's all we know."

"Just so we're a hundred percent clear on this, you're claiming you didn't come up here to meet him because he happens to be Michael L. Tribue, chairman of the board of Southeastern Trust Banks. The banks your son, Jacob Panther, has been blowing up. That had nothing to do with this little rendezvous?"

Charlotte made an effort to keep the shock from her face. Parker's lips drew apart as if he meant to bellow across the valley, but no sound emerged.

"Yeah, like you two didn't know."

"Michael Tribue? You're sure of that, Sheffield?"

"Damn sure," Frank said. "Older brother of the congressman, uncle of the sheriff, which also makes him the uncle of our blowgun victim at Miami International. Pieces starting to fall into place for you now, Counselor? Your prodigal son coming into better focus?"

Charlotte stepped close to Parker and took his hand in hers.

"Just yesterday," Frank said, "Agent Roth and I paid a courtesy call on the good gentleman. Bringing him up to speed on the bombing investigation. He was dressed in his Brooks Brothers pinstripes, spunky little bow tie, not this deerskin bullshit. Desk he was sitting behind had to be worth what I knock down in a year, and then, twenty-four hours later, we find he's been up here on the mountaintop dancing with wolves. Not that I'm making light of Mr. Tribue's death, but finding him whacked like this, well, it kind of snaps some of the pieces into place."

Frank scribbled some more on his pad.

"What pieces would those be?" Charlotte said.

"Pretty obvious. The old man's bank turned Panther down for a loan, foreclosed on a relative's house, screwed him one way or another. Who the hell knows, but whatever it was, it pissed Panther off big-time and sent him on his bombing crusade.

"One by one he's been blowing up the old guy's banks. Then he finds, shit, that's not getting rid of his itch, so he whacks the nephew, Martin, and like we've all seen it happen plenty of times before, once the guy crosses that line, gets some blood lust going, Panther can't help himself, he's got to come up here and blow up the old guy himself."

Charlotte held up her backpack and turned it around so Sheffield could see the two-inch gash the first slug made.

"How about us, Sheffield? It's just a coincidence Parker and I happened to be here? Maybe we were the targets."

"Oh, come on. Your daughter's a runaway, and granted, that's a shitty thing. But it doesn't make the sun start orbiting around your navel."

194

"After Uncle Mike was dead the shooter kept firing."

"So? Maybe he wasn't sure he got him."

"From the distance he was shooting his rifle had to be scoped. So he could damn well see what he was shooting at, and he saw the result. He put a second slug in Uncle Mike, and then he kept on firing."

"So? Nothing weird about that. Guy didn't want to leave behind any witnesses. Maybe he knew it was his father in here, maybe he didn't. With a guy like Panther, I don't see that making a lot of difference."

Parker stepped forward.

"And where does my mother's murder fit into your neat little package?"

"And Gracey," Charlotte said.

Parker shook his head in disgust.

"And tell us, Agent Sheffield, in your vast experience with the patterns of criminal behavior, have you ever come across an offender with so many differing methods of attack? Jugs full of gasoline, blowgun darts with exotic poison, a hatchet, then a sniper rifle. It should be clear to you, as it is to me, that we're dealing with multiple parties here."

Frank glanced down at his notebook, and his mouth twisted into a sour smile. He tore off the page he'd been doodling on and wadded it up and stuck it in his pants pocket.

"Oh, by the way," Frank said, "we made some progress on that hatchet."

"Yeah?"

"Turns out the weapon used in your mother's murder came from up here."

"Up where?"

He told them about the missing ax from the Cherokee museum.

"It was in Tsali's hand?" Parker said.

"Yeah, stolen right out of the museum. You got any ideas how that might be relevant? I mean, that's what this place was called, right, Camp Tsali? I know the story about the guy, but is there a connection here I'm not seeing?"

Charlotte and Parker exchanged a glance, but neither spoke.

"Okay, fuck it, that's it," Sheffield said. "I keep sharing all kinds of fascinating shit with you guys, expecting a modicum of professional quid pro quo, but what do I get? Dick."

"We don't know what it means, Frank," Charlotte said. "Something occurs to us, we'll call you. We're not withholding. We're just absorbing."

"Yeah, right." Sheffield looked over at the knoll where his men were working. "So Sheriff Tribue said he wants to meet you two. Don't ask me why. You up for that?"

Charlotte took another look at her watch. Still over an hour until their meeting with Gracey.

"Why not?" she said.

"He's an odd duck," Frank said. "Makes me look downright normal."

Sheffield told them to wait there, and he walked over to the hillside and brought back a large, dark-haired man with a long, narrow face, prominent ears, and hollow eyes.

He was trailed by two white poodles, standards, though to Charlotte's estimation, they were considerably broader in the chest and heavier than was usual in the breed, as if they might've been mixed with mastiff or Great Dane.

Dressed in the local no-frills blue police uniform, the sheriff was stern-faced and walked with the ramrod formality of a revival preacher about to call thunderbolts down on his flock.

Sheffield made the introductions, and the sheriff nodded and touched a finger to the brim of his hat.

"Mr. and Mrs. Monroe, I'm sorry about your unfortunate brush with violence. This is not a customary event in our peaceful corner of the world."

Charlotte accepted his stiff courtesy with a nod.

"Our condolences on your brother's death," Charlotte said. "And now your uncle."

The man was eyeing her with a faint lift of eyebrow, as one might appraise the value of horseflesh whose fitness was in question.

With a curt nod in her direction, he turned to Parker.

"So I understand, sir, that you're the son of Charles Andrew Monroe, Chief as he was known."

Parker said yes, he was.

"I was nineteen that summer," Farris said. "Just married with a newborn son. Those events stand out starkly in my memory. The idea that Standing-dog Matthews would resort to such savagery was deeply shocking to us all—setting fire to your father's house, killing those others. I think our sheltered community lost its innocence that summer."

Parker said, "I know I lost mine."

As she watched the sheriff, the flesh on Charlotte's shoulders had grown cold and prickly. There was nothing in Tribue's expression that fitted Fedderman's coding list, and nothing in his strict demeanor she could put a simple name to—but the sensation was there, one she'd had only twice before.

Most recently when she'd looked into Jacob Panther's eyes a few days earlier—his cold, invasive stare. The other time was years ago, when she'd been one of several cops in the interrogation room when a middle-aged married man confessed to raping and murdering eleven adolescent girls in the course of a year, and after he finished his admission, he began telling knock-knock jokes, one after the other.

Charlotte swallowed back the knot in her throat and said to the sheriff, "Agent Sheffield seems to think your uncle's murder and your brother's are connected. That Jacob Panther is at war with your family. Is that how you see it, sir?"

Farris was about to reply, but Sheffield thrust a hand between them.

"Hold it right there."

The sheriff eyed Frank uneasily and retreated a half-step.

"You're not part of this investigation, Monroe. Don't forget that."

Charlotte caught a microexpression flitting across Tribue's face. His nose wrinkled, he flexed his levator labii superioris, alaeque nasi. For the briefest of instants his teeth were bared, brows raised then lowered. Equal portions of disgust and anger. AU 9 was Fedderman's code for it.

As his rage flickered, then dissolved into a serene facade, Charlotte had a tingle of recollection. Mildred Pierce on the stairway. Her fury revealed for that brief moment, then hidden again behind her lifetime mask of phony geniality.

It might've been taken for nothing more than a flash of testiness at Sheffield's pulling rank. But it looked like more to Charlotte. A lot more.

She stepped over to the larger poodle.

"Are they friendly?"

"Usually." The sheriff's smile was still shaded with anger. Not as adept at masking his emotions as Joan Crawford.

"What are their names?" Charlotte patted the larger one's head. The dog bore her touch without response, staring ahead at the open field.

"They don't have names," Tribue said. "They're dogs, not people."

Sheffield suppressed a smile and shook his head.

"So, Monroe," Frank said. "Where can I find you two if I need to get in touch?"

"You've got my cell number."

"And locally?"

"The Holiday Inn."

"Well, if anything comes to light on your girl's whereabouts, I'll call. Otherwise, you stay clear of the Panther investigation. You've got no official status here. And let me be clear, if you bump into the asshole and don't inform us immediately, you're going to have to start considering a new career path."

He tried for some menace in his blue eyes, but couldn't muster much.

"Always a pleasure, Frank," she said. "Always a pleasure."

She and Parker were crossing the open field, headed for the footpath down the mountainside, when a black SUV, one of those engorged monsters with tires a half-story high, bounced over the rise and in a cloud of red dust skidded to a stop a few feet in front of them.

A man in khakis and a black polo shirt jumped out of the passenger's side and blocked their path. From his sun-spotted arms and crow's-feet, Charlotte made him for late sixties, but his hair was a perfect black and his dark eyes had the quick gleam of a man twenty years younger. He was a lean six feet tall with the self-satisfied bearing of a military man, or country squire.

Ignoring Charlotte, his gaze locked on Parker and he strode forward. From the driver's side, a woman half his age hopped down, a cell phone hard against her ear. She had whitish blond hair and was as wispy as an adolescent. In gray capri pants and a snug black top and backless sandals, she might've been heading for a luncheon at the country club.

"You Agent Sheffield?" the man demanded of Parker.

"That's Sheffield over at the cabin, jeans and white shirt."

"And who, may I ask, are you?"

"I'm Parker Monroe. This is my land you're trespassing on."

A flinch of surprise passed across the older man's face.

"Charles Monroe's son?"

"That's right."

198

"Yes, yes, I was fortunate enough to know your father rather well. An excellent gentleman. That was a terrible business. The fire, all that."

The young woman approached with the cell phone pressed to her ear.

"A funeral with all the trimmings. It's his son, for godsakes. Strings, harps, hell, whatever you can dig up."

"I'm Otis Tribue," the gentleman said to Parker. "I was informed my brother, Michael, was shot. Is that correct?"

"Yes, it is," Charlotte said. "A rifleman in the woods."

"A hunter?"

"More like a sniper."

"It's Panther, isn't it? Jacob Panther, that goddamn Indian."

"That seems to be the general view."

He gave her a sharp look, then turned back to Parker.

"Is he going to make it? Did he survive?"

"No," Parker said. "He's dead."

The congressman slowly rocked his head back and gazed up at the sky, which was full of birds and tattered clouds, indulging in a moment of hammy grief. She could almost see him counting to ten before he brought his steely gaze back to Parker.

"And what brings you back to these hills, boy, after all this time?"

"Personal matters," Parker said. "No concern of yours."

The congressman's lips wrinkled at Parker's impudence.

Parker held steady under the politician's withering inspection. Finally the old man lost interest and caught his staffer's eye and sliced a finger across his throat. With a curt "ciao" she clicked off and stepped forward to do his bidding.

"If I believed in such things, Mr. Monroe," the congressman said, stinging each of them with a final look, "I'd say this land of yours is cursed."

Then he and his staffer stalked away toward the people in charge.

TWENTY-SIX

PARKER AND CHARLOTTE WERE SILENT on the trek back to the car. Silent on the snaking drive down the mountainside. She watched the dashboard clock, its green digital numbers counting off the minutes till their reunion with Gracey. She was trying, with little success, to throttle back the wild swings of emotion, one minute a surge of giddy optimism, the next moment a blinding flash of anger or dread. Trying to restrain herself as her training had taught her to do in moments such as these, when she might be called upon to be the one reasonable mind at the gathering.

"Nice family," she said. "Uncle Mike the airy-fairy hermit. High-and-mighty Otis, and his son Li'l Abner from Planet Weird."

"That white pickup I saw," said Parker. "We're being stalked, Charlotte. Somebody's trying to kill us, and you're making jokes."

She looked over at him. His breath was ragged, his forehead gleamed with sweat.

"Relax, Parker."

"Relax? What? You don't believe Uncle Mike?"

"That gibberish? Hell, I'm not sure who I believe anymore."

"And Tsali's hatchet? What the hell's that about?"

"I don't know, but I suppose it means we're going to have to do what

Uncle Mike said, and go see that pageant. This is about more than Jacob Panther blowing up banks. That's for damn sure."

"That's your professional opinion? We're not being targeted?"

"At the moment I just want my daughter back. I'm trying to keep my focus on that. I'm not discounting anything."

She was silent for a while, watching the shadowy woods flash by. Only a few miles away was the tacky tourist strip, but the landscape up here was prehistoric. Fertile and lush, the trees and underbrush so dense they appeared impenetrable.

A forest very much like this one had been her refuge as a child in Tennessee. A vine-tangled realm of perpetual dusk where she'd hidden for hours, perched on rotting logs or sitting cross-legged on the beds of pine needles, plotting her escape from her mother's double-wide trailer. When she grew weary of fantasizing, her attention turned to the action close at hand. The fierce clash of ants and spiders and beetles and moths—the clandestine warfare of birds and creatures with teeth and claws. Predators and prey whose every second was an ordeal, a test of reflex and strength, a hunt for food, mates, supremacy.

What she absorbed in those lonesome hours in the forest near her home laid the groundwork for what minimal belief system she had. It was her conviction that on some level the human condition was forever rooted in that same unruly soil. A destiny based on dirt and blood and unceasing conflict. Try as we might to rise beyond the earth, lift our bodies into the faultless sky in airplanes and antiseptic high-rises, dress for the opera, pray to our civilized gods, pretend we've refined ourselves beyond those primal urges, still, the earth and its feral laws and endless skirmishes were rooted in our cell memory. As far as she was concerned, it was inescapable. Every corner of the world was as perilous and unpredictable as the forest floor. Our blood forever howled with its animal song.

And then out her window the blur of the forest gave way to Farris Tribue's curious face. She turned to Parker.

"I've seen that condition before."

"What condition?"

"The sheriff, his face. Close-set eyes, protruding ears, long, narrow bone structure. It's got a name."

"What're you talking about?"

"A month ago we had a seminar at work. Genetic disorders. Things we might encounter on the street. Autism, Down syndrome, that sort of thing. The sheriff's face, that's a marker for one of them. Close-set eyes, protruding ears. I can't recall the name. It was something I'd never heard of before."

"You saying the guy's mentally impaired?"

"No, with this one, you can be a carrier, have that appearance, but be okay yourself. That much I remember. Recessive genes."

"How's that relevant?"

"I don't know. But the guy creeped me out. When we get back to the hotel, I'll dig around on the Net, try to find the name."

"Creeped you out?"

"It's cop talk. You wouldn't understand."

She meant it to sound droll, but it came out with a harsh tang. Parker flinched and was silent. Just like that, the tension between them was back. Or maybe it had never gone, and was simply dwelling beneath one layer of skin.

They drove through the town of Cherokee, past the tourist shops and casino. Kept going up U.S. 19, Charlotte staring out at the farm implement stores and more souvenir shops and mom-and-pop motels.

In her backpack Charlotte's phone sounded, and she dug it out and answered.

"This is the guy you talked to."

"Which guy is that?" Charlotte said.

"Standingdog's cell mate. The one made you as a cop this morning. You left me your card, remember?"

The reception was scratchy, breaking apart, coming back.

"So what do you want?"

"I got a name for you," the man said.

"I'm listening."

Parker was staring at her, shrugging a question.

"Jeremiah," said the inmate.

"And who is that?"

"He's the one you're after. He's the one that did the deed."

"I'm dense," she said. "You need to spell it out."

"The handyman," he said. "The fire at that goddamn summer camp."

"Jeremiah?"

"Yeah, and there was another one, too. Boss of the operation. Mr. Big. He planned it, made it happen, but that guy got away clean."

"You got a name for this Mr. Big?"

"Don't know. But those were the two that did it. Jeremiah and this other guy. Not the Dog. He just took the fall, don't ask me why."

The connection broke. She held the cell phone in her lap and waited. But he didn't call back.

"Standingdog's cell mate," she said. "He remembered a few things."

"What?"

She repeated the fragmentary conversation.

"Call Miriam," he said. "Dig up the trial transcript for Standingdog Matthews. Capital murder, it's got to be archived. Trial exhibits, appeals, the whole record. We need to know who this Jeremiah fellow was."

"Miriam's got a lot on her plate already. I have somebody I can use."

She called Marie Salzedo, Lieutenant Rodriguez's secretary who'd swooned over Sheffield. Beneath her bimbo act, Marie was the best researcher in the department.

"Awful quiet around here without you, Charlotte," Marie said.

"Quiet's good."

"You want to talk to the boss?"

Charlotte explained what she wanted. Had to spell out *Jeremiah* twice.

"I'm not all that busy. I can pull it while you're on the line."

Charlotte waited. The reception was so good she could hear Marie's fingers clicking the computer keys. Explain that. Cherokee to Miami crystal clear. Cherokee to Cherokee was half-static.

"You still there?"

"I'm here."

"A little longer. There's not much stuff. It was only a one-day trial. I'm running a search for the name in the transcripts. It's taking forever."

Five minutes later, entering Maggie Valley, Marie came back.

"Sorry about that. Computers are bogged down today."

"You find it?"

"Tribue," she said. "Jeremiah Tribue, he died in the fire, him and a kid named Nathan Philpot and Charles Monroe. Does that help?"

Charlotte was silent for a moment, absorbing it.

"You still there?"

"Yeah, Marie, thanks. Do me one more favor, okay? E-mail me the link to the Web site you were just on, or cut and paste the files into an e-mail attachment, whatever's easier."

"The whole trial transcript?"

"Yeah, and listen, see if you can dig up the police reports, too. Find out who handled it—State Bureau of Investigation, county sheriff's department, tribal police, whoever. When you find them, see if they'll fax you the background stuff. And there had to be an arson investigation, too. Scan it and e-mail it to me so I can get to it from my laptop."

"I'll take care of it right now."

"And listen, if you wind up talking to Carolina police, be nice. They're different up here. Not city folks."

"I'm always nice."

"I know that. Just be extra nice."

"Not so Cuban, you mean."

"You're a peach, Marie."

"A peach?"

"You're sweet," she said. "And oh, hey, one more thing. Call the North Carolina department of motor vehicles, see if you can locate a special application. Somebody requesting a license plate with the last four digits, 1773. Probably happened in the last twelve months."

Marie wanted to know if all this involved a Gables PD investigation.

"The plates, the trial transcripts, all of this relates to the murder of Diana Monroe. Parker's mother."

"But Metro's doing the homicide work, not us."

"We're assisting," Charlotte said.

"Right, right. We're assisting. You think Rodriguez will buy that?"

"Better if he doesn't know what you're up to."

"Roger that."

"Thanks, Marie. I'll bring you back a souvenir. A jug of cider."

"Make it a hundred proof, okay?"

After she relayed the information to Parker, he was silent, eyes fixed on the car ahead.

"Jeremiah Tribue," she said. "Probably Mike and Otis's brother."

"Could be another Tribue family altogether."

"That a common name up here?"

"Not really. It's an old pioneer name."

"So this is all connected. What happened the night of your father's murder and the fire, the banks blown up, two Tribues dead in one week. And Jacob Panther and us in the middle of it somehow."

"Look, Charlotte, it's totally immaterial what some ex-con claims. If Jeremiah was Uncle Mike's brother, it wouldn't surprise me. But it doesn't mean anything. Standingdog killed my father. End of story."

Charlotte grabbed her backpack from the floor and held it up. She stuck two fingers through the gash in the fabric.

"And this?"

"That wasn't Jacob."

"Oh, come on. Think about it. How did we get to Uncle Mike's cabin? By following the bread crumbs Jacob laid out for us. He mentions Sequoyah Caverns to you, so we go there first. Maybe he was in the woods last night with his rifle, but Sheffield and his boys got in the way."

That got Parker shaking his head.

"Sequoyah Caverns is plan A, Echota is plan B," Charlotte said, "and just in case those don't work out, he gives himself a C. Gracey calls, tells us to go to the barbecue place. Jacob's pulling her strings. If we make it this far, then he knows where we'll head next. To that restaurant. Another ambush."

Parker gave her a deadpan look. "That's not Jacob, goddamn it."

"You're willing to bet your life on that?"

"I spent more time with him than you did. That's not Jacob."

"What? Like five minutes more?"

Parker kept his eyes forward, but she could read the strain in his forehead and saw the muscles working in his jaw. As though the doubt had formed a lump that he was trying to grind away.

Charlotte looked out her window at the first trickle of summer tourists, families with young kids going in and out of souvenir shops along the strip. A steady stream of retirees heading toward the casino.

Then she remembered something else and dug the road map out of the glove compartment, checked the index, found the street, flipped the map over, and took a minute to locate it.

"What're you doing?"

"Make a U-turn, go back five blocks, maybe six."

"That's not the way to the barbecue place."

"We still got an hour. Humor me."

He retraced their course west on U.S. 19 until she told him where to turn.

"One of the bomb sites," she said. "It's along here somewhere. Water Street. I thought we should have a look, it's so close."

"What's that going to tell us?"

"Jesus, Parker. You don't solve a crime without at least taking a look at the crime scene. I know, I know, that's Miriam's job, going out on the street. You just sit in your office all day and fiddle with your briefs and filings. But this is how we cops do it. We see things. Touch them."

"Oh, come on. I get out on the street."

"Yeah, on the way back and forth to the courthouse."

Parker swerved the car over to the curb and slammed the shifter into park. His lips were flat, forehead creased with an anger as hot as she'd ever seen in him.

"Look." He raised his finger and pointed at her. "I'm not going to argue with you. You're right. I'm not out on the street like you. But what I do all day, getting the words right on the page, that's just as important, okay? If the words aren't right, the sentences, the paragraphs, the fucking logic, then it doesn't matter if you have all the goddamn evidence in the universe on your side. You understand what I'm saying? It's the right words in the right order, just as much as it is hair follicles and fingerprints and DNA."

She reached out and took hold of his finger and folded it down into his fist and she cupped it in both her hands.

"Okay, I'm sorry," she said. "We have different skills, different points of view. You're right, I was needling you. I'm sorry."

He let go of the breath he'd been holding, and gave her hand a half-hearted squeeze, then eased back onto the street.

They passed a hardware store, a hair salon, a bar, a tiny bookstore, and a burrito joint. Circled the block, then the next one.

One left turn and two stop signs later, they saw it on the left corner—the blackened shell of a two-story brick building. Parker drew up to the sidewalk. A couple of men in yellow hard hats prowled the edges of the site, drawing out spools of measuring tape and writing on clipboards.

"Panther's file is back at the motel," she said. "But I think this was the most recent one, maybe February. A night watchman died."

Parker stared at the building.

"You wouldn't think a jug of kerosene would do so much damage."

"No sprinklers."

"They're a little slow rebuilding," he said. "Four months, still rubble."

"Bomb team probably had the site shut down for a while."

Charlotte stared at the blackened ruins. Part of the second floor was still intact, with interior doors opening onto twenty-foot drop-offs. Surrounding the property, a chain-link fence glistened in the bright sun.

"Seen enough?"

"Do the whole block," she said.

He circled, getting the full 360 of the damage. They passed a small white sign and Charlotte told him to stop, back up.

It was the building-permit display board, with several documents encased in plastic, thumbtacked to a sheet of plywood.

"Just be a sec."

She hopped out, jogged over to the board, and read the permits down to the fine print. Afterward she tracked down the two hard hats, got clarification, and trotted back to the car.

"So?" Parker said.

"So our blowgun victim, Martin Tribue, happened to own the company rebuilding the banks Jacob Panther blew up."

"Allegedly blew up."

She waved away his quibble.

"I can see your wheels spinning," she said. "Let's hear it."

Parker took another few seconds to get it straight, and said, "Okay, so, big deal, we got a little nepotism going on. Nobody's going to give that a second look. Backwoods area like this, it's only natural Uncle Mike tosses the rebuilding work to his nephew. Every month another bank blows, and the contracts start stacking up."

"Insurance fraud?"

"An intriguing possibility. Some free remodeling, close relative makes a ton of profit, maybe kicks back a few bucks to Uncle Mike."

"Which would make Jacob Panther their fall guy."

"Right. A unique-looking local kid, blond-haired Cherokee, you hire a bomber to dress up in a wig and do the job. One brother controls the security cameras, the angles, the film. Another Tribue, the sheriff, IDs Jacob from the security videos, then big daddy congressman steps in and uses his clout to promote Jacob onto the Most Wanted list. You got a nifty all-in-the-family scheme, and together they frame Jacob Panther. The longer he stays on the run, the more money they make. Which all fits with the war thing. The Tribues declared war on Jacob, and he's just fighting back."

"I don't know, Parker. That's one hell of an elaborate plot to remodel their goddamn banks."

"Could be somebody's got financial problems. Construction company's in trouble, bank could be having accounting issues, issues with the IRS. And Jacob knows it's a frame, and he's simply fighting back."

"And Diana? And Gracey? And all that stuff Panther said to you at our house? You're next. The red war club. And Uncle Mike claiming we're in grave danger. How does that fit into insurance fraud? Where do we come in?"

He was quiet for a moment, concentrating on the traffic. Then he looked over at her and grimaced.

"Okay, okay. It needs some tweaking."

They drove in silence back to U.S. 19 and found Butts on the Creek barbecue. Chose a table with a view of the parking lot.

"You don't want to sit on the creek?" the waitress asked them.

Charlotte looked out the back of the restaurant. A dense wood ran along the opposite shoreline of the creek. Excellent concealment for a sniper.

"This is fine," she said.

"Sunny day for a change, it's pretty out on the creek."

Charlotte shook her head, and she and Parker turned their attention to the parking lot.

"Suit yourself."

The waitress shrugged and left them with menus and ice water.

Parker said, "Why the hell would a handyman try to kill my dad? That's just jailhouse bullshit. Standingdog trying to pin it on somebody else."

"He said it was Jeremiah plus another guy," Charlotte said. "The guy running the show got away. Maybe Mr. Big was Uncle Mike. Two brothers working together."

"Absurd. Uncle Mike was my father's closest friend, like a brother."

"You were fifteen years old. Were you that good at reading adult dynamics?"

"It's jailhouse bullshit, Charlotte. It's meaningless. He confessed to the whole thing at the goddamn trial."

"So Standingdog did it. Everyone else in the universe is innocent, but he's your one exception."

"Standingdog hated Dad. He was poisoning the community against the camp. He was a violent man who beat his own daughter because she was dating a Monroe. He organized that boycott, sabotaged equipment around camp. He wanted to drive us out of there."

"Because he believed the land was sacred."

"Hell, every square inch up here is sacred. Some Cherokee event happened anywhere you look. Standingdog hated my dad for owning a chunk of his homeland, a man who knew more about his past than he did himself. He hated my dad, hated my whole family. There's always men like him keeping alive some ancient hatred. The white invaders, the poor exploited Cherokees. Oh, it was Standingdog. Not some handyman and his mysterious boss."

They stared out the window, watching the cars come and go.

TWENTY-SEVEN

JOAN CRAWFORD THOUGHT THE WHOLE setup was pretty shabby. The tiny camper with the duck-your-head ceiling, the half-assed Kmart dinnerware, the food, my God the food, who can eat Vienna sausages and Cheez Doodles? Forget the crappy nutrition and all that sodium, how can you get those horrible things past your taste buds, come on, Gracey, were you born without a gag reflex?

Joan was critical of the whole thing, even Gracey's decision to run away from home. It surprised her to find Joan throwing in with her mother. A girl shouldn't go off on her own into the world until she'd sorted out the essential issues with her parents. Fathers, too. Though mothers mattered most.

And Barbara Stanwyck had been there off and on last night, whispering in her ear, hottie things about how Gracey could go about seducing Spielberg. He's talking to you, yeah, he's interested, but to push him over the top, you got to do something extra, go that extra sexy mile.

First thing was to ditch that blue top, find a sweater a size too small, show him what God gave you, girl, there's nothing to be ashamed of. You got it, flaunt it. How else you going to get ahead? You think it's about talent? Gimme a break. It's about sweaters, deary. It's about shapely calves and uplift bras and it's about a thing you need to work on in your eyes, a certain light, a knowing glance, a waywardness you got to stand in front of the mirror and practice.

The eyes, honey, the eyes were what the camera looked at, that light shining inside them, that sneaky, flirty, come hither, but don't hurt me too bad, you big brute thing. That's what she needed. Look at a mirror, work on it. You think this shit comes natural? Maybe for the women on Mars, but not you and me, kid. It's work. It's practice and ambition.

Gracey had been off her meds for three days, or was it four? Who could remember? It was late afternoon, she thought, getting close to time to meet her mom and dad. At least she thought it was late afternoon. There weren't any clocks in the camper, and she'd left her watch behind in Miami.

Ever since Gracey'd arrived the night before, Lucy didn't want to talk much. She just lay on her bunk looking out the window, and fiddling with her pistol.

Gracey didn't know anything about them. Mom would know the make and model, all about it. Her dad knew guns, too. One of his clients had probably used a gun just like it to kill somebody, and now the guy was back in school, or at his job like nothing happened. Which was okay. If her dad got somebody off, then he was innocent. A jury said so, so there. Forget it. But the gun Lucy had was lying right out on the table where anybody could see it.

Not like guns at her house. Gracey wouldn't know where to look if she needed one, maybe a closet, or a drawer, but they were probably locked up somewhere, knowing her mom.

Lucy had it sitting on the little fold-down table. The pistol sitting there when Lucy wasn't cleaning it or loading it or unloading it. Like she couldn't make up her mind now that Gracey was around, was it more dangerous to have it loaded or unloaded, her being a kid? Gracey said something to her about it.

"I'm not afraid of guns. I've shot them."

And Lucy came back with, "That's a good thing. You might need to do that again. But shooting at a beer can isn't the same as between the eyes."

Getting all testy, like Gracey had stepped over the line somehow. Not even knowing a line was there. Like at home with her mother. Lines everywhere, always pissing her mother off about some damn thing.

Gracey spent that first night before she fell asleep babbling to Lucy about her meeting with Jacob. So exhausted from her bus trip, but also so hyper she wasn't sure why she was saying what she did. Blab, blab for an hour in the dark, not sure if Lucy was awake or not. Telling her what she and Jacob talked about in Miami, the thing Jacob said about her skin looking softer than a marshmallow. Which all happened before she knew Jacob was her half brother and made him officially off-limits as boyfriend material.

But she told Lucy anyway to see if she got a jealous twinkle, so Gracey could find out what the deal was. Was Lucy his girlfriend, his sister, or what? Gracey could've come right out and asked, but it seemed stupid. Are you his girlfriend? It seemed so high school and now that she was out in the world with adults, she totally didn't want to seem high school.

Last night in the dark, when Gracey finished talking, Lucy said nothing. Maybe asleep. So she just shut up and went to sleep herself and in the morning there was bacon frying and eggs and coffee. So they sat and ate breakfast with the gun between them on the table, loaded, unloaded, Gracey couldn't tell.

"He's my son."

Gracey was looking out the window swallowing some toast and wasn't sure who said it. Joan Crawford? Barbara? More like something Barbara would say, that juicy, saucy way she had.

"Jacob's my son, in case you were wondering."

Gracey turned from the window and looked at this dark woman in the green sweatshirt and wheat jeans. Her hair pulled back in a teensy ponytail.

"Your son, really?"

"In case you were curious."

"So that means you and my dad? You were like boyfriend-girlfriend?"

"Like that, yes."

"Wow. So you could've been my mother."

"But I'm not." Lucy got up and started cleaning off the plates even though Gracey wasn't finished.

"I'm sorry, I didn't mean . . ."

She wasn't sure what she was sorry about or what she'd meant in the first place. And she didn't know why Lucy started scrubbing the dishes, then swung around and picked up the pistol and set it on the counter beside her.

And that was the last thing Lucy said the rest of the day.

Gracey spent all morning being bored. She had her cell phone, but had no one she wanted to call. Another cell phone sat on the unmade bed where Lucy slept.

But nothing else to amuse herself with. Browsing through Lucy's teensy bookshelf but finding only books on Cherokee Indians. All of them about the same thing. Family-tree stuff, with lines connecting one name to another, branches running down the page. Booooring. Indians reading about Indians, how weird was that? And it was weird to Joan Crawford, too.

I was up for an Indian part once, she told Gracey. They wanted me to wear this getup, Howard Hughes, he had this deep-cut blouse made by his wardrobe people, and I said to him, honey, for you in private maybe I'd wear that rag, but when I'm in front of the camera I'm an actress, not a slut. There isn't an Indian alive would be caught dead in this outfit.

So she didn't get the job, Howard Hughes chose somebody else, some unknown with big knockers, a fresh girl he wanted to screw. That's what Joan said, out there in Hollywood it was all sour grapes and blowing smoke and sex, everyone hiring somebody they wanted to screw, then, when they'd screwed them, they fired them and hired somebody new, a different kind of screwing. But the whole deal with Howard gave her a bad taste about Indians in general.

That's how Joan was, everything had to be about her. Ranting about tidbits, gossip, things behind the scenes. Nothing classy like you'd imagine from looking at her.

Like right out of the book Mr. Underwood had them read for class this semester, *Hollywood Behind Closed Doors*. All the dirt. To get them ready for the business side of things, show them it wasn't all glamour and art. It was casting couches, too. Same things Joan was saying.

And then Steven was back, faint at first, voice far away, but clearly him.

Gracey lay still on the bunk and closed her eyes and listened. Indians weren't going to work in the movie he had in mind. He wanted to do a modern noir, an urban, down-and-dirty street film. That's what was happening now. Back-alley tough guys with Kevlar skin and rottweiler girlfriends.

Hard-edged action. A moody and passionate protagonist, like Bogart in *Maltese Falcon,* an antihero. Only speed up the pace. Bing, bing, bing, something happening every second, like MTV, flash, next image, flash, next and next. Zipping here and there like city traffic. Not this syrup-slow pace of the mountains. Man, that was like watching a glacier move. Who was going to go out on Saturday night and pay to watch Indians sitting around in pint-size campers eating Vienna sausages?

We need more movement, more gritty reality. Look where your mass audience lives, in L.A., Manhattan, Boston, D.C., in four-room apartments with a couple of yellowing plants in the corner, horns honking down on the street, sirens wailing all hours of the night, car alarms going off. Nobody wants all this green mountains and birds and sky and streams rushing. Big deal. It was like so hokey. So long ago and far away.

Gracey saw his point. She'd been bored all day waiting for Jacob Panther to show up. He was supposed to be there by now. Lucy was fretting, with a strained look on her face, angry, impatient, ready to go.

Steven told Gracey she should get up and stir things up. Get the blood flying. She was acting like a prisoner who'd surrendered to her captors. Plot an escape, for godsakes. Hatch a plan, a clever scheme. Let him see her act a little.

Enough of this passive, thumb-sucking stuff. Make something happen. Cause and effect. Get the hell moving, head back to Miami, where things were hip and edgy. This whole Indian-in-the-woods thing was never going to fly.

Lucy's cell phone rang then and she rolled over and picked it up and looked at the caller ID but didn't answer. It rang a few more times, then Lucy pressed the Answer button, then clicked it off without saying a word.

"Was that Jacob?"

"No," Lucy said.

"Who was it?"

Lucy frowned, like who-did-she-think-she-was-asking-personal-stuff-like-that?

"Come on. Who am I going to tell?"

"A friend of mine," Lucy said. "Woman named Nancy Feather."

"How come you cut her off?"

"It's our all-clear sign. Now you can stop with the questions."

Lucy lay back on her bunk and stared up at the ceiling.

"Isn't it time to see my dad at the barbecue place?"

"We're waiting for Jacob."

"Well, where is he?"

"I told you, he's stealing a car. He's down in Asheville picking out something good. Dark windows, big engine."

"What? You planning on making your getaway?"

"Maybe," Lucy said.

"How long does it take to steal a car? Could be he's in trouble. Maybe you should call him, see if he needs help."

Lucy sighed.

"Why'd you want my dad to come up here anyway? What could he do?"

"We thought he was a big-deal lawyer. He had clout."

"He *is* a big deal. He's on TV all the time, because he gets people out of trouble. He's got plenty of clout. And he's smart."

"Hasn't been so far," Lucy said. "Seems a little slow."

"That's not true. Dad's amazing. He never loses a case."

"He's losing this one."

"Are you a criminal, too? Like Jacob?"

Lucy drew a couple of breaths, then said, "Yeah, I guess I am."

"There a reward for your capture?"

Lucy stared at her but didn't say anything.

"I bet there is. I bet it's a lot, too. Maybe I should turn you in, buy a nice car with the reward money. A BMW or something."

After that Lucy shut up and wouldn't respond to any more of Gracey's questions. So she shut up, too. Angry at herself that she'd misunderstood Jacob's words to her. Angry she'd come all this way, suffered through that bus ride from hell, and for what? Because she thought Jacob wanted her, that they had a spark between them. But all he'd wanted was to use Gracey's dad for his attorney, get some cheap legal advice. Jesus, she felt like bawling. But she didn't, she held on, clamping her teeth, concentrated on fighting back the tears.

A while later a car drove up to the campsite.

Lucy jumped down from the bunk, grabbed her pistol, peered out the window, then set the pistol down.

A chunky Indian woman got out of a little beat-up Hyundai with plastic bags of groceries in each hand. Tight black jeans and a green shirt that showed off her plump body. Short black hair and a pug nose. She brought the groceries inside, and Lucy introduced her. Nancy Feather. Nancy said hello, then said to Lucy in a rush, "Farris has been asking about me."

"Asking what?"

"At work," Nancy said. "He came to the office and talked to Julius and Jacqueline heard through the wall and told me. He asked Julius if I did Martin's travel plans. He knows, Lucy."

"You weren't followed, right?"

Nancy looked over her shoulder out into the muddy campground.

"No, no. I was careful. Like usual."

Lucy thanked her for the groceries and told her she should go. It was probably better they didn't meet for a while. Gracey could see Nancy was sad about it, but understood.

"Farris is a bloodhound," Nancy said.

"If he comes to talk to you, just act normal. You and I used to be friends, but you don't have any idea where I am. You can lie, Nancy, can't you?"

"Sure, I can lie. I been married, haven't I?"

The two women shared a smile and hugged and Lucy walked with her back to the car. Gracey thought she could see tears in Nancy Feather's eyes.

Then Steven was in her head again, telling her to get busy. Take charge, make something happen. Remember, bing, bing, bing. Get the hell out of the mountains and back to the city. That's where the action was. The grit, the grime, the tawdry underbelly. The angst and existential misery of urban culture.

Okay, okay.

So while Lucy and Nancy Feather said their good-byes, Gracey picked up her cell and dialed.

TWENTY-EIGHT

THEIR BARBECUE SANDWICHES ARRIVED A couple of minutes after they ordered them, accompanied by dishes of coleslaw and heaps of French fries. The food grew cold on their plates while they stared out at the parking lot.

After twenty minutes the waitress came back and asked if anything was wrong with their food.

"Food's fine," Charlotte said. "Just having a serious conversation."

"Well, I'll scoot, then. You shout out, you need anything." The waitress gave Charlotte a sympathetic smile. Damn these men.

It was almost five when Parker got up. He needed to stretch, he said, his feet were going to sleep. He wandered the deserted restaurant, reading the headlines inside the newspaper vending machine, glancing at the mass-produced Indian artwork, then studying the bulletin board by the front door.

Charlotte watched him for a while, then stirred the cold French fries with her fingertip and turned her eyes back to the parking lot. Slow afternoon at the barbecue joint. A young couple with three noisy kids sat outside along the creek. Otherwise, the place was empty.

She forced herself to draw a complete breath. Let it out slowly and did that again. She roamed her memory for a prayer, some incantation that might attract God's mercy. But nothing came. As a teenager she'd been a

Baptist for a month, a Presbyterian for two. Trying it out at fourteen to see if religion might be an escape from the hellhole of her mother's double-wide trailer and the whiskey-driven men endlessly coming and going. Neither religion had taken root. What she had instead was fifteen years of police procedure and her philosophy lifted from the forest floor. Helpful enough for day-to-day functioning, but not much use as solace.

"You sure you heard her right?" Parker said. "Five P.M. today?"

"I got it right," Charlotte said. "Apparently her plans changed."

It was almost six when the waitress came over and took their plates and asked if they'd like some pecan pie or ice cream.

Parker shook his head and the waitress gave Charlotte another commiserating glance. The crap we women had to endure.

When the waitress was gone, Charlotte said, "She's not coming."

The words ached in her throat. But they needed saying.

"Yeah," Parker said. "I'm afraid you're right."

Charlotte told him she had to use the john and scooted from the booth and located the restrooms down a long shadowy hallway.

She locked the door and in the bathroom mirror gave herself a thorough look. It'd been forever since she'd turned her critical eye to her own expression. The face she saw in the mirror was a train wreck of emotions. The heavy eyes and sagging cheeks of despair, a repressed fury pinching her brow, twitches at the corner of her mouth signaling her helpless dread.

She ran the tap and cupped a handful of water and splashed her face. Far colder than Miami water ever was. She rubbed away the last traces of her makeup, then scooped another handful and dropped her face into her hands and kept it there, let the frigid water numb her flesh.

With her head bowed, she felt a tremor in her gut working upward.

She shook the water away and pressed her palms flat to the wall on either side of the mirror, and brought up the hot bulge that had been growing in her bowels for days. It rose into her chest and filled her throat, then broke from her mouth in rumbling sobs. Her eyes burned, and she was suddenly lost in the weeping, hands against the wall, feet back, hips pressing the sink like a suspect being frisked.

She let it come. Her only child lost. Her own abilities in doubt. Her faltering love for Parker. The daily agony she'd witnessed on the city streets for years. All the losses, the regrets whirled together. But it was Gracey's face she saw inside the storm of weeping. Gracey's face at ten, before the diagnosis and the drugs and the voices in her head. A birthday party at the beach at Key Biscayne. Balloons and kids and a magician. Gracey smiling. Gracey innocent and smart and full of fun. And the magic white doves that appeared from the top hat and exploded into flight, lofting into a perfect ocean sky.

Gracey's scream of delight.

Charlotte let it have its way. Purging everything she'd so faithfully stored up, years of fitting edge against edge, the neat parcels of grief. Always room for one more. And one more on top of that. They broke from her throat like that flock of white doves, sob after sob.

From far away, inside her weeping, she heard the trill of a phone.

She blinked the tears away and listened. For a moment she was lost. Like waking to a strange room, having to track back through the hours, reconstruct the route she'd taken to this moment.

She blew her nose in the towels, wadded them, dropped them in the hamper, and plucked the cell phone from her backpack and flicked it open.

"Mom?"

"Oh, God. Where are you, sweetie?"

"I'm ready to go back to Miami," she said. "Steven thinks it's best. This Indian stuff is so hokey. The mountains, the slow pace. It's not filmic. It just won't work."

"Oh, Gracey," Charlotte said. "Are you okay?"

The connection felt so fragile, her daughter's throaty voice was solid in her ear, but she didn't trust the filmy web of electrons bouncing around the unstable atmosphere, those erratic peaks and valleys.

"Jacob didn't want me anyway," Gracey said. "He wanted Dad."

"Just tell me where you are, honey, and we'll come get you right now. Just give me a landmark, anything."

"There's guns lying around. Right out in the open. Like any minute there could be a shoot-out or something. Which bothers me, you know, makes me nervous, then Joan, she's been after me to check in and tell you I'm okay, but it wasn't till Steven went off about Miami and how much better it would be for the film if we were back there, you know, that's why I called. So you can come get me now. Or I'll call Earl. He'll do it. Earl was nice. You remember Earl, right? No, you don't know Earl, do you? That was just me alone in his truck. Right? Just me and Earl."

It was the scattered, hyper way she got when she'd been off her meds and was beginning to stagger toward chaos.

"Gracey, okay, now listen. Just give me some idea where you are, and Dad and I'll be there as quick as we can."

On Gracey's end there was noise in the background, a door slamming, then an adult's angry voice.

The phone rattled, and Gracey squealed as if she'd been struck. Charlotte called out her daughter's name, but all she could hear was a muffled voice behind the covered mouthpiece.

Then a woman's voice spoke in her ear, "Who the hell is this?"

"This is Gracey's mother. What're you doing with my daughter?"

The silence lasted for several heartbeats, then as Charlotte was summoning her hard-ass cop voice, the woman spoke.

"Where are you and Parker staying?"

Charlotte hesitated a second too long, and the woman said, "You want your goddamn daughter back or not?"

"The Holiday Inn on Route Nineteen."

"Tomorrow sometime," the woman said. "And if there's any sign of cops around, or FBI, or anything that looks a bit strange, forget it. That clear?"

"I want her now, goddamn it."

"Tomorrow."

"Jesus Christ, what're you doing with her?"

"She showed up at my door, and I took her in, okay? Just be there tomorrow."

"Is this Lucy Panther?"

For almost half a minute Charlotte listened to the woman breathing. Then the connection broke.

TWENTY-NINE

IT WAS DARK NOW, AND from his vantage point across the parking he had a perfect sight line on Room 118. He was in a dead zone behind a defunct motel next to the Holiday Inn.

To his immediate right was a Dumpster and a yard away to his left was a white church van that appeared to be abandoned. Two of its tires were flat, and the front windshield was broken out.

In front of him, the security lights of the Holiday Inn illuminated the parking lot, but the yellow halo faded to shadows by the time it reached his position. He was standing in almost total darkness, and would fire into a brightly lit arena.

His rifle was a variant of the MSG90 outfitted with several custom features, including a threaded muzzle that wore a screw-on silencer and a low-signature flash hider. Although in the past he had never fired the weapon in such close quarters, the sound suppressor functioned admirably, so once he had made his shots, all he had to do was walk briskly for twenty paces until he was beyond the corner of the building where he'd parked the stolen car.

It was a quarter to eight, and the lamps were on in the Monroes' room. He saw figures moving behind the curtains. For a while he tracked their shadows through his light-gathering sight, moving the barrel smoothly inches to the left, then inches to the right. His hands so steady, the crosshairs showed only the slightest quiver.

From such close range, making the shots would be a near certainty. The Heckler & Koch MSG90 had a five-round magazine and was outfitted with a Hensoldt telescopic sight. Equipment that was far more sophisticated than his current needs required.

He lay his backup magazine on a ledge of the Dumpster. Ten shots to achieve his purpose. This time nothing would interfere.

"We're going to be late," Parker said. "If you miss the first ten minutes of this play, you miss Hernando de Soto and some great plumed helmets and blunderbusses."

"You seem pretty blasé."

"I'm just repressing, Charlotte. Putting one foot in front of the other, just like you. I don't see we have a lot of choice in the matter."

Charlotte made one last uninterested pass with her lip liner, gave her hair a final scrunch, then stepped into the bedroom.

As Parker reached for the doorknob, the motel phone rang.

He sighed, marched over and snapped it up, listened for a moment, said, "Okay," then set the receiver back.

"Front desk," he said. "An envelope addressed to you. They're sending somebody around. It'll just be a minute."

Charlotte perched on the edge of the bed and stared at the blank TV. The jangle in her veins was so loud she could barely form a coherent thought.

She realized now that she should've handled the phone call with Gracey differently. Not attacked Lucy Panther. If she'd used her negotiating skills, played it calm, Gracey might be with them now.

Her goddamn instincts were failing her. Or maybe she'd just been kidding herself all along about her abilities. She'd totally misread Frank Sheffield, not seen the con job he was pulling with his tracking device. Her first impression of Uncle Mike had been grossly distorted by her impatience and escalating irritation. And then she'd blown it with Lucy Panther—letting her emotions override years of training.

The discipline and control she prided herself on were unraveling. Her so-called gift for reading faces struck her now as a fraud. Some statistical accident that Fedderman had misinterpreted as genius. She was an imposter. Put her under stress and her skills vanished.

When the knock on the door came, Charlotte pushed herself to her feet and joined Parker. The ground seemed to be buckling beneath her, the first seismic tremors as the plates shifted far below the earth. A forewarning that the ground was about to split apart and swallow her and all those she loved. But Charlotte's faith in her own intuition was so badly shaken, she ignored that needle jiggling against the graph paper, that shiver in the concrete beneath her feet. She followed Parker out the door.

At first his mind would not accept the reality of what he was witnessing. He watched with growing alarm through his telescopic sight as the day manager of the Holiday Inn, Myra Rockhill, rounded the far corner of the building and came striding down the sidewalk, then stopped outside Room 118 and knocked.

Myra was six feet tall and nine months pregnant. Word around town was that she was having triplets. With her massive body obscuring the doorway, he lowered his rifle for a moment to make certain his eyesight was working properly.

The door immediately opened, and Charlotte and Parker Monroe stepped into view.

He caught the rest of the action through his sight, but managed only fleeting glimpses of his targets as the pregnant colossus handed Charlotte Monroe a white envelope, then spoke briefly to her.

Despite the startling event, he managed to hold his emotions in check, for he was certain a clear shot was approaching.

But instead of walking back down the sidewalk in the direction she'd come, Myra, the gargantuan, must have just gone off duty, for she took a path that headed directly toward his own position, crossing the parking lot with long strides, and effectively blocking his view of the Monroes as they entered their car.

Flattening his back against the Dumpster, he hid his rifle behind his leg and watched the woman proceed in his direction. As she came closer, he inched backward, deeper into the shadows, but still visible from the parking lot, where the woman reached into her purse and drew out her car keys and chirped the alarm on her pickup. Its headlights flared and trapped him in their beams.

He staggered back behind the Dumpster, dragging the Heckler & Koch, and only at the last second did he remember the additional magazine clip he'd left behind.

Peeking around the edge of the Dumpster, he watched Myra Rockhill struggle into her truck and start the engine, then sit for a moment with a cell phone at her ear. Clamping the phone in place with her shoulder, the woman lit a cigarette, then put the vehicle in reverse and backed out of the space. When she was safely out of sight, he reached back and snatched the extra clip.

The entire affair unfolded in less than half a minute, yet he was badly shaken. His hands rattled and his throat burned with each breath. His plan had been foiled by a sequence of the sheerest coincidences. As he stood in the darkness, composing himself, the only consolation he could muster was that the Monroes had not been carrying suitcases, so in all likelihood they would be returning sometime later that evening.

All was not lost. His quarry had merely gone out for dinner or a movie or some other form of rustic entertainment. They would return.

Parker handed Charlotte the envelope and she ripped it open and glanced at the business card. Then she switched on the map light and read the scribbled note on the back.

"What?" Parker said.

"Sheffield. He wants me to call him."

"What is it?"

"Doesn't say."

"So go ahead, use the cell."

"The jerk can wait."

They parked outside the amphitheater, bought their tickets, and prowled the theater gift shop for a few minutes, then bought programs and made their way down the aisle to seats near the front.

A group of spirited college kids in Western costumes warmed up the crowd with American show tunes and gospel.

By the time the drama began, the outdoor theater was only a quarter filled. Maybe five hundred people. A decent crowd in most auditoriums, but that cavernous arena felt empty. A natural valley surrounded by woods, with the spring night damp. Some faint stars showing in a chilly sky.

The nightly performances of *Unto These Hills* had once been the largest tourist draw in that part of the state. Fifty years earlier, in a simpler, more moralistic age, the play's sappy treatment of the Cherokee's history would have been solid dramatic fare, and it still seemed to please the crowd around her, though to Charlotte the play's tragic mood and overblown message had little bite in the current age of greater horrors and catastrophes.

The story was simple and familiar. The white man barged into paradise, and almost overnight the innocence of the Cherokee was destroyed. Their nation was portrayed as more advanced and civilized than those of their Native American neighbors, and their people far more enlightened than their conquerors. Cherokee leaders were temperate and blessed with unfailing wisdom.

And finally, an hour into the play, there was Tsali's story.

Isolated on his farm in a remote valley, Tsali and his family of five lived a simple, idyllic life, until that day when the soldiers rode in and took them prisoners, marched them off toward a stockade where the others of their tribe were being assembled for their long trek west to Oklahoma. But when one of the soldiers used his bayonet to hurry up Tsali's wife, wounding her, it set off a fierce struggle that resulted in two dead soldiers. The other two escaped.

Fleeing into the mountains, Tsali and his family hid in a tiny cave. For weeks dozens of soldiers combed the dense forests without finding a trace.

But Tsali's mutinous behavior could not be tolerated. The army was determined to take whatever measures were necessary to capture the Cherokee and make an example of him. An entire regiment was sent into the mountains to seek the fugitives.

Weeks passed, but every effort failed. As winter approached, the U.S. Army circulated an offer among the remaining Cherokees. If Tsali could be convinced to emerge from hiding and give himself up to execution, the few hundred Cherokees still living in the western Carolina mountains would be free to remain in their homeland.

Learning of the proposal, Tsali spent days in deliberation. At last he and his family came down from their hiding place and turned themselves over to the military. Tsali and all but his youngest son and wife were placed before a firing squad and shot dead.

Despite all its sentimental excess, Charlotte was caught off guard by the story. Maybe she was a sucker for altruism, or maybe it was just the strain from Gracey's absence, but as Tsali gave up his life, Charlotte found she had to rub a finger hard across the bridge of her nose to keep the tears from flowing.

"So?" Parker said, on their way up the aisle. "You see anything?"

"I need to take a look at that gift shop again," she said.

"What is it?"

"Give me a minute. I'm mulling, okay?"

While Parker looked idly at Cherokee knickknacks, Charlotte prowled the two shelves of books. She skipped the kids' stories and oversize illustrated volumes and concentrated on the handful of academic studies, chapbooks, and pamphlets. She paged through the shop's complete collection, then chose four that struck her as having potential and took them to the checkout.

"What's going on?" Parker stood beside her as she counted out the bills and got her change.

"Uncle Mike said there were two sides to every story."

"Yeah? So what are they?"

"The conquered and the conqueror."

"It wasn't about the soldiers. They were the bad guys."

"They probably didn't think so."

"Okay, so I'm blind. I don't know what the hell you're talking about."

"Give me a minute."

Back inside the car, Charlotte switched on her map light and started paging through one of the pamphlets. *A Brief History of Tsali* by Dr. Julie Milford.

Parker found a restaurant still open, and they squeezed into a booth and ordered salads. When they arrived, the salads were nothing but iceberg lettuce topped with a pound of shredded cheese, and tomato slices that looked like fried rubber. Parker nibbled at his and drank coffee, and Charlotte pushed hers aside and continued to read.

Parker picked up one of the books and fanned through the pages.

"Minute's up. Spill it, Charlotte."

Without looking up from her booklet, she said, "I'm wondering who they were, those soldiers, where they came from. Their families."

"Why?"

"It's the other story," she said. "The one they didn't tell."

Charlotte turned the page and skimmed the next one.

Parker took a bite of one of the dinner rolls, then set it aside.

"Okay, here's something," Charlotte said. "A contrary opinion."

Parker shut his pamphlet and fiddled with his salad while she read.

" 'Current thinking among most scholars is that Tsali did not give himself up to execution as the popular myth describes. More likely he was betrayed by his own people. After the removal had begun, many Cherokees remaining in the mountainous areas believed that Tsali's murderous behavior would bring down the Army's wrath on them, so they voluntarily hunted down Tsali and his family and turned him over to the U.S. military for execution. Most of these Cherokees had already made private covenants with the government to stay in North Carolina. Contrary to the widely held view, Tsali wasn't their savior at all. He was simply a renegade who threatened their own exclusive arrangements.' "

"Big deal," Parker said. "That's how historians make their reputations, debunking previous views."

Charlotte got back to her book. Ten minutes later, as Parker was finishing his salad, she found a passage that punched the breath from her lungs.

"Oh, shit," she said.

Parker drained the last of his coffee and pushed the mug forward.

"This is a narrative account of Tsali's capture and the killings. Same author as the other one." Charlotte read the sentence slowly. " 'On October 19, 1838, two U.S. soldiers were struck down by Tsali and his sons. Corporal Morgan Jessups and his superior officer, Sergeant Matthew Tribue.' "

The waitress reappeared to fill their mugs. They were silent till she was gone.

Parker took the pamphlet from Charlotte and read it for himself.

"Holy Mother of Christ."

She looked around the restaurant to see if anybody was paying them any attention. No one was. She eased the booklet from Parker and found her place.

"A couple of pages farther on, there's this. 'After Sergeant Tribue's death, Molly, his wife, who was pregnant with their first child, having no family or means of support, fell into poverty and was forced to suffer a life in sordid circumstances. As tragic as Molly Tribue's existence was, later generations of the Tribue family managed to transcend these destitute beginnings and gain major prominence, making great social and economic contributions to their communities and their nation.'"

"So it's a puff piece for the congressman. Among other things."

"I'm interested in those 'sordid circumstances,'" Charlotte said.

"Maybe a saloon girl, something like that."

Charlotte slid the pamphlet across to Parker. It was opened to a page that showed a black-and-white oval miniature portrait of Molly Tribue. She had curly hair and a fleshy face and pouty lips.

"Not your decorous church lady," she said. "More like a strumpet."

He flipped through the pages for several minutes, working his way to the end. He read for a moment, then handed the book back to Charlotte.

"The bio," he said. "Did you see it?"

It was a few sentences about Professor Milford's academic background, followed by a brief acknowledgment of gratitude. Undergraduate degree from Emory University with a master's and Ph.D. from Duke in American history. The professor was now affiliated with Asheville Women's College as the executive director of the Tribue Institute, whose generous sponsorship by Roberta Tribue provided both time and other forms of support necessary to complete the research for this book.

"Which one is Roberta?" Parker said.

"I don't know. But apparently the Tribues have their own vanity press."

Charlotte flipped to the last page, the list of Milford's other publications.

"*Tracing Your Cherokee Roots,*" she said. "Also by Dr. Julie Milford and also published by Tribue Institute."

"That's what we legal types call a nexus. Tsali, Tribue, Cherokee ancestors. Some serious overlapping with our own concerns."

"We flatfoots call it suspicious."

"So we have a family who appear to be the ancestors of the soldier Tsali killed. The Tribues apparently govern this little corner of the universe, but they're getting knocked off one by one. Martin, Uncle Mike. And these are the same people who have singled out Jacob Panther as their target, the fall guy for some kind of insurance swindle."

"I don't know, Parker. The insurance thing, it doesn't fit."

"Money always fits. It's the great motivator. The everlasting why."

"Not this time," she said. "Think about it. That ax was chosen for a reason that had nothing to do with money. Why go to the trouble to steal a murder weapon from a museum unless it was to send a message? That ax is about history. About something that happened a long time ago. This is about Tsali and the man he killed. I don't know where we fit, or how Jacob enters the picture, but we're closing in on that part. I feel it."

"The way your mind works," he said, "so tidy and rational, you could make a damn fine attorney, Charlotte."

She closed the pamphlet and laid her hand over it like it might fly away.

"I believe we already have all the lawyers we can handle in this family."

The smile they shared at that moment seemed imported directly from the old days, when their connection was unshakable and everything was effortless and clear.

THIRTY

GRACEY AND LUCY PANTHER SAT in a white Lincoln in the shadowy parking lot of the Holiday Inn, waiting for Jacob to return to the car.

Lucy was behind the wheel, with Gracey huddled in the backseat listening to Steven Spielberg going over the entire movie scene by scene.

While Steven brainstormed, changing things on the fly like he did, Gracey was speechless, honored he'd try out something as important as this on her before putting it down in a script.

Steven was more excited than she'd heard him before.

This was going to be a major departure for him. No more goody-goody E.T.-phone-home bullshit. Forget dinosaurs or sharks gobbling people down, this film was going to make all that look like a Goldilocks tea party.

This was going to be edgy and mean and hot, and Gracey was going to be right in the thick of it. A teenage femme fatale swept up in a complicated plot with lowlife bad guys the likes of which the film industry had never seen. Forget *Maltese Falcon, Body Heat, Scarface,* Joan Crawford's *Sudden Fear.*

This was going to be violent, dark, and dangerous, but very hip, smart, cool, full of dissonance. She knew about dissonance, didn't she? Of course, Gracey told him. Mr. Underwood did a whole class on it last semester. It was like when your teeth didn't line up right. Things grated, got off center, weird, over the top. Like when someone was about to die with an avalanche coming down on top of them and they were making ironic jokes.

Close enough, Steven said. So what did she think? She'd seen *Scarface,* right?

Over and over, Gracey said. It was on Mr. Underwood's top-ten list.

Good, so there's your model. Michelle Pfeiffer, that icy blonde look, eyes way out there on the horizon. Coasting above it all, but talons ready.

Barbara Stanwyck whispered to Gracey. That Pfeiffer bitch, she stole me blind from *Double Indemnity*. Everything but my ankle bracelet.

I have an idea, Gracey said. What if instead of the femme fatale thing, which is done to death, the girl in the movie is a schizophrenic?

What, like nuts? A split personality?

Not nuts, Gracey had to tell him. And multiple personality disorder is something else completely. Schizophrenics are a whole different ball game. They hear voices, can't tell what's real from what's not sometimes. Though sometimes they can act just fine, get by, nobody knows what's going on.

Never work, Spielberg said.

And this little schizophrenic girl, Gracey said, she goes through the whole movie and everybody thinks, poor girl, she's all screwed up, but it turns out, bingo, she sees things more clearly than anybody else and solves the whole deal, and is, you know, kind of redeemed in the end.

Steven was silent, considering it or fuming. You could never tell with him.

Gracey knew redemption was uncool. It was one of Mr. Underwood's pet peeves. He was always mocking movies with epiphanies. Where somebody found peace or landed on a new planet of understanding.

But the truth was, Gracey kind of liked them. She liked to believe people could hack their way through the jungle and come at last to a sunny beach, transformed. She never admitted it out loud, but she liked those movies. They made her cry, gave her hope. But she knew they were totally unhip. Usually she kept quiet about it or scoffed at what she secretly loved.

Fuck redemption, Steven said. Fuck redemption and the lame horse it rode in on.

I could maybe live with a troubled teen, Spielberg said. But a schizoid, no, that's over the top. Too extreme. Mainstream audiences, no way, unless it's the bad guy. Psychotic bad guy, that could work. But a teenage girl, no, it's too much. Too much of a downer. Bleak, depressing.

So Gracey just shut up.

Truth was, she had major doubts about the whole project, the story line, so complicated, so many twists. Not to mention there was way way way too much gore for her taste. More Tarantino than *Maltese Falcon* or *Sudden Fear*. Very graphic, slice and dice, shotguns blowing people inside out. Bullyboy writing, one tough guy getting in another tough guy's face, backing him down. Motherfucker this, motherfucker that.

It wasn't like Gracey was into girly-girl romantic comedies, and she wasn't prudish, but all the guns bothered her, all the people murdering each other without any good reason, blink-you're-dead, and Gracey's character was caught in the middle of everything, also for no reason she could see. Young girl put at risk. Like nothing had changed in a hundred years since virgins were lashed to train tracks with the locomotive bearing down.

Gathering her nerve, Gracey went ahead and told Steven about her doubts. Did it in a quiet way, trying to sound adult, not be sarcastic or super critical. Not wanting to hurt his feelings, but she told him the truth, that the whole thing lacked heart. Where were the people to care about? The story was just a lot of sharp knives and shotgun blasts and bad guys going after badder guys. Had he forgotten about normal people? It made her brain numb. None of the characters mattered. They could've been hand puppets.

And then, with all due respect and everything, there was an even bigger problem. The nudity thing. Half the time Gracey's character is on screen, she's topless, or else totally naked. Just like she'd told Steven she wouldn't do.

She couldn't believe he'd gone ahead and put it in, like she didn't have a say, or he hadn't cared about her feelings. Well, she might be just starting out in her acting career, but she had her values.

Sure you do, kid, Barbara Stanwyck told her. Stick to your guns. Show as much tit as you're comfortable with. Or none at all. I mean, hell, a little cleavage can be sexier than the whole enchilada. And then Joan chimed in with, didn't I tell you this was going to happen? I saw it coming from the

232

start. This business never changes. Actresses come and go, but it's always about tight flesh and sex appeal. Nipples, honey. They got to have their dose of hard little pinkies.

All of it was churning around and around in Gracey's head. She sat there waiting for Steven to say something, defend himself, convince her she was wrong. But he was silent. Doing the passive-aggressive thing.

Meanwhile, Lucy Panther wasn't saying a word, just sat staring ahead out the windshield of the big white Lincoln that Jacob stole in Asheville, and taking worried looks every now and then in the rearview mirror. Like Gracey had just cursed out loud, which maybe she had.

She wasn't sure. That's how it happened sometimes. That membrane started leaking, the one that was supposed to keep outside out and inside in. It got perforations in it and then what Gracey was thinking was sometimes coming out of her mouth and sometimes it wasn't.

Sometimes it stayed sealed up tight inside her brain, but from how Lucy kept frowning at her, Gracey figured she must be babbling.

But hell, how could she stop something she didn't even know for sure was happening?

Screw redemption, Spielberg said. Redemption is so last century. So faith-based bullshit, high-carb goofy. Irony is what's happening. Dark irony, human misery, the inherent corruption of the human spirit. You know about tragic irony, right, Gracey? I'm not talking to an uninformed little girl, am I?

"Are you okay?" Lucy Panther said from the front seat.

Gracey had to think about it for a few seconds, sorting through the voices, before she figured out it was Lucy.

"I'm okay, yeah, I'm fine. What's Jacob doing?"

"Don't worry about it."

"Who's worried? I'm just asking."

"He's doing a job," Lucy said. "It'll be finished in a minute or two."

"What job?"

"What he should've done in Miami if he hadn't gotten run off by your mother."

"Tell me."

"You sure you're okay? You're making noises like you're not right."

"You just figuring that out?" Gracey said. "Of course I'm not right. Who would want to be right in a screwed-up world like this?"

"Good point," Lucy said. "Very good point."

Then Spielberg was back, sounding grim. Telling her straight out that the nudity was absolutely essential to the plot. A girl tied up with all her clothes on was simply not the same thing as a girl tied up naked. The vulnerability, the pathos were totally different with the naked girl. The film's entire artistic integrity was at stake.

They all say that, Joan Crawford said. They been saying that since the Stone Age. Artistic integrity my ass. It's tits, pure and simple. I told you, Gracey, I told you how it was. You wouldn't listen.

Their parking space outside Room 118 was still vacant, and Parker eased in and shut off the ignition. They sat there for a moment. Parker seemed as exhausted as she was. They'd been working it over for the last hour but had gotten nowhere. Their situation was connected to Tsali and the Tribues. But the rest of it was a muddle. Bank bombings, insurance fraud, blowguns, axes, and a sniper in the woods. Jacob Panther, Martin Tribue, and Uncle Mike and Diana Monroe. They tried to wrestle the ingredients into some coherent tale, but there was no thread that seemed to weave it all together.

Finally, Charlotte shut off further discussion, saying there was only so much they could understand by sorting and re-sorting the data they already had. They were missing some crucial pieces. What they needed was to turn over some different damn rocks. Like this Milford woman for one thing, Asheville Women's College, pick her brains, And hear what Marie Salzedo and Parker's investigator, Miriam Cardoza, came back with.

Though she didn't admit it to Parker, Charlotte was still fixed on Standingdog's trial, the fire at Camp Tsali, Diana's status as a Beloved Woman. With growing certainty she felt that something happened the night Parker's father died that was central to what was unfolding now. But that part was all too raw for Parker to hash it out. So she kept silent on the issue.

"You all right?" she said. "That had to be rough on you back there, seeing Uncle Mike shot down. A guy you used to respect so much."

"Rough, no. Rough doesn't begin to cover it."

"You're feeling numb, spacey. Startle reflex on high alert."

He gave her a feeble grin.

"And you?"

"Ditto."

"So where's the tough cop?"

"Huddled up in here." Charlotte tapped on her sternum. "With a temporary case of the shakes. It'll pass."

He leaned over and kissed her on the lips. Drew away and smiled faintly. "We'll get Gracey back. I know we will."

She held his eyes and nodded, hoping he couldn't read her dread.

They were getting out of the car when Charlotte saw the man stalking across the parking lot. In the shadows she could tell he was medium height and thick-bodied, then he entered the light and she saw he'd trimmed his blond hair into a short military cut and dyed it dark, but even in the murkiness there was no mistaking that bone structure, those hard, probing eyes.

She drew her handgun and let her backpack fall to the ground.

The sulfur light gave his face an eerie sheen.

Parker yelled at her across the roof of the car to put her gun down. But she held her aim.

Panther's hands were hidden in the shadows at his side.

Charlotte ordered him to halt, to show his hands, but Jacob kept coming, fifteen steps away and closing fast with steady strides, his right hand drawing away from his belt and starting to rise, creases deepening in his forehead, jaw grinding, the desperate look of a man resolved to go down firing.

At his current pace, she had about ten seconds to decide.

She shouted again for him to stop, but he kept coming and his bleak look hardened in the orange light and his right hand rose swiftly and Charlotte caught the flash of silver in his palm, but held her fire, not positive what she'd seen, no longer trusting her own biased eyes, watching him, struggling to decode that face, that look, its potential for harm, until Jacob closed to within ten feet, just two, three seconds from the decision point, Charlotte feeling her finger tighten.

From somewhere behind Panther, she heard a hard snap like a chicken bone breaking in half, then Jacob Panther lunged. It was an awkward move, a half-stumble, but he came at her faster than a man off balance, like he was shoved from behind.

She checked his face in the last second before he was on top of her and it was fixed in some kind of otherworldly mix of agony and horror. In that instant she flashed on Fedderman's video of the state trooper who hadn't seen the machete blade coming. She was hesitating just as the trooper had, unwilling to accept the inevitable.

As Panther covered the final few yards between them, Charlotte heard another sharp crack from across the parking lot.

He was two steps away, coming fast, and Charlotte watched with disbelief as a bloom of meat and blood broke through Jacob's forehead. Her finger tensed reflexively and she put two rounds into Panther's chest. He whiplashed backward, then forward, throwing his arms outward as if he meant to embrace Charlotte in a last, reckless act of affection.

She heard screams from the motel behind her as she was driven to her knees under Jacob's weight, and more screams as she rolled his body away, and came up with her pistol swinging from side to side toward the darkness across the parking lot.

With another two snaps, the back window of the minivan exploded and a rear tire blew out. Another round whistled above her, and still another scraped a long gash across the Toyota's door only an arm's length away from Charlotte's head.

She returned fire, once, twice, raising sparks on the Dumpster. Ducking down, then coming up for a third shot.

At the first sound of gunfire, Gracey thought, Damn, Spielberg had started the movie without her. Doing it out of spite, just to put her in her place.

Gracey was opening her door to get out and run over and get in his face, when Lucy rammed the shifter into drive and gunned the big engine and went screeching forward. Gracey was thrown back into her seat and her door slammed shut.

A second later they were rounding the corner of the building, Gracey leaning forward to see Steven in his director's chair, the cameras set up, the light crew, the sound guys with their booms, all the others who were always on the movie sets, listed in the long roll of credits.

Peering out the windshield, she saw nothing but darkness, then the yellow flash of a pistol.

Lucy roared up to the back of a white car and slammed on the brakes. And there was Gracey's mother crouched down with a pistol in her hand, and her father lying flat on the sidewalk as the windows of cars exploded all around them. But Gracey wasn't sure. Was this real? Or was she seeing this because she'd been off her meds, somehow making this all happen inside her head and projecting it out on the world like her doctor said she did sometimes?

She stared out the side window and saw her brother, Jacob Panther, lying flat on his stomach, big ugly bullet wounds in the back of his head.

Lucy saw him, too, and moaned and just then the back window of the Lincoln exploded.

"Gracey!" her mother screamed. "Gracey, jump out, stay down. Jump out, sweetheart."

But Lucy floored it, tires screaming, and there was nothing to do but hang on.

"Here." Charlotte held out the Beretta. "Give me the car keys."

As Parker raised himself up from the sidewalk, behind them a motel-room window shattered.

"Don't be crazy, Charlotte. It's too dangerous."

"Give me the goddamn keys."

He dug them out and handed them over.

"You can defend yourself, right?"

He took the pistol and rose up to a squat.

"Damn right," he said.

"Keep him busy. All this gunfire, the sirens should be on their way."

Charlotte scrambled to the Toyota, got the door open and the engine started before the shooter noticed her. She reversed, spun the wheel, slipped it into drive and hammered the accelerator, head down. She heard the heavy thunk of two slugs hitting the passenger's side, but she was around the building a few seconds later.

The exit road made a long S before it reached the highway, and she could see across the bordering hedges that the Lincoln was already out on U.S. 19, traveling east. Only one shortcut she could see.

Charlotte cut the Toyota hard to the left, aimed through an open parking space between two vans, bounced over the curb and tore through the shrubs, and slid down a steep, grassy embankment to the highway.

Saved maybe a half a minute.

The two-lane highway was solid with traffic in both directions, but she flashed her lights, held down the horn and swerved in front of a delivery truck, and got the Toyota rolling east. About a half-mile behind the Lincoln. Only five or six cars separating them, no traffic lights for at least a mile. She mashed the gas and kept her hand on the horn and passed two dawdlers and had to slam the brakes for a semi that was stopped in front of her, making a left turn. Traffic was heavy from the opposite direction. No way to pass, so she cut right, bumped onto the rough shoulder, got a rear wheel caught over the lip of the ditch, spun on empty air for a second, then the tire grabbed, and she skidded back onto the road.

She could still see the Lincoln up ahead, caught in a slow stream of casino traffic. Passing three more cars, getting some angry honks, using her cutthroat Miami driving skills, Charlotte bulled ahead till there was only one car separating her from the Lincoln, maybe a hundred yards ahead.

As she pulled out to pass the final car, a pickup turned out of a side street into her path and Charlotte wrenched the car back into the right lane, but clipped a bumper on the pickup. The driver in front of her must've seen it all and, realizing Charlotte was out of control, pulled to the side to let her by.

She flattened it, flirting with eighty in a thirty zone and caught the Lincoln on the long straightaway just before town. Pumping her brakes in measured strokes, she closed the gap until she was riding the Lincoln's rear bumper.

In her headlights, Gracey was staring back at her. She was in the rear seat, talking fast, turning back to Lucy Panther, then looking out at Charlotte. Excited, but it was impossible to tell if she was angry or frightened or what. Impossible to know if she was actually speaking to Lucy or someone else, maybe one of those rowdy characters who populated her head.

Then a moment later her daughter was leaning out of the rear window with a pistol in her hand. Her lips were moving fast and her face was contorted, as if she were screaming curses. Had to be hallucinating, or maybe they had mistaken Charlotte for the sniper on their tail.

Gracey's hair was whipping in the wind, a long streamer of blond. She raised the pistol and aimed at the Toyota, wagging it back and forth as if trying to scare her off. Then her other hand came up to steady the weapon.

Charlotte cranked open her window and yelled out Gracey's name, but it had no effect. She flashed her brights, once, twice, three times. She caught a quick look of Gracey flinching and turning her head away, thinking at first the headlights had blinded her daughter, then realizing it was not that at all. Gracey was turning away, anticipating the concussion of the pistol shot.

As Charlotte nailed her brakes, her windshield exploded, and in the dazzling spray of glass she lost her grip on the wheel and the Toyota steered itself across the oncoming traffic, and she heard tires screaming but saw nothing for a moment as she slid sideways into a parking lot, spinning a full 360 and coming to a stop in front of a souvenir shop, where in her headlights a stuffed black bear stood on its hind legs, waving its giant paws at the chilly Carolina night.

THIRTY-ONE

WITH THE RIFLE PRESSED TO his right leg, he strolled back to his car, leaving the murder scene. He wasn't rattled as he'd been earlier in the evening, when Myra Rockhill blocked his shot. Nor was he disappointed by tonight's outcome. Even though the other targets had been arrayed before him briefly like a platter full of delectables, there was no profit in faulting himself for his mediocre shooting.

There would be time enough for the rest of them. Here in the mountains or back in Miami, or wherever on earth he had to go to finish the mission. He'd taken down Jacob Panther, and he'd had a decent shot at the Monroe girl, the crosshairs settling on the side of her pale face, but as he squeezed, he'd jiggled the weapon and missed. A little overexcited, perhaps.

But those jitters had passed, and now a satisfying peacefulness settled over him as he climbed into his car and headed back to the highway.

No hurry. Indeed, when he considered it more fully, it was actually preferable this way. One at a time, with breathers in between. A measured approach, no orgy of violence. Plant the seed of fear in each of them, let them marinate in dread, knowing he was coming ever closer. A nameless avenger.

At first he'd toyed with the idea of leaving notes. Words or phrases cut from newspapers. Or perhaps assume a titillating nickname. Taunt them and toy with them as the Hollywood villains did. But after a few moments' consideration he dismissed the idea. He was by nature and by choice a drab and simple man. Such gaudiness was not his way, not his personality.

Better to be as anonymous and invisible as the air.

Another good reason to draw out the cycle of killing for as long as possible was his mother. Because when his mission was completed, and the last of them was dead, then the wire strung tight inside his chest, the wire that had been droning for weeks, would slow its hum and finally cease to vibrate, and in the ensuing stillness his mother's voice would regain its prominence. Her shrill nagging. Every hour, every day.

Not that he didn't love his mother, or pine for her, or honor her in her afterlife, but her harsh voice, which rose inside him at night when the house grew quiet, when he was sinking away into sleep—well, if he was honest, that voice distressed him, put unmanly flutters in his pulse.

A year after her death, his mother continued to badger him over the pettiest issues. She was forever after him to keep the toilets spotless, scrub out the tubs and sinks, floss his teeth at least once a day, clear the dead rats from the traps in the barn, all the obsessive trivia that had constituted her own daily routine for seventy years, the endless chores that consumed her right to the end of her days, when she lay on her deathbed in cancerous agony, and finally as she stared into the remorseless eyes of her Maker, and issued her last commands to those surrounding her deathbed.

In her dying moments, his mother had revealed to him the true nature of his ancestry and the ruinous toxin that streamed through the family's veins, revelations that he'd had no inkling of previously. And it was those final words of hers that launched this deadly quest. Their echoes that drove him every hour.

But even in the very moments after the good woman passed along those weighty revelations, as she lay panting for breath, her next admonition, the last words she spoke, concerned the health of his teeth and gums.

As he drove along the highway, staying well under the speed limit, he still felt in the meat of his hands the pleasant throb from the Heckler & Koch. True, all but one of his shots were errant, yet a kill had been achieved. A kill that was as crucial as any of the others. His mother should be pleased.

It was when he stopped for a traffic light that he heard her voice, hardly more than a tickle of noise in his ear. Had he flossed after breakfast this morning? Had he?

No mention of his shooting. Just the flossing.

Had he?

Honestly, he couldn't remember if he had or not. A day so full as this one. A day of momentous actions. Deaths and escapes and near misses.

Plaque never stops growing, was her reply. It is always there. Always. Working below the gum line, eroding the solid bones. And the rattraps? Had he checked them today? Had he? Had he?

THIRTY-TWO

OUTSIDE THE MOTEL ROOM A dozen blue lights were flashing. Charlotte sat in the chair at the desk and stared at the wall. Parker and Sheffield had been pacing the room, asking her questions, where had she gone, how the hell did the car get shot up, but she'd not replied. Couldn't find the words. Her own daughter had come within inches of killing her.

She wanted to bawl. Wanted everyone to leave her alone so she could dig under the blankets and sob. But they kept after her with their questions until she turned in the chair and looked up at the two of them and said, "The asshole is stalking us, Sheffield—he had our motel room staked out."

"Okay," Sheffield said. "I'm willing to entertain that possibility."

"So who knew we were staying here?"

"Small town like this," said Sheffield. "The fry cook at the Waffle House probably knew."

"I don't think so, Frank. With all the feds coming and going, why would anybody notice us? No, there's only two people for sure who knew where Parker and I were."

"Me," Sheffield said. "That's one. So now I'm a suspect?"

"You and the sheriff. He was standing right beside you when we said the Holiday Inn."

Sheffield shook his head and waved his hands, enough already.

"The sheriff, Frank."

"Okay, okay, there's no denying our boy Farris is a little backwoods creepy. I give you that. But come on, Monroe, that doesn't make him a shooter. He's the law, for godsakes. What's his motivation? If he shoots down Panther, J. Edgar would rise from the dirt and pin a medal on him. He'd be on *Good Morning America,* talking to Charlie."

"He was after us, not Panther. Panther got in his way."

"Jesus Mother and Mary. I wish sometimes I'd done like my father wanted and gone into the ministry. Once a week, give a sermon, go home, and watch ESPN for six days straight. No hassles, no crackerjack cops to deal with."

Charlotte said, "I got a strong reaction to the guy, Frank. A very strong reaction."

"What? Like this Fedderman bullshit? Your Geiger counter clicking?"

"Go get him, Frank."

"So you can interrogate him?"

"So I can take another look at him."

"This may be Coral Gables PD procedure—hunches, gut instincts—but this isn't how we do things, Monroe. We like some shred of probable cause before we go off on somebody."

"I been taking your shit, Frank, since this started. Do me this, okay?"

"Jesus Christ."

When Frank was gone, Parker came over and sat near her on the edge of the bed. He held out his open hand.

"Jacob was holding this. It was on the pavement next to his hand. I'll give it to Sheffield if that's what you want."

Lying in Parker's palm was a heart-shaped silver locket.

She hesitated, but Parker extended it to her and she took it and flicked the locket open.

"I believe it's the woman from the pamphlet," he said. "Molly Tribue, wife of Sergeant Matthew Tribue."

It was a miniature portrait in muted colors, the work of some journeyman artist who must have traveled those hills almost two centuries earlier.

Charlotte studied the woman with the chubby face, the tightly curled hair, the promiscuous grin.

She snapped the locket shut and handed it back to Parker.

"Your call," he said. "Give it to Sheffield?"

"Put it in your pocket."

He nodded.

"When Jacob was coming toward me, I saw something in his hand. A flash of silver. I thought it was a knife or gun. But it was that locket."

"You weren't sure, so you held your fire. That's how you're trained."

"I choked."

"Look, you waited till the last possible second. And, Charlotte, he was already dead when you shot him. I watched it happen."

"I froze," she said. "I read his face, believed he was dangerous, but I didn't shoot until he was almost on top of me."

"You're all knotted up. Thinking too much. And give yourself a break. Jacob wasn't just a random suspect. He was my son. Of course you hesitated."

"Still," she said. "My training. My instincts."

"Tell me what happened, Charlotte, when you were chasing Lucy."

She shook her head.

"Not now."

"Knock, knock," Sheffield said from the doorway. He waited a second, then said, "Sheriff Tribue has a couple of questions for you, Officer Monroe, if you'd be so kind. About the shooting. His people are giving us an assist."

Charlotte rose and Parker followed her to the door. Outside on the sidewalk they stood for a moment or two watching the techs work. Flanked by the two large poodles, Farris Tribue walked toward them across the parking lot.

"Those dogs go with him everywhere?" Charlotte asked Frank.

"Hey, it's a different world up here, Monroe."

"So I've noticed."

Touching the brim of his hat, Farris gave Parker and Charlotte a nod.

"Again," he said. "I express my deep regret."

"We gave our statement to Sheffield," Charlotte said. The prickling on her shoulders had begun again. "But if there's anything else."

"I would be intrigued, Ms. Monroe," Tribue said, "to have your professional estimation of the shooter. Since you experienced his abilities firsthand."

"Yeah, Monroe," Sheffield said, with a droll look. "Give us your professional estimation of the shooter."

She stared off at the Dumpster.

"He's an amateur," she said. "And he got rattled."

The sheriff took off his hat and wiped the inner band.

"And how do you draw that conclusion?"

"Guy puts Panther down with the first two shots, then started spraying rounds all over the place. Same as this afternoon. Is the guy just a bad shot? Or maybe he's some kind of gutless nutcase? He panics, then unloads his whole clip. I don't know. But my bet is, when you do the ballistics, you'll find the shooter tonight is the same freak who killed your uncle."

The sheriff set his hat back in place. He looked at Charlotte, his eyes smoldering briefly, then fading like the glow of a lightning bug.

Sheffield rubbed at the gray stubble on his chin. He was looking haggard, the mountain air not treating him well. He hadn't been getting his eight hours, maybe a few too many rum-and-Cokes to knock himself out in the evening. Droopy lids, a slump in his shoulders, a downward slide in his mouth. Gravity winning this week's tug-of-war.

"So the gunman's not a master criminal," Frank said. "Thirty years on the job, I still haven't met one of those yet."

"From what I can surmise," Sheriff Tribue said, "it was a bit chaotic at the time. If indeed that was the case, it strikes me as doubtful that even the most proficient marksman would have scored well in such fluid circumstances."

"You're sticking up for the guy?" Sheffield said.

"I'm hypothesizing," Farris said. "I believe it's referred to as playing devil's advocate."

"Chaos or not," Charlotte said. "Given the bad shooting after Panther went down, you can't even be sure Jacob was his real target."

The two poodles sat down on the pavement behind the sheriff. Both of them looking at Charlotte as if they sensed something about her, some threat.

"So, big deal, the guy's a moron." Sheffield gave her a sly look, having fun with this, then turning back to Tribue to see how the sheriff would come back.

"Moron?" the sheriff said. "Why would his intelligence be at issue?"

"I don't mean dumb, just sloppy."

The sheriff turned his eyes toward the Dumpster.

Sheffield said, "So you satisfied, Monroe?"

"One more thing, Sheriff," she said. "Who is Roberta?"

The name stunned him. His jaw muscles loosened, eyes slid sideways toward the dark, and a vein in his temple rose like a blue worm to the surface.

"Why do you ask?"

"Roberta Tribue," Charlotte said. "Do you know her?"

Farris brought his eyes back from the darkness. The earlier emotion had drained away, and now his eyebrows were drawn close and his eyes had clenched and his lips puckered with restrained rage.

"Roberta Tribue was my mother. She died a year ago. Where did you hear her name?"

"Oh, I came across a pamphlet in a local bookstore that mentioned her. I understand she was something of a philanthropist."

"You apparently have the wrong Roberta. My mother was as parsimonious as a stone. I doubt she spent a hundred dollars in her lifetime."

"I'm mistaken, then."

Sheffield looked back and forth between Charlotte and the sheriff, then cleared his throat.

"Look," he said. "I know this is in poor taste, but truth be known, whoever the shooter was, I frankly don't give a rat's ass what his motives were. Far as I'm concerned, the asshole performed a valuable public service. He should be pursued and arrested and prosecuted to the fullest extent of the law, yeah, yeah. But personally, just from this federal agent's point of view, I'm glad the dead guy's out of action."

"Amen," Tribue said.

"For chrissakes, Frank," Parker said. "You can't take five minutes off from being an asshole?"

Frank bowed his head and raised an open hand as if he were swearing off glib remarks forever.

The four of them were quiet for a while, watching the tech guys down on all fours scouring the asphalt.

Charlotte caught Farris glaring at her with open contempt. That spike of rage at the mention of his mother's name was clear enough. But there was something else about him she was having trouble naming. Something gawky and incongruous, like an ill-fitting suit. Or maybe it was like that movie Gracey enjoyed so much, where the ten-year-old kid wakes up one morning to find himself in a body three times his natural age. Moving through the rest of the film in a clumsy Frankenstein walk.

"You sent me a note, Frank—what was that about?"

"Oh, that. It was nothing really. A guy was asking some questions about Parker and you, I wanted to give you a heads-up."

"What guy?"

Sheriff Tribue had turned his face toward his forensics people, but she could see his attention had not strayed from their talk.

"County chief of police over in Murphy. Guy named Brody Maxwell, he wanted to ream somebody a new asshole. I think that's how he put it."

"Why?"

"Seems a friend of yours at Gables PD, a Marie Salzedo, called his office today, started bullying one of his secretaries about some police report Panther supposedly filed last year."

"Marie doesn't bully people," Parker said.

"Miami manners, then," Sheffield said. "A little culture clash. In any case, this guy Maxwell had a bug up his ass and wanted to yell at somebody, so I thought I better give you the caution flag. He doesn't like out-of-town cops and their lawyer husbands running investigations in his neighborhood."

"What crime was Panther reporting?"

"It was bullshit."

"What was it, Frank?"

"Brody wasn't giving out lots of detail, but it was some loony horseshit about a murder conspiracy going on forever, somebody killing Cherokees. Unexplained disappearances. That kind of thing. Total wackjob."

"Ah, yes," the sheriff said, drifting back into their circle. He had his hat off again, fingering away sweat from his brim. "My department receives that same report on a regular basis. Naturally we treat each one with the utmost seriousness, though they clearly spring from the deeply superstitious nature of the Cherokee people. 'Please help me, Sheriff Tribue, my Uncle Joe disappeared, and we believe he's a victim of the ancient campaign against our people.' And then, more often than not, a week later we locate Uncle Joe sleeping off a two-week drunk in the Atlanta county jail. Personally, I believe the outbreaks may be related to the lunar cycle."

The sheriff attempted a smile.

"Don't you just love getting out of Miami," Sheffield said. "All this funky local color."

"It's my daily reality," the sheriff said with a meager grin. "To live among people who believe the wings of giant buzzards created the mountains and valleys."

"You mean they didn't?" Sheffield said.

By the time the parking lot was clear of law enforcement, it was four in the morning. Parker took a long time in the bathroom, then finally lay down in the dark beside her.

"It's not too late. We could move to an inside hallway. It'd be safer."

"This is fine," Charlotte said. "He's not coming back."

He was quiet for a while. Charlotte stared up at an orange stripe on the dark ceiling. The security lights sneaking around the curtain's edge.

"Are you all right?"

He touched her shoulder, stroked her bare flesh.

"I'm fine," she said. "Considering."

Parker shifted beside her, raised himself up on an elbow, and brought his lips to hers. They completed the ritual kiss. A few seconds longer than usual.

She lay flat on her back, staring up at nothing.

Parker's voice was quiet in the dark.

"I was terrified out there. I was frightened out of my skin."

"Yeah, so was I."

"And Jacob. That must have been horrible. Dying in your arms."

"He's your son, Parker. You're the one I'm worried about."

"Don't be." He was quiet. She wondered for a moment if he was going to cry again. But when he spoke into the darkness, his voice was firm. "You and Gracey are my family. Biology by itself doesn't make someone a father. I didn't know the kid. I mean, let's face it, someone can't just walk into your life out of the blue and make claims on your emotions. It's not possible."

It sounded like high-grade bullshit to Charlotte. Trying to argue himself out of the grief before it had a chance to take root. But who was she to argue? It was Parker's call. His way of dealing.

Charlotte lay still and waited for him to pronounce the other name. But when he didn't, she whispered a question to him.

"And seeing Lucy again? How difficult was that?"

He lay still for a moment as if he were picturing her. Charlotte had only seen her for a few frenzied seconds, but her impression was vivid. Lucy Panther was not as exotic as she'd imagined. She had a well-structured face and flawless skin and lush lips, but it was her eyes, their dark primal energy, that set her in a class apart from the merely beautiful. A woman who could stir men in ways Charlotte could only guess.

Parker rolled onto his side, the sheets rustling around him, and he reached out beneath the covers and touched her bare upper arm. Keeping his voice low, he said, "The memories came back, yeah. But I was a fifteen-year-old kid. The world was simple. The feelings I had for Lucy were simple, too."

"Nothing's simple anymore."

"No, it's not."

His hand roamed up her arm, smoothing his palm lightly across her skin, but she halted it with her own.

"I was wrong about Jacob," she said. "He meant us no harm. He was coming here to explain things. The locket. Show-and-tell."

"I know," he said.

"And when he was done, they were going to hand over Gracey."

"That's my guess, too," he said.

"Lucy will bring her back tomorrow. She'll find a way."

"I think she will, yes. I think you're right."

"Unless she believes it was me who shot her son."

"She knows it wasn't you. She probably knows who it was, and that's what she and Jacob were trying to tell us. Who it is, what it's about."

250

"So we'll stay around here tomorrow and wait. Just sit in the room where she can find us."

"I think that's our only choice."

She released Parker's hand and reached out and drew his face to hers. And though she would never have believed it could happen, the day's horrors fell away as their kiss lengthened, and all the accumulated grief and uncertainty and frustration gave their hunger an urgency it hadn't had in years. Even with the name of Lucy Panther hovering over them.

The jealousy she'd felt for Lucy had been stupid, sophomoric. Everyone was the product of all the loves they'd known, all they'd lost and still hungered for. Knowing Parker's secret, his long-ago passion for that young girl gave a new dimension to this man she loved, and even if some part of Parker's desire for Charlotte was seasoned by his memories of Lucy Panther, it mattered not at all.

They came together with such fierce need that within seconds Charlotte lost touch with the disastrous day. His hands moved across her flesh lightly but with the craving of someone starved for human touch. The exact pressure and pace she longed for and that he had always been so adept at providing. But something more this time, something that seemed to spring from deeper within, as if their mutual need to obliterate the images in their heads, erase the bloody visions, had stripped away years of habit and restraint.

Sweaty and struggling for breath, they reached that familiar place together, then gradually they went beyond it to another altitude, a place where light and air and gravity dropped away entirely.

THIRTY-THREE

IT WAS NINE ON FRIDAY, a sunny morning, the lawn glistening with dew, and in the Hensoldt telescopic sight of the Heckler & Koch, Congressman Otis Tribue's head was magnified so vividly that Farris could make out three dark hairs sprouting from the tip of his right ear.

Farris stood in his mother's bedroom, aiming out the open front window, sighting on his father's skull as Otis Tribue worked his way through a bucket of golf balls, driving them off the cliff edge into Raven's Gorge—showing off his manly swing for Shannon Muldowny.

One after the other the white orbs arced upward, then stalled and plunged into the steep valley, disappearing a half-mile below into the scrub pines and boulders.

The cliff edge where his father stood was fifty yards across the broad green lawn from the front of the Tribue home. Built eighty years before, the house was a brick two-story with eight white columns and a majestic front porch. A sunny, many-windowed dwelling with gleaming maple floors and elegantly detailed banisters and filigreed trim throughout. Lush views from every window stretched for miles. It was in that airy house Farris and Martin had been born and several generations of Tribues before them took their first and last breaths.

Adjusting his sight an inch to the right, Farris captured Shannon's pale blond hair in his lens. He centered the crosshairs on her thin, arching neck, the upper knobs of her spine. Shannon was a year younger than Farris, with a boyish build and shoulder-length hair and crisp blue eyes. A Boston native, Shannon had spent the last twenty years in single-minded devotion to the political career of Otis Tribue. Somewhere along the way Otis promoted her from his chief of staff to his full-time concubine, a nubile, city-bred replacement for Roberta Tribue, Otis's lawful wife and Farris's beloved mother.

Never legally divorced, Otis resided in Georgetown and ventured back to his home district only to campaign for reelection. It had been well over a year since Farris last saw the old man, though Otis was rarely out of his thoughts.

Farris despised the two of them—as much for their betrayal of his mother as for their current indiscreet displays of affection. That they would fondle and steal kisses on this land where Roberta's dying wails still echoed was an unforgivable blasphemy.

During the long torture of his mother's dying, as the tumor sprouted its poisonous vines inside her, her husband, the esteemed congressman, paid not a single visit, nor had he once inquired by phone about her condition.

So cold was he to his estranged wife and so complete was his removal from family life that when Roberta died, Otis did not even make an appearance at her funeral, though four dozen white roses were sent in his name, a bouquet that in a fit of rage his brother Martin promptly carted outside and pitched over the edge of Raven's Gorge at almost the very spot where Otis Tribue stood at this moment, teeing up another ball and driving it out into that green abyss.

With two curls of his fingers, Farris Tribue could remedy this portion of his torment, and send the two of them pitching over the cliff. Their bodies would free-fall for half a mile and vanish into the pine and rocks below. Farris was confident the corpses of the two sinners would never be discovered. The canyon was so steep and impenetrable that, as far as Farris knew, no living soul had ever attempted to rappel its walls. Positioned as it was, almost dead center in the three hundred acres the Tribue family owned, it was as secure a dumping ground as any place on earth.

Out on the cliff edge, Otis handed Shannon the driver and she took her turn, teeing up a ball, setting her feet, and swinging with clumsy enthusiasm.

Through the sight, Farris watched as Otis stood behind her, smoothing a vain hand across his healthy mane. In a Washington salon it was tinted twice a month to the shade of a man thirty years younger. No doubt Shannon had canvassed a thousand registered voters to choose that exact hue.

Farris lowered his aim a fraction and lined up the crosshairs, his finger tightening against the trigger just as Shannon was taking a backswing. Timing the shot with her downstroke, Farris fired his weapon a half-second before the club head reached its nadir. With the highly effective sound suppressor, the blast was reduced to no more than a gentle clap of hands.

At Shannon Muldowny's feet the white ball disintegrated on the tee. With its sudden disappearance, the young woman's club whiffed through the air, and in her shock and loss of balance she staggered forward toward the precipice.

Otis Tribue stabbed out his hand and grabbed his mistress's arm and held her at the teetering edge, one of his cherished drivers slipping from her grip and disappearing into the chasm.

Farris stepped away from the window and lay the rifle on his mother's deathbed. Her quiet voice resounding in his ear, a chuckle of approval.

He had another use in mind for these two. Something far more inspired than a bullet through the skull.

Yesterday, when his father had arrived, he advised Farris that he'd scheduled his return to Washington in two days.

There was to be a quick, public funeral for his murdered son, then a couple of speeches to local VFW and Rotarian groups, a chance to bask in the pity of his constituents, and he would be off.

So Farris could bide his time at least for a little while. And though it was tempting to send the tumbling slug exploding into the old man's brain, Farris wanted his father to linger in some degree of pain approaching, if possible, what his own wife had suffered.

For Shannon Muldowny, Farris had another treat in mind. Retribution that perfectly matched her crimes.

Such brutish thinking was new to Farris. For all of his adult years he had lived a life of moral rectitude, abiding by the same law he enforced. It was only recently that he had discovered a profound and fundamental truth at odds with all he'd once believed. When a man's heart has been completely hollowed out by bereavement and he has made his unwavering pledge to follow those he loved into the endless hereafter, all one's petty worries and moral restraints evaporated.

With his mother gone, his cherished brother torn from him as well, Farris had lost forever the dual tethers that had anchored him to the practice of principled behavior. And what was left after those losses? His only remaining blood relations were a grimly defective son and a father who wallowed in self-indulgence.

There was no hope for Farris, no future he imagined or desired. Love was lost to him, joy of any kind had flown beyond his grasp. The ghastly knowledge his mother had given him in her last moments had seen to that. Farris Tribue had discovered himself to be a man poisoned by circumstance and history. For all these years, without his knowledge, a dark curse had festered in his blood. A silent worm gorging on his bowels.

But along with that dire knowledge came a liberation beyond any he might have imagined. He was now free to do and say whatever he would. Untroubled by inner commandments or the petty rules of law he was sworn by his profession to uphold. Emancipated of all earthly obligations.

Yet as emboldened as he was by his willingness to depart this world, he was nonetheless still dedicated to discipline and stealth. For he wanted to leave this earth with maximum effect. At a time and place of his choosing, he would pull down the pillars of the temple so when it collapsed around him, it would take as many of the guilty as possible.

"That's your idea of a joke, Farris? Shooting at your own father and his guest. What the hell is wrong with you, boy?"

Otis Tribue met Farris at the bottom of the porch stairs, armed with a nine iron.

Shannon Muldowny hung back a dozen feet, her flesh a deathly pale.

255

Gray trousers and a pink silk top, a sprinkling of gold and diamonds at her wrist and throat. Urban finery that was as grossly out of place in that rough country as she was herself.

"Amusing you, Father, was the last thing on my mind."

At the hostile tone of Farris's voice, his two white poodles roused themselves from their slumber in the damp grass nearby and approached the group. Shannon gave the dogs a nervous look—as well she should.

"You owe Shannon an apology, Farris. She'll take it now."

Farris's lips formed a smile, and he gave the woman a cold and empty nod.

"I raised a heathen," Otis said, and waved his hand as if dispersing a foul gas.

"Any raising that was done around here, sir, was accomplished by a woman ten times your equal."

"I can see this was a grave mistake," his father said. "We'll be moving to a motel in town, so as not to intrude on your tender sensibilities."

His father turned toward the porch.

"I know your secrets, old man."

Otis halted and came around slowly.

His father's mouth twitched, but his eyes remained dull and vacant. The politician in him could will his face to play a host of tricks.

"I saw you speaking to Parker Monroe yesterday. That must have aroused some poignant memories."

"I don't know what your game is, boy, but I'm not having any of it."

"Did you realize, Father, that Parker Monroe is married now to a police officer named Charlotte? They have a daughter who is sixteen and apparently suffers from psychological instability. Now, isn't that ironic? Wouldn't you say, Father? Very ironic."

"This conversation is at an end."

"I know everything, Father. Every last secret."

Otis blinked, then turned to stare out at the rim of the gorge.

"Your mother told you wild stories."

"Wild, perhaps, but completely credible."

"Your mother lived in the foul dust of the past."

"You may try to wave this all aside, Father, like a puff of smoke. But it can't be done. Whether we're mindful of it or not, our history lingers about us. Some of us taste it in every breath."

"Horseshit. We're two centuries removed from all that nonsense."

Shannon stared at the two men, her fine-boned face tightened into puzzlement.

"When you're ready to discuss this, Father, you know where to find me."

Farris turned away and the two dogs trooped behind him to their work zone, where Farris and Martin had long ago erected a mannequin that they used as the dogs' target. Today the effigy was dressed in blue-jean overalls and a white shirt and baseball hat.

Some years earlier, it had been Martin's idea to train attack dogs. He cast about for weeks before settling on that particular breed. Martin found it amusing to be a breeder of poodles.

With their white coiled fur, expressive eyes, and long, narrow snouts, they appeared deceptively harmless. A deception, Martin liked to say, that just might prove useful one day.

After a regimen of rigorous schooling and highly selective breeding, Martin corrected the poodles' passive streak until this current crop of canines was every bit as fierce as any pit bull. Though Farris was slow to warm to the enterprise, eventually he came around, and now that Martin was gone, the dogs quickly transferred their loyalty to him.

Outwardly the pair was quiet and subdued. Visitors to his home rarely noticed the difference between his dogs and ordinary poodles. They relaxed around the canines, admired their poignant brown eyes and their soft coats, which were scented of freshly mown hay. And the dogs displayed a fondness for humans, licking faces, nuzzling. But all that folderol would cease in a heartbeat if Farris commanded the dogs otherwise.

On that early June morning, with Otis and his whore looking on, Farris retrieved the dummy's head, replaced it on the slender neck, wedging the ravaged fiberglass skull back into its slot, then reset the baseball hat at a jaunty angle. With a hand sledge Farris fixed the mannequin's feet to the soft earth with stakes. To knock the target over, the dogs had to be moving at a decent clip and then leap high, throwing themselves in tandem against the chest.

While Otis and Shannon huddled on the porch, whispering amid sips of morning coffee, Farris led the dogs across the lawn so he was in full view of the front porch.

Farris commanded them to sit and they obeyed promptly, with their eyes fixed on Farris's every move.

For a signal, Martin had long ago settled on a simple salute. The inside edge of his right hand raised to his forehead and chopped forward a few inches in the direction of the target.

Now, as Farris raised his hand, the two animals quivered with excitement. After holding them for a few moments more, Farris sent his salute toward the dummy, and the dogs broke into casual lopes across the grass, just as they had been trained, no snarl, nothing savage in their demeanor to arouse suspicion or alarm, no sign that this was an attack until it was too late.

When the poodles reached the mannequin, they sprang in unison, high and hard, and knocked the dummy flat. Then the dogs heaved forward and fastened their jaws onto the throat and face and shook their heads from side to side. Five seconds, ten at most, and it was concluded. The mannequin's head broke loose and spun away across the grass and lodged against the base of a sugar maple. The dogs trotted away from the decapitated dummy and lay down to lounge beneath the white, quivering blossoms of a dogwood tree.

"I wonder about your mental health, Farris," Otis called.

Farris stood for a moment, holding his father's stony gaze.

"Are you ready to discuss this matter, sir?"

Otis spoke a few words to Shannon and stood. He was wearing black jeans and a blue work shirt and boat shoes, the attire of a man who labored at appearing more youthful than he was.

Otis joined him on the lawn, and they strolled in silence toward the cliff edge. The congressman still clutched his nine iron in one hand and swung it idly, clipping the tips of the grass and beheading dandelions.

When they were safely out of Shannon's hearing, Farris halted and looked out at the distant mountain ranges. The sweet green zest of spring was spreading across the peaks. Two hawks coasted high over the adjacent valley. On another day earlier in his life, Farris might have drawn in a lungful of that unsullied breeze and absorbed a strong dose of vitality from it. But now the endless spread of wilderness that stretched before him was a lifeless canvas, flat and dull and devoid of interest. Nature's redemptive power, which had always sustained Farris in his darker moments, had lost its sway.

Farris turned his gaze from the miles of green and looked into his father's dark eyes.

"My question to you, sir, is this. Why did you leave it to our mother to inform us of our condition? Did you lack the courage, Father?"

Otis sighed and dodged Farris's eyes and shook his head sadly as if these were words he'd long dreaded.

"You left your children in ignorance of their damaged state. You told us nothing about our birthright. If it weren't for Mother's last-minute confession, Martin and I would never have known. How could you do that, Father? What possible reason did you have for hiding such a thing? Letting me marry without forewarning, bring my boy Shelley into the world. Was it cowardice?"

His father took another small swing at the tips of grass, and Farris reached out and twisted the golf club from his father's grasp and tossed it into the yard. The poodles came to attention, focused on Farris's hands.

Otis composed his face, though his cheeks darkened with fury.

"You should ask yourself, Farris, what your mother's motives were in telling her outrageous stories. That woman devoted herself to keeping the embers of blame and guilt constantly aglow, searching always for scapegoats for her many complaints. Eventually I found it unendurable, but I had the good grace to wait till you and Martin were mature adults before departing. That wasn't easy, knowing how close you were to the woman, risking the loss of my boys. But I could endure her no longer. Although her condition was never diagnosed, I believe the woman was unbalanced in some fundamental way."

"Stop it," Farris said. "I won't hear your slurs. I'll strike you down where you stand."

Otis Tribue took a measuring look into his son's eyes, then his gaze shied away toward the cliff edge, where his golf club lay in the grass.

Farris said, "Mother informed us of what you did, Father. The botched job you made of it. I know every detail of that fateful evening. In fact, it is the lingering aftereffects of your failed exploit that caused my brother's murder. You may deny it all you want, old man, but the past haunts us still. And now it is left to me alone to finish what you failed at."

"No, Farris. You must not do this. It's not true. She lied to you."

"It's true, all right. I have the proof. My damaged son, a brother murdered. I have all the proof I need to finish what you so poorly began."

He burned the old man with a final look, then marched over to the fallen mannequin and wrenched it from its moorings and hoisted the dummy over his shoulder and carried it thirty yards to the lip of Raven's Gorge and heaved it over.

He stepped close to the rocky edge, and leaned forward to follow its flight until it crashed into the boulders and scrub pines a half-mile below. For several years the mannequin had served its purpose well, but it was now time to test the dogs on more challenging quarry.

THIRTY-FOUR

CHARLOTTE WOKE WITH A JERK at five that morning. Another dream of detached heads. These were floating bodiless in the air. And this time they were all jabbering at once, ridiculing her, cursing her ignorance, screaming at the pain she had caused them, or crying out in ecstasy as if to mock her pleasure of the night before.

She lay there for a while, staring up at the dark ceiling, and knew she would not be able to slide back into sleep. While Parker continued to snore, she rose quietly and dug her laptop from her bag and plugged it into the phone line.

She accessed her e-mail, then used the link Marie Salzedo sent her to retrieve the trial transcript from the North Carolina archives. Charles Andrew Monroe's murder, the fire at Camp Tsali.

On the slow phone line it took several minutes to download the thirty-page document of supporting material Marie managed to sweet-talk from the State Bureau of Investigation. Police reports, autopsy files, even some handwritten notes of the detectives working the case that had been scanned and added to the electronic file.

Parker woke just as Charlotte was filling the last of her legal pad with notes. When he came out of the bathroom, he asked if she'd had any luck.

"I got a few things, yeah. Not quite finished."

"I'll go get coffee, maybe call Miriam on my cell, see what she has."

"Good plan."

He was back in fifteen minutes with two black coffees. He set one beside Charlotte's laptop.

"Done yet?"

She nodded that she was.

"I got a little from Miriam. Who goes first?"

Charlotte straightened her notes.

"You," she said.

He cleared his throat and reset his shoulders the way he did when he was about to make a summation before the jury.

"A year ago, about this time, something major happened. Something that set this whole thing off."

She took a sip of the scalding java and set it down.

"I'm listening."

"Last June, Lucy Panther was teaching her class at the tribal school, and Jacob was working in Cox's sawmill a few miles from here. He'd been on the job for over ten years, ever since he graduated high school, already promoted to assistant foreman. Making almost twenty thousand a year, which is a damn good wage around here. New pickup truck, renting a trailer not far from his mother's place. Had a few friends, dated some women. He'd had that one brush with the law. Stole a car, but that was years earlier, just out of high school. A kid thing. But otherwise, no sign of trouble in their lives. Then bam."

"The banks started blowing up," she said.

"Not exactly," he said. "First thing that happened, Lucy quit her job and Jacob walked away from his."

"Before the bombings?"

"Yeah, a month or two before. Left their homes, started moving around—motels, friends' apartments. Vagabonds. Something happened, they reacted. Then seven, eight weeks later the bombings started. It was during that period that Jacob filed that police report in Cherokee County. Not with the tribal police, mind you, but the county police chief. Like maybe he didn't trust Farris."

"Can't blame him."

"Miriam got the same story Sheriff Tribue was selling last night. This whole murder conspiracy thing is old news. People had been bugging the cops on and off with this stuff for years. Some kind of urban legend that crops up every so often, Cherokees being murdered in some kind of plot. Somebody gets a wild hair and runs off to the police and starts babbling."

"Where there's smoke," she said.

He nodded.

"So Lucy and her son were doing the good-citizen thing, living a normal life, then something happens, they go on the run, somewhere in there they take a shot at going to the cops for help, and get nowhere."

"Then the banks start blowing," she said. "And shortly thereafter the sheriff IDs Jacob for the crimes, and the entire U.S. Cavalry is chasing Jacob Panther."

Parker closed his eyes and ran it through a couple of times, then opened them again and shrugged.

"This isn't about banks and insurance fraud," she said.

"No, it's not."

"Something bigger. Something weirder."

"It's about Tsali, the camp, the Tribue family."

"That much we know."

"And you? What'd you dig up?"

She drew a breath. This wouldn't be easy.

"I did the trial," she said. "*People of North Carolina versus Standingdog Matthews.*"

"Jesus, Charlotte. You just can't let that go. Determined to prove he's innocent."

"He is, Parker. He didn't do it."

"You read the transcript and now you're certain. This I got to hear."

"First thing you should know—your dad didn't die from the fire."

"What?"

"He died of gunshot wounds. Same with Jeremiah Tribue. Gunshots."

"Bullshit."

"Gunshots, Parker."

"Impossible. You got the wrong transcript."

"Nope. I got the right one. *State of North Carolina versus Standingdog.*"

"Death by asphyxiation," he said. "Injuries they suffered in the fire."

"The Philpot kid, yes, that was his official cause of death, but not your dad. And not Tribue."

Parker stared down at the carpet, shaking his head.

"You were fifteen years old, sweetheart, in shock, you'd just lost your father, almost died yourself, and you didn't know anything about the law. It's not surprising you'd get things wrong."

"I remember every goddamn word, Charlotte. I don't have it wrong."

"Transcript's right here. Check it out if you want. You understand the technicalities better than I do."

He waved the thought away.

"Go on," he said. "But damn it, there were no guns mentioned in the trial, I was there."

"Well, that part you got right. The guns weren't mentioned because Standingdog wasn't being tried for your dad's death or Tribue's."

"Do that again?"

"Standingdog was on trial for the Philpot kid alone. He took a plea deal, put up no defense, and took life in prison, but it was for the fifteen-year-old kid. Not your dad or Jeremiah Tribue."

Parker stood up and did a quick turn around the room, then went back to his coffee, finished it off, and sunk into his chair.

"Because Philpot died of asphyxiation and there was lots of testimony about that, you probably assumed your dad's cause of death was the same. But it wasn't. They didn't even introduce it in Standingdog's trial."

Charlotte shut down her laptop and stood up.

"I'm assuming," she said, "the DA went with Philpot instead of your dad because they had an eyewitness. You might remember him, he was your cabinmate that summer. Jeremy Banks."

"Vaguely," Parker said. "Some prissy kid from Knoxville."

"DAs love eyewitnesses. Never mind that Jeremy was a fifteen-year-old boy, awakened from a dead sleep, in a dark cabin. He wore glasses but confessed he wasn't wearing them. And the abductor was in and out of the cabin in a second or two. Even with all that, the government still liked Philpot better than what they had with your dad and Tribue. A kid pointing his finger at Standingdog. It makes for such good theater. And hey, what's the worst that can happen? They lose the Philpot case, they could still indict Standingdog for your dad and Tribue. But as it turned out, they didn't need to."

"Where does the gun come in?"

"Not *gun*. *Guns*. Two different ones."

"Whoa, whoa."

"All of it's in the police reports, the coroner, medical examiner. It's all there. Go ahead and read it if you don't believe me."

"Just tell me."

"Your dad took two shots to the chest. Different weapon than the one used to kill Tribue."

"This is crazy. This is a whole different story."

"Exactly."

Parker bent forward in his chair, elbows on his knees.

"I know Dad had an old Colt he kept in his bedroom."

"That was the weapon used on Jeremiah Tribue, registered to your dad. The gun that killed your dad was a small caliber, probably a twenty-two. It wasn't found."

"All right, okay. So let's say Dad brought his Colt down. He wrestled with Standingdog, the gun goes off and kills Jeremiah Tribue, who'd come there to help put out the fire."

She shook her head.

"Listen to me, Parker. The only prints on the Colt were Diana's."

"No."

"It's all right here." She tapped the lid of her laptop.

Parker stared at the far wall for several long moments, breathing slow and deep, as though he might be shouldering large boulders of memory from one place to another, rearranging the foundations of his past.

Charlotte walked over, and moved behind him. She settled her hands onto his shoulders and began to massage. An old formula between them, a prelude to lovemaking on more than one occasion. Easing his tension, then easing toward the bed.

"Just go with this for a second, okay? Say Jeremiah and Mr. Big set the fire."

She dug her fingers into the tight muscles, kneading upward to the base of his neck.

"One of them has already grabbed the Philpot kid from your cot, mistaking Philpot for you, drags him over to the house and starts splashing kerosene around. They want to wipe out your family. So far it's the same story as yours, but with Tribue and Mr. Big instead of Standingdog.

"Your dad is upstairs, sleeping, he hears something, goes downstairs, sees the Philpot kid lying there, the fire going. Tribue is splashing his kerosene. But before Chief can do anything, Mr. Big shoots him."

Parker laid a hand on hers and stopped the massage.

"And Mother?"

"She hears the gunshot, grabs your dad's gun from the bedside table or wherever, runs down, starts firing. Kills Jeremiah and scares away Mr. Big. That's how the second weapon leaves the scene."

"And when did I come in?"

"I put it about now. Diana's up on the stairs, working on your dad, trying to revive him maybe, stop his bleeding. The flames are spreading fast, you walk in, the smoke's so thick you don't see the bodies. You head toward the stairs, beam falls, knocks you out. Diana hauls you outside to safety."

Parker ran through it for several moments before replying.

"Couldn't happen," he said. "Standingdog's attorney had access to all this. The two guns, Diana apparently using one, the other disappearing. All of it exculpatory or potentially so. But they didn't use any of it, didn't even try."

Charlotte finger-combed his sandy hair back in place, realigned his part.

"It's because of the plea deal, Parker. Standingdog pled to the Philpot murder, but wouldn't go along with a joint trial on the other two."

"No defense attorney worth two cents is going to let him take that deal."

"Maybe somebody else had Standingdog's ear. Telling him how to play it."

"No way," Parker said. "No DA's going to leave two murders dangling like that. Especially somebody like my dad. Well-known in the area."

"So they keep his file open," Charlotte said. "Happens all the time.

They wait for Standingdog to confess to somebody in prison, wham, they're back in court."

"They had enough to indict him then. I don't see why they'd wait, much less why they'd make any deals."

"You're the expert, Parker. But I've seen my share of trials. And this case looks too damn messy. Too many different facts. Diana's prints on one murder weapon, no sign of the second weapon. Most DAs I've met would be happy to take a deal like that. They got an eyewitness for Philpot, and they've got a strong motive for Standingdog. The DA gets to tell a simple story and Standingdog hangs. Everybody goes home happy."

"Okay, so why the hell would he go along? Standingdog pleads guilty, winds up sitting in prison the rest of his life for something he didn't do. What is he, some kind of masochist?"

"Maybe he's a martyr."

"Bullshit. The guy's no martyr."

Parker was shaking his head to all of it. In full-blown denial.

"When you described this Beloved Woman thing, Parker, you said one of her roles was to make life-and-death decisions. Thumbs up, thumbs down. Which prisoner was executed, which went free."

"That's ancient history, hundreds of years ago."

"I'm just brainstorming, Parker, trying to work with what's here."

"So what're you saying? Diana told Standingdog to take the fall? And he went along? That's ridiculous, Charlotte. Completely absurd. Why would he agree? What's in it for him? You didn't know the man. He was ruthless, mean. The man you saw the other day, dying in his wheelchair, that's not who he was when he was young. You're sentimentalizing the guy."

Charlotte smoothed her hands across his knotted back muscles.

"I remember you said Standingdog was silent during the whole trial."

"That's right. He just sat there. Gloating or furious, who knows?"

"That's another thing you got wrong. The transcript says different. After the verdict, when the judge asked if he had any final statement, an expression of remorse or an explanation for his actions, he spoke in Cherokee. A single word."

Charlotte gave him a parting pat and walked over to her desk and found the note. She spelled out the word and Parker pronounced it for her.

"*Ga-du-gi.*"

"Court reporter didn't bother to translate it in the transcript. You know what it means?"

He nodded.

"Common Cherokee custom. Working together for some mutual goal. Communal generosity, something like that. Dad was always preaching it. Many hands are better than two."

"Like I said. Sacrificing for the greater good."

Parker sighed again and took a calming breath. He cleared his throat, looked back at her with fresh clarity.

"So what's the motive? Standingdog was battling with my father. But these other two guys, what in the hell is pushing their buttons?"

"I don't know," she said. "We're still missing something."

Parker leaned back in his chair and peered up at the ceiling.

"A hundred and fifty years ago an illiterate Cherokee sacrifices his life so his people can stay in their homeland. And because of that somebody kills my father, and thirty years later they murder my mother and now seem to be hunting down the rest of us? What the hell is this, Charlotte? What the hell?"

She logged off her computer and looked at him while it cycled down.

"If Uncle Mike was telling the truth, they were hunting Diana and you and Gracey, but not me. That tells me something, Parker."

But he wasn't listening to her.

"*Ga-du-gi,*" he said. "Standingdog said that at the trial?"

He'd taken his eyes out of focus and didn't seem to be waiting for an answer. So she gave him none.

THIRTY-FIVE

AT A QUARTER AFTER TWELVE, flustered and uncertain, Nancy Feather arrived at the Tribues' estate. Farris met her at her car, led her to the front porch, and installed her in a rocker that was angled away from the dog-training area.

He offered her a half-sandwich from the tray on the side table, and Nancy, somewhat unnerved by the enormity of the occasion, snatched it up and took an immediate bite. When she'd chewed and swallowed, she patted her mouth with one of the linen napkins and tried to compose herself.

Nancy Feather ruffled the fur of one of the dogs. Standing still with strict patience, the dog gazed off toward the wide view of wilderness, range after range of mountains stacked behind one another into the hazy distance. Another spring storm was darkening the southern sky, some distant rumbles rolling up the valley.

Sprawled nearby, the other dog assumed a position of tranquillity, but his eyes continually darted in his master's direction.

Farris extended the serving tray, and Nancy Feather selected one of the glasses of iced lemonade.

"I wish I had longer than an hour for lunch, Farris. But you know how it is. We working girls."

She took an anxious peek at her watch.

"We have plenty of time. Not to worry."

"I was kind of surprised, you calling. All hush-hush, don't tell anybody where I was going. Kind of scared me, I guess. Thinking maybe I'd done something wrong. I was going to get interrogated or something."

Farris shared a laugh with the woman.

Nancy Feather wore white jeans and a green blouse that was rigidly ironed. Chopped short, her black hair lay flat and lifeless on her skull as if it, too, had been ironed until it had lost its will.

She had a round, homely face with a stubby nose, plump cheeks, and a chin with a deep cleft.

In his crisp blue uniform Farris sat down beside her, and had a sip of his lemonade. She took a dainty bite of her sandwich and made a "yum" noise.

"You're a good cook, Farris. Most men can't boil an egg."

He gave her thanks and bit into his own sandwich.

Nancy, in her anxious desire to please, had not dared to change her chair's position. Though a simple turn of her head would have brought Shannon Muldowny into view, Nancy had shown no interest in looking beyond Farris's face or the mountain range.

They ate their sandwiches and drank their lemonade and watched the thunderstorm roll northward, dragging with it several long curtains of rain.

"It's so beautiful here," Nancy Feather said. "I can't hardly imagine what it would be like to have every day free just to watch the weather and play with my dogs."

"Are you applying for the position?" Farris said.

Some magazine or insipid friend had coached her to laugh frequently and with gusto at a suitor's remarks, and Nancy Feather applied the lesson with yet another whoop of laughter.

"Tell me about your work, Nancy."

"Oh, it's nothing really. Typing contracts, filling out forms. Nothing very demanding. I always wanted to be a schoolteacher, but I didn't have much of a head for books."

"But travel," Farris said, bringing her flighty mind back to the issue. "Surely that must be an exciting benefit to your work."

"No, I don't get to travel. I just buy tickets for other people."

"I see." Farris looked over at the dogs and they both stiffened.

"If I lived in a place like this, I'd never travel. Why would I want to when I could just sit out here all day and all night and never be bored?"

"Eating plate after plate of bonbons," Farris said.

She looked at him with momentary alarm, then again resorted to a hearty laugh at his display of wit.

"I believe you handled my brother Martin's bookings, did you not?"

"Oh, poor Martin. Everybody is so shocked. Struck down like that right out in public in a big-city airport. I've heard terrible stories about Miami. I don't know why anyone goes there at all. Though if they came into the office saying they wanted to travel to Miami and I was to tell them how dangerous it was down there, Mr. Weatherby would fire me in a minute."

"You arranged Martin's trip to Miami?"

She was not so dense that she failed to hear the harsh authority in his voice.

"Yes, sir. I did all his plans."

"Call me Farris, please, Nancy. No need for such formality."

Now Nancy was thoroughly befuddled. Was this police business or a social call or something else entirely? The moment had tipped precipitously, and her round face was pinched with worry.

"I didn't know young Mr. Tribue that good. But he always asked for me. I guess he thought I was nice or something."

Nancy took a hurried sip of her lemonade and plucked the rest of her sandwich from the plate and bit into it in such haste that she appeared to believe she was about to be evicted.

"Do you have any friends, Nancy? Women you talk to sometimes?"

"Sure, I have friends."

"Do you ever discuss your work with your friends?"

"It's usually so boring at work, there's nothing to talk about." Then she laughed again.

One of the poodles stood up and walked over, its nails clicking against the oak planks. It stopped in front of Nancy and stared at her.

"I'm curious," Farris said. "Mr. Weatherby told me he thought one of your friends might be Lucy Panther. Is that true?"

Nancy Feather looked at the poodle standing just two feet in front of

271

her. She reached out and patted its head with a hand so stiff she might have been flattening dough. The dog could tolerate her touch no longer and turned and rejoined its littermate.

"Me and Lucy were in the same class at reservation school. We knew each other from a long time back."

"Do you still see her, talk to her?"

Farris watched as she wrestled with the question. She looked at the poodle, then out at the distant storm.

"I see her," she said quietly. "Sometimes."

"Did you by any chance discuss Martin Tribue's recent travel plans with Lucy Panther, your friend from long ago?"

She swallowed and set the remains of her sandwich back on the plate.

"I'm not supposed to talk about the personal affairs of our clients. That's one of the rules. Mr. Weatherby's very strict about his rules and regulations. They're on the bulletin board in big letters."

"Don't worry about Julius. This discussion is strictly confidential."

"Okay." Her breathing had become shallow and irregular. "Well, yeah, I might have said something to her about Mr. Tribue going to Miami."

"Why did you do that? Did she query you on the matter?"

"Query?"

"Did Lucy Panther ask you to keep her informed about Martin's plans?"

She shrugged and licked her lips and looked longingly at the remains of her sandwich.

"I guess so," she said. "Lucy knew Martin, and I guess she was curious what he was up to. You know, his comings and goings."

"Where can I find Lucy Panther?"

She shook her head, mouth clamped like a child refusing medicine.

"You won't tell me such a harmless thing as that?"

"Those FBI men, they've been hounding her for two years, tracking her everywhere she goes. I swore not to say where she was living, not tell anyone."

"But I'm not just anyone," Farris said.

Again Nancy Feather shut her mouth tightly.

When he stood up from his chair, both dogs rose in unison.

Farris reached down and gripped the back of Nancy Feather's rocker and wrenched it ninety degrees to the left.

She looked over her shoulder at Farris. Eyebrows arched, her mouth a dark, perfect hole of shock.

"Now watch," he said.

Nancy turned her gaze to the clearing where Shannon Muldowny was gagged and bound to a wooden fence post, her arms and legs loose so she could make some attempt at defending herself.

Farris had taken care to plant the post in a shallow footing, so it would collapse when sufficient force was applied. Thus the dogs would be less likely to injure themselves when they flung their bodies at her.

With the dogs focused intently on his every move, Farris raised his hand to his forehead, held it there for a moment, then he saluted the young woman from Boston. His father's concubine, his mother's replacement.

Without hesitation, his two poodles rushed from the porch, scampered across the lawn, and did their silent duty.

It was the first time he'd substituted human flesh for the mannequin, and Farris was pleased to see the dogs appeared to notice no difference.

Martin would have been thrilled.

Nancy Feather closed her eyes and ducked her head, but Farris ordered her to open them and she obeyed, however briefly.

"Now tell me, Nancy, where I can find Lucy Panther."

THIRTY-SIX

GETTING OUT OF THE BATHTUB was the easy part.

Nancy Feather got her duct-taped feet over the edge of the tub, and she wedged her back against the other side and straightened out as much as she could. Inch by inch she shifted her balance farther toward the open side of the tub until she got her knees over it and scooched down toward her thighs, then she had to press hard with the back of her head and thrust her skull against the wall. With a loud grunt she seesawed out.

She crumpled onto the white tile floor. Outside, in the hallway, she could hear the dogs pacing. Their claws clacked on the wood as if they were standing guard.

She got to her knees and wriggled into a standing position.

Farris was gone. She'd heard his police cruiser pull out about ten minutes before. Only reason she was still alive was because he probably doubted she'd told him the truth, and wanted to be able to come back and torture it out of her later if she'd lied.

She hadn't lied. She told him where Lucy Panther was staying. So scared he was about to feed her to his devil dogs like he'd done that pale-skinned girl. Confused and telling herself it was her only chance, she'd confessed to this evil man where her friend was hiding.

She was mortified. She should've been smarter and sent him on a wild-goose chase, and tried to escape before he returned. But seeing the girl die made her head swirly, and she'd done the totally wrong thing.

Now her only way of fixing it was to get free and warn poor Lucy. It was maybe a twenty-minute drive down the mountain and into the town of Cherokee, past the casino and out a couple of narrow roads, then into the woods a piece to the campground. Maybe twenty-five minutes total if he did the speed limit. So Nancy Feather guessed she had somewhere around ten minutes left. Ten minutes to save her best friend's life.

Earlier, out on the porch, Nancy Feather watched the pale blond woman go down and watched her kick and wriggle in the dirt and smack at the dogs while she was crippled up and hopeless from being fastened to a pole. Farris made her watch the last part, when the two dogs got the woman's throat and face and yanked their heads from side to side and then they stopped all at once and walked away into the shade and licked each others' faces, more like they were comforting each other than because they liked the taste of human blood.

After the woman was dead, he dragged Nancy Feather over to the body and made her see it close up. Then he hauled it out to the lip of the gorge and heaved it over, and told Nancy that's where she was going if she didn't tell him where Lucy Panther was hiding out.

So she'd done a Judas on her only real friend.

Now she stood in the bathroom, hands duct-taped behind her, ankles taped, mouth wrapped up tight so she could barely breathe through her nose. She looked around for scissors or a nail file or anything sharp but saw nothing sitting out. With her chin she opened the medicine cabinet and found it empty.

On the landing the dogs were rustling around, making a little more noise than before, like they knew she was up and around. Nancy Feather didn't know if they'd go for her without a signal from Farris. But that was getting ahead of herself. What she needed now was some way to get free and do it fast enough so she could call Lucy's cell and warn her what god-less thing was on the way.

Around the reservation there'd long been talk about Farris and his family, talk of evil doings, but she'd never taken it serious. Now she knew, by

God. Now she knew it was all true and more. More than anyone had guessed.

It didn't take her long to search the whole bathroom and see it was useless. Nothing anywhere. And the door was locked from the outside, so it looked like she was stuck. She went back to the sink and looked at herself in the mirror, her sad face, her eternal pudginess. Then the idea came to her. The one thing Farris hadn't thought about. Smart man, yes. But Nancy Feather saw something he hadn't seen. Little fat squaw like her, she saw a way to beat him. She saw herself. Her reflection.

She leaned her waist against the front edge of the sink and cocked her head back and bashed her forehead against the reflection, and the mirror spider-webbed. She saw about a hundred Nancy Feathers then, all with blood running from their hairline down their foreheads toward their eyes.

She bashed her head into the mirror again, and this time it all came loose.

She blinked the blood from her vision. Her head hurt bad, but it didn't make her groggy or slow her down. She saw a few likely pieces near the tub, so she lowered herself until she was kneeling on the cold tile and rummaged around behind her until she found a piece that felt long enough and sharp.

She couldn't get the angle right to saw at the tape on her hands, so she worked on her ankles. It was slow going. And she could feel the hundred pieces of broken glass under her knees and shins, slicing and jabbing through her jeans, but that was all right, too. Because now it wasn't just about saving Lucy, or herself, but about beating Farris. The prideful son of a bitch.

She rocked her body to put more pressure against the sticky, thick tape, then had a better idea and jabbed the pointed end through the tape, puncturing it and opening a hole in it, then backing out and opening another one and then connecting them. That worked. Still took a while, but eventually she could feel her ankles loosening, feeling the sticky, slimy film of blood on her hands and running into her mouth, tasting that. But she got it done.

And she was up on her feet with her hands still behind her.

Door locked, window locked. Hands still bound. She hadn't thought that far ahead, but now it seemed stupid to be on her feet and still just as imprisoned as she'd been.

Then she figured it out. It was another special skill she had on top of her limberness. That thing with her toes that her ex-husband, Albert, hated so much. The way she could grip things. Prehensile, he said, malting an ugly face. He'd asked somebody about it at work, thinking she might be part ape. The way she could hold a fork with her toes, tweezer up pennies off a flat floor. A trick she'd been able to do since she was a kid.

She kicked off her shoes and got down on her knees again, and looked around her and picked the piece of mirror glass she wanted and then commanded her toes to pick it up and turn the piece around and get it set tight. The damn toes were bleeding before she'd even begun to saw at the tape around her hands. The skin between her toes was splitting but it looked worse than it felt. She had to lean way back, like some kind of swami on the yoga channel. Bent backward, hands out, toes gripping the glass.

Five more minutes at least. And the pain was finally starting to make her dizzy, and her stomach was moving around.

When she got the tape off her hands, first thing she did was pull the rest of it off her mouth, and then she didn't even bother with trying the door. Between the lock and the dogs, there was only one good choice.

She undid the window lock, raised the sash, and climbed out onto the rusty tin roof. A cold rain had started, and the roof was slick with it, shining like a playground slide except for one thing—the screw heads sticking up everywhere. Which at that point, hell, it didn't matter. What pain? Pain was burning her toes and her butt and every part of her, and even after wiping the blood out of her eyes, she could still only half see.

She pointed herself right, then let go and slid down the roof and got going so fast she couldn't stop at the gutter but went over and landed in a mountain laurel. One of the screw heads ripped her jeans and tore a chunk of meat from her thigh. But thank God for the laurel bush, or there'd have been bones broken.

The dogs were out the door by then, and they came for her.

Not looking mean, but then they hadn't looked mean when they killed the woman in the clearing. Real slow, like a sleepwalker, she headed toward her car. Not making eye contact, showing no fear, not saying anything. One of the dogs got close behind her and started licking blood off the gash in her jeans, the other one nosing her butt. But she didn't push it away or acknowledge it. And she thought maybe the dogs had a conscience after all, were good and sweet and fine down in their dog hearts and the bad things they did were just because they were ordered to. Left to themselves, they'd just lick and play and howl at the moon like any old dogs.

She was only about ten yards from her car, thinking now that there wasn't no master alive could train a dog to do something later on, after he left, if X, Y, or Z happened, and expect them to remember to do it. No dog was that smart. No master, either.

She walked to her car, opened the door, and got in.

The dogs lay down beside the car in the light rain, finding comfortable positions, then closed their eyes, resting like dogs do when they've had an active day.

Nancy Feather got her cell phone out of the glove compartment and turned it on. Her bloody fingers were getting the keypad all red and gooey. And now her head was spinning, really spinning. Eyes fogged over so bad she had to scrub them with the back of her hand before she managed to punch in Lucy's number.

Then she listened while the phone rang and rang and rang again.

THIRTY-SEVEN

"I NEED TO GO HOME," Gracey said. "I need to go back to Miami. Like right away. It's a career thing."

Since last night at the motel, Lucy had barely said a word and she didn't say one now. Seeing Jacob shot down had switched her off.

After they got away from the motel, they dumped the Lincoln at the casino parking lot and spent two hours hiking back to the campsite, Lucy dead silent the whole time. Walking like a zombie on Thorazine. Which gave Gracey a serious case of the creeps.

Sure, it was terrible seeing Jacob lying there on the pavement with bullet holes. Sure, it had freaked her out, too, and it was still making her sad, but Lucy, man, Lucy was somewhere else. Moving around like she was a mile underwater, sluggish and sleepy.

"Maybe Jacob's not dead. Maybe he survived," Gracey said. "It happens, you know."

Lucy rose up on an elbow and looked at Gracey. Her eyes were red, her face drained, the way people got when they ran out of feelings, cried themselves empty. Gracey had seen that same face in the mirror a few times and recognized it right off.

"I've seen it happen," Gracey said. "A guy gets shot, three, four times, he survives."

"Where'd you see that?" Lucy Panther said. "In the movies?"

"The movies are as real as anything else."

"Sure they are."

Lucy closed her eyes and pressed her head back into the pillow.

"I'm ready to go," Gracey said. "What're we waiting for? You said you were taking me back to my parents. So let's go."

But Lucy just lay on her bunk, taking breath after breath but not saying anything else. Catatonic. Gracey had been that way a few times and knew how it felt. Nothing you wanted to do. Nobody you wanted to see or talk to.

In her head Steven was quiet, too. But not Joan Crawford. She was yakking about *Sudden Fear,* that movie she did with Jack Palance. In the film her character was a rich heiress and she married Palance, then found out he was going to murder her for her money. She should've known better. Anybody could look at the bone structure of Palance's face and know he was a killer. All those sharp angles. My God, you could slice steel cable with those cheekbones. But no, Joan fell for him because the script said so. She had to act like she was in love with the troll for half the movie. Play kissy face.

But if Gracey wanted to learn something, really learn something important about acting, she should look at the scene where Joan hears on a tape recorder Jack Palance's plot to kill her. She's alone in her room, hearing her lover's voice plotting her murder. No dialogue, just his recorded voice and Joan reacting. Look at my face, the way I go through about ten octaves of emotions. Look at it, Gracey. Study it. What I did with my eyes and mouth. Play that over and over and analyze it, girl. And was I naked one time in that movie? No, sir. I was in my nightgown, sure. I was in robes and silky things but never any flesh. And tell me how sexy I was. Get your big-shot director to take a look at that movie, why don't you? See if I wasn't sexy as hell.

Joan got quiet, and at the same moment Lucy popped straight up in the bunk. Then Gracey heard what Lucy had heard: a car coming up the drive, then its engine shutting off. Gracey rolled over on her cot and peeked out the tiny window high up on the mobile home. A porthole, like.

"Aw, shit," Lucy said. "Christ Almighty."

A man was climbing out of a cop car. It was a tall, gawky guy with black hair and a big jaw and a blue policeman's uniform with gold all over it. He walked over and stood by their barbecue pit, looking at the camper, just standing there like a gunslinger out in the middle of the street waiting for the other guy to show. That's the look he had.

"Get on the floor. Face down, flat," Lucy barked at her. "Do it, don't ask why. Get the hell on the floor."

Gracey got on the floor.

Snatching her pistol, Lucy duckwalked toward the front seat, reached out, and touched the keys hanging from the ignition. Then drew her hand back, changing her mind.

On Lucy's cot the cell phone rang. It rang and rang, but Lucy just stayed crouched behind the bucket seat, peeking out the windshield at the man standing there. Gracey raised herself up so she could see. This was something she could use later. This was one of those high-octane moments Mr. Underwood was always raving about. Gracey could feel it.

But that damn Joan Crawford kept jabbering about another movie of hers, a part she'd played, not an Indian, but a disfigured woman with a face so scarred up that she hated everybody she came in contact with. Bitter about how she looked, taking it out on everybody else because of how ugly her face was. And the wardrobe in that one, hell, it was still with the deep cleavage, but what were you going to do? You couldn't fight every little thing.

Gracey got up, scooted over to the bed, and picked up the cell phone and pushed the On button. Thinking maybe it was Jacob, calling from the hospital, letting them know he was still alive.

"Hello?"

Lucy hissed and waved for her to get down.

"Lucy?" It was some woman on the line.

"Lucy can't come to the phone right now. Can I take a message?"

The woman was silent for a second, then said, "Who's this?"

"I'm Gracey. I'm visiting from out of town."

She said she wanted to talk to Lucy, sounding sleepy and weird, the phone cutting out, part of her sentence missing in the static.

"You're breaking up," Gracey said.

"Get the hell down on the floor," Lucy screamed at her. "Do it now."

Flat on the floor again, on her tummy, Gracey kept the phone at her ear, but the woman's voice was going in and out, Gracey catching a word here and there, that was about it. Gracey twisted around to see what Lucy was doing. She was in the driver's seat, turning the key, the motor coming to life but not sounding good, a sputter, a knock, like it was running out of gas before it even got going.

Gracey clicked off the phone and tossed it onto the cot.

"Stay down." Lucy turned, gave Gracey a quick look, then slid the pistol down the floor toward her. "Use this if you have to. Whatever you do, don't let this guy get you. He comes within ten feet, start shooting. Ten feet, you hear me?"

Lucy shoved the gearshift and hit the gas, and the camper lurched forward. It bumped over a rut and dishes came spilling down. Gracey covered her head with her arms and stayed down. Heard glass breaking, and then her hair was showered with something. There was a gunshot and Gracey looked at the pistol in her hand, thinking it'd gone off, but it hadn't because there was another gunshot and more stuff sprinkled her head and itched against her neck.

She felt back there and it was wood chips or something and she turned her head a little and saw a big gash in the fiberboard next to her head and looked the other way and saw the rip in the metal side of the camper, like about two inches above her head. Big hole you could put your hand through.

"Hold on!"

Gracey lifted her head to see out the windshield, shattered now, but she could see the roof of the police car coming up fast, Lucy aiming the camper at its side and holding the gas down and crashing hard into the truck and driving it sideways into bushes and trees, then ramming the shifter into reverse, backing, and swinging the big, top-heavy thing to the left.

Woo-woo, she heard in her head. One of the voices. Could've been any of them. Woo-woo, hang on tight. Woo-woo.

The camper was weaving down a gravel road, then it started slowing down, slower and slower. That wasn't right.

Gracey looked up from the floor and saw Lucy slumped sideways, still holding on to the wheel, but not steering anymore. Gracey could see trees coming at them through the windshield, she scrambled up there and bent down beside Lucy and took over the wheel. A ditch coming, too, ten feet ahead, deeper than a regular ditch, more like a valley.

She was frozen, just holding on to the wheel, until Barbara Stanwyck said, Do it, be brave, make your mark. You're too young to die, kid. Do it.

Gracey yanked the wheel to the right and got the camper back on the gravel. She leaned over Lucy and looked into the big rearview mirror, and she couldn't see the man anymore, so she figured he was running to his car to see how bad it was smashed up.

Lucy looked at her, eyes groggy but open. Blood ran down her neck. Gracey's breakfast started to back up into her throat, the eggs, the toast.

"Can you drive this thing?" Lucy crowded past her and dropped into the passenger's seat, holding the wheel until Gracey was in the driver's seat and got her hands set and found the accelerator and got them going somewhere, she wasn't sure where, Lucy telling her, "The left coming up, yeah, this one, here, now look for the first right, a highway, be careful. It's busy." Her voice fading on every word.

Talk about blood, Joan said, you should've seen me when I went under the knife, and lo and behold the surgeon performed a miracle and I came out of the anesthesia and I was beautiful, and it completely changed me, I was well for the first time in my life and I started being good to people, loving and kind. Then, Joan's voice got sarcastic and she said, best acting job of my career, hell, I only had to be sympathetic for the last five minutes of the film.

Gracey got them to the edge of the highway, lots of cars going past.

"Which way?"

She looked over and Lucy had closed her eyes, but she got her hand up and waved to the left, so that's which way Gracey turned, going somewhere, she didn't know where. But she had them rolling along, settling into the stream of traffic and that seemed good enough for now.

Woo-woo, somebody said. Sounded like Steven. Blood and bullets and car crashes and chases. Woo-woo.

Nancy Feather was dialing Lucy's number again. Using her thumb. Her head was foggy, eyes misting over. Steering her little Volkswagen down the twisting highway, going fast on that familiar road, knowing every switchback, every pothole, every damn passing lane.

But her heart wasn't firing on all cylinders. Too fast, too irregular. Mind whirling. Who could she call for help? Who would believe her? Farris Tribue's dogs killed a young woman. Farris Tribue, the sheriff for the Eastern Band of the Cherokee Nation. Farris Tribue, the way he'd toyed with her, mocked her. That remark about bonbons. She was hearing it all again, his snotty, bigoted tone. Treating her like a fat dumb squaw. She got the numbers punched in, and it was the wrong number, some old woman answering, wanting to talk to Nancy, ask who she was, shoot the breeze, and Nancy apologized to the woman and said she had to go and started dialing again, focused on the keypad now so she got it right and missing that Z turn, just going straight out over the edge, no guardrail, no trees, nothing but free fall.

The car tilted forward so Nancy saw straight out the windshield, straight down into the river valley, a man down there fishing, casting his line, and she was aiming right for him, and Nancy tried turning the steering wheel, but of course that did nothing. Nothing at all. It was all so quick she didn't even have time to scream.

A few miles down the highway, Lucy pointed out a muddy side road and told Gracey to pull off. With gauze and adhesive tape from the first-aid kit, Gracey bandaged Lucy's wounded ear. The bullet had torn off most of her earlobe and scraped her neck, but it wasn't like she was going to die or anything.

"Who was that guy shooting at us?"

"The same man who killed Jacob."

"Why'd he want to kill you?"

When the bandaging was done, Lucy traded places with her and got behind the wheel and started the camper and headed back out to the highway.

"Why'd he want to kill you, Lucy?"

"He didn't want to kill me."

"He sure acted like it."

"He was after you," Lucy said.

"Me? What'd I do?"

"Nothing," said Lucy. "Absolutely nothing."

"I must've done something. People don't try to kill you for no reason. There's got to be a motivation. That's how it works."

Lucy looked over and her mouth softened a little, almost a smile.

"You're on a list," Lucy said. "You and Jacob and your father."

"What list?" Gracey leaned forward to see Lucy's face.

"I said too much already. You're just a kid."

"If I'm going to get shot at, I should know what's going on. What list?"

Lucy stopped for a red light. They were getting closer to town.

While they waited, Lucy took a long look at her. The way her mother did sometimes when she was trying to gauge if Gracey could be trusted, or if she was old enough to handle something.

"This man wants to murder you because of who your father is. Like they already murdered your grandmother and your grandfather before that."

"My grandmother? Diana? She's dead? When?"

Lucy sighed.

"This man," she said. "Jacob tried to tell your dad about him, so maybe Parker could help, but that didn't pan out. That's as much as I can tell you."

Steven Spielberg was talking to her again in his low-key, serious way. The most amazing thing. He was officially offering her a part. Not the lead, of course, she was too young for that, too inexperienced, but he'd decided she was ready for a supporting role.

The gunfire decided it for him, the incident in the camper. The way she'd acted, so brave, talking to the woman on the phone when all that craziness was going on around her. He was excited. Did you see Melanie Griffith in *Night Moves*?

Of course she'd seen it, Steven. She'd told him that once before and they'd talked about it for hours, didn't he remember? Gene Hackman, he's a football player turned private eye. Yeah, yeah, Steven was off again. It was Melanie's first movie. You could tell she was going to be a star—that mousy voice, that look, those eyes.

Those tits, said Joan Crawford. Don't kid yourself, Gracey, it's the tits that did it. You think that little twit has talent? That girl was blond and she had the firm young knockers all those adolescent boys in Hollywood drool over.

Don't listen to that old crone, Barbara Stanwyck said. It's all sour grapes with Joan. Look at her. Of course she hates women with tits. She hates any woman. Everybody's a threat. Who wouldn't be a threat to an ugly bitch like her? Look at those eyebrows, my God, throw away the tweezers, get out the hedge clippers. Don't listen to her, Gracey, with her tit phobia. If it takes a good set of boobs to get you in the door, then fine, don't worry. So you're well-endowed, great, enjoy it, be happy, stand up straight, show them off. Joan's just picking on your vulnerability. She knows you're sensitive about them.

"I am not," Gracey said out loud.

Lucy turned and looked at her.

"I'm not sensitive about my breasts. I don't know where you get that."

Yes, you are, deary. Don't try to lie to me. It isn't possible.

How the hell did she know what Gracey was sensitive about?

Because I'm in here, my little elf. Inside. What you know, I know.

"In here? Inside where?"

Barbara said, where you are right now, that's where.

Don't tie yourself in knots. Just relax and enjoy. Bottom line is, when it comes to acting, however you get your start is just fine. Listen to Spielberg. He's a class act. Not some adolescent tit man. Crawford's a mean, mean woman. Spent her entire career trying to fake a smile, cover up what a perfect bitch she is. Can't trust someone like that. You listening to me, honey?

"You okay?" Lucy asked her.

"Sure," said Gracey. "I'm great. Fantastic."

"You're talking to yourself."

"No, no. I just got offered a part in a movie. A major motion picture. Steven Spielberg wants me for a supporting role, like Melanie Griffith."

Lucy was quiet.

"What? You aren't happy for me?"

Lucy nodded, but she didn't look very enthusiastic.

"I have to get back to Miami," Gracey said. "This is huge."

"I'm taking you to your parents," Lucy said. "Right now."

"And listen, I'll tell my dad about the guy and his murder list. Dad will nail the guy. You don't need to worry anymore, Lucy."

"I'm not worried."

"What's the man's name? The one who was shooting at us?"

"Farris Tribue. He's the sheriff around here."

"Okay, good. I'll sic my daddy on him and, look out, that guy won't know what hit him."

"You do that, Gracey."

"Now what're you going to do? Make a run for it? Blow town, go on the lam?"

"After I take you to your parents, I'm going to do what I should've done months ago."

"What's that?"

"Finish this thing. Finish it once and for all."

THIRTY-EIGHT

"FRAGILE X," CHARLOTTE SAID.

"What?"

She was scrolling through an Internet article on her computer. A Web site devoted to genetic disorders. Killing time in their motel room, waiting for Gracey to appear.

" 'Characteristic facial features include long, narrow face, narrow inter-eye distance, highly arched palate, and enlarged ear size.' "

"Farris Tribue," Parker said.

For most of the morning he'd been lying on the bed, drawing an elaborate chart on a yellow pad. His usual way of sorting out riddles: doodling circles, connecting them with branching lines, tracing the chains of causality, trying to see relationships, which sequence of events might have triggered the current situation.

Charlotte hadn't told him about her theory. She wanted it to settle for a while, let the murky water clear, see if it still made sense.

It felt right. It answered everything, but still she wasn't ready. She had to make sure it was solid before she spoke the words.

Charlotte read some more from the Web page.

" 'Prominent thumbs, hand calluses, enlarged testicular volume, also known as macroorchidism, particularly noticeable after puberty. Approximately one in seven hundred males will be born as a fragile X–permutation carrier. Carrier males are at high risk to pass on the fragile X mutation and to have affected offspring. Fragile X is the leading hereditary cause of mental retardation and second to Down syndrome as a specific genetic cause, and it may also have a significant association with autism.' "

Parker absorbed the information quietly, then said, "So?"

"So that's what Farris's got. Fragile X."

"I repeat," Parker said. "So?"

"So, nothing. It was bugging me."

"So Farris has big nuts. I could've guessed that."

He went back to diagramming on his legal pad. Charlotte killed the Web page, tried to think of something else to occupy her mind.

"Wait a minute." Parker sat up. "Sissy, Uncle Mike's daughter."

"Yeah? She was spying for him somewhere."

"Back when I was a kid, Sissy used to show up at camp now and then for the big ceremonies. She loved the Indian lore stuff, the dances, the bonfires. She was maybe a year or two older than me."

"And?"

"She's a high-functioning autistic. A smart girl, but emotionally stunted."

"So maybe it's in the family, this fragile X thing. Farris, his twin brother, his cousin."

She could see Parker drawing another circle on his legal pad, making an X in the middle of it, factoring that into his visual equation.

Turning back to her computer, she was about to check her e-mail for the twentieth time that morning when the knock came on the door. Three sharp raps.

In two seconds Charlotte was at the peephole and saw Gracey standing there, bobbing her head as if counting off the seconds impatiently.

Charlotte whipped the door open and grabbed Gracey by the upper arm and dragged her into the room. As she was shutting the door, she saw a white camper pull away from in front of their room, heading for the parking lot exit.

Gracey was bedraggled, wearing the same outfit she'd had on earlier in the week in Miami. A million years ago. Parker and Charlotte took turns hugging her, and Gracey stood it as long as she could, then pushed away and said, "I need a shower. I stink."

"How about some food? We can order room service, whatever you want."

"I need a salad, a big green salad. I've been eating junk. I'm all puffy."

Parker was smiling, heading for the room-service menu on the desk. He hadn't noticed yet what Charlotte had just seen.

Gracey's eyes were icing over. She was heading inward. Standing at the foot of the bed, tilting her head to the side as if listening to some high-pitched whistle.

"Look," Gracey said. "I need the whole script. If I don't know how it comes out, how'm I supposed to play the role?"

"Gracey?" Charlotte said.

Parker turned from the desk and stared at his child.

"Okay, sure, this is my first time, and you have all the experience and everything, yeah, but I don't see how you expect me to play a role without knowing where my character's headed."

Parker looked over at Charlotte, his face suffused with naked grief.

"No, no, no," Gracey said. "Forget it, Steven, I'm absolutely not doing any nude scene. No, not even topless."

She shook her head and muttered something below her breath. Then she leaned forward in Parker's direction.

"If that's all you want, just to see my breasts, then never mind. Forget the whole damn thing, okay. I'm not some slut. I know, I know, Melanie Griffith, Melanie Griffith, yeah, yeah."

Charlotte spoke her name again, but it didn't register.

"She needs her meds," Parker said.

"I'm not whining," said Gracey. "I don't know where you get that. I'm just stating my case. If you don't like it, tough. Find some bimbo with big tits. Make her a star."

Charlotte tugged on Gracey's arm and led her over to the bed and eased her down till she was sitting on the edge.

For the next few minutes she talked to empty air, bitching at Steven Spielberg. Holding firm on the topless issue. Saying she might be willing to compromise a little, maybe consider a quick, tasteful butt shot, but anything more than that was out. From what Charlotte could gather, Gracey had gotten him on the defensive. Apologizing, backtracking. She reminded him that she was only sixteen years old and he could get in trouble. Had he forgotten about that whole Brooke Shields, *Pretty Baby* thing? What was he, some kind of pervert?

Maybe Charlotte was starting to lose it, too, but despite everything, she felt a surge of pride in Gracey. Her tough daughter, standing up for herself against an intimidating big-time director like that.

While Gracey was undressing in the bathroom, Charlotte got through to Gracey's psychiatrist, who approved a one-time double dose of her medication. However, he advised, because of the interruption in her treatment, it would be as long as a week before the drugs began to take hold again. In any case, that extra pulse at the beginning would probably help.

With only a minor fuss, Gracey swallowed the capsules Charlotte had brought along, then spent the next fifteen minutes in the shower. Steam pouring from around the curtain. Afterward, she dressed in a pair of Charlotte's jeans and a long-sleeved jersey and curled up in their bed and fell into a soundless slumber.

For a time Charlotte watched Gracey sleep while Parker sat at the desk and stared at the front curtains.

Maybe Parker was right. Maybe Diana had been, too.

All Charlotte had to do was love the girl. Not that it would fix Gracey's condition. But it might, if she was lucky, fix Charlotte's.

For the last year, Charlotte had wanted more than anything to recapture her healthy, happy daughter. She would always want that. Dream of it. Never give up that hope. But maybe she'd gotten things badly confused. In wishing Gracey were right again, she'd been discounting the girl Gracey had become. As if to acknowledge her daughter's new self would mean yielding to the illness. She could blame it on the shrink, just following his orders not to indulge Gracey's fantasies. But it was more than that. For little by little Charlotte had withdrawn her emotional support, held back her affection, begun to give Gracey an almost constant torrent of disapproval.

Goddamn it, they *were* right. Charlotte had been handling it all wrong. Mourning her loss of the old Gracey with such fervor that she had nothing left to give the new one.

She went over to the bed and bent over her daughter and pressed a kiss to her forehead. The flesh was cool and dry. Her face softly composed, as if her dreams had liberated her momentarily from the torment of her waking hours.

She made a silent vow. Whoever Gracey was when she woke, that was the person Charlotte would love. As challenging as that might be, it seemed at the moment her only chance to recover some portion of the girl she'd lost.

THIRTY-NINE

LUCY PANTHER CAME UP THE Tribues' gravel driveway on foot, her pistol in hand. The big meadow out front had been recently mowed, and the scent of grass hung thickly in the air. A song sparrow trilled its haunting, off-key melody from the hemlocks. Somewhere nearby a towhee called out, "Drink your tea." In the high grass near the trees, she heard a buzzing sound, a timber rattler or a nest of yellow jackets waking from their winter sleep.

Lucy climbed the front steps. The two broad-chested poodles rose to meet her but showed no hostility. One of them nosed her butt as she passed by.

Lucy used her pistol butt to break the narrow windowpane, and then she reached through the jagged glass and unlocked the door to the Tribue house.

When Farris returned, he would see the broken glass by the doorway, be instantly on guard, throw open closets, kick in doors. Even though she'd parked the camper a mile away in the trees and trekked up, he'd still know.

Which was fine. At this point any way it went was fine.

She'd lost her boy, the only man who'd ever meant anything to her. Aside from Parker for that one short summer. Off and on for years Parker had barged into her dreams, which left her thinking maybe he'd show up at her door one day, smile the way he had that first time, shy, awkward, full of reckless heat, and he'd want to know all about his son, and eventually he'd touch her, and the fire would flare again. She'd imagined that so much, it was almost like it'd happened. But it hadn't and it wouldn't, and now she didn't care.

That was done, too. Parker wasn't the same. And the woman he'd married was Lucy's equal. Took her only a second to recognize that. Both of them from the same race of fighters. Tooth-and-nail women who'd die before they surrendered what they loved. He'd found himself a substitute, as good or better than Lucy. Fine.

Didn't matter. None of it did.

Lucy moved through the dark house, seeing just well enough to keep from knocking over furniture. The dogs stayed out on the porch, didn't even try to follow. Lazy beasts.

The house was quiet, and for a moment she stood in the foyer and listened, absorbing the vibrations of the place.

A large part of this ruinous state of affairs was Lucy Panther's fault. She could trace nearly everything back to that summer dalliance thirty years ago. Now her son was dead. Even her father, Standingdog, had, in his own way, lost his life to this thing. This thing she was resolved to end today.

Unless he killed her first. But even that didn't concern her much. Live or die, at this point it was all the same. The world was poisoned. Every last thing that mattered was gone.

What she needed to do now, the only thing that counted, was to find a place in this house, the right vantage point from which she could see Farris's face when she gut-shot him, when he crumpled and died. That was the single thing in the entire universe that interested her. Finding that place.

She was leaving the bathroom when she heard the noise down the hall. Voices in conversation. It took a second more to discern that it was only TV people talking.

Two doors down the corridor, a light shone from a cracked-open door. Lucy wiped the sweat from her shooting hand, then reset her grip.

Moving forward, she walked a line on the edge of the hallway to keep from creaking the boards. And she made it to the door itself before the floor planks crackled underfoot.

She didn't wait for a reaction, but shouldered through and came in the room pointing the pistol left, then right, then left again.

Old man Tribue was tucked beneath the white sheets, propped by pillows so he could watch the cowboy movie playing on his TV across the room. John Wayne in Technicolor riding a white stallion across a prairie.

Congressman Otis Tribue stared at Lucy, his eyes frantic.

Hanging from a freestanding metal pole was a plastic bag, an IV drip. The tubing ran to his right arm, a vein near the joint of his elbow. Lucy had heard the gossip around town of Otis Tribue's wife, Roberta, sustained by endless bags of morphine through her final days.

Lucy moved closer to the bed and checked the side table for weapons. Nothing.

She kept the pistol aimed at him while she stripped back the white sheet.

The congressman was wearing only undershorts. He was lashed to the bed by ropes and duct tape. His ankles knotted to the bedposts, from his waist to his sternum a crisscrossing of silver tape kept him motionless.

The old man closed his eyes slowly and kept them closed like he was taking a moment to commune with his Maker.

On the TV, John Wayne was riding at full gallop, firing back at a war party of Apaches, a six-gun in each hand, while the Indians were blown backward, one by one, from their ponies onto the rocky ground.

"What's going on here?"

The old man's voice was hoarse and weak, as if he'd been shouting at the empty room for hours.

"My son," he said. "He's killing me."

"Killing you?"

Otis Tribue nodded at the IV bag.

"Pull out the needle," he said. "It's bleach or gasoline. I don't know what."

Lucy Panther stood close to the footboard and looked down at the man. Even in his old age, he was handsome. His face had the weathered vigor of the men on the walls of his room. Black-and-white photographs and tintypes of other Tribues with their side whiskers and full beards, the stern pioneers who had preceded him in this bedroom, and on this land. Frontiersmen, they called themselves, tamers of the wilderness. As if wilderness ever needed taming.

Otis Tribue and people like him had homesteaded Cherokee land since long before the Civil War, and they founded the stores and banks and blasted corridors through solid rock for roads and dams and they clear-cut the forests, and their modern versions built the hundreds of money-grubbing businesses that completed the conquest their predecessors began centuries before—the soldiers with their muskets and diseases and baubles.

It was all lost now. No going back. No fixing it.

When this white warlord died, he would be replaced by one as bad or worse. Nothing Lucy Panther could do would change the landslide. Casino money was just the latest fraud, promising paradise and giving them shit.

"You know who I am?" Lucy asked him.

He closed his eyes and shook his head.

"I'm the daughter of Standingdog Matthews, mother of Jacob Panther."

The old man moved his head in sad acknowledgment of her words.

"Pull out the needle," he said. "I'm dying."

"Why did Farris do this to you?"

"To punish me," he said. "Now pull it out, goddamn you."

His eyes were as deep and murky as the caves of ancient bears.

"No," she said. "Not until I have some answers."

"Have mercy, woman."

"I don't have a nickel's worth of pity for you, old man. What you did there's no forgiveness for. Nothing but brimstone's in your future."

"What do you want to know?"

"The story. The whole story, back to the beginning of time if that's when it got started. Tell me and I'll shut this poison off."

"Shut it now, or I'll be dead and there'll be no telling anything."

Lucy considered it for a moment, then moved to the IV bottle and twisted the clamp. She sniffed the air around the plastic bag, and, yes, she could detect the sharp reek of a flammable liquid.

"Water," the old man said. "Water."

Lucy looked back at John Wayne. He was behind a boulder now, blasting away with his endless bullets. More Apaches flew backward in their last immortal seconds.

She went to the tiny bathroom and poured him a cup and held it to his lips and watched him gulp it down.

"Now tell me," she said. "Or I turn on the drip again."

"I need a doctor. I need medical attention now. A transfusion."

"You'll tell the story first."

"Goddamn you, woman."

"Oh, he has already, yes, you bet your ass he has. Now tell me."

He closed his eyes, summoning his strength, and a moment or two later, in his croaky voice, he began the tale. From one fall afternoon two centuries ago until that very evening they shared. He compressed it, left out most of the names and particulars. Those things she could find out on her own, he assured her.

In his story, dozens of her people were murdered. More than she'd imagined. More than any of the tribal scandalmongers had reckoned. Last of all, he told her where to find the remains of many of those Cherokees his ancestors had killed. A stone's throw from his very bed.

In the last twenty-four hours she had watched her son die, seen her lover Parker again, and then received this dreadful tale, and now there was more weight on Lucy Panther's heart than her heart had ever carried.

When Otis was finished, he looked at her for a long minute. She was not about to give the old man her forgiveness, and he was clearly asking for none.

"I'm dying," he said. "Call an ambulance."

But even if she'd wanted to, it was too late for that. The first convulsion came and went only a few seconds later, followed by another and another.

Lucy Panther stood unmoved and unmoving as she watched the seizures cease and the old man dwindle, and slowly lose his place on earth, watched him slap the air a final time, twist once more in his sheets and fall still.

When he was gone, she prowled the room, opening drawers and pawing through a woman's carefully folded undergarments and sweaters and white aprons. In the bottom drawer of the dresser she found what she was searching for. Otis Tribue had mentioned it prominently in his story. And here it was, an antiquated, small-caliber revolver. A tangible memento from Otis

Tribue's wicked past. She tucked the pistol in the waistband of her jeans. Legal evidence, in case she survived the evening.

So now it was one Tribue down and one left to go.

Lucy drew up a chair close to the TV, and she watched what was left of the John Wayne movie. She'd seen this one a couple of times before. It didn't end well for the redskins.

It never did.

FORTY

FARRIS RADIOED FOR A DEPUTY to bring him a fresh cruiser and gave the dispatcher directions to the campground, but told her nothing further about his situation.

"Somebody smashed you up pretty good," the Cherokee deputy said when he got a look at Farris's car.

"Stay here and watch the car, son. I'll send back a tow truck."

Before the deputy could object, Farris climbed into the cruiser and left.

He drove straight away to Stillwell Branch Road, parked beside the familiar field, and took the bridge and path into the dusty basin where Margie Hornbuckle's double-wide trailer was planted.

It was the boy's nap time, so Farris tapped lightly on her door. Her domicile was tidy and smelled of lemon air-freshener, and she welcomed him without complaint or question.

"He's sleeping," she said. "And I been after him with that antiseptic like you said. But he fights me on it. Burns him something fierce, he says."

He went into Shelley's bedroom and looked down at the snoring boy. The light from the living room threw a slash across his face. His stubbled cheeks needed tending, but beyond that the boy seemed in decent shape.

Farris took a look back at the living room and saw Margie slouched in her recliner before the television with a can of iced tea in her hand.

In silence, Farris stooped forward and brought his face to the boy's and hovered there only an inch away, tasting the heat and scent of his son's spent breath. Those molecules, which had journeyed into the boy's lungs and out again, were charged with an intoxicating fragrance.

Such intimacy with his son aroused in Farris a sense of overwhelming injustice. Although his own blood circled in the boy's veins, and Shelley would pass into a distant future that Farris would never know, the boy would never reproduce, never send the Tribue bloodline forward into the years. In his crucial life's work, Farris had utterly failed. He had passed on nothing to this angelic child but an empty life and a world of fruitless dreams.

Farris brought his mouth to the boy's scalp and pressed his lips against the rough bristles, lingering there for a moment until Shelley stirred and grunted and Farris drew away.

He remained in the bedroom a moment more, recovering from the act. He listened to the ceaseless babble of the television, the nameless tune of a bird outside. He tasted again the scent of his son, which lingered like the burn of sour mash at the back of his throat. Inside his chest he felt the immensity, a blank, cold universe, starless and moonless, which stretched to the borders of his being and throbbed beyond endurance. An unspeakable yearning.

If that sensation pulsing in Farris's breast was not what mankind defined as love, then Farris was truly damned to never know its name.

With a final look at his boy, Farris walked back into the living room and stood next to Margie's chair.

"I've spoken to John Gathers at the bank," Farris said.

A stricken look passed across Margie's face. Fear of eviction, no doubt, an end to her life of ease.

"From this point on, you'll receive a monthly retainer directly from the bank," Farris said. "It should be sufficient to provide for the boy and yourself. Upon your death, the bank will select a new caretaker for my son and that person will live here where you have lived. I have asked Mr. Gathers to appoint a watchdog to make regular visits to check on my son's health and well-being. As well as your own."

"You going away somewhere?"

He looked at the television, then back at the room where his son slept.

"Buy the boy a drawing pad," Farris said. "And a box of colored pencils. And those chigger bites, take care of them."

Margie looked up at Farris and was about to reply when he turned from her and without a backward glance left the trailer.

Lucy heard his car. She heard his step. She didn't move. By now he had seen the broken glass and knew his house had been invaded.

The TV was telling other movie lies. A John Wayne anthology—this time he was a U.S. Marine, leading his men into the teeth of machine-gun fire, taking a Pacific beach. All about him his loyal men were chewed to bits by a hail of lead, but soldiering on for John Wayne's sake. Heroes, heroes, everywhere.

Lucy lost Farris's tread somewhere in the house. He was moving down corridors she didn't know. He was circling, hunting her, coming closer by slow degrees. A board creaked, hinges squealed. He was headed her way.

She didn't take cover. Tired of all that. The hiding.

She kept her seat in the comfortable leather chair across from the dead congressman and watched John Wayne rally his grubby troops, hacking through jungle vines, his valiant Americans picked off one by one by a ruthless, invisible sniper high in the treetops.

The door swung open, but Farris was not there.

She waited, her aim fixed on the empty space.

The gray halo of the television gave her sufficient light. Since the first shot she'd ever fired, Lucy Panther had been known as a sharpshooter, better than any boy in the tribe. She propped her pistol hand on her knee to keep from tiring the muscles. Aiming for the middle of the door.

"You're dead," Farris called out.

"That makes two of us," she replied.

That set him thinking for a moment. While he was distracted, she could hazard a guess about where he was standing, attempt a shot through the wall, but then again she didn't want to waste the shells. More than that, she wanted the satisfaction of seeing him the second he went down. So she waited.

"Father!" Farris called out in a full and untroubled voice. "Father!"

"You'll have to wait a while to talk to him. Till you join him in hell."

The boards creaked again. Farris reacting. She couldn't imagine how. Surely he wasn't weeping for that old devil. Was he crouching for a dive and roll? It didn't matter to Lucy. However it unfolded from here was fine. Glad it was almost over.

Farris had slunk away, for she could hear the creaks of his departure. Off concocting a scheme, or calling reinforcements.

For the moment she relaxed. Rocked her neck from side to side, took a peek at the marines. Airplanes flying low and strafing. Explosions, fire, the jungle burning. His men cowered, but John Wayne stood sure and tall.

God, she missed her Jacob. Her brave boy. How smart he was, how strong and loving. Only hours ago she'd watched him die, but it seemed like forever. Seemed like he'd never lived, never held her in his strong arms, comforted her. None of those years together ever happened. All of it was nothing but a movie played out to its finish and dissolved into darkness.

In a while Lucy Panther heard Farris coming back. She heard him stop outside the door, and she waited in her chair.

Seconds passed, then there was the snap and flare of a match and an odor that took her a second to give it a name.

Gasoline.

Lucy stood up and aimed at the empty doorway. The pungent smell grew stronger.

Another moment passed, then the ceramic jug rolled through the door, the rag in its mouth on fire. A gallon of explosive sloshing in its belly. The same strategy they claimed her boy had used against the banks.

Or perhaps the jug was simply filled with water, a trick to drive her from the room.

Motionless, she watched the jug roll across the floor, watched the blue flame eat up the length of cloth. Would a man like Farris destroy his own ancestral home, his father's remains, and all he owned to kill a simple woman? From the madness she'd heard detailed tonight, she had no doubt that such a thing was possible within this family.

An inch of fabric was left as she made her hasty calculations. Death here and now in a burst of flame, or take her chances at the doorway or beyond?

The prospect of watching Farris die won her over.

Lucy Panther sprinted for the door and headed down the empty hallway toward the head of the stairs.

She made it a dozen feet before Farris heaved himself from a nook and threw his weight into her and slammed her body against the wall. A pistol fired. But she felt no pain, and then he bashed her chin and everything went soft and simple.

FORTY-ONE

THEY WERE ON THE OUTSKIRTS of Asheville, and by Charlotte's map reading, not more than ten minutes from the college. Gracey was in the backseat of the new Pontiac rental, staring out her window at the crystal afternoon, the faultless blue sky.

At Charlotte's insistence, it was to be a quick stop to ask a few questions of Professor Milford, then on to their four P.M. flight back to Miami. Parker wanted to know what possible value such a side trip would have and Charlotte said, "Just ten minutes, that's all I want."

Before leaving the motel she'd called her old partner, Jesus Romero, and he'd agreed to take charge of Gracey for a few days while Charlotte and Parker returned to Carolina to unravel the last few knots.

"There's a list," Gracey said quietly. "A murder list. We're all on it. Grandmother was, too."

These were the girl's first words since she'd awoken from her nap, grouchy and uncommunicative.

Charlotte swung around and rested her left arm on the seat back.

"A murder list?"

"Lucy said so. A list. And our names are on it."

Gracey crossed her arms over her chest, sunk into her seat, and began to mumble as if she were about to drift away again into another fit of gloom.

Charlotte looked over at Parker. He was watching Gracey in the rearview mirror.

"Later," he said to Charlotte. "Don't press."

She shook her head. It was a now-or-never moment. Worth the risk of pushing the girl deeper inside herself. She turned back to Gracey.

"Do you remember anything else Lucy said?"

"You don't believe me, do you? You think I'm making it up."

"Not at all," said Charlotte. "Your dad and I would like to hear anything else you remember from the time you were with Lucy."

"You know, Mom, I can tell what's real from what's not real." She hugged herself tighter and kept her eyes on the rugged landscape. "I can tell when people are faking and when they're telling the truth. Even you, Mother, even you."

"It runs in the family," Parker said.

"Well, if you don't want to talk about it, Gracey, that's fine. But later on, if you remember anything, sweetheart, we're here, you can always tell us."

She was about to turn back around when Gracey said, "Jacob went to the police to tell them what was going on, but everybody laughed at him."

Charlotte nodded.

"We heard something about that. Yes."

"And Jacob and Lucy thought Dad had clout. That he could fix everything, and that's why he came to Miami, to warn us we were in danger, but Mom called the FBI on him before he could do it. And he had to run."

Parker gave Charlotte a quick look, but said nothing.

"Anything else?"

"The man that shot at me and Lucy when we were in the camper, the one that wounded Lucy, I forget his name, but he's the sheriff."

"Farris Tribue?"

Parker slowed the car and turned off the interstate down a ramp.

"That's right," Gracey said. "A tall man with the Elvis hair. All geeky and gross. That's the one who shot at us."

"You're sure of that, Gracey?"

"See what I mean? You never believe me."

Parker assured her they did believe her. And what's more they loved her very, very much.

Charlotte reached back and patted Gracey's knee, but the girl recoiled from her touch.

"You don't believe anybody. Everybody's a liar. Making things up, imagining things."

"I believe you, Gracey. One hundred percent. I swear."

She tried to hold Gracey's eye, but the girl looked away. So after a moment more, Charlotte turned back around.

"Call Frank?" Parker said.

"Not yet. We need to fill in a few more blanks."

"You're not going to tell me why we're here."

"If what I think is true, we should know in a few minutes. If it isn't, I don't want you getting in an uproar over nothing. Okay?"

Parker looked over at her, his stern face melting into a smile.

"Whatever you say, Officer Monroe."

Five minutes later, as they pulled off the two-lane country road onto the college grounds, Gracey was quiet, looking out her window, occupied by the scenery.

Asheville Women's College was a brick and ivy affair that seemed mired in an antebellum fantasy with Southern belles in hoopskirts and tight corsets moping for hours with their girlfriends about the total lack of suitable beaux.

From what Charlotte could see on the shady entrance drive that led to a plantation mansion and a cluster of charming dormitory buildings, the college occupied the only land for miles around that wasn't mountainous.

The rolling green pastures were fenced for the dozen or so horses that nibbled at sprigs of new grass or basked in the clear spring sunlight. Snaking through a grove of poplars and maples were pathways overhung with trellises that would probably soon be tangled in wisteria and honeysuckle.

As they approached the main buildings, they saw college girls strolling here and there, hugging books to their chests and chatting with their friends.

"Jeez," Gracey said as Parker eased into a visitor's parking slot, "they're all wearing dresses."

"This is the factory," said Parker, "where they make the Stepford wives."

"Funny, Dad."

"Don't look now—we've been spotted."

A uniformed security guard came marching across the lot and stopped just outside Parker's door.

"Help you?" he said through the open window.

"We're looking for a Professor Milford."

The guard made no reply but walked to the rear of the car and jotted down their plate number.

He stayed back there and used his walkie-talkie.

"Are we under arrest?" Gracey said.

"It feels that way," said Parker. "We may be needing a good attorney."

"Too bad we don't know any," Charlotte said.

Parker smiled at her. What grieving he was doing for his lost son, he was concealing down in some secret canyon of his heart. The manly way. Only the faintest echoes of pain lurked in his eyes.

The security guy had red hair and a twitchy mouth.

"Dr. Milford's in class," he said, this time without stooping down.

"Is there somewhere we can wait?"

"You got an appointment?"

"Do we need one?"

"For tribal assessment you do."

"What's that?" Parker asked.

The guard made no reply, so Charlotte leaned across Parker and smiled up at the young man.

"We're deciding on colleges for our daughter. Dr. Milford suggested we have a look at where she worked."

The guard bent down and gave Charlotte a careful appraisal, trying for a moment to peer past the surface of her smile. But she kept it rigidly in place.

"Her office is over there. One-oh-four Tribue Hall. Somebody'll help you."

"Tribal assessment?" Parker said as they walked down the shady path.

"I wouldn't go to this college for a million bucks," Gracey said. "You can't force me."

"I just made that up, Gracey, so the guard would leave us alone."

"Not for ten million dollars," she said. "Look at all these goofballs."

Gracey matched Charlotte's stride, and the two of them followed Parker to Tribue Hall, a two-story version of the main house, an outbuilding that once might have housed the favored slaves.

In the foyer, a family of Native Americans sat on a bench in jeans and matching flannel shirts. The father stood up when they entered.

"I'm Rufus Youngdeer and this here's my family. Sally, the wife. Flora Mae and Bailey. I come back with the right figure this time."

With a shy smile, he extended a white envelope fat with greenbacks.

"She's the wrong one," the man's wife said. "That's not her."

"You Milford? The professor lady?"

"No, I'm not," Charlotte said. "Sorry."

The man drew back the cash and hunched forward into a bow.

"Sorry," he said. "Sorry, missus."

She and Parker and Gracey trooped down the polished wood hallway and found 104 at the very end. Charlotte knocked, then tried the door, but it was locked.

"Kick it in?" Parker said.

"I'm tempted."

Gracey stared out a hall window at the college girls in their spring frocks. Passing to and fro like bright reef fish cruising an aquarium.

"Hello?"

It was a woman in her late forties with pink cherub cheeks and flat blue eyes. Her curly hair was permed into a tight mass of jet-black curls. She was barely five feet tall but probably outweighed Parker by twenty pounds. Her black suit looked expensive but was a size too tight, buttons straining. She was studiously avoiding eye contact.

"We're here to see Dr. Milford."

"For assessment?"

The woman's eyes were circling the room as though following the flight of an invisible bee. For a moment Charlotte wondered if she was blind.

"What's an assessment?" Charlotte said.

The woman paused for a moment and her face hardened, then just as quickly it relaxed as if a jolt of voltage had passed through her system. She looked at the air just above Charlotte's head and smiled.

"Tribal registry," the woman said. "Validating roots."

"That's what Milford does? Decides who's Cherokee, who's not?"

"Oh, yeah. It's big around here."

"What does that cost?" Parker said. "Validating your roots?"

"Varies," the woman said.

"A hundred dollars, five hundred?"

"Oh, more than that. I don't know exactly. But they make it all back with the casino payouts in a couple of years."

The woman giggled, then it turned to a real laugh. Then ceased abruptly.

"What's so funny?" Gracey said.

Charlotte held up a hand and sent her a look. Don't ask.

"I'm Charlotte and this is Parker, and this is Gracey, our daughter."

"Oh, I know Parker already," the woman said. "Remember me? I'm Sissy Tribue."

The woman put out her hand, then immediately withdrew it, her eyes still following the spiraling path of the insect.

"Hello, Sissy. It's been a long time."

"A long time," Sissy said. "A long time, yes, a long time."

"You work with Dr. Milford?"

"I'm her gofer." A smile came to her lips, then slipped away.

"Could we talk to you while we wait?"

"Don't see why not."

They followed her into a sunny office space. Books neatly shelved, a single framed picture on the wall. Sissy and her father, Uncle Mike, standing side by side in their Sunday best.

"We were very sorry about your father's death."

Sissy beamed at the wall.

"Oh, that's okay. He was old, and he knew he was going to be killed. He expected it."

"He did?" Charlotte said. "Why?"

"For telling Jacob Panther the truth about his lineage. But Daddy had to do it because it was the right thing to do. He always did the right thing. Daddy was a good man. He was good."

Gracey stood at the window and looked out at the stream of campus beauties passing by.

"What was Jacob's lineage? What is it your father told him?"

Sissy settled into the swivel chair behind her oak desk. Her eyes were roaming the upper quadrant of the room. She swiveled to the right, then swiveled back to the other side like a kid trying out new furniture.

"Genealogies, that's hard work. Tracking down ancestors."

Sissy chortled again. Then her face went neutral.

"It's very, very hard work," Sissy said. "Marriage records, birth certificates, Civil War pension archives, different reservation rolls the government did over the years. Land transfers, police records. These days, she's super busy. So many people pretending they have Indian blood, wanting a cut of casino cash. But Dr. Milford can always tell who's who. Weed out the bad ones."

"Yeah," Charlotte said. "The ones without envelopes."

Charlotte was having little success reading the young woman's face. Her empty smile, and those senseless laughs, and eyes that glistened without depth or guile.

"Tell us about Tsali's relatives," she said.

The question hit an inflamed nerve. Sissy stiffened and went still. Her dazed look hardened into rock.

"Is she okay?" Gracey said.

Charlotte dug through her backpack and found her wallet, flipped it open, and laid it on Sissy's desk with the badge exposed.

"Sissy, I'm a police officer. You can talk to me. It's okay, it's safe."

Sissy rocked sideways to glimpse the badge, eyes hidden, chin down.

"I'm not allowed."

Charlotte drew her Beretta and laid it on the desk beside the badge. The least threatening threat she could think of. But Parker still looked aghast.

"When a police officer asks you questions, Sissy, you know you have to tell the truth. Or you could go to jail."

"I know," she said quietly.

"So, tell us about Tsali's ancestors?"

Sissy considered it a moment more, and shot another glance at the pistol, then she reached into the collar of her blouse and drew out a key on a gold chain. Grunting, she wrestled the chain over her head. Her face was flushed, and sweat glistened on her upper lip, her jaw locked.

Parker leaned close and whispered angrily.

"You're terrifying the girl."

Sissy rose from her chair and walked on tiptoes around her desk, her hands raised to her shoulders as if she were being held at gunpoint.

Charlotte scooped up her wallet and pistol and tucked them into her backpack, and she and Parker followed Sissy out into the hall where Sissy used the key to open Dr. Milford's office door.

She stepped through the door with her palms held at shoulder height.

Milford's office seemed to be professionally decorated, with pale blue curtains and marching chairs and an Oriental rug that felt two inches deep. Her cherry desk was wide and gleamed with fresh polish; her leather chair was high-backed and deeply padded. On her shelves, the books were lined up with the spines perfectly flush.

Moving with the languor of the weightless, Sissy eased around behind the professor's desk, slid open a drawer, and drew out a small booklet.

"That's good, Sissy," Charlotte said. "Now pass it over here."

Sissy slid a slim document to the edge of the desk. Printed in bold type on its cover was THE TRIBUE PROJECT.

Charlotte opened the booklet and found that the pages unfolded to triple their width. On each one was printed an intricate diagram. Names with dates of births and deaths on solid lines that branched into other solid lines. Cause of death was listed for many of them or else labeled "unknown." Fathers and mothers and their children. From a quick look, it seemed that each page covered maybe a quarter century. The booklet was apparently a single family tree that ran back to 1800.

Charlotte paged through the document for several moments, then stopped near the end, tilted it up for Parker to see, and jabbed her finger at a name on one of the final pages. *Walkingstick.*

Gracey appeared in the doorway and came over to see.

"What is that thing?"

"What we've been looking for. The list you mentioned."

Parker said, "The last page. Look."

And there were the three of them, the final three branches of the tree. Diana, Parker, and Gracey Monroe.

"This is why you insisted on coming here? You figured this out."

"I had a hunch."

"You were the hardest, Parker," Sissy said. "You and your mother and your little girl. Like somebody went to the courthouse and stole all your birth records and other documents. That's what Dr. Milford thought, but she located everything eventually, on microfilm stored away in the basement of some courthouse. She's good, she doesn't give up. She found you like she always does. Sooner or later. Sooner or later. Sooner or later."

"Oh, she found us all right," said Parker.

Sissy watched the imaginary bee circle the overhead light.

"Aunt Roberta wasn't nice," Sissy said. "She wasn't a good person."

"She died last year about this time?"

"Everybody dies," Sissy said. "My mother died, my father died. Everybody dies. Animals die. Pets and birds. There's nothing that doesn't die, unless you count rocks."

"Tell us about Roberta. Why do you say she wasn't nice?"

Sissy scrubbed both hands hard across her face as if trying to wipe away a nightmare. She took her hands away from her reddened flesh and said, "When Aunt Roberta was sick, Farris and Martin went into her room and closed the door and she told them things and when they came out they were different."

"How were they different?"

Sissy's eyes were growing cloudy and vague.

"They were angry after that. All the time. Angry, angry, angry."

Sissy bent forward and chopped the side of her hand against Milford's desk several times to demonstrate what *angry* looked like.

"There's our major event," Parker said. "The thing that set this off. Roberta dies."

Charlotte nodded but kept her eyes trained on Sissy. The girl wouldn't meet her gaze, but somehow she seemed to know that Charlotte's eyes were bearing down on her.

"Do you know what your aunt told Farris and Martin?"

"My daddy told me. My daddy tells me everything. He never hides things from me like most people do. He treats me normal. He told me."

"What did he tell you?"

"There's sick blood in our veins. It's the reason I'm like I am and the reason Farris and Martin are like they are and the reason Shelley is like he is."

"Who's Shelley?"

"He's retarded. He's got a mental deficiency."

"Who is he?"

"He's my cousin Farris's little boy. Shelley. He's mentally deficient."

"How old is Shelley? When was he born?"

"That summer," she said. "The summer of the fire, when camp closed."

Parker's jaw was working as if he were chewing a wad of gristle.

"Shelley was born, then the fire happened?"

"Yeah, Shelley, then the fire. Shelley's mentally deficient."

Charlotte dug through her backpack until she found the silver locket. She clicked it open and passed it across the desk. Sissy snuck a look at it, then hid her eyes again, staring at the bookshelves.

"Who is that, Sissy? Do you know?"

"That's Molly Tribue. She was a prostitute. Lived in a cathouse and got syphilis. Aunt Roberta blamed everything on her, on the venereal disease she got. But my daddy said she was wrong, the sick blood was in her veins before Molly ever went to the whorehouse. There was something wrong with her, and she passed it on. And we all caught it."

"But your cousins didn't believe that."

"Martin and Farris were angry. Very, very angry."

"And they blamed Tsali. And Tsali's ancestors."

"They were very angry. Men do things when they get that way. Bad things."

Gracey had moved to the window and was holding aside the curtain to stare out at the silent sashay of all those entitled young ladies. Their spring dresses glowed more vividly than the blooming flowers, brighter and cleaner than anything natural.

Charlotte moved over beside her and put her arm over her Gracey's shoulder. Her daughter, the last descendant of a Cherokee martyr.

313

The clack of heels echoed on the wooden floor of the corridor and Charlotte turned to see a rail-thin woman coming into the doorway. Her black hair was knotted in a bun, and her suit so severely cut it didn't give her room for a full breath.

"Sissy? Is there some good reason why you're in my office?"

Flustered, Sissy rose, and her face went scarlet. She took a deep breath and shut her mouth like a diver about to submerge. Eyes looking heavenward.

"And who are your friends?"

With painful shyness, Sissy began to sputter something, but Charlotte cut her short.

"We were just leaving."

Milford had the impatient eyes and rigid mouth of a woman rarely challenged. There was nothing innocent in her face, and when she saw the pamphlet in Parker's hand, all vestiges of civility vanished.

"What have you been doing, Sissy?"

She reached out and snatched the booklet from Parker. Then rattled it at the petrified girl and was about to launch into a tirade when Charlotte stepped between the professor and Sissy Tribue.

She leaned in close and, though Milford held her ground, some of the arrogance in her expression took flight when she took a closer look at Charlotte's face. Charlotte twisted the booklet from her hand and passed it to Parker.

"Professor," she said quietly, "when my husband and I are finished dealing with the rest of this, the two of us are going to sit down and research the law that applies to your accountability. And I promise, you'll be hearing from us again. In the meantime, I suggest you find yourself a very good attorney."

FORTY-TWO

THEY WERE HEADING OUT THE college drive when Charlotte said, "Tsali and his ancestors were the Tribues' personal scapegoats. That's what Jacob was coming to tell you when I chased him away."

"Don't go bending this around, looking for some way to punish yourself."

"I know, I know. But still."

"Go to the airport, or stay here and close this down?"

"Do we have a choice?" she said.

They were quiet for a minute, Parker steering them back the way they'd come, the narrow road through cow pastures and apple orchards.

Her cell phone rang, and Charlotte answered. Marie Salzedo again. Just a single bit of information. Charlotte thanked her and hung up.

"A fax from the North Carolina DMV," she said to Parker. "A special application for a license plate with the last four digits of one seven seven three was made by Mr. Martin Tribue in June of last year."

He nodded.

"Not like we needed anything else."

"But when it goes to trial," she said, "every little bit helps."

"Something occurred to me on the motivation side," he said.

"Yeah?"

"That play, *Unto These Hills.* Imagine how you'd feel if you were a Tribue and every night, all summer long for the last fifty years, thousands of people saw your ancestor reviled as a villain while Tsali, who actually murdered your blood relative—he's held up as a saint."

Charlotte was quiet for a while, then said, "Now I see why Diana was so worried about you being in the limelight."

"What?"

"I didn't mention it to you at the time, but she was anxious about your high profile. All the television and newspaper stories."

"That's how Martin and Farris found us. My goddamn career."

"They would have found a way, Parker. Sooner or later."

"I'm ready to go home," Gracey said.

"I know, honey," Charlotte said. "I'm ready, too."

"I'm sick of this place. I miss Miami. I miss the heat."

"We do, too, sweetheart. We'll go as soon as we can, I promise."

Parker drove for a while, then said, "Mr. Big, Jeremiah's partner."

"Had to be Otis Tribue," she said. "He nearly gets killed, loses his nerve, gives up the fight."

"And it would've stayed that way," Parker said. "Except that his beloved wife, Roberta, was dying and decided to poison another generation."

Charlotte turned around to see if Gracey was paying attention, but the girl was looking out her window, muttering softly to one of the people who inhabited the scrambled universe within her.

"How's it possible?" Parker said. "Somebody can keep alive that kind of hate for all those years?"

"Seems pretty obvious to me."

"I don't get it."

"You and I had different backgrounds, Parker. You were a summer-camp boy. You had conscientious parents, nice spiffy prep-school friends. You didn't ride to Florida with Teddy Miles in a rusty Olds Cutlass, get sent to jail as an accomplice to felony murder. I knew a rough crowd."

Parker concentrated on the thickening traffic.

"Take the people you work with, your clients," she said. "You listen to their stories, you evaluate the evidence against them, then you do your magic rain dance and all their problems go away."

"I wish it were that easy."

"Thing I'm saying is, Parker, in a job like yours you have to keep a positive view. For you it comes natural. You believe people deserve a second chance because they're essentially good. Next time they'll get it right."

"I know there's evil. Don't make me out as some idiot Pollyanna."

"I wouldn't have you any other way, Parker. It's just that you're not as familiar as I am with what's out there. Not just the white-sheet crowd, some wacko in his apartment making pipe bombs to blow up women's clinics. I'm talking ordinary people so beaten down they know, goddamn it, there's a conspiracy working against them. They're pissed off, got all this frustration boiling and nowhere to put it. Searching for somebody to blame."

"But this is different. So systematic. So long term."

"Is it any different from racism, any other kind of bigotry?" she said. "Same low-grade fever festering below the surface, always ready to flare up when the right spark comes along to set it off. All it takes is some kind of trauma. A mother dying, bringing her boys close to her deathbed, spreading a hateful folktale. Your own son is mentally retarded, and now suddenly you have somebody to blame. That would be enough to light the fuse. A guy like Farris. His brother.

"I mean, look at that Drury kid you got off last week. Shooting the basketball coach. You think that kid sat down and sketched it out in his notebook, ran through the moral pros and cons? Should I, shouldn't I? Hell, no, he had so much hair-trigger rage and despair and God knows what else banging away inside him, all that coach had to do was yell at him one time that he was being lazy on defense, not moving his feet quick enough, and the kid runs home and gets his Glock. There's thousands of Drury kids. Millions. Just looking for the right cause, the right spark to set them off."

"Your years on the beat," he said. "That's darkened your view."

"It's more than that, Parker. More than what I see on the street."

She looked back at Gracey, but the girl had her eyes closed, still mumbling to herself.

"Mother should have told me the truth," he said. "Told us all. Let us decide how to address it."

"She thought it was over, Parker. She thought it had run its course and was finished. She didn't want to contaminate our lives with fear. I give her credit for that."

Charlotte stared ahead at the mountains rising before them. Green and fresh and staggering in their dimension. A landscape that mocked human pretense, immense and ancient and unknowable.

She felt the words rise from her unbidden.

"I lied about the Qwik Mart."

"What?"

"I knew it was going to happen. I knew exactly what Teddy was up to."

"Come on, Charlotte, no reason to dredge all that up."

"Let me finish, okay? Just let me get it out."

He looked over at her with such undiluted dread it was as if he could see a web of cracks forming in her face, the woman he loved about to split wide open.

Charlotte hadn't thought this out, had never let the words take shape in any logical way, but they came in an unstoppable rush, a flood of truth that had gathered for so long against the bulwarks of self-control that, as painful as it was to admit, there was an equal measure of relief.

"I wasn't some innocent kid on a spring-break lark. I was eighteen, and every bit as pissed off and spiteful as Teddy Miles, right down at my core. Both of us headed nowhere. I was sick of the sour gray Tennessee winters, sick of my mother sleeping with guys for a six-pack of beer and a carton of Camels. Sick of picturing my future and seeing nothing but repeating the same damn life my mother had.

"We spent that thousand-mile drive cranking each other up, taking big slugs off the same bottle of venom. All the crap we hated, all the people standing in our way. This conspiracy of the haves against us poor pitiful have-nots. The unfairness of it all. Bitching about how we were trapped, like there was this big barbed-wire fence running around the city limits of our town. You could escape, but they'd track you down and drag you back and force you to stay the rest of your life there and do the same damn thing your mother did and your father. Live that same way.

"Then we hit South Florida, saw that skyline sparkling in the distance, and both of us started howling, not from joy or excitement but like a couple of starved wolves ready to tear flesh from bone. When Teddy pulled over and walked into that Qwik Mart with a dead-eyed look, I knew it was going to happen. I read it in his face, Parker. This was the big breakout we'd been raving about for all those miles. I knew what was coming down. If that's not an accomplice, I don't know what is."

Parker was quiet for a few seconds, then said, "Did you discuss the crime itself, plan it out with him in advance?"

"Oh, forget the lawyer crap. You already got me off once. But you can't sweet-talk the judge this time. I know what happened, how I felt. I know how Teddy felt and why he blew like he did."

"Understanding someone's motive doesn't incriminate you, Charlotte."

"It was more than that. I was rooting for him. Teddy was trying to change his luck. Attack the source of his misery. That's how it happens, Parker. Even if they become congressmen and sheriffs, it doesn't go away. That sense of injustice, of being wronged, that fury."

Parker drove with his eyes fixed straight ahead. They were silent for a mile or two.

When he spoke, his voice seemed to come from far away, a foreign land where he'd just arrived, its landscape more harsh and severe than any he had prepared himself for.

"A hundred and fifty years," he said. "It's unthinkable."

"Welcome to the Confederacy. All that rebel blood soaked in the topsoil. People live and breathe it every day. The conquered nation, forced to serve a foreign master. Sure, there's a new South. But the old one's still there, too, living right alongside it."

Parker looked over at her.

"Jesus, Charlotte."

He hadn't known all that was inside her. She'd barely known it herself.

"Let me ask you something." He cut a quick glance toward Gracey. The girl was still muttering to herself, but Parker lowered his voice anyway. "If somehow you found a person you were convinced was responsible for her condition, would you do what the Tribues have been doing? Would you?"

Charlotte looked out her window at the rolling countryside.

"No, I wouldn't," she said. "But, by God, I'd have the urge."

Gracey slouched in the seat and blocked out her parents' voices. She was feeling dull and stupid. Steven had gone off looking for a bimbo willing to strip naked for his new movie. He'd given up on her. And Mr. Underwood, he wasn't anywhere around. Joan and Barbara weren't ragging at each other anymore either. All quiet.

She looked out the window and thought about the college. All those girls with bright dresses and boyfriends and futures. She'd never have any of that and she knew it. The drugs were hammering her. Taking her down into the silent place. Sluggish and dreary and lightless.

She watched the hills turn to mountains and her father and mother yakking in the front seat while Gracey waited for something to happen inside her head. But the drugs had driven everyone away. Everyone, even Jacob Panther. Even her half brother wasn't speaking to her anymore. Off in heaven or wherever. She didn't know about any of that religious stuff. Didn't have a clue where people went when they died. She'd tried to imagine it, but all she could see were clouds. Lots of clouds. And she knew better than that. She'd been up on plenty of airplanes and there was no one sitting around. No harps. None of that.

The drugs were killing her. Making everything gray and stupid. She felt heavy in her seat. Like some big-titted goon that no one would ever love because she was too weird, too lost inside her own head, too doped up and dull and going nowhere. Not to any college. Not off on her own, living with roommates, going on dates, kissing boys and the rest. None of that. Maybe a mental hospital, that was where she was headed. Strap her down, do those shock treatments she'd seen in movies. Be a zombie with all the other zombies, wearing nightgowns all day. *Night of the Living Dead* for the rest of her life. The cuckoo's nest.

She waited for someone to speak. But the only voices were her mother and father talking and debating. The two of them doing what they always did, taking opposite sides.

She'd always be a little girl. She'd never grow into a woman. Her body was there, but her head was never going to catch up. She knew that. She wasn't right. She was a strange little girl like they called her at school. Spacey Gracey.

Joan and Barbara and Steven and Mr. Underwood. They'd been good to her, treated her like she was somebody special. But nobody else did. And now they were gone. Driven off by the drugs, the stupid stupid pill her mother handed her, made her swallow. Her stupid stupid mother with her stupid stupid pills.

Gracey? Are you okay? You still on board?

The voice was so faint, she could barely make it out. She clenched her eyes tight to hear better. And good God, if it wasn't Steven.

He was saying the script was finally finished. He'd cut out the naked part, okay? He decided he could live without it.

Gracey had chills. It wasn't the drugs after all. Steven had just gone off to consider the issue. She'd challenged him, pushed him to change.

I've decided you're right about the nudity. And there's that age issue you mentioned. I mean, I didn't realize you're only sixteen. Sure, we could get in trouble. It would be controversial.

She sighed. She'd won him over, convinced him.

But then again, Steven said, controversy sure had a way of perking up the box office.

Gracey was quiet. Steven was starting to wobble back the other way. Giving it with one hand, two seconds later taking it back with the other.

Box office, Joan said. That's how it starts. They work around to money, profits, bottom line. Bottom line, my ass. It's tits. Always with the tits.

Gracey looked out the window as her dad drove. They were back in the mountains now, up and down, one switchback after another. She remembered the black guy on the bus. Excuse me, excuse me, every time they bumped. And she remembered that her grandmother had been murdered. And her half brother shot down five feet away. And Lucy shot and bullets whizzing by her head. And now her name was on a murder list. Being hunted by somebody. And she held that up alongside all the stuff Mr. Underwood and Steven were always saying about exposing herself to the harshness of the world, and here's what she thought: She thought they were both full of shit.

Two little boys. Two adolescents who didn't know what the hell they were talking about. Not a damn thing. Gracey had driven that goddamn camper while Lucy Panther bled from a gunshot wound, for chrissakes.

And then they were gone. Steven disappeared. She could feel it. Blink— he's not there anymore, whooshed away back to the Hollywood world he came from. And Joan Crawford, too. Not that she'd miss Joan particularly. Gracey wasn't sure about Barbara Stanwyck, but she listened and didn't hear anything except the sound of her parents talking and the wind rushing past the car and big trucks blowing by in the opposite direction.

Gone. Snap your finger, like that, it's finished. Her big movie break. Melanie Griffith, all that. Gone, gone, gone.

Spielberg, jeez, what was she thinking? He was just another spoiled kid who didn't know shit about real pain or danger or anything. Parents getting divorced? An unhappy childhood? You call that trouble? I'll show you trouble.

In only a few days, Gracey had changed and they hadn't. Simple as that. She'd moved on.

"Good riddance," she said aloud.

Her mother looked back at her.

"Screw them," Gracey said. "Screw all of them."

"Who?" her mother asked. "Screw who?"

It sounded funny, that rhyme coming out of her mother's mouth.

"Screw who?" Gracey repeated. And she laughed.

A second later her dad joined in, laughing, too, and finally her mother.

All of them said it one more time, "Screw who?" Practically in unison.

Then when the laughing died down, her mother said to her dad, "I think it's time to call Frank."

FORTY-THREE

"YEAH, I'M STILL HERE," SHEFFIELD said. "Another bucket of shit hit the fan."

They were passing through a town named Dellwood, about halfway between Asheville and Cherokee. The mountains starting to flex their muscles.

Charlotte asked what happened.

"Congressman Tribue died. I figured I should stick around, double-check a few things."

"Suspicious circumstances?"

"You might say that." She could hear other men speaking in the background.

"You can't talk now?"

"That would be correct."

"Parker and I have something heavy to unload, Frank."

"How heavy is heavy?"

"Trust me, this is serious weight."

"I'm listening."

"Has to be face-to-face."

"Well, right now I'm out in the front yard at the Tribues' estate. Should be here the rest of the day. You know where that is?"

"Is the sheriff there? Farris?"

"Does the pope shit in the Vatican?"

"How about Roth and your other guys?"

"Yeah, they're around, why?"

"Can you keep Farris there? Make sure he doesn't go anywhere?"

"What the hell's this about?"

Charlotte looked over at Parker and gave him a reassuring smile. He returned it, but his had a forlorn edge. She'd given him a peek into the lower regions of her heart, and it had shaken him. Truth be known, it shook her, too, hearing herself say those things, knowing they were true.

"Give me the directions, Frank. We'll fill you in when we get there."

For the rest of the drive, they were silent, Charlotte studying the *Tribue Project* pamphlet. Tracing the half-dozen branches of Tsali's family tree that sprouted from his one surviving son. Each branch ended abruptly, except for Diana Walkingstick and her son, Parker, and his offspring, Gracey.

An hour later, winding up the steep entrance drive to the Tribue estate, she said, "It's possible Milford called Farris by now, and he knows we're on the way."

"So how do we play it?"

"Get Sheffield alone. Tell him what we know. What else is there?"

"He won't buy it, nobody in their right mind would. All we've got is a bunch of disconnected facts. A booklet with our names in it, a locket with an old drawing. No clear connection to Mother's murder. No connection to Jacob. Just a pound and a half of speculation. Nothing hard."

"Gracey saw Farris shooting at her."

"Put Gracey into the middle of this? You're not serious. And is Sissy a reliable witness? Not on your life."

"Okay, look, I've been studying this booklet, Parker. And the way it seems, at least three-quarters of the people in this book, Tsali's ancestors, died before the age of twenty. Violent deaths, knife wounds, falls from high places. Gunshots. Disappearances are common. Three-quarters of them, Parker."

He shook his head and half-closed his eyes, unimpressed.

"So you got a long history of accidents, high incidence of violent deaths, it could be random for all we know. Take that to a DA along with this crackpot tale, he'd laugh you out of his office, pure and simple. Who knows, maybe those death stats are the normal life expectancy for the tribe. These are hard-living people, not famous for their healthy lifestyles."

"You don't believe any of this?"

"Oh, I believe it," Parker said. "But we need something a little more concrete. Like a signed confession."

"One look at Farris, you know that isn't gonna happen. Guy's got antifreeze pumping through him."

"Suggestions?"

"Get inside his house," she said. "Locate the rifle he used on Jacob."

"Come on. You're going to steal a weapon from the sheriff's house to run a ballistics test? Jesus, Charlotte. You're not thinking straight."

"There's got to be something."

"Give it to Sheffield. This is his world."

"Sheffield," she said and groaned. "God help us."

He parked alongside a group of white Fords like the ones Frank's people had been using. Through the hemlocks and pines, she could make out a grassy lawn where the two white poodles and a half-dozen local police were milling around.

"You sure about this?" he said. "Nothing says we have to do it now."

"Why don't you and Gracey stay in the car? I'll lay it out for Frank, then the three of us can chew it over later."

"I got to take a whiz, Mom. Big time."

"Can you use the bushes?"

"No way," Gracey said. "There's snakes everywhere up here."

Charlotte looked back at Gracey.

"I'm serious, Mom. I got to go like right now. I can't hold it."

"Okay, so you go with her," Parker said. "I'll handle Frank."

Charlotte didn't like it, but Gracey was squirming, so she hitched her backpack over her shoulder and they set off through the trees to join the gathering.

Halfway across the field, the two poodles spotted them and trotted over and gave them all a good sniff. The dogs homed in on Gracey, nosing her crotch, pawing her jeans for attention. She squatted down and they nuzzled her neck while she giggled and dug her hands into their coats.

A moment later Farris arrived with Frank at his side. Farris was dressed in black trousers and a dark collarless shirt. Frank sent Charlotte a strained and questioning look, but Charlotte made no attempt to respond.

"Once again," Parker said, "our condolences for your loss, Sheriff."

Farris bowed his head in mock gratitude.

"A release from his earthly pain. A better place and all that."

Charlotte drew Gracey away from the dogs.

"Is there a bathroom we can use?" she said. "Gracey's in need."

"Forensics are finished," Frank said, "the body's out, you're free to go inside. Long as Sheriff Tribue says yes."

Farris said, "I'll be happy to show you the way."

"You're most gracious." She shot Parker a parting look—make it fast.

Trailed by the dogs, they walked in silence across the terraced lawn, and Charlotte halted at the front steps. She looked back to see Frank listening intently to Parker's story.

"Mom, I gotta go. Come on."

Farris raked Charlotte with a tight-lipped scowl, and for some reason she was reminded of the red-haired boy in Fedderman's videotape, the single scenario she'd gotten wrong. The kid aiming his pistol at that cornered cat. *Here, kitty kitty.*

"Down the main hallway," Farris said, "second door on the left. That's the guest bath."

She thanked him, and she and Gracey, trailed by the dogs, mounted the porch. When the two of them pushed through the screen door, the dogs halted outside.

Gracey went into the tiny lavatory, and Charlotte stood guard in the foyer, looking back through the screen. Parker and Sheffield were bent close, but when Farris arrived, they stepped apart and gazed out at the distant peaks. She tried to read Frank's face, but at that distance his features were a blur.

Some of the FBI guys were out near the edge of what looked like a ravine, while Farris's tribal police squatted down in the grass in the shade of a grove of poplars. It was a standard cooling-off time at a death scene. The work done, but nobody ready to leave the area quite yet.

The toilet flushed and a moment later Gracey reappeared.

"Better?"

"I heard a voice," Gracey said.

"What voice?"

"Upstairs, a voice. Through the plumbing or something."

"Gracey, come on, we're leaving. We can't stay here."

"I recognized it. Lucy Panther's in trouble."

Charlotte took Gracey by the elbow and steered her toward the screen door, but she yanked away.

"I heard her voice, goddamn it, in the pipes, I heard her groaning, Mother. I did. I'm not hallucinating, okay?"

She was halfway up the stairs before Charlotte recovered and followed.

When she made it to the landing, she found Gracey standing still with her head cocked to listen. The room at the head of the stairs was crisscrossed with yellow police tape.

"She's in there," Gracey said and started toward the front bedroom.

"Gracey, we'll send Sheffield in. It's not our place."

"You're a cop, right? Isn't this what you're supposed to do, save people?"

Gracey stormed past her and halted outside the door and tried the knob, but it was locked.

She pressed her ear to the wood.

"Listen if you don't believe me."

Charlotte sighed and stepped beside her and flattened her ear to the door, and yes, there was a muffled grunt. Two feet away, the sound was lost.

"You inherited your father's hearing."

"I told you."

"Okay, step back."

The girl dodged away, and Charlotte retreated two steps and threw herself forward, planting her kick near the knob. The door gave but didn't break. She repeated it and, on the third try, the edge splintered and the door flew inward. Gracey rushed inside with Charlotte two steps behind.

Spread-eagled on a double bed, Lucy Panther was naked, her wrists and ankles lashed to the posts, her mouth covered with layers of gray duct tape, her head tipped to the side near a tiny sink. Her grunts had not made it beyond the door, but somehow they'd found their way down the pipes to the floor below.

She looked at Charlotte and Gracey with a composure that belied her situation.

Charlotte peeked out the edge of the front window and saw Farris and Sheffield and Parker engaged in conversation.

Charlotte hurried back to the foot of the bed and pried a green comforter from beneath Lucy's bound legs, then shook it out full length to cover her nakedness.

Lucy nodded her thanks.

Making a quick search of the dressing table for something sharp, Charlotte found nothing, then remembered the nail scissors in her bag.

When she snipped the gag loose, Lucy's first words were, "Get the hell out of here, both of you. He'll find you. Go now."

Charlotte set to work on Lucy's right wrist. As she sliced the gummy fabric, Gracey said, "What happened, Lucy?"

"More than I can tell. More than anyone should have to hear."

"Like what?"

"You need to get out of here. I'm serious."

"So am I," said Charlotte.

She tipped her bag to the side and showed Lucy the Beretta.

Lucy Panther said, "Last night I got the whole damn history lesson. Back to the beginning of time. You wouldn't believe the shit this family's been up to the last two hundred years."

"Oh, yeah," Charlotte said. "We've been putting it together ourselves." She had the right wrist loose and was working on the ankle.

"You know about Molly Tribue?"

"Wife of Matthew," Charlotte said. "The soldier Tsali killed."

"You hear about the whorehouse?"

Charlotte said yes, she'd heard that part, too.

The tape on the ankle was thicker, five or six layers deep, straining the scissors.

"The reservation was the Tribues' private hunting club, you know what I mean, one of those places where they stock all this wild game in a fenced-in area. They go out with their high-powered rifles and bag a rhino. Only it was Tsali's bloodline they wanted."

Lucy wriggled the right leg loose, and Charlotte moved around the bed to work on the other side.

"That gun loaded?" Lucy said.

"It is."

"You're going to need it. Getting out of here, you're damn well going to need it. You can't trust Farris's deputies. Not one of them."

Charlotte looked up and saw Gracey standing at the front window.

"Get away from there, Gracey, before someone sees you."

The girl ducked aside and grinned.

"Nobody saw me," she said. "Nobody but those stupid dogs."

One of the poodles had begun a listless barking.

"Two more things I gotta tell you, in case I don't make it out of here alive," Lucy said.

"Don't say that. You're going to make it."

"The gun Otis used on Parker's dad, some old cheap-ass revolver, it's in that drawer over there."

As Charlotte worked on the remaining tape, she heard a distant crow cawing and another answering back in a minor key. Outside in the lawn, the poodle continued to woof in a lazy tempo like the background bass of late-night jazz.

"Mike Tribue's the only one in the family worth a damn."

"Far as the law's concerned," Charlotte said, "Mike's an accomplice. He knew what was going on, but did nothing. He'd be treated the same as the doer of the deed."

"That accomplice saved your life."

"If he knew the truth, he should never have let it get as far as it did."

"Old Mike was a gentle spirit," Lucy said. "Men like that don't come at things like you and me, head on. They're roundabout. But that doesn't make them guilty. It's just a different approach. He sat on the sidelines, watching the rest of his family, knowing someday it might boil up again, and when it did, he came to me and Jacob and laid it out. I give him credit. Not much, but some."

"And then he sent you off to do what he lacked the courage for."

"Men do the best they can with the gumption God provided."

Charlotte got back to work and stripped another layer of tape away.

"And the banks?" she said. "That was Farris and Martin, too?"

"Yeah, Jacob went and ran his mouth to the police about the Tsali story, and Farris got wind of it."

"Why the hell blow up the banks?"

"Sons of bitches," Lucy said. "Once Farris and Martin heard Jacob was yammering about that old conspiracy, those two boys figured a way to get Jacob on the run so nothing he ever said again would be believed. Or me either, for that matter."

Charlotte jabbed her fingertip with the needle point of the scissors and had to suck away the blood before going on.

"And your father, Standingdog? He took the fall, why?"

"My goddamn fault," Lucy said. "I got pregnant and he found out."

"I don't follow."

"Standingdog went barging in to see Chief and Parker's mom at the summer camp, ready to kill them for what their son did. And Diana had no choice but to tell him who she was. The whole Tsali thing. Her being an ancestor. Which meant my baby was going to be one, too."

"So if the truth ever came out about who Jacob's daddy was, Jacob would become a target."

Lucy nodded.

"So your daddy went to prison to protect his grandson."

"Far as I know," said Lucy, "that was the one good thing he ever did."

"It kind of outweighs a lot of bad."

While she worked with the scissors, she ran through the snarl of secrets and motives and sacrifice and deceit and got stuck on one simple question.

"Why couldn't Diana and Charles go to the police? A couple of upstanding people like them, they'd be taken seriously."

"What're they going to say? A boogeyman's after me? I don't care how upstanding they were, no cop I ever met is going to waste a second on that kind of superstition. Up here, where everybody's married to their second cousin, isn't any way to know who to trust. So Parker's mom did the one thing she could after the fire, she ran off and hid herself and Parker. It's what I would've done myself."

Charlotte's head swirled. Trying to imagine Diana's daily dread as her son rose in his profession, became a subject of headlines and news stories.

"You said you had two things to tell us," said Gracey.

Her left ankle was free, and Charlotte had the left wrist almost done.

Lucy started to speak, then grimaced and shook her head as if the words had thickened in her throat and lodged there.

"Go on, Lucy. It's okay."

Lucy puckered her lips and whistled down a long breath.

"A bunch of the Cherokees they killed over the years, Tsali's people, the goddamn Tribues heaved their carcasses into that gorge out there. That's where my own body was headed soon as Farris had enough of it. That ravine goes straight down a half-mile and ends in scrub pine. It would take a mountain climber with ropes and pulleys to get down there. Bones from a hundred years ago mingled with last week's kitchen trash."

Lucy Panther was free, struggling to rise. Charlotte gave her a boost, and Lucy sat up and began to rub at her hands and feet, getting the blood back.

"Someone's coming up the stairs, Mom."

Charlotte took a glimpse out the window and saw Sheffield and Parker still standing on the lawn. A single white poodle was pointing its snout up toward the window where she stood, barking and barking.

FORTY-FOUR

WHEN HE SAW THE MONROE child in the front window, Farris knew it was finished. Not that he'd ever doubted it would end badly. His father's autopsy would be impossible to explain. Gasoline in his veins. His fate was sealed.

Farris knew his mother would approve of that part at least. The IV, the torturous agony her husband had to endure. Although it fell well short of her own months of misery. As he walked toward the house, he looked through the trees toward the barn. When had he last emptied the rattraps? Their bodies rot, you know, and the smell, oh my God the smell, once it permeates those old pine planks, it will be there forever. And your teeth. The plaque, the floss, and the toilets. Don't forget to clean below the rim. That's where it accumulates, the scum. You've got to stay on top of it, or the porcelain will be ruined. How many times had she told him? The toilets, his teeth, the rattraps. How many times?

Farris marched toward the house, knowing it was almost over. A relief of sorts. A quiet serenity suffused him. If all was lost and Farris was never again to see his boy and breathe his breath, then, at the very least, he would accomplish some last portion of what he'd been charged to do. One of the Monroes would die. Which one, it hardly mattered anymore.

If she'd had more than thirty seconds to plan it out, Charlotte would have devised something more creative. But as it was, she worked with what she had in the fleeting seconds available.

She stashed Gracey in one closet and Lucy in another.

Then she flattened her back against the wall, just beyond the range of the door's inward swing.

All she wanted was a second of distraction, maybe two.

Lucy had barely shut herself inside her closet when Farris kicked the broken door open, his SIG Sauer coming through at shoulder height. There was a pause as he absorbed the scene before him. An empty bed, an empty room.

Charlotte chose her spot and hacked the pistol's steel casing across his knobby wrist. His handgun went skittering across the floor, and she hopped away from the wall with a two-handed grip, sighting on his sternum. Giving him orders to put up his hands, turn around.

Farris obeyed without comment. She saw twin flickers pass across his face, the grim sag of defeat morphing into desperate fury and then back again.

Lucy came out of her closet wearing a green robe. Standing at a distance, Gracey looked on in a soundless rapture.

"Get his gun, Lucy. Cover him while I pat him down. And if he flinches, you empty that thing, okay? Don't worry about hitting me."

"I won't be hitting you."

With her Beretta jammed against his spine, Charlotte frisked him one-handed, feeling through the black funeral clothes the tense, wiry body beneath, but finding no more weapons, nothing, not even a wallet or keys.

But still her right first finger was curled with four pounds of pressure against a five-pound trigger. Twitch and he was gone.

"This isn't over," Farris said. "As long as there are Tribues on this planet, there will be one to hunt you down."

"He's lying," Lucy said. "The Tribues have played out their string. Now with Otis gone and Martin and Uncle Mike, there's just this last one left."

"What about this boy, Shelley?" As she spoke the name, Charlotte felt Farris's back grow rigid against her gun barrel.

333

"Oh, him," Lucy said. "You got nothing to fear from that one. Way I hear it, that boy can't wipe the snot off his own nose."

Charlotte prodded Farris forward with the pistol.

He took two steps into the hallway and said, "This isn't finished. This will never be finished."

"You may be right about that," she said. "But *you're* finished. That's for damn sure."

Charlotte walked him down the stairway and outside onto the porch and told him to go on down into the yard. Sheffield and Parker spotted them and came running, followed by a swarm of deputies and agents. Guns were drawn all about her, questions shouted, but Charlotte didn't respond. Lost in the moment, watching Farris's shoulders for any sign of that twitch.

She prodded him out into the center of the lawn. His men stepping forward to block her further progress. The two white poodles wriggled through for a view of the proceedings.

"Now halt right there," she said. "Keep the hands up, don't move."

"They're growing heavy," Farris said.

"Lower them and you die."

"What happened?" Sheffield said. "Are you out of your mind?"

"I'll explain later. Somebody cuff this guy."

"I gotta have a reason here, Charlotte. Talk to me."

"It's what Parker told you."

"Not credible, Monroe. Now put the gun down."

One of the deputies made a threatening feint in her direction, and Charlotte waggled the pistol at him. He halted, and she resumed her aim at the center of Farris's back.

"Farris killed Parker's mother. That morning when he learned his brother had been murdered, he ducked into the museum, stole Tsali's hatchet, then flew down to Miami and killed Diana on Tuesday night and he was coming for Parker and Gracey, too, but it all got a little too messy, so he turned around and flew back home and slid behind his sheriff's desk and decided he'd just bide his time. But, lo and behold, the next day he hits the jackpot, because the whole Monroe clan suddenly shows up right in his own backyard."

"Isn't that how it went, Farris? Tell Agent Sheffield. Unburden yourself, Farris. Go on, let it out."

"She's insane," Farris said. "Someone disarm her."

"If that's how it was," Sheffield said, "then we can check the airline passenger lists. Fine. We'll do that, Charlotte. But right now, you're going to have to put that weapon down. Do you hear me, Officer Monroe? Now."

A few feet to her right, the dogs watched, alert to the unfolding events but showing no inclination to protect their master.

"Keep your hands up, Farris, and turn around so I can see you."

Farris revolved slowly, his hands sagging to his ears.

"Hands higher!" she said. "Above your head."

"Won't anyone stop this outrage?" Farris said.

"Somebody give me some goddamn cuffs," Charlotte shouted at the officers.

But no one moved to help. Roth and his team had drawn their pistols as well and were in a standoff with the deputies. Everyone, it seemed, was trying to decide who threatened them most.

Farris got honey in his voice and said, "Gracey, your granny is over there in the trees. I see her."

"Shut up," Charlotte told him.

"Granny?" Gracey said.

"Parker, come get Gracey."

But one of the deputies blocked his way, gripping him by the arm.

"Put your weapon down, missus," the deputy said. "Or we'll be forced to fire."

"Nobody's going to shoot," Sheffield said.

"Your granny. She's over in the trees. Don't you see her? Diana."

"Another word, Farris, and you're dead. It's that simple."

He smiled at her, and Charlotte saw again the boy in the videotape, the redheaded punk, his flattened lips, the fixed, lightless eyes. *Here, kitty kitty.*

The circle of police officers was tightening around her. Ten feet and inching closer.

Gracey took several wandering steps toward the grove of poplars.

"No, Gracey, you stay here, right here. Go to your dad."

"She's calling for you, Gracey. Don't you hear her, your granny?"

Her daughter turned her back on Charlotte and headed at a trot across the field toward the trees. The dogs stared at Farris, and Charlotte felt a clock begin to tick in her chest, twenty seconds, nineteen. *Here, kitty kitty.*

Farris held her eyes and dared her. An unarmed man standing five feet away, threatening no one, doing nothing.

Then she saw it. His right hand drifting downward to his ear, curving forward toward his forehead.

An unarmed man. A man endangering no one. Ten seconds, nine, eight, seven.

"Where?" Gracey called out. "Where is she?"

Farris touched his right hand to his forehead, the beginnings of a salute, and Charlotte put two rounds in his gut that knocked him sideways and spun him to the ground.

The dogs shied back a step but continued to observe the fallen man.

The deputies were in a frozen panic. She panned the pistol across the group and behind the men saw Lucy Panther trot away toward Gracey.

One of the deputies in the back of the pack broke into a sprint for his patrol car. But Charlotte could tell from Farris's wounds that he was beyond the help of paramedics.

"Mom!" her daughter screamed. "Mom, what's going on?"

"Drop your weapon, Officer Monroe," Sheffield called out. "That's a goddamned order. Drop it now."

"He was going to kill my daughter," Charlotte said.

"The man's unarmed, Monroe. You shot a defenseless man."

Farris groaned and heaved up a stringy mix of blood and slime.

"He was going to kill Gracey. I read it in his face."

"His goddamn face? Are you nuts? She's over there, fifty yards away."

Sheffield was coming toward her, one hand extended for her pistol, the other aiming his .357 at her chest.

Struggling onto his left elbow, Farris groaned and brought his hand up and completed the salute and the two white poodles loped away toward Gracey.

Charlotte fired twice more into Farris and settled her aim on the dogs, but before she could squeeze off a round, Lucy Panther stepped into their path and opened her arms wide. The dogs leaped onto her, knocked her to the ground, and tore at her head and neck and shoulders.

It lasted only seconds, then they fell away from Lucy's broken body and ambled into the shade of the poplars and lay down to lick each other's muzzles.

Lowering their pistols, the deputies parted for her and Charlotte sprinted across the field and dropped to her knees beside her weeping daughter. Parker and Sheffield were there seconds later.

"What?" Gracey sputtered through her sobs. "What did I do?"

"You were fine," Charlotte said. "Just wonderful, Gracey. You did exactly right. It's over now. It's over."

"Lucy Panther saved my life. She saved my life, didn't she, Mother?"

"Yes, she did. Lucy was very brave. Very, very brave."

FORTY-FIVE

MORE THAN SIXTY SKULLS WERE found among the refuse at the bottom of Raven's Gorge. Shattered human bones of every sex and age, and even the recent remains of a young woman from Congressman Tribue's own staff. A mass grave of such proportion that it would take years to excavate and sort out.

Before they returned to Miami, Charlotte and Parker went to meet Shelley Tribue. Margie Hornbuckle, his caretaker, led them out to a sunny field where they found Shelley sitting in an old lounge chair that someone had dragged into the middle of the meadow.

The gangly young man had a drawing pad balanced on his knees and was using a box of colored pencils to draw circles on the white sheet.

"He says that's his father," Margie said. "The boy can't get enough of drawing his father."

The circles were the size of quarters, and there were two dark dots in each one that Shelley must have intended to be the vacant eyes of Farris Tribue.

"He misses that man already," Margie said. "Don't ask me why."

. . .

Officer Charlotte Monroe went back to work with Dr. Fedderman and applied herself to becoming one of his disciples, learning his mystifying muscle groups so she could teach others the skills she still didn't fully believe she possessed. It was the bargain she'd made, so she honored it, but her heart wasn't in the daily grind of videotapes and flashing microexpressions. The detailed diagrams of skinless faces, with strands of muscles and tendons and branching nerves, all to be memorized.

She decided she owed them a year. After that she would press the button on her ejection seat and parachute back to the streets. There'd be pressure for her to stay, but she could handle that. In the meantime, she watched faces for eight hours a day and learned what they asked her to learn.

In early July, Marvin Drury, the teenager Parker had successfully defended in the Miami High coach's shooting, was involved in another incident.

A math teacher tutoring Marvin in summer school pissed the kid off and took two rounds in the shoulder for his misstep. The teacher survived, but Marvin was charged with attempted first degree. The boy's mother pled with Parker to take her boy's case, but Parker informed her that he wasn't that kind of lawyer. Second chances were within his province, but beyond that he would not go.

In early July, Charlotte found a camp for Gracey out on Key Biscayne. Not a sleepover place like Camp Tsali, no charismatic director, but a good-hearted woman who specialized in artistic types. They would be performing *Othello* for the closing ceremony, and after a week of grueling auditions, Gracey won the female lead.

When the kids weren't rehearsing or memorizing lines, they swam in the Atlantic and learned to scuba dive. Gracey seemed okay with it, as okay as she was with anything. Not ecstatic, not glum, but going dutifully each morning and coming home each afternoon smelling of salt water and sunscreen.

The beaded disk arrived in early August. It appeared in Charlotte's mailbox at the Gables police department. The envelope was flimsy and water-stained. It was addressed in a scrawl that was barely legible, like the quaking hand of someone two hundred years old. No address, no zip code. Simply: TO CHARLOTTE MONROE, BELOVED WOMAN. CORAL GABLES POLICE DEPARTMENT. The disk was woven with a different design than Diana's. A face with two large blue eyes staring out at the world with such simple wisdom that Charlotte could only wish that one day she might approximate such sight.

Middle of August, there was a hurricane out in the Atlantic. Harold, a Category 4, spinning their way. The TV weather guys were hyped. Its path looked like a direct hit on Miami, so Gracey's dad was putting up the aluminum shutters. Him and the guy he used for yard work. Hernando Gonzalez, maybe eighteen or nineteen years old, a Cuban rafter who'd made it across the ninety-mile stretch of open ocean so he could live in Hialeah with his cousins and do tree-trimming for her dad and people like him.

Gracey thought he was cute. Tall with long lashes and a funny smile. That smile would start to take shape on his lips, then he'd swallow, his big Adam's apple bobbing, and he'd made the grin disappear like he was afraid someone might see how happy he was and deport him back to Cuba.

She was in her room studying Shakespeare. Trying to get her lines down. But something was nagging at her. How could Othello be so stupid as to fall for Iago's bullshit? How could Desdemona love a guy that completely dumb? But she was trying to make herself believe it. Iago keeps whispering and whispering into Othello's ear, making him crazier and crazier. Okay, so that was something she could identify with. A start.

Working on her lines while out her window Hernando Gonzalez and her dad did the shutters. Her part had her saying:

> *My noble father,*
> *I do perceive here a divided duty*
> *To you I am bound for life and education,*
> *My life and education both do learn me*
> *How to respect you: you are the lord of duty,*
> *I am hitherto your daughter. But here's my husband;*
> *And so much duty as my mother show'd*
> *To you, preferring you before her father,*
> *So much I challenge that I may profess*
> *Due to the Moor my lord.*

She understood some of it, the divided duty part anyway. Boyfriend versus Dad. But the rest was giving her trouble. Looking out the window at the skinny Cuban guy with those lashes. Then coming out of the goddamn blue, there was Steven Spielberg. After all these months of silence, then bang, there he was again like nothing had ever happened.

Telling her about that scene with Lucy sprawled naked on the bed. Wasn't it better that she was naked? Didn't that scene have a little extra oomph? Didn't it? Come on, Gracey, admit it. I was right, wasn't I?

What it had was a little extra tit, Joan said, if you call that oomph. But Joan sounded meek and far away, like her heart wasn't in it anymore. Off in the clouds. And Barbara Stanwyck said, now, now, don't let them bother you. Do your lessons. Read your play. Shoot higher, girl. Tits and ass, explosions, all that thrill-a-minute carnival ride bullshit, that's written *by* little boys, *for* little boys. You're a woman now. So start acting like one. 'Cause that's how it is, right? You act a part well enough, you become that person.

But Gracey didn't buy any of it. Not even the woman thing. As nice and supportive as Barbara Stanwyck was, Gracey told her, along with the others, that she was busy. She had work to do. A play to memorize. A part, a good part, juicy, something to sink her teeth into. Shakespeare, for godsakes.

And that boy out her window, there was him, too. That funny smile he had. Smiling, but sad somehow, like there were things he'd seen he'd never get over. Gracey knew about that. Oh, yes, she knew all about that.